BY THE SAME AUTHOR

Simple Justice

John Morgan Wilson

# Revision
# of Justice

A Benjamin Justice Mystery

DOUBLEDAY
New York
London
Toronto
Sydney
Auckland

PUBLISHED BY DOUBLEDAY
a division of Bantam Doubleday Dell Publishing Group, Inc.
1540 Broadway, New York, New York 10036

DOUBLEDAY and the portrayal of an anchor with a dolphin are
trademarks of Doubleday, a division of Bantam Doubleday Dell
Publishing Group, Inc.

Library of Congress Cataloging-in-Publication Data

Wilson, John M., 1945–
Revision of justice: a Benjamin Justice mystery
John Morgan Wilson.—1st ed.
     p.   cm.
I. Title.
PS3573.I456974R48   1997
813'.54—dc21   97-17850
CIP

ISBN 0-385-48235-3

Printed in the United States of America
December 1997
First Edition

10  9  8  7  6  5  4  3  2  1

In Memory of Vito Russo

I must express . . .

My enormous gratitude to Alice Martell, my smart, hardworking agent; Judy Kern, my courageous and supportive editor at Doubleday; Ali Berliner, Brandon Saltz, and others at Doubleday, past and present, for their assistance; Irv Letofsky and Pat H. Broeske, for their helpful Hollywood savvy; Tom Meyer, for supplying the beer; and John Langley, for providing the cigar.

My special thanks to novelist Melodie Johnson Howe and the students in her UCLA Extension mystery writing workshop for their invaluable feedback on the early chapters of this book.

As ever, my love and appreciation for Pietro, for always being there, and being himself.

Special mention must be made of the nonprofit AIDS Healthcare Foundation (6255 West Sunset Boulevard, Sixteenth Floor, Los Angeles, CA 90028), which depends on the generosity of donors to continue its good work helping so many living with HIV and AIDS.

# Revision of Justice

# One

ALEXANDRA TEMPLETON and I made our way up the narrow, twisting streets of Beachwood Canyon, toward a party I didn't want to go to, on a night, like most, when I wanted to be left alone.

In the distance, moonlit against the dark hills, the Hollywood Sign looked as innocent as a picture postcard.

"Promise me you'll try to have a good time, Justice."

She stretched out a slim brown arm and opened her pink palm to catch the passing breeze.

"You know I don't make promises I can't keep."

Her sly brown eyes slid in my direction.

"Then at least promise me you won't try to have a *bad* time."

"You're asking a lot this evening."

She smiled a little, which made her more beautiful than she already was. Then she closed her eyes and tipped back her head, letting her black braids hang free and the warm air bathe her long, slender neck.

With each turn in the road, the letters spelling out *H-O-L-L-Y-W-O-O-D* loomed larger across the canyon, like a beacon of hope for the lost and lonely.

Then the famous landmark disappeared as we hit a stretch of road that ran straight for what looked like half a mile. I pressed down on the gas pedal, and the old Mustang rose like a slow rocket, leaving behind a sea of city lights.

Templeton grew quiet, which was usually my role.

"Thinking about What'shisname?"

Her eyes remained closed, her lips pressed together.

"We don't have to talk about him, if you don't want to."

"Why so curious, Justice?"

"Just making conversation."

"Frankly, he's not worth it."

"You sound a little pissed off."

"We dated for a few months. I caught him two-timing me. It's history."

"I never liked the guy much, anyway. Terrible choice on your part."

She opened her eyes and sat up, suddenly full of sass.

"You only met him twice, Justice. Of course, for a recluse like you, that's a deep friendship."

When I didn't say anything, her mood shifted again, losing some of its spunk.

"What was so bad about him, anyway? That is, before I discovered he was a deceitful, two-timing sonofabitch."

"I didn't like the way he was always flaunting his heterosexuality."

She smiled serenely.

"Mmmm. I did."

"So you do miss him."

She sighed, settled back, and stared out the pitted windshield, across the rust-ravaged hood.

"It's nice when you have someone in your life you care about. Instead of just your work."

"At least you've got that."

I had the top down and we could hear dogs barking from the deep shadows of the canyon and the desolate tinkle of music from one of the houses that clung awkwardly to the hillsides like would-be suicides waiting to jump. I'd always found the canyons above Los Angeles to be lonely places, and I liked them for that. Templeton considered them picturesque and romantic.

We saw a lot of things differently. Maybe it was because I had more than a dozen years on her, and had seen things, both as a reporter and as a man, that she hadn't yet seen even in her worst nightmares. Or maybe I was just a jaded ex-reporter who drank too much and spent too much time feeling sorry for himself.

"So here we are," I said, "two souls without mates, on our way to a party full of strangers. What could be more fun?"

I glanced over at her.

"That's why you were so insistent that I come along tonight, isn't it? So you wouldn't have to be alone so soon after breaking up with What'shisname?"

"Frank. His name's Frank."

She hadn't answered my question.

"Templeton?"

"Not exactly."

She was avoiding my eyes.

"What exactly does 'not exactly' mean?"

"I'm working on a freelance assignment. For *Angel City*. I'm having some problems with it. I hoped you might be able to give me a hand."

My eyes went back to the road.

"An article for *Angel City*."

"It's a Hollywood piece, nothing very heavy."

"Oh, Templeton."

"You know how I've wanted to move up from the crime beat at the *Sun*. Get into general features. Break into the magazines."

"Better money. More prestige. More depth and style to the writing."

"And a wider range of subject matter."

"So you're writing a Hollywood piece for a fatuous monthly like *Angel City*? That's progress?"

"*Angel City* is not fatuous. Trendy, maybe. But not fatuous."

"Debatable."

"I could use some help on this, Justice. Do I have to grovel?"

"Of course you have to grovel."

Her lips stretched into a smile that had *fuck you* written neatly between the lines.

"So what's the problem, Templeton?"

"I'm in over my head. Can't get a handle on the story."

"You said Hollywood. Be more specific."

"It's a trend piece, on the screenwriting trade. The ruthless competition, awesome money, success stories, shattered dreams. That kind of thing. Four thousand words and a sidebar, due in two weeks."

"It sounds like you're all over the place with it. What's your focus?"

She hesitated, which told me a lot.

"The intense competition, I guess."

"Not much of an angle."

Her brow furrowed in thought.

"How about—how far some people will go to get their hands on the hottest new script."

"It's an improvement. Still a bit vague, though—and rather lightweight."

Templeton met my blue eyes straight on.

"Think of it as a story about greed, power, and reckless ambition. Is that worthy enough for Benjamin Justice?"

"At least I hear a theme."

She faced forward again, crossing her arms over her shapely chest.

"God, you can be a pompous ass."

"Enough with the compliments, Templeton. Let's get back to the problem."

"As you've already articulated with such incomparable brilliance, I can't figure out how to tell the damn story."

"No focus. No framework."

She suddenly sounded weary, her defensiveness gone.

"The piece is a mess, Justice. And I've got a deadline breathing down my neck."

"And Harry, too, I'll bet."

Harry Brofsky—my former mentor at the *Los Angeles Times* and now her editor at the less prestigious *Los Angeles Sun*—worked with a paltry budget and a minuscule staff. He also frowned on outside freelance work.

"And Harry, too."

The road twisted, and my headlights caught the yellow eyes of a scrawny coyote just before it slipped away into the dry chapparal. The Hollywood Sign was in front of us again, then gone with another turn of the wheel.

I glanced at my watch, which told me it was a few minutes before nine. I felt them ticking away.

"And this gathering we're going to?"

"It's a networking party. Lots of aspiring screenwriters, Hollywood wannabes. A few agents, maybe a producer or two."

"God, I can hardly wait."

"I figure I might pick up some colorful background material, maybe connect with some good sources. Gordon Cantwell's publicist suggested we come."

"I should know who Gordon Cantwell is?"

"Teaches screenwriting, has a book out. Started back in the early seventies when the marketplace became wide open for original screenplays and the money started getting big. He's made quite a success of it."

"Writing scripts? Or teaching people how?"

"The latter, from what I gather."

"What's his gimmick?"

"He offers a technical approach to screenplay structure that he calls the Cantwell Method. It's apparently had quite an impact on how screenwriting is taught and executed, on how contemporary movies are written."

"One of those writing gurus, with ambitious young groupies lapping up his every word."

"He has his following, but from what I hear, his time has pretty much come and gone."

"Maybe we'll be the only ones at the party."

"Don't get your hopes up, Justice. Cantwell's been hosting this thing every month for more than twenty years. It's become something of a Hollywood institution. Anyone can attend, and a lot of people do."

"And where do I fit into this mad social whirl?"

"I'm going to meet Cantwell around nine. We'll do a get-acquainted interview of fifteen or twenty minutes, during which he'll tell me how much he's done for his screenwriting students and plug his book on screenplay structure ad nauseam."

"And *moi?*"

"You'll wander around, not talking much. Sipping white wine in that pensive, controlled way you have. Seeing everything while revealing nothing. You'll take endless mental notes that you'll commit to memory and later share with me. Snatches of conversation, colorful details, telling anecdotes—the stuff of great feature writing. All of which I'll use to craft a smashing piece and launch a glorious freelance career."

She'd managed to get a smile out of me, which wasn't easy.

"I see you've got it all figured out."

"I consulted the Psychic Hotline."

I glanced at a street sign as we sped by.

"I didn't."

"Turn right at Ridgecrest."

We passed a road sign showing a forbidden match and cigarette, reminding drivers of the fires that plagued these canyons when the winds blew hot and dry. Moments later, another street sign loomed. I swung the wheel hard, turning onto Ridgecrest

Drive, where the pointy silhouettes of thorny cactus fronds jutted out daggerlike from the roadside.

The nose of the Mustang was now pointed directly at the Hollywood Sign, which looked big enough and close enough for us to reach out and touch.

"Cantwell's publicist told me the sign was just across the canyon from his house."

"We must be getting close, then."

I said it tightly, drawing a concerned look from Templeton.

"You're sure you're all right with this, Justice?"

"You brought a bottle?"

"In the backseat, with my purse."

"That should help."

Her eyes stayed on me, but I kept mine on the road, thinking about the party that was only minutes away, then of parties long ago, in better times. Finally, inevitably, of Jacques. My mind must have stayed on him awhile, because I heard Templeton beside me, a million miles away, asking if I was paying attention to a single word she was saying, asking me if I was losing my nerve.

"I'll be all right."

We reached the end of a line of parked cars, from which partygoers trudged the rest of the way on foot. Most clutched bags shaped like bottles, and a few toted what I would later learn were freshly printed film scripts. One earnest-looking young woman carried a knapsack filled with them on her back.

I eased the Mustang to the shoulder of the curbless road and shut off the engine. I didn't get out right away. Instead, I sat staring out at the night ahead, feeling empty and anxious.

Templeton reached over to run her fingers through my blond hair. It was thinning on top but still thick in back and it felt good to have her fingers there, now that she knew me well enough to know I had no interest in going to bed with her.

"You're thinking about Jacques, aren't you?"

*Yes,* I wanted to say, *I'm thinking about Jacques.*

About the way he had of turning a dull party into a wonderful adventure, total strangers into instant friends. How he got me to stop drinking when I'd had too much, saying just the right words, something no one else could do. His quick and honest laugh, the smile that came with it, and the flash of humor in his dark, Latin eyes. What it had been like, tumbling into bed with him at the end of the night, when the world disappeared and he became my world, safe and welcoming and warm.

"Let's go in," I said, "before I change my mind."

We got out, leaving the top down. Templeton grabbed her purse and a bottle of Pinot Grigio from the backseat. I hadn't tasted alcohol yet that day, and when she handed me the bottle in exchange for my keys, my hands were shaking a little.

We started hiking with the others.

Up ahead, across the road, an ancient woman descended, dragged by a shopping cart heavy with reclaimed bottles. She was peering suspiciously over her shoulder, back up the road at an oddly shaped house where the party was apparently in progress.

A wild tangle of white hair made it difficult to see much of her face. She wore a battered pair of running shoes and a full-length coat, old and heavy, despite the warm August air.

Suddenly, she pulled on the handle of the cart, slowing it to a standstill, and showing surprising strength for someone so old and thin. She bent to pick up a dusty bottle from beside the road, inspected it, and added it to the others, before glancing back at the house and hurrying on.

"Flames across the canyon!"

She was a small woman, but her voice was strong, and beneath the tumbling white hair, her eyes were fierce.

She pointed a bony finger at the two of us as she passed.

"Smoke and fire! For the betrayal of Genesis!"

Then she descended around a curve, rattling her load of bottles, until she was out of sight.

We turned and followed the others up the hill, no more troubled by the old woman than we were by the hundreds of other crazy street people who roamed the city, speaking their personal vision of reality in a language that sounded like madness to the rest of us.

As we climbed, my attention gradually focused on the house at the top of the rise, where the voice of a torch singer crooning "Haunted Heart" floated above the crowd's chatter.

"Sounds like a party," Templeton said, and found my hand with hers, offering comfort.

I didn't say anything. I was preparing myself for the first party I'd been to in at least a decade without Jacques at my side.

The house was on the right, separated from the road by a short wooden bridge and a wide expanse of healthy, leaf-littered lawn. The bridge spanned a drainage ditch cleverly designed with stonework to resemble a medieval moat. Templeton and I made our way across, taking it all in.

"Welcome to Fantasyland," she said.

We found ourselves looking up at a two-story stucco in the shape of a European castle, probably built in the movieland heyday of the twenties or thirties, decorated with dramatic archways, pointy turrets, and arched windows of leaded colored glass. Soft light bathed the walls, at least those we could see. Behind the house, pitch-black slopes ran down into the canyon.

My first thought was that it was garish, ostentatious, and silly. My second thought was that Jacques would have loved it.

"Beauty before the beast," I said.

Templeton crossed the bridge ahead of me, to a serpentine flagstone walkway that traversed the well-watered lawn.

It was then that we heard the scream.

It was ragged and shrill and probably came from a woman, though it might have escaped from a nervous man skating on the thin ice of hysteria.

It also carried the unmistakable sound of desperation, the kind that, given the setting, sounded like too much alcohol and dwindling career prospects.

Raucous laughter immediately followed.

"They must be discussing box-office grosses," Templeton said, as we ascended the final steps. "Or maybe superstar salaries."

"What could possibly be more important?"

"Are you sure you're up to this, Benjamin?"

Through the rounded doorway of Gordon Cantwell's quaint house, I could see bodies massed in chatty little groups or drifting alone, looking awkwardly unconnected, desperate for a place to land. I clutched my bottle a little tighter.

"I wouldn't miss it for the world."

We stepped inside to a burst of machine-gun laughter that riddled my guts with dread.

# Two

YOU MUST BE Alexandra Templeton. I've been expecting you."

The voice was on the deep side, direct and self-assured, and came from a diminutive young woman whom I first mistook for a pretty teenage boy.

"I'm Christine Kapono, Gordon Cantwell's assistant. Call me Chris."

She extended her hand, looking up into Templeton's face with almond-shaped eyes as bright as they were dark.

"And you can call me Alex," Templeton said. "Shorter and simpler."

"The name you use on your byline at the *Sun*."

"Right."

"Alex, then."

Christine Kapono wore her black hair cropped into an efficient ducktail; her skin was as smooth and brown as a hazelnut, suggesting island blood. She was trim but sturdily built—strong shoulders, wide hips, small breasts—and looked quite at home in her Gap T-shirt, snug jeans, and leather sandals. Bony protrusions showed atop the arches of her small feet, "surfer's knobs" caused by years of kneeling and paddling on a surfboard, if my guess was right.

"You must have been watching for us," Templeton said.

"You weren't hard to spot. Gordon's publicist described you as tall, black, and beautiful." Kapono's eyes lingered on Templeton as they shook hands. "He was right."

Templeton, accustomed to admiring looks from both women and men, glanced my way.

"This is my friend Benjamin Justice."

"Welcome to the party." Kapono's grip was formal and firm, her eyes less interested. "Are you a screenwriter?"

"I'm not much of anything these days."

"Sounds like an aspiring screenwriter to me."

That generated a small laugh all around. Kapono glanced at the diver's watch on her wrist.

"Gordon's running a little late. Celebrity softball game for charity. He should be along any minute."

"I didn't know Gordon Cantwell qualified as a celebrity," Templeton said.

"Only in his own mind." Kapono followed the remark with a smile, but the edge in her voice had been unmistakable. "He's filling in for someone who couldn't make it. Center field, his favorite position. They called him day before yesterday. Needless to say, he was thrilled to be asked."

"I take it he likes the spotlight."

"You'll meet him soon enough, Mr. Justice. I'll let you judge for yourself." She indicated my bottle. "You'd probably like to open that."

"More than you can imagine."

She led us through a maze of men and women toward the kitchen, turning it into a guided tour along the way.

"The bedrooms are upstairs. Gordon uses the downstairs primarily for business and entertaining."

The lower level of the house was a collection of high-ceilinged rooms separated by arched entries, decorated with framed movie posters going back six decades and furnishings salvaged from the sets of famous movies and later sold at memorabilia auctions. A stone stairway with an ornate wrought-iron railing, worthy of a descending Norma Desmond, led to the second floor. Near the foot of the stairs was a gaping fireplace that reminded me of the one in *Citizen Kane.* Above the mantelpiece hung a framed one-sheet from *Gone With the Wind,* in mint condition, without so much as a fold or crease within its borders.

Off the dining room, we could see a crowded patio lighted by candles and tiki torches. A few partygoers spilled out onto the lawn, but not far, because of the darkness extending to the edge of the canyon.

"The pièce de résistance," Kapono said.

Across the brush-covered divide, on the upper slopes of Mount Lee, the white letters of the Hollywood Sign rose five stories high. From the flats not quite two miles below, the sign had looked modest and unprepossessing. Now, from a hundred yards straight across the canyon, even without lights, the huge letters looked monstrous, dwarfing the surrounding houses, riveting the eye.

"Impressive, isn't it?"

"That's one way of putting it."

"It looks positively indestructible," Templeton said. "Wood?"

"Sheet metal."

"On a steel frame," I added, "set in concrete. Four hundred and fifty feet across. At one time, it was illuminated at night by five thousand high-powered bulbs, until the local residents complained."

Templeton threw me a curious look.

"How do you know all that?"

"I wrote a short feature on it once, when I was at the *Times.* Don't look so surprised, Templeton. I had my share of frivolous assignments when I was starting out."

As we moved on, I felt more and more imprisoned by bodies, and suffocated by the buzz of conversation that filled the rooms. The chief topics seemed to be the Sundance Film Festival, the odd career of a director named Quentin Tarantino, and how much a writer named Jake Novitz had been paid for his latest script.

I was older by a good decade than most of those around me, who ranged in appearance from clean-cut to scruffy, from carefully businesslike to self-consciously bohemian. For all the varied styles on display, however, I sensed that the group was bound almost religiously by a singleminded social zeal. More than anything, I was struck by the restlessness of the eyes, most of which seemed to be searching the room.

As we neared the kitchen, the babble and laughter rose in my ears like discordant music, and the crush of bodies began to feel claustrophobic. Kapono's husky voice cut through the din.

"You can usually spot the agents. They tend to be better dressed and more confident looking. Just as intense, but without that sense of anxiety and neediness. At least the successful ones."

We slipped past a small group that included the young woman with the knapsack we'd seen marching resolutely up the hill. She was handing fresh-looking, vinyl-covered scripts to two thirtyish men who resembled Armani models from the neck down but ambitious young salesmen from the neck up.

"It's very castable," I heard the young woman say eagerly. "I think you'll see plenty of foreign potential in the action scenes. I'm sure that pre-sell could cover half the budget."

We reached a breathing space in the big kitchen, which was mercifully free of bodies, except for a brown-skinned housekeeper who busied herself opening bags of chips. Kapono took the bottle of wine from my hands, found a corkscrew, and put it to work.

"The party looks like quite a success," Templeton said.

"Give it more time. By eleven, it'll be wall-to-wall people, every one of them with at least three new ideas for next year's box-office blockbuster, and ready to pitch to anyone who will listen."

I glanced around at the faces.

"It's certainly a young crowd."

"And white," Templeton added.

Kapono's eyes flickered knowingly.

"Welcome to Hollywood."

I heard the pop of the cork as it came out and felt a surge of desire for the alcohol. Kapono poured the wine into a clear plastic cup, looking up and waiting for me to tell her to stop. I didn't.

When it was full, she handed it over.

"Most of the people are here to make some kind of connection," she explained. "Screenwriters looking to hook up with an agent or a development person, development people hoping to find a hot new script before someone else does. It's a very social business, moviemaking. Connections and relationships count for a lot."

"And why are you here?" Templeton asked.

"Why do I work as Gordon's assistant?"

Templeton nodded. Kapono fixed her with clear, confident eyes.

"My goal is to meet enough people and acquire enough knowledge to work myself into a position of influence."

"Influence or power?" I asked.

"I suppose they're one and the same, aren't they?"

"And what is it that you hope to influence?"

"What kind of movies get made. What kind of images we put on the screen for the world to see. How we reflect and shape the consciousness of the next generation. From a woman's point of view."

"An Asian woman's point of view?" Templeton asked.

"Possibly." Kapono cocked her head thoughtfully. "And a lesbian's viewpoint as well, when it's appropriate."

Kapono's frankness surprised me, especially in front of a journalist gathering material for a story. Either times had changed more than I realized, or Kapono had lots of backbone. Maybe both.

"You sound very serious about it."

"Dead serious, Mr. Justice."

She offered Templeton some wine, but Templeton requested mineral water instead. Kapono found two bottles of Evian, handed one to Templeton and kept the other for herself, then glanced out toward the party.

"Why don't I introduce you around?"

I followed them out, but quickly excused myself to find a rest room. Kapono pointed toward the stairway.

"There's one at the top of the stairs, or below, at the end of the hall."

"We'll be mingling," Templeton said. "Don't hide too long."

I took the shortest route into the downstairs hallway, leaving the press of humanity behind. On either side hung more framed posters: *Tootsie, The Graduate, To Kill a Mockingbird, The Wild Bunch, On the Waterfront, North by Northwest,* one or two others.

Halfway down, I heard voices.

They came from a half-open doorway near the end of the hall. One was male and deep, distinguished by an accent that had the map of Australia printed all over it. The other, a California monotone delivered with precise diction, came from a woman who sounded as tight as an angry fist.

Male: "I'm telling you, I didn't know! I swear!"

Female: "Where is he?"

Male: "Believe me, I'd like to find the little bugger myself!"

Female: "He's evil, Dylan—you have no idea."

Male: "I know enough to want to kill the bastard!"

Female: "That makes two of us, believe me."

Through the partly open door, I saw a bearded man in dark clothes with an oversized can of Foster's Lager in one hand and a cigar shaped like a torpedo in the other. He faced a slim, elegant woman in a white summer dress and gold jewelry, with a helmet of frosted blond hair that looked lacquered down to the last strand.

She caught me looking at her, then said quickly to the man, "If you see him, tell him he *must* call me!"

The door opened wider and she stepped past me without a word, disappearing quickly down the hall. The Australian tipped the can of Foster's to his mouth, draining half of it, then puffed angrily on his tapered cigar.

He glared through the open door, then moved toward me.

"You seen Ray Farr by any chance?"

The Aussie was of moderate height, two or three inches below my six feet, but closer in years to my thirty-nine, maybe older. His shoulders were hunched and powerful, and he sported a long mane of well-conditioned auburn hair that matched his luxuriant beard. Furious green eyes fastened on me from a chiseled, sunburned face.

"I asked you a simple question, mate."

He poked my shoulder in a way I didn't like.

"I don't know anyone named Ray Farr."

"Everybody knows Ray Farr!"

The sound was more mocking now than belligerent, and inside the bushy beard his mouth curled into a grin. I relaxed a little.

"I assume Farr is the same man the lady wants to talk to."

"The lady used to be his agent."

"He's a screenwriter, then?"

"Ha! That's a joke. He's a scam artist and a bastard is what he is."

He tipped the can again. I watched the muscles of his throat work as the beer went down. After that, he toppled a bit toward me on the toes of his snakeskin boots.

I put a hand on his arm to steady him. Beneath his black silk shirt, I felt a bicep as thick and hard as the rounded end of a forty-pound barbell. The shirt was creamy soft and looked expensively Italian, the kind worn by a man who thought a lot of himself and was accustomed to getting his way.

"Maybe you should slow down," I said, holding him steady and indicating the big can of lager.

"Maybe you should fuck off, mate."

I wasn't in the mood for trouble, so I turned away toward the bathroom, leaving him to wobble on his own.

He grabbed my arm, stopping me and steadying himself again. Then he placed his hand on my shoulder, close enough to my face that I felt the heat of the cigar's orange ash. He switched the cigar to his other hand, showing it to me.

"Montecristo Number Two, lovely smoke. Six inches long to the centimeter, fifty-two-ring gauge. Cuban, of course. Torpedo's the common name, but the rollers call 'em a *pirámide.* You a cigar man?''

"I'm afraid not."

"I smoke 'em for the rich flavor, the spice. Some blokes smoke 'em because they like to play the big shot."

"Are you a big shot?"

"I was until they took my picture away from me last month."

He said it pitifully, the way drunks can get in the blink of a bleary eye.

When I said nothing, he pushed the subject.

"You must have read about it in the trade papers."

"I guess I missed it."

"Locked me out of the damned editing bay!"

"Hardly seems fair."

"*Thunder's Fortune* is now in the hands of some other bloke." His grin grew crooked, sad. "Or some bloke-ette."

"You're a director, then."

"Not just any director, mate. Dylan fucking Winchester! Brilliant young director from Down Under. Only he's not so young anymore and he doesn't look too fucking brilliant at the moment, does he now?''

He laughed uneasily and swigged from the can. The Foster's frothed over onto his beard. He belched, wiped a meaty hand across his mouth, kept talking.

"Your movie's too fucking long, they said. Behind schedule. Over budget. But that wasn't the reason they took it away from me. I've been behind schedule and over budget on every fucking studio picture I ever made!"

He thrust his hairy chin at me, fixing me with his bold, dangerous eyes.

"You want to know the real reason?"

"Sure."

"Raymond Farr is the reason." The humor had drained from his voice like blood from a dead man's face. "Raymond fucking Farr! And when I find the little prick, I'm going to kill him!"

He flung the empty beer can at the bathroom door, hard enough to leave a mark. Then he turned and stomped away down the hall, out into the mass of bodies, leaving the spicy aroma of his Montecristo Number 2 behind.

I picked up the can and set it on a small table next to a Mickey Mouse telephone. The bathroom door was locked, and I picked up a different aroma, the sweet scent of burning marijuana, so I didn't bother to knock.

Instead, I leaned against the wall and drank my wine, studying Paul Newman's anguished face on a poster for *The Verdict* and digesting Dylan Winchester's unexplained fury at the man named Raymond Farr.

# Three

N O MORE than fifteen minutes had passed when I saw Dylan Winchester again.

This time there was a pane of glass between us, framed by tall window curtains of heavy dark velvet that reminded me of *Rebecca*.

I was standing in the shadows of the breakfast room, on the southern side of Cantwell's house. The lights were off and I was working on my second glass of Pinot Grigio while I took in the view.

A thorny hedge of cactus had been created down the slope, decades ago if the density of its growth was any indication. I could just make out the shapes of beavertail, barrel, and prickly pear, with a scattering of smaller, pincushion cacti at their base.

Beyond lay darkness, all the way down the canyon to the illuminated windows of other homes, which led to an explosion of lights in the distance, city after city, as far as the eye could see.

Suddenly, off to my left and below, Winchester emerged from the deepest shadows of the yard, looking even more agitated than before. His fancy Cuban cigar was gone and his head was down, but his beard and mane of auburn hair were unmistakable.

He hurried toward the side of the house, into the fringe of the light, looking like he wanted to get away as quickly as possible.

Then a younger man appeared from the same dark section of the yard, several steps behind. He was slim and blond, wearing shorts and sandals and a rather smug look on his pretty face.

He dashed after Winchester, grabbing at him, the way Winchester had grabbed at me in the hallway only minutes before. Winchester shook him off, disappearing around the side of the house while the younger man stared sulkily after him.

Before another minute passed, he turned away, toward the flickering light of the patio, and the lively silhouettes of men and women socializing there.

I glanced at my watch: 9:32. I couldn't very well keep putting Templeton off—"hiding," as she had put it with a fair degree of accuracy. I drained my glass, refilled it, and wandered back into the party, carrying the bottle with me.

The wine had begun to do its job. The cacophony around me, which had sounded so maddening earlier, had settled into a pleasant hum, and the packed bodies began to feel almost comforting, even sexy.

I spotted Templeton in the living room, taller and darker than any other woman in sight, standing with Christine Kapono in a knot of chatty types gathered around bowls of chips and guacamole dip.

As I made my way toward them, I saw Dylan Winchester yet again, through an arched window that looked out across the yard to the street. He was behind the wheel of a black Mercedes convertible, pulling out fast.

"You're back among the living."

It was Templeton, greeting me as I approached, with Kapono at her side. I raised my glass to them both, feeling the glow.

"Ladies."

"Come," Kapono said. "I see two friends I'd like you to meet."

We followed her to the middle of the room, where I found myself face to face with the tightly coiled woman who had slipped past me in the hallway, making a hasty departure from Dylan Winchester. Next to her was a dapper, white-haired gentleman old enough to be her grandfather, who held a stemmed glass of red wine in his well-manicured fingers, one of which was adorned with a gold wedding band.

"Roberta Brickman and Leonardo Petrocelli," Kapono said, "I'd like you to meet Alexandra Templeton and Benjamin Justice."

Then, quickly, like a warning: "Alex is on assignment for *Angel City*—a piece on the industry."

"We'll have to watch what we say, then, won't we?"

Roberta Brickman seemed to be looking more at me than at Templeton when she said it. Her voice was cool and controlled now, which fit the rest of her—the elegant, conservative clothes, the flawless coiffure. She appeared to be in her early thirties, with intelligent brown eyes and a well-shaped face that might have been attractive had it not been so pinched and severe.

Kapono informed us that Brickman was an agent with International Talent Associates, in Kapono's estimation one of the major "players" in the industry. Leonardo Petrocelli, she told us, was a "screenwriting master, the kind you don't find too many of anymore."

Petrocelli, trim and courtly, raised his bushy eyebrows in acknowledgment, along with his glass of red wine.

"Surely you're not here looking to make connections or pitch ideas," Templeton said to him.

"Why not, dear—because of my age?"

"Because of your experience, Mr. Petrocelli. I assume you're well established in the industry."

"At one time, Miss Templeton. Unfortunately, that doesn't count for much when you're dealing with studio executives two or three generations behind you. These young agents and producers today—mention the word 'classic' and they think you're talking about *Animal House*."

Everyone laughed except Brickman, who managed a pained smile.

"Present company excluded," Petrocelli said, bowing slightly in her direction. He winced, and raised himself upright with effort, struggling to conceal it.

"And you, Roberta?" Templeton asked. "Conspiring with Leonardo on a new film project?"

"As a rule, Alexandra, I don't talk to the press."

"Why is that?"

"I prefer the attention go to my clients."

*Translation: Because the media are always looking for an angle, usually negative. Talking to you can do me no good, but could do me harm. So why bother?*

Templeton decided to test the agent's resolve.

"Have you picked up any clients at one of Gordon's parties?"

Brickman smiled tightly.

"Not that I recall."

"Roberta's always made herself accessible to new writers," Kapono said, sounding like a publicist. "She even returns phone calls."

"An agent who returns phone calls," Petrocelli said. "They should give you a special Oscar for that, Roberta."

"It's simply good business."

"Is that what screenwriting is?" I asked. "A business?"

"For some, it's buying and selling product, Mr. Justice. For others, it's trying to make the films they want to make. But, yes, bottom line—it's a marketplace."

"Sad but true," Petrocelli concurred.

He offered us a weary, knowing smile.

"Perhaps you'd like to share your insights with Templeton," I said, "for the article she's putting together."

Petrocelli studied me carefully.

"If I'm not mistaken, Mr. Justice, you're a reporter yourself."

"Not for some time."

"In the eighties—you wrote for the *L.A. Times*. Mostly investigative pieces, I believe."

"That's right."

"Pulitzer problem, if I recall correctly."

"You do."

"I thought I recognized the name."

From the silence that fell momentarily over the group, it seemed as though the others now recognized it as well.

"Maybe we should talk about it sometime," Petrocelli said. "It might be the premise for a good movie."

There wasn't a hint of meanness in his voice. It was all said matter-of-factly, with the kind of frankness writers and reporters display so easily when discussing others, but rarely when discussing themselves.

"It was a series of articles, actually."

I heard the tension in my voice, and didn't like it.

"On AIDS, wasn't it?"

"It was about two gay men who were lovers. One was dying. The other was caring for him. Not my usual nuts-and-bolts reportorial style."

"Quite touching, if memory serves."

"And largely fiction, as I'm sure you're aware."

"Which is why they made you give the Pulitzer back."

"And why you haven't seen my byline since."

"At the heart of every tragedy, Mr. Justice, there's invariably poignance. As I said, perhaps a film. If not for theatrical, then maybe for HBO or Showtime."

"Frankly, it's not something I enjoy dredging up."

Petrocelli's face softened with sympathy.

"I suppose not. Forgive me if I spoke out of turn."

We'd stumbled into one of those awkward moments that can shatter the artifice of a social gathering like a hammer on glass. Kapono moved quickly to pick up the pieces.

"Leonardo, I believe you're out of wine."

"So I am, dear."

I held out my bottle.

"Pinot Grigio, Mr. Petrocelli?"

"Thanks. I'm a burgundy man."

Kapono reached for his empty glass.

"I tucked a bottle away for you in the kitchen, Leo."

"While you're at it, if you should run into Raymond Farr—well, tell him I'd like a moment of his time, if it's possible."

"Raymond Farr," I said. "That's a name that keeps popping up."

I glanced at Brickman. The muscles around her mouth tightened into a grotesque version of a smile.

"He does seem to get around, doesn't he?" Petrocelli said. "Just before you joined us, Roberta was telling me that—"

"Raymond is a former assistant of mine."

Brickman regarded me harshly, the way she had when she'd caught me eavesdropping in the hallway.

"According to Dylan Winchester, Farr was also your client."

"That would be an overstatement."

"Ah."

"I've neither seen nor heard from him in some time."

"We've each independently been trying to reach Farr by phone," Petrocelli said. "All we get is his infernal answering machine. Doesn't anybody in this town answer their damn telephones anymore?"

"I'd hoped to clear up some old business with him," Brickman said. "I thought perhaps I'd find him here tonight."

For someone so press-shy, she was suddenly volunteering more than her share of information.

"He's a party regular, then?"

"A former student of Gordon's," Kapono said. "He worked at ITA until—"

Brickman silenced her with a glance sharp enough to cut the Hope diamond.

"Until what?" Templeton asked pleasantly, in the even manner of a reporter who smells an interesting lead.

"Until a few weeks ago," Brickman said, her voice as frosty as her lacquered hair.

"And Dylan Winchester?" I asked. "An ITA client?"

"Until recently."

"Interesting."

"Not really. Clients jump agencies more often than they change therapists."

Brickman's monotone pelted me like small, cold stones.

With noticeable relief, Kapono turned toward the doorway.

"Look who's here!"

There was a commotion in the foyer as the youthful crowd parted to clear a path for the new arrival.

He was a pudgy, florid-faced, middle-aged man dressed incongruously in an orange-and-white baseball uniform, complete with cap and cleated shoes. The words *Tinseltown Tyros* were stitched across the chest, and his snug baseball pants were smudged with grass stains and infield dirt.

In the crook of one arm he carried a grocery sack, an economy-sized bag of taco chips peeking out the top; under the other arm, a well-used outfielder's mitt.

The young people around him raised their bottles and beverage glasses, offering high fives and calling out his name, all in earnest pursuit of his attention.

Gordon Cantwell, the absent host, had finally made his entrance.

# Four

H E SEEMS to know everyone," Templeton said. We watched Gordon Cantwell work his way through the room, juggling his outfielder's mitt and grocery sack to shake hands along the way, tossing nods and smiles to grateful greeters the way a wealthy matron dispenses token gifts to the poor.

"King of his castle," Kapono said, making it sound pleasant enough.

Cantwell was a fiftyish man of average height, with a soft middle and skinny legs but solid in the shoulders. His mustache and beard were badly trimmed and looked dyed to match the reddish-brown toupee crowning his sunburned head, as if he'd done both jobs himself at the bathroom mirror. Despite his age, he wore his orange-trimmed baseball outfit with unabashed pride, brimming over with the effusion of someone whose team has just won a close one.

I was filling my cup with wine as he approached, beckoned by Kapono's upraised hand.

"Let me guess," he said as he joined us. "Alexandra Templeton, ace reporter."

His appraising eyes were all over her in an instant, and he was clearly pleased with what he saw.

"Mr. Cantwell," Templeton said.

His busy eyes finally settled on her face.

"Never did I expect anyone quite so lovely. Someone should put you in the movies, Miss Templeton."

He sounded like a second-rate actor auditioning with a third-rate script, yet blissfully unaware of it. Petrocelli piped in to save Cantwell further self-embarrassment.

"Are you going to tell us the score, Gordon—or shall we assume that your team took a drubbing?"

"On the contrary, Leo. As you've probably heard, I played on Tom Hanks's squad. I'm pleased to say we pulled out a victory—two runs, bottom of the ninth, to break a tie, thanks to a Jimmy Smits double."

Then, to the rest of us: "Not to sound immodest, but I personally put my glove on fly balls hit by Kevin Costner, Billy Crystal, and Wesley Snipes."

Cantwell had managed to drop five well-known Hollywood names in less than half a minute. He was nothing if not well rehearsed.

"The question is," Templeton said, "were you able to hang on to any of them?"

Laughter rippled through the group.

"She's quick," Cantwell said to the rest of us. He winked in Templeton's direction. "I like that."

Then, leaning toward her ear: "I can assure you, when something comes my way that's worthwhile, I grab it and hang on."

This time, Kapono stepped in to save him.

"Gordon, this is Alexandra's friend, Benjamin Justice."

Cantwell asked immediately if I was in "the business," and when I replied in the negative, lost interest in me just as quickly.

"I'd love to chat longer," he said to the group, "but I promised Alexandra an interview." He turned back to her. "There's a terraced garden down the hill with a spectacular view of the Hollywood Sign and the city lights. We can talk there, if that's all right."

Templeton showed him her notebook and tape recorder.

"Whenever you're ready, Gordon."

Cantwell hoisted the grocery sack.

"I'll just leave this in the kitchen, then I'm all yours. Chris, you'll see that our guests have whatever they need?"

"I'll take care of them, Gordon."

We watched him cross the room, shaking hands along the way.

"He's quite sociable," Templeton said.

"Especially with attractive women," Kapono replied. "Be sure to holler if you need help."

She was smiling again, but exchanged a silent look with Templeton, the kind between women that speaks volumes.

A minute and some small talk later, Cantwell appeared in the dining room, clutching his baseball glove under one arm, as if clinging to the memory of the evening's victory. He caught Templeton's attention with an upraised hand, and gestured toward the yard, where the outdoor lights had come on.

"I think that's my cue," Templeton said.

She handed business cards to Brickman and Petrocelli, said her good-byes, and made her way through the throng. Cantwell slipped an arm through one of hers and guided her out the dining room doors.

They traversed the patio to the yard's southern boundary, where they descended a lighted trail of steps that led them quickly out of sight.

"I promised you a glass of burgundy," Kapono said to Petrocelli.

"No rush, dear. Two glasses is my limit these days."

Brickman stepped to Kapono's side.

"I'll go with you, Christine. I could use something for this headache."

"And I'm off to the rest room," I said.

We left Petrocelli alone, looking like a pillar of dignity and decorum amid the hubbub of the younger crowd.

I took the stairs this time, climbing past yet more film posters— *Casablanca, Singin' in the Rain, The Third Man, Witness.* The last poster along the staircase, a step from the top, was from *The Blue Angel,* featuring a leggy blonde born Maria Magdalena Dietrich von Losch, but known more famously as Marlene Dietrich.

On the same step, coming down, was another slender young blond, of the male variety.

I recognized him as the man I'd seen a few minutes earlier, pursuing Dylan Winchester across the yard.

He was one of those smooth, pretty types with good genes and fine hair, who might be twenty or thirty-two or anywhere in between, depending on the quality of the light. The sleeves of his silk T-shirt, pale blue to match his eyes, were rolled up sissy-style, revealing long, boyish biceps. The thumbs of his fine-boned hands were hooked into the side pockets of his white summer shorts, which showed off a pair of legs that were surprisingly muscular and hairy, out of synch with the rest of him.

He looked me over as he came down, searching my face with something other than professional interest, yet protected by a coolness that bordered on disdain. Yearning to be admired yet unapproachable. I pegged him immediately as an actor.

As I reached the top of the stairs, two more framed posters faced me from either side of the bathroom door, one from *Rocky,* the other from *Frankenstein,* which made me wonder if the juxtaposition was a comment on bodybuilding and plastic surgery. Down the hall in either direction were more—*The African Queen, King Kong, Bonnie and Clyde, Lawrence of Arabia, The Searchers, It Happened One Night.* Cantwell's house was beginning to feel more like a museum of movie memories than a home.

I glanced over my shoulder and into the pale blue eyes of the young man on the stairs. He stood midway down in his sandaled feet, peering up with an insolent look that told me he found me attractive, but not so much that I should expect him to make the first move. I laughed to myself, enough to let him see it, then turned away and moved on.

I drank the remainder of the wine slowly but straight from the bottle, sitting on the toilet seat with the door locked, savoring the isolation. Gradually, as the bottle emptied, it dawned on me that I was surrounded by freshly minted screenplays.

Stacks of them sat atop the toilet tank and the laundry hamper, on a small side table, the edge of the tub, even the floor, where one or two of the piles had spilled, scattering scripts across the clean tile. They were all encased in variously colored vinyl covers and bound by golden brads that glittered with optimism. Business cards bearing the names of the writers were paper-clipped to some or tucked inside. On others, Post-it notes informed the reader that the attached script was for sale or option or in need of an agent; several of the notes signified genre—romantic comedy, suspense thriller, action-adventure, mystery, horror, sci-fi. There were also a few résumés, all rather skimpy, emphasizing cinema school degrees and awards I'd never heard of, with the credits limited mostly to student films.

Atop one stack was a hand-printed sign: *Just read the first five pages—no longer than it takes you to take care of business and flush—and I guarantee you'll be hooked.*

The shortest script I flipped through was ninety-two pages; the longest, 124. Each began with the words FADE IN: and ended with FADE OUT, FADE TO BLACK, or THE CREDITS ROLL. In between were fifty or sixty scenes, designated interior or exterior—*Int.* or *Ext.*—filled primarily with action and dialogue, and the sparest description. Screenwriting appeared to be a minimalist's craft—a case of *less is more.*

I drained the bottle and thought about all the work that must have gone into so many scripts that would probably never be sold, let alone produced. It depressed me, for all kinds of reasons, so I switched my thoughts to the young man on the stairs.

I had no doubt he was attracted to me, although I wasn't sure why. Maybe he had a thing for hairy-chested men who were pushing forty with thinning hair and paunchy waistlines. Maybe he was drawn to me because I didn't go gaga over him on first sight, and he liked a challenge. Maybe he mistook me for a producer with a studio development deal.

It didn't really matter. I'd seen the look; I knew the look. The question was whether I wanted him.

I peed, zipped up, and flushed, then opened the door expecting to see him at the bottom of the stairs, leaning casually against the railing with his eyes carefully averted, as if he'd forgotten me entirely.

He was considerably closer, standing just outside the door pretending to study the *Frankenstein* one-sheet.

I passed him without a word.

"I've seen you around West Hollywood."

His voice was baritone deep, on the cultured side.

I stopped and turned, already resenting the power of his youth and beauty, the way it had seized a weak part of me.

"Have you?"

He nodded, then turned away as if it didn't matter in the slightest, as if the conversation was over. The dance of narcissism was underway; the next step was mine.

"You have a name?"

"Lawrence Teal."

He tossed it at me like a scrap.

"Live in the neighborhood?"

"Hilldale, just off Dicks."

"Dicks Street—where the sign's always being stolen."

"That's the one."

"I'm on Norma Place—just around the corner. I guess that makes us neighbors."

"I know your face." He said it flatly, distantly, reminding me that he didn't really care. "I've seen it before."

"I believe you already said that."

I matched his offhand tone, which forced him to play it a little cooler.

"Don't let me keep you, if you have better things to do."

"Thanks, I do."

I turned back to the stairs.

"Wait."

I waited.

"What's your name?"

"Benjamin Justice."

His soft, pink mouth curled at the corners.

"That's it. That's where I know you from. The Pulitzer business."

"I didn't know actors paid attention to such things."

"How do you know I'm an actor?"

"Aren't you?"

"At the moment, I'm in a one-act at the West Hollywood Playhouse."

"Drama school?"

"Yale."

"Which means you probably make a living waiting tables."

It stung; his nostrils flared.

"I park cars, actually. Parties, mostly. It allows me to audition during the day—take time off if I get a role."

"You sound very committed, Teal."

I started down.

"Maybe we could have a drink." He said it quickly, giving more away, I suspected, than he wanted to. "Talk a little. See what develops."

I looked him over the way a picky shopper sizes up the hothouse tomatoes.

"I've had more to drink than I need. And we *have* talked a little."

Half a dozen steps separated us when he spoke again.

"Fuck you, Justice."

When I looked back up at him, his hands were thrust into his pockets and his eyes fixed on mine with a look that was part glare, part seduction.

I stepped back up to the landing, grabbed him roughly by one arm, and hustled him toward a closed door at the end of the hallway. With any luck, it would be unlocked, with a big bed behind it.

I shoved him against the door, grabbed his hair, and pressed my mouth against his, hard enough to bruise his pretty lips. My other hand went directly to the front of his pants, where I found a lump that was alive and moving.

"Justice!"

I turned to see Templeton standing at the top of the stairway. She moved down the hallway toward us.

"I hate to interrupt a tender courtship," she said. "But we've discovered Raymond Farr, down on the terrace."

"It's about time someone found him."

"Justice—he's dead."

# Five

EXCEPT FOR scattered whispers, a hush had fallen over the party as Templeton and I reached the bottom of the stairs.

People moved aside to let us pass.

"I called 911 before I went looking for you," Templeton said. "Cantwell's down on the terrace, attempting CPR."

She led me across the patio and yard to the steps where I'd last seen her disappearing with Cantwell.

"I couldn't find a pulse. His skin was on the clammy side. I think he's been dead awhile."

"You OK?"

"A little queasy."

The steps were brick, bordered on each side by low, Oriental-style lamps. They lighted our way through a break in the cactus hedge to a thick stand of oleander that opened up to a terraced patio not visible from the house.

Cantwell knelt on the bricks, frantically attempting CPR on a lean young man who stared into the starless sky with dead eyes.

The amber glow from a circle of Malibu lights was dim, but I could make out certain features—a clean-shaven, sharply angled face with a shadow of heavy beard; long, straight dark hair fanned out behind the head; eyes as black as coal; thick hair on the forearms and upper chest, where two buttons were open Hollywood-style. Greek, Spanish, Middle Eastern, Italian—I couldn't tell which. But rather good-looking, for a dead man.

Cantwell tilted back the young man's head and blew four blasts of air into his mouth. When he was done, he placed his hands on the man's belly, just below the rib cage, and pushed forcefully several times.

"How are you doing?"

Cantwell looked up at me with anxious eyes. He was breathing hard and his ruddy face glistened with sweat.

"I could use a break, to be honest."

I knelt down and took over.

Christine Kapono appeared and immediately pushed aside a couple of patio chairs to make more room.

Down the darkened canyon, flashing blue lights could be seen snaking up the road while a siren wailed above a chorus of barking dogs.

"We'll need more light," Cantwell told Kapono. "There are flashlights in the garage."

Kapono took off at a run.

"I can't believe this is happening," Cantwell said, sounding seriously shaken.

"Why don't you sit down?" Templeton suggested.

"I think I will."

Templeton touched my shoulder as I pumped on Farr's flat belly.

"Let me know if I can help."

I nodded without pausing to look up.

I worked on Raymond Farr, getting no response, until the paramedics arrived. They took over, went quickly to work, but eventually pronounced him dead.

Templeton and Kapono stood dutifully by with Cantwell's big flashlights, beaming them down on the body. Templeton had the intent look of a reporter, her eyes and ears alert. Kapono seemed more in her own world; her mouth had taken on an odd twist, barely noticeable, that suggested a private smile.

Under the added light, the victim's skin looked unexpectedly pink, as if he were embarrassed by all the trouble he'd caused. There were no wounds or blood on the body that I could see, no external signs of blunt trauma. I did notice a series of old scars on Farr's left wrist and hand, pronounced enough to indicate deep cuts at some point in his distant past. The fingers on his right hand were slightly curled and rigid, while those on his left hand were open, looking more relaxed.

Next, I surveyed the patiolike enclosure.

Beneath a shade umbrella, a half-empty bottle of imported Grolsch beer sat upright on a table, distinctive with its emerald-green glass and hinged, reclosable cap. Near it was Templeton's handbag, notebook, pen, and bottle of Evian water. Cantwell's outfielder's mitt lay forlornly on a chair, a telling counterpoint to the somber turn the evening had taken. Cantwell himself sat in the adjacent chair, looking pale and upset.

I lifted my nose. The air had grown calm and the smell of beer was strong, along with an odd, fainter scent I couldn't quite identify. The terrace itself had recently been swept clean, and was free of litter or noticeable debris, with one exception—the remains of a torpedo-shaped cigar near the entry, chewed wet on one end, cold ash at the other. A half-smoked Montecristo Number 2.

By the time I spotted it, a small crowd of the curious or concerned had come down from the house to look on, pushing forward to form a ragged group just inside the passageway.

Roberta Brickman, Leonardo Petrocelli, and Lawrence Teal were among them. Of the three, Teal appeared the most troubled, though I caught Brickman exchanging a look with Christine Kapono that was as steadfast as it was impossible to read.

Teal's agitated eyes were pointed where mine had been only moments before, at the half-smoked cigar that lay a foot or two from where he stood.

The paramedics asked the onlookers to move back and a shuffling of feet followed. When it settled, I looked again for the cigar, but didn't see it. Teal was slipping a hand into a pocket of his white shorts. When my eyes went looking for his, they took off faster than a long-legged rabbit in hunting season.

Moments later, uniformed police arrived and, minutes after that, a homicide detective.

His name was Claude DeWinter. He was a huge, jowly black man in a dark suit who stood two or three inches above six feet, with a lieutenant's badge on his belt and a big man's bellicose manner that instantly put me at odds with him.

The first thing he did was to pop a stick of sugarless gum into his mouth. The second was to order everyone off the patio who did not personally know the victim or have something pertinent to offer that might explain his death. Everyone else was to leave a name and phone number, and go home.

Brickman, Petrocelli, Teal, and Cantwell stayed, along with several others I would later learn were former Cantwell students who had met Farr once or twice. Templeton and I also remained.

Of all the civilians, I was standing closest to the victim.

"You," DeWinter hollered at me. "Over there with the others. And watch where you step."

"That Grolsch bottle," I said, as I crossed the terrace. "You should probably have the contents lab-tested."

He threw me a look.

"No shit, Sherlock."

DeWinter stood his ground like a mountain, making me go around him while he followed me with his dismissive eyes.

He softened a bit when Templeton approached with her press credentials. If she'd been male, or not so strikingly attractive, I'm not sure her press card would have made a difference.

DeWinter actually smiled a little, and lowered his voice a decibel or two. Templeton pointed to me as I took my place with the others.

"That gentleman is with me."

DeWinter regarded me critically.

"Professionally or socially?"

"We sometimes work together on stories."

"Stay out of the way," DeWinter said to me, "and we'll get along."

He directed a uniformed cop to begin taking names and information, and scanned our faces.

"Anyone here occupy the house?"

Cantwell stepped forward in his baseball outfit, his cleats clacking on the bricks.

"That would be me."

"Name?"

"Gordon Cantwell."

"You know the victim?"

"He was a student of mine."

"What do you teach?"

"Screenwriting."

"Victim's name?"

"Raymond Farr."

From the back of the pack came an unfamiliar male voice.

"His real name is Reza JaFari."

Everyone turned at once, like movie extras on cue, as if Dylan Winchester had been there directing us.

Standing at the edge of the terrace was a gaunt young man with shaggy hair down to his collar and a sparse beard scattered over the lower portions of his face. The hair and whiskers were dark, like his eyes. His look suggested Hispanic, but his face was curi-

ously pale. I immediately saw Jacques in the face and in the slender, slouching body.

"You knew the victim?" DeWinter demanded.

The young man nodded. He made his way forward, excusing
himself, until he was face to face with DeWinter.

"Relationship?"

"Roommates."

"Give me an address."

While DeWinter scribbled in a small notebook, the young man
gave his street and apartment numbers on Fountain Avenue.

DeWinter slipped a fresh stick of gum into his mouth and
glanced from the roommate to Cantwell and back again.

"So is he Reza JaFari or is he Raymond Farr?"

"He's both," the roommate said. "He was born Reza JaFari—
he's Iranian. Came here when he was, like, fourteen. Later, he
figured Raymond Farr would work better in Hollywood. At least
that's what he told me."

"He seems to have confided a lot in you."

"Like I said, we're roommates."

"What's your name, pal?"

"Daniel Romero."

"You came with him?"

"I dropped him off earlier."

"Dropped him off at what time?"

"Around seven, I guess. Earlier, maybe. He had an appointment to meet somebody."

"Who?"

"Didn't say. Just said there was a party and he wanted to get
here early, before it started. Asked me to come back around nine,
give him a ride home."

"You're late."

"I went to run my dog over in Runyon Canyon. I fell asleep."

"In the park?"

"In my truck."

"Anybody with you?"

Romero shrugged.

"Maggie."

"Who's Maggie?"

"My dog."

"Don't get cute, Danny."

"I guess nobody was with me, then."

"Anybody see you?"

"Maybe. At the park."

"After that, when you slept."

"I doubt it."

"You don't seem too shaken up, seeing your buddy lying here dead."

Romero said nothing, didn't even flinch. There was a remarkable calmness about him that was almost eerie.

"I asked you a question, Danny boy."

"No, sir. You made a statement."

DeWinter didn't like that, not a bit.

"You stay here."

The big detective crossed to the body and bent slowly down, wheezing as he strained for air with his huge gut trapped between his knees and his chest. As he reached out to examine the victim, Romero spoke again.

"You might wanna be careful how you handle him."

"I'm always careful," DeWinter said gruffly, his jaw working hard at the gum. "I been doin' this for twenty years."

"I mean extra careful—he's HIV-positive."

"Jesus!"

DeWinter rose with amazing quickness, considering his size. I saw Cantwell wipe furiously with a sleeve at the lips that had been on Reza JaFari's mouth just moments before my own. Petrocelli and Teal also registered surprise, but Roberta Brickman never even twitched.

DeWinter was looking straight at Daniel Romero.

"How do you know he's got HIV?"

Romero shrugged again.

"I know, that's all. He told me."

"Did he tell you if he liked girls or boys?"

"He was what you'd call bisexual, I guess."

"And you, Danny boy?"

"I'm gay, if that's what you're asking."

DeWinter regarded Romero with eyes full of disgust, then turned away to peer down at Reza JaFari.

"AIDS," he said, half under his breath. "At least we know what killed him."

"Romero didn't say JaFari had AIDS," I said. "He said he was HIV-positive. Big difference."

"Do me a favor," DeWinter said. "Butt out until you're asked."

He pointed a finger toward the rear of the crowd.

"And you, Romero. You stay put. Maybe he died of AIDS, or

maybe this was some kind of lovers' quarrel. Either way, we have some talking to do."

"He didn't have AIDS," Romero said. "And we weren't lovers."

Daniel Romero stood several inches shorter than Claude De-Winter, and probably weighed half as much. He was, quite possibly, in a bad situation. Yet he had just discounted the detective's two pet theories regarding the cause of Reza JaFari's death, and there wasn't a hint of acquiescence in his voice. I liked him for that, if nothing else.

DeWinter nailed Romero briefly with one of his patented hard looks.

"Yeah, yeah, yeah."

He pulled on latex gloves as he turned away to attend to the body, muttering to himself.

"Jesus, I hate these fuckin' fag deals."

# Six

LIEUTENANT DEWINTER questioned us one by one in Gordon Cantwell's study.

Templeton was the first to be interviewed, leaving her enough time to phone in details afterward for a short news story in the next day's *Sun*—a favor DeWinter granted her after she'd dropped hints that she was single and found police work fascinating.

In between, I grabbed a few seconds alone with her, just enough time to tell her that Dylan Winchester, the director, had attended the party but left before the body was found.

"Don't you think DeWinter should know that?"

"If he asks."

She raised her wrist, looked at her watch.

"I'd better find a phone and file my story."

The rest of us waited our turn in the living room, while Cantwell's housekeeper laid out a table of sandwiches and coffee in the dining room to sober us up and help us stay awake.

I was pouring a cup when Lawrence Teal sidled up next to me. All the lights were up, and his narrow face had lost some of its youthfulness, especially around the eyes.

"Please don't say anything about the cigar."

Even at a whisper, Teal sounded seriously worried.

"Not if you turn it over to me, Teal."

"Why would you want it?"

"I collect crime scene evidence as a hobby."

"What makes you think there was a crime?"

"If there wasn't, why did you snatch up Dylan Winchester's cigar before the police could find it?"

We had orders not to talk, and a uniformed cop was giving us the eye from across the room.

"I'll explain later."

"Where's the cigar?"

"I flushed it."

"You're a fool, Teal."

The cop was on his feet, eyeing us more closely. I grabbed a sandwich, showed Teal my back, and found a chair near the fireplace, waiting my turn to face the inquisition.

I passed the time stealing glances at Daniel Romero while Lawrence Teal did the same to me, his eyes looking increasingly uncomfortable as my meeting with DeWinter drew near.

Finally, I stopped sneaking peeks and simply stared. Romero's face haunted me that much; it reminded me so of Jacques's. Once or twice he looked up from his magazine, smiling a little in my direction, but without a hint of coquettishness or calculation. After a while, he stretched out on the floor with his hands behind his head and his eyes closed, his T-shirt raised just enough to reveal a flat belly between bony hips and a wispy trail of dark hair descending from his navel into his low-slung jeans.

I was imagining what the rest of him might look like when I heard DeWinter bellow my name.

I got up and crossed to the room under the stairs. DeWinter faced me from across Cantwell's antique desk. A small engraved plate facing me on the front panel informed me the desk had been used in newsroom scenes for *His Girl Friday*.

DeWinter was no more cordial than he had been earlier, and during his terse questioning, I recalled his previous command— *Butt out until you're asked*. I volunteered nothing, including what I knew of Dylan Winchester's tirade against Raymond Farr/Reza JaFari, and the cigar that had later disappeared into Lawrence Teal's pocket.

Since I had neither met nor seen JaFari before his body was discovered, my interview with DeWinter was over in less time than it took him to chew the life out of a fresh stick of gum. He kept Daniel Romero behind for more interrogation, but let the rest of us go.

The last I saw of Romero that night was DeWinter escorting him into Cantwell's study. He stopped at the doorway just long enough to glance back toward the living room, where I stood with

Templeton as she gathered up her things. His dark eyes searched my face a moment, revealing little more than curiosity, and then he was gone.

Templeton and I made our exit a few minutes past midnight. The coroner's van was parked out front and a criminalist was setting up lights on the terrace.

"Make your deadline?"

"With time to spare."

We strolled down Ridgecrest Drive toward the Mustang, which was parked a short distance up from an old pickup, which I assumed belonged to Danny Romero. All the other party vehicles were gone. Templeton talked on, pumped up from her involvement with a breaking story.

"I fed the desk enough to fill a ten-inch hole. They're boxing it somewhere on page three. An unexplained death at a Hollywood party always spices up the page."

"Especially if famous names are involved."

"Unfortunately, Dylan Winchester is the only household name I had to work with. And he's not exactly A list anymore."

"You're starting to talk like a Hollywood type, Templeton."

"Am I?"

I nodded.

"How should I talk?"

"Like a reporter type. Tell me what you got out of DeWinter."

She raised her eyebrows.

"Getting interested in the story, Justice?"

"I might be."

We'd reached the Mustang and faced each other across opposite doors. Since I was sober, she tossed me my keys.

"DeWinter feels JaFari's death could be natural or accidental, maybe an overdose. And he hasn't ruled out AIDS. But he seems to think Romero is involved in some way."

"What makes you say that?"

"Romero's name kept creeping into his conversation. And the fact that he's got no alibi."

"What else?"

"DeWinter told me the house was unlocked after six P.M. Anyone could have come and gone without being noticed."

"Somebody must have seen something."

"Between six and seven P.M., Cantwell was in the early innings of his softball game. Kapono was down the hill picking up ice. The housekeeper was in different parts of the house, getting ready for the party."

"They leave the place wide open?"

"On party night. It's pretty much BYOB, come when you want. Cantwell leaves Kapono in charge."

"According to Romero, he dropped JaFari off sometime before seven. JaFari took a beer with him down to the terrace, either with someone or alone, to keep his appointment."

"And died there."

"Leaving Romero the last person to see him alive."

"At least that's how DeWinter figures it."

"You and DeWinter have gotten pretty chummy pretty fast."

"There are certain advantages to being female."

She said it with a crafty smile.

"At least when the cop's straight," I said, recalling a few of my own police sources from the old days who weren't.

The driver's door groaned as I pulled it open. I slid in behind the wheel.

"So, you think DeWinter's zeroing in on Romero?"

"He says it's not uncommon when the murder victim is gay to find out a lover is involved."

"Gosh, just like heterosexuals."

She smiled ruefully, with a shrug of her shoulders.

"And presuming it is murder," I added.

"Presuming, yes."

"Only Romero says he and JaFari weren't romantically involved."

"DeWinter doesn't buy it."

"He can't imagine two homosexuals living together and not fucking like bunnies?"

"He does seem to have his preconceptions."

"If Romero's guilty, why would he come back the same night so openly?"

"By DeWinter's reasoning? For exactly that purpose—to give himself the appearance of innocence."

We buckled our seat belts, and I slipped the key into the switch.

"So, are you going to work with me on the magazine piece, Justice?"

I punched the accelerator twice and turned the key. The carburetor choked and gave up. Three attempts later the engine kicked over and I goosed it with a little gas until it idled.

"Here's your lead, Templeton: *Screenplays were stacked up knee deep around the upstairs toilet, and there was a dead man down on the terrace. Just another Hollywood party.* You can take it from there.''

"It's cute. But I need more than an opening, Justice. I was in over my head to begin with. Now the story's complicated by an unexplained death.''

"Not complicated, Templeton—*enhanced.* You've got more to work with now. Makes your job easier.''

"I don't know if I can sort it all out.''

"That's what outlines are for.''

"There's still some hard research to be done, and several interviews. I'm running out of time.''

"You're a pro, Templeton. You'll handle it.''

She sat in silence for a moment, then took a deep breath before she spoke.

"Harry's already spoken to my editor at *Angel City*. He's gotten you cleared to join me on the assignment.''

"Harry did *what?*''

"They're old friends, back from Harry's early days at the *Times.* Harry asked if you could assist me, to take some of the load off. Said he needs me back on my regular beat at the *Sun*. Officially, you'll be my research assistant. You might even get a tag credit.''

"Harry's meddling in my life again.''

"*What* life?''

I slipped the Mustang angrily out of park, then twisted the wheels through the angles of a Y-turn until they were pointed downhill. I was shifting into drive when I heard Lawrence Teal's voice from up the road, calling my name.

We turned to see him trotting toward us, his sandals slapping the asphalt.

"Your blond friend,'' Templeton said.

"You got the hair color right.''

Teal leaned against the driver's door, catching his breath.

"I was wondering if you could give me a lift down the hill.''

His eyes were searching mine again, telling me we needed to talk.

"I've been waiting for a cab, but I'm not sure it's coming.''

"Sure, get in.''

He climbed into the backseat, and I introduced him to Templeton. I started down the hill, while Templeton leaned over the seat.

"I understand you knew Reza JaFari.''

"As Raymond Farr.''

"How well?"

"Saw him around now and then. That's about it."

I glanced at Teal in the mirror.

"What was his connection to Dylan Winchester?"

Tension passed like a shadow across Teal's face.

"Why do you ask that?"

"You and Winchester are pretty close, aren't you?"

"We're acquainted."

"I saw the two of you together earlier this evening."

He looked away, and kept his mouth shut.

"I also know that Winchester was looking for Farr. Angry with him, as a matter of fact."

"You didn't tell me that," Templeton said.

I kept my eyes on Teal in the mirror.

"Teal?"

"I wouldn't know about that."

"Justice, watch out!"

My eyes darted back to the road as we came off a curve. I stomped on the brake pedal.

Directly ahead, caught between my low beams, was the old lady with the shopping cart full of bottles. I twisted the wheel hard and the nose of the Mustang veered sharply to the right. I heard the sound of worn tires sliding with a soft *swish* across the pavement, then a clatter of metal against metal as my car door made contact with the wheeled basket.

The Mustang stopped sideways across the road. The old woman hobbled after the cart as it rolled downhill on wobbly wheels.

All three of us were out of the car in seconds. Teal went after the runaway cart while Templeton and I raced to the old woman's side. When we took her arms, she shook us off.

"Let me go," she said. "I want my bottles!"

"We'll get your bottles for you," Templeton said. "Are you all right?"

"My bottles!"

Teal caught up with the cart and held on to it until we reached him.

"Thank the Lord!" The old woman patted Teal's cheek, then smiled at Templeton and me. "Not a single one broken."

"I think we should get out of the road," Templeton said. "Before another car—"

"The road is the problem," the old woman said. "They made

it wider. Paved it. All the cars. Houses everywhere. So beautiful before that. So unspoiled."

"Let me take you home," I said.

"My home is the canyon! Until the flames come!"

Templeton and I exchanged a glance. We guided the old woman to the side of the road.

"You live in the canyon?"

"Seventy years I've had my house—since 1927. The house my husband built."

Templeton lay a hand gently on the woman's shoulder.

"Why don't you show us where it is?"

"Why should I do that?"

"We love old houses. Don't we, Justice?"

I nodded.

"Come, then!"

The old woman was already moving down the hill behind her cart. I climbed back into the Mustang and moments later pulled alongside.

"She says her name is Constance Fairbridge," Templeton said. "Her house is just down the road."

I followed slowly behind, while the old woman recited passages from Genesis. Before long she crossed the road to a dirt-and-gravel drive, where the wheels of her cart settled into familiar grooves. A white mailbox with the name Fairbridge scrawled in pencil stood at the entrance.

The drive led through a stand of oak so thick no moonlight pierced it into a clearing of wild grass and a carpet of ivy coated with dust. A two-car garage built of split logs stood off to the right, leaning badly from age and neglect. Next to it was an ancient gasoline pump with a crank handle and metered numbers frozen in another time.

A two-story cabin that resembled a small hunting lodge stood on the left of the property, with a broad porch running all around. It was a generous, untended piece of land that had some-how survived the ungentle subdivision that had carved up the rest of the area over the decades. Beyond the house was a private stretch of canyon well hidden from the road.

Glass bottles were everywhere, hundreds of them. Clear bottles, colored ones, all shapes and sizes. They lined the porch, the steps, the railing. More could be seen inside, on the ledges of the windows.

I parked and climbed out.

"Are you sure you're all right, Mrs. Fairbridge?"

"The cars," she said. "I forget about the cars."

"Do you live alone?" Templeton asked.

The old woman's eyes scanned the trees, then the dense underbrush.

"I have the birds. The little animals."

"Anyone else?"

"You'll find all the truth you need in the book of Genesis."

"Would you like us to call anyone?" Templeton said.

"Why?"

The old woman looked at Templeton like she was crazy.

Templeton smiled.

"No reason. As long as you're all right."

"I'm just fine. You've been very nice."

Her face grew troubled; she took Templeton by the wrist.

"Come, let me show you."

Mrs. Fairbridge tugged Templeton along, while Teal and I followed. The old boards creaked under our weight.

When she reached the front of the house, she raised a thin, scabby arm and pointed up the canyon with an unsteady finger.

"Sodom and Gomorrah!"

She looked around at the three of us, fierce emotion showing inside the pink rims of her watery eyes.

"Sins of the mother and the father, visited on the child! Oh, the shame, the unpardonable sin!"

"Maybe she's upset about the Hollywood Sign," Teal said. "Some movie she saw?"

Mrs. Fairbridge shook a gnarled finger in Teal's face.

"Not the sign!"

She swung her arm and pointed back up the long, jagged ravine.

I stooped to follow the direction of her finger more carefully, and realized it was fixed on Gordon Cantwell's hillside house.

A hundred feet below, the criminalist's lamps could be seen on the terrace, casting their eerie light into the canyon's shadows.

# Seven

W E EMERGED from the lower slopes of Mount Lee onto
Beachwood Drive, which took us in a straight line through
the Hollywoodland Gates to the flats below.

The sandstone gates, with their arched passageways for pedestrians and peaked columns for show, had been erected in 1923 as
the entrance to a prestigious new subdivision. The Hollywood
Sign had gone up the same year—as HOLLYWOODLAND—an enormous billboard advertising the sale of real estate, which would
not lose its last four letters and some of its crassness until a much-
needed renovation in 1945.

By day, the Hollywoodland Gates had a fairy tale quality. Now,
after the unsettling events of the evening, they looked hulking
and gothic.

"I'm glad to be out of there," Templeton said, as I hit the last,
flat mile of Beachwood Drive and the sign became a row of
crooked teeth in my rearview mirror.

With the hills behind us, I picked up the signal for KLON-FM
at 88.1 and we listened to some lush Saturday night jazz while
gliding through a scabrous section of Hollywood down to Santa
Monica Boulevard.

At the intersection, several patrol cars were pulled up at a gas
station, pinning down a three-toned Dodge van. The cops had
two young white men spread-eagled against the side panels; two
more were being handcuffed on the ground, their pimply faces
pressed against the greasy pavement.

"Just what we need," Templeton said. "A little more drama."

"What we need is a party."

It was Teal, from the backseat, sounding petulant.

"We just came from a party," Templeton said.

"Yes, and there was a *dead* person there."

I turned right onto Santa Monica Boulevard, pointing the Mustang past a string of Latino bars and equity waiver theaters toward West Hollywood. It was 1 A.M., and this part of the world belonged to dancers, drinkers, cabbies, and whores, along with roving vehicles filled with jumpy-eyed teenagers on the prowl.

Three miles and a few dozen curbside hustlers later, we crossed La Cienega Boulevard into the heart of Boy's Town. The first busy bar we passed was the Powder Room, overflowing with women rather than men; another lesbian enclave appeared soon after, a cozy little coffeehouse called Eleanor's Secret.

After that, as West Hollywood began edging up against Beverly Hills, the street was crawling almost exclusively with men.

We slowed to a stop in the heavy traffic and felt a sonic disco boom hit us from one of the clubs, where a line had formed to get in and music blasted through the open doors.

"Christian extremists could launch a SCUD missile attack on West Hollywood," Templeton said to me, "but the bars in Boy's Town would stay open for business."

"With most of the customers making jokes about the size of the incoming missiles."

I turned right at Hilldale, pausing as a stream of young men crossed between the bank and the bagel joint. Two or three blew kisses or made lewd propositions to Teal, who now sat perched atop the backseat like a prom queen, pretending not to notice. He told me he'd get out at my place and walk home from there.

A minute later I was pulling to the curb in front of the small house owned by my landlords, Maurice and Fred. A gleaming new Infiniti, a twenty-sixth birthday gift from Templeton's ever-doting father, sat in the driveway. A light was on in the living room—unusual at that hour for Maurice and Fred—and I could see them huddled in earnest conversation on the sofa.

"Remember my offer," Templeton said, as she faced me on the sidewalk. "I could really use a partner on this magazine piece."

"I'll think it over."

"Did I mention that *Angel City* pays a dollar a word?"

"Not that I recall."

"They do."

"It's a decent rate for a city magazine."

"That's more than two thousand apiece, Justice—after we split."

"And more than four thousand for you if we don't."

"Don't tell me you're not strapped for cash."

"I'm always strapped for cash, and you know it."

"Any work lately?"

"I ghosted a few trade journal pieces last month. For a real estate executive who writes like a lawyer."

"You must have loved that."

"It was a job. No byline. No background check. No questions asked."

"What did this job pay?"

"Not a buck a word."

"We definitely should talk, then."

She pecked me on the cheek and started toward her fancy new car.

"Templeton—I'm not looking for charity. Not from you, not from Harry."

"Don't worry, Justice—if you come aboard, you'll earn every penny."

She drove off waving a hand out the window, as if having me back in her life was already reducing What'shisname to an inconsequential memory. I wasn't sure I liked that. But I did like the sound of a buck a word.

"I was hoping we could talk."

Teal stood next to me, looking fidgety.

"Really? What about?"

His eyes flashed mild contempt.

"You're enjoying this, aren't you, Justice?"

"Somewhat."

Slowly, like a chameleon changing colors, his manner grew soft, deferential.

"Maybe I could buy you a drink."

"Congratulations, Teal. You said the magic words."

We walked to Rimbaud's, three blocks down in the thick of the action. It was Teal's choice, not at all the kind of place I would have picked. I was doing my best to stay out of bars these days, away from the siren call of hard liquor, but if I was going to be in one, I preferred a long, dark counter with beat-up bar stools, sawdust and peanut shells on the floor, kick-ass music, and a pool table where good-looking young men had to bend over to make their shots, showing their shape.

I suspected Teal was looking for a comfort zone and, for someone like Teal, Rimbaud's would be the place. It was a small, polished, continental restaurant with linen tablecloths and fresh-cut flowers where you could hear soothing Sinatra and Nat King Cole tunes in the background and listen to bitchy comments at the bar about Drew Barrymore's hair and Tom Selleck's marriage. It was also popular with the kind of older gentlemen who dote on cute young men like Teal the way lonely matrons do small, fluffy dogs.

The breathy voice of Carmen McRae singing "A Taste of Honey" welcomed us as we entered. Heads swiveled, eyes drawn immediately to Teal's blond, youthful head, before moving down to see if the rest matched up.

We squeezed into a corner of the bar that looked out on the street, where hundreds of young men made their final move to one more club before the 2 A.M. curfew, the way thousands of straight men and women were moving with quiet desperation in other parts of the city.

The bartender wore tight shorts and a tighter tank top. His skin was flawless, his hair peroxided, and he clenched his butt so tight when he walked that it looked sutured. After some silly small talk that included a sexual innuendo or two, he took our orders and sashayed away.

Teal leaned close, indicating he was ready to talk, or at least negotiate. I tossed out the first chip.

"So tell me, Teal, just how long have you known Dylan Winchester?"

"Suppose I don't want to discuss certain things?"

"Suppose I give Lieutenant DeWinter a call and tell him you disposed of Winchester's cigar?"

"Maybe he wouldn't believe you." Teal had turned snippy again; it seemed he couldn't help himself. "After all, you're fairly notorious when it comes to making things up."

"Let's try another scenario, Teal. Suppose DeWinter does believe me. What if he decides to ask you some tough questions—putting you in the position of having to lie to a cop?"

I leaned close to his ear.

"Destroying evidence is a felony, Teal. That cute ass of yours would get quite a workout in Men's Central."

Teal's Adam's apple performed a little jump as he swallowed.

Then, unhappily: "Anything I tell you is strictly off the record."

"I can live with that."

The bartender placed a generous glass of fumé blanc in front of me and a double scotch rocks in front of Teal, and took Teal's cash away.

Teal raised his glass in a toast, though he wasn't smiling.

"To our new relationship."

He couldn't have made it sound any less warm. I tapped his glass with mine, and we sipped.

"Tell me about Dylan Winchester, Lawrence."

"Private or professional?"

"Professional I can get from his résumé."

The recitation that followed—delivered coldly, with a trace of venom—was not what I'd expected.

"Dylan likes slim, smooth boys with brown skin. Light or dark, as long as they're pretty. Asian or Mexican, in the fifteen to twenty range—although he's been with his current boyfriend for a decade. Which you'd understand if you saw him."

"You're telling me Dylan Winchester's gay?"

"What did you think I was doing with him when you saw us? Auditioning for his next movie?"

"It crossed my mind."

"Up yours, Justice."

"We'll discuss that later."

He gave me a sour smile and drank more scotch.

"Dylan looks like rough trade and likes to act tough. But in bed he's almost exclusively a bottom."

"You seem to know a lot about him."

"I get around."

"You still haven't told me what you were doing with him in the yard."

Teal hesitated; anxiety kept his eyes moving.

"A few minutes earlier, I'd seen him going down the steps."

"Toward the terrace."

"Yes. He was calling out Ray Farr's name. Dylan sounded drunk, angry. I followed him, even though it was dark."

"Why?"

"The awful truth?" Teal attempted nonchalance. "I wanted to get him alone so I could give him a blow job."

"How romantic."

"I'm not the romantic type, a trait I believe we share." He smirked. "Judging from your earlier behavior."

"It depends on whom I'm with."

"That makes two of us."

So we loathed each other; that was out of the way.

"What happened when you followed Winchester down to the terrace?"

"I never got that far. I ran into him as he was coming back up."

"What was his mood?"

"Upset, in a hurry."

"Without his cigar, I take it?"

"Yes."

"You tried to talk to him?"

"He brushed past me, determined to get away. I went after him. That must have been when you saw us."

"So you never saw JaFari's body until—"

He cut me off, sounding both sincere and scared.

"I didn't know he was down there until your friend Alexandra came upstairs to tell you. I swear, that's the truth."

"How well known is it that Winchester likes boys?"

"He doesn't advertise it. After all, he makes a living directing action pictures for the major studios. But it's no secret in gay circles that he's queer."

"Maybe it's just rumor. That's common enough."

"I speak from firsthand knowledge, Justice."

"But you're as blond as a baby chick. You told me—"

"Dylan makes exceptions if you're young enough and he's had enough to drink. At the time, I was and he had."

"When was that?"

"More years ago than I care to count."

"Count anyway."

"Nine, ten. Somewhere in there."

"And now you're trying to rekindle the old flame?"

"I'm turned on by butch men. Let's just leave it at that."

"For now, maybe."

He turned to stare out at the street, looking haughty again.

"Why was Winchester looking for Reza JaFari tonight?"

"You'll have to ask him that."

"What was their relationship?"

"They slept together briefly when Raymond—that is, Reza—was a teenager. You know, before that heavy beard and all the body hair. Body hair is a big no-no with Dylan."

"How long did it last?"

"Dylan got tired of Ray after a few weeks and started looking for someone new. He was a hot young director back then, handsome as hell. Boys were all over him, not to mention girls. He had his pick of hopeful starlets, of which I was one."

"And Reza?"

"He didn't have the patience for acting. He was just one of those pretty boys who slip into the gay Hollywood circuit and date older men with money."

"And eventually he met Winchester."

"It was at a party up in the hills thrown by Nando Sorentino, the set designer. Schlesinger was there and Vidal and Jim Bridges, the writer-director." Teal shook his head, as if to himself. "He's dead, isn't he? Nando, too, come to think of it. God, it's time to weed out the old phone book again."

"JaFari connected with Winchester that night?"

"Out by Nando's pool. The light reflecting up through the blue water, the city lights twinkling below—it was the perfect setting. Here was this kid, seventeen or eighteen, slim, nice face. He had this incredible long dark hair that he brushed straight back like Bo Derek when she still had a career. New to the scene, waiting to be plucked. Dylan started drooling the moment he saw him."

"And they were together by the end of the night."

"Raymond fell hard. He figured Dylan was his romantic fantasy and his ticket to the easy life all wrapped up into one."

"You make him sound awfully naive."

"Don't get me wrong. Ray was no virgin. He'd been fucked by plenty of men before he came to this country. Sexually, he was quite experienced."

"How do you know all this?"

"He talked about it once—about certain sexual practices in the Middle East. Ray said it's not that uncommon for young boys to be used sexually by older men, especially married men. It's just not talked about."

"But emotionally—"

"Ray was as ripe as a summer peach. Full of romantic notions when he came here, like a lot of immigrants. He didn't understand that to men like Dylan, he was just another good-looking kid to be used and tossed away like Kleenex during the cold season."

Teal's voice and face suddenly grew bitter.

"Needless to say, Hollywood is littered with used-up boys and girls like that."

"After Winchester dumped JaFari, you still saw him around?"

"He was different. After Dylan, Ray became more calculating.

Started sleeping around a lot more, with both men and women, to get what he wanted.''

"And what was that?''

"Who knows? He talked about being a screenwriter, a producer, a director. Mostly, he was a hustler, out to get what he could with the least amount of effort. He had the looks, but there are thousands of young men in this town with great looks and no more talent than it takes to sell shoes.''

"JaFari must have had something going for him. Roberta Brickman hired him as her assistant.''

Teal reacted with a snort.

"I don't think so.''

"That's what she told me at the party.''

Teal raised his eyebrows, seeming to accept it.

"I knew Farr had a low-level job at ITA. Working as a runner or something. But working for an agent of her caliber?'' He paused, then shrugged a little. "Maybe he finally got his act together. Stranger things have happened.''

The bartender announced last call. Teal raised his glass, set it down next to mine, and the bartender whisked them away.

"You still haven't told me why you picked up Winchester's cigar.''

He kept his eyes averted, saying nothing.

"Talk to me, Teal. Unless you'd rather talk to DeWinter.''

He dropped his head for a long moment, staring at the bar. When he looked back up, his eyes blinked back tears. He might have been acting; I suspected not.

"Obviously, I did it to protect Dylan.''

"Then you think he's connected to JaFari's death.''

"I didn't say that.''

"Why then?''

"Dylan went down there looking for Ray Farr, who's gay. Or bisexual, whatever. I followed him down hoping for a quickie. If the police find that out, the press finds out. You know how reporters are. You people won't leave it alone until you've dug up every choice little morsel. The more tawdry, the better. You guys live for that stuff.

"They'd connect Dylan to me, to JaFari, to half the kids he slept with. Straight directors can get away with sleeping around like that. Look at Polanski—he diddled a thirteen-year-old girl and he still works, even sits as a judge at film festivals. So do a few hundred other breeders like him who never got caught. But Dylan's career would be over with the first headline. He'd be lucky to make a living shooting commercials back in Australia. I don't think he could live with that."

A tear spilled over; he wiped it quickly away.

"You fell as hard for him as JaFari, didn't you, Teal? You still carry a torch."

He glared at me for a moment, then looked away as the bartender set fresh drinks in front of us. Teal gave him more money, and we drank in silence for a minute or two. The bar was slowly emptying out.

"I never liked being the last one out of a bar," I said.

"You haven't finished your wine."

I picked up my glass and drank it down. Then I shoved the glass away and slid my other hand up Teal's thigh.

"My place or yours?"

Teal was staring straight ahead, into the empty dining room.

"Maybe I don't like being taken for granted."

"It's supposed to be the other way around, isn't it, Teal? You're supposed to take *me* for granted."

His mouth curled unattractively. Then he tipped his head back and swallowed the last of his scotch.

He set his glass down and looked at me in a way that suggested desire behind the hatred.

"You really think you're something, don't you, Justice?"

I stroked the inside of his thigh, then reached deeper, where I felt the meat between his legs getting hard.

"Shall we go?"

Back on Norma Place, the house was dark; Maurice and Fred had finally ended their earnest conversation and gone to bed.

Teal followed me up the gravel-strewn drive to the garage. We mounted the stairs to the small apartment at the top, where I'd lived rent free for more than a year, since ending a six-year drinking binge that somehow had failed to kill me.

Inside, I left the lights out. Our shirts came off first, each of us handling that step ourselves, quickly and efficiently.

When I reached out, I was surprised to find Teal's body firmer than his soft looks had suggested. We dropped our pants and shorts to our ankles and left them there. Teal's torso was tightly muscled and hairless down to his lower belly, where an erection rose up that was well out of proportion to his slim frame. At its base, large, droopy testicles were furred with soft curls. When I touched them, I heard Teal draw in his breath sharply through clenched teeth.

We got each other off standing up, my right hand on his cock, his right hand on mine. There was nothing remotely sweet or gentle about it; it was all heat and desire and burning pleasure, driving us into a single, frenzied rhythm of which we were both well-practiced masters.

Teal groaned and erupted, gasping as he came. I followed seconds later. We clung to each other for a few moments more, Teal's fingers grasping the thick hair on my chest, my hands molded to his tight, smooth buttocks, until the momentary madness of sex had subsided.

Then he pried himself away, speaking crisply.

"That went well. Towel?"

I handed him one, he cleaned up and put his clothes quickly back together.

"I guess this means we're not getting engaged."

He smiled a little and turned toward the door, buckling his belt.

"See you around."

"One more question, Teal."

He waited with his hand on the doorknob.

"Dylan Winchester went to the party tonight looking for Reza JaFari."

"I believe we already established that."

"Roberta Brickman and a screenwriter named Leonardo Petrocelli were there for the same reason."

"So?"

"It strikes me as quite a coincidence—three different people looking for the same man, an unimportant one at that, who later turns up dead."

"Not really."

"I don't follow."

"To outsiders, Hollywood may seem like a big place. But it's actually a very small world, built on the most unusual relationships. You might even say incestuous."

"Thanks for your insight."

"Not at all."

He stepped out the door and trotted down the stairs.

I watched him until he reached the end of the driveway, disappearing as he hit the street.

Back inside, I found a notebook and filled several pages with what Teal had told me.

Then I took a shower, trying to wash away the smell of him, the memory.

# Eight

I WOKE Sunday morning to a telephone that wouldn't stop ringing, no matter how long I ignored it.

When I finally answered, I wasn't surprised to hear the grating voice of Lieutenant Claude DeWinter at the other end.

He had read Templeton's news item in that morning's *Sun*, called her at home, then called me. He wasn't happy.

"She wrote that Dylan Winchester was at the party last night. The movie guy."

I let out a monstrous yawn.

"How interesting, Lieutenant."

"She tells me she got the information about Winchester from you."

"True enough."

"Where did you see him?"

"In Gordon Cantwell's downstairs hallway. Later, outside the house."

"Where outside?"

"The south side."

"Where the terrace is located."

"That general area, yes."

"What was he doing?"

"Leaving."

"When was this, roughly?"

"Nine thirty-two P.M., roughly."

"Why are you so sure about the time?"

"I looked at my watch."

"Why?"

"I wanted to know the time. Look, Lieutenant—"

"Why didn't you tell me this last night?"

"You didn't ask."

"That's not how it works, Justice."

"On the contrary, Lieutenant. You told me in no uncertain terms to butt out until I was asked. Like I said, you didn't ask."

"I don't put up with this kind of shit, Justice. I bring the hammer down on jerks like you."

"If you want people to cooperate, Lieutenant, maybe you should be more careful how you talk to them. For starters, I'm not enamored of the word *fag*. Not when it comes from someone who isn't one."

"How about *punk*?"

"Sorry, don't care for that one, either."

"I could toss your ass in the can for obstruction. You know that, don't you?"

Another yawn got away from me.

"I haven't had my morning coffee, Lieutenant. Can't this wait?"

"Where can I find Winchester?"

"What am I, his agent?"

"Suppose you tell me who his agent is."

"Until recently, he was with ITA—International Talent Associates. They can probably help you find him."

"And if they can't?"

"Call the studio that's releasing a movie called *Thunder's Fortune*. Winchester directed it."

"What else can you tell me that might be useful to this investigation?"

"Try calling later in the day, Lieutenant, when I've got some caffeine in my system. Better yet, don't call me, I'll call you."

I hung up. The phone started ringing again. I shoved it under the pillow and left it there until it stopped.

By then I had on a pair of sweatpants and was drawing the string as I made my way down the stairs.

"Coffee, Benjamin?"

It was Maurice, down in the yard with Fred, sorting and packing donations they'd collected for Out of the Closet, a small chain of thrift stores operated by the AIDS Healthcare Foundation. It was the new focus of their volunteer work, since the foundation had closed its hospice, now that more and more people with AIDS were living longer and healthier lives.

"Desperately."

"I just made a fresh pot. Help yourself. You know the way."

They went back to work while I crossed the patio. Maurice, slim and agile, scurried about moving the lighter items and organizing the packing. Fred, big and beefy, handled the heavy stuff. They were working on their forty-second year as a couple, and moved together like the pistons of a well-oiled Packard Deluxe.

When I emerged from the house, gulping hot coffee, Maurice looked up from taping a box.

"We need to talk, Benjamin."

He sounded a bit anxious, which wasn't like him. The three of us took chairs at the patio table under the leafy branches of the jacaranda, sharing the shade with two chubby cats. Fred picked his teeth with a twig while Maurice drew back his long, white hair and bundled it into a ponytail.

"I may as well get right to the point, Benjamin. I've lost my job. They're closing the dance school."

"Jesus. I'm sorry."

"After thirty-three years, I'm out of work. Classical dance instructors aren't in great demand these days, certainly not at my age."

I knew where he was going, and he had every right to go there. I just wasn't eager to make the trip with him.

"I'll be sixty-six in April. The two of us have our Social Security and the house is paid for. Fred has a small pension. But there's not a lot left over."

Fred grunted, which was about as much as I ever heard from him.

"I'll start paying rent," I said.

It was a humiliating thing to have to say at the age of thirty-nine, something more appropriate for a kid graduating high school. But the fact was, I hadn't earned more than a few thousand dollars a year in the seven years since I'd left the journalism business following the Pulitzer mess.

"We're not going to throw you out," Maurice said. "It was Jacques's old apartment, after all, and we haven't been eager to have anyone in it but you. But we would like you to start exploring more income possibilities."

He said it as gently as he could, and Maurice was the gentlest of souls. But it still felt like warm piss in the face. Some people actually enjoy warm piss in the face, but I've never been a golden shower queen myself.

"I'll have something for you by the first of the month. Would five hundred do for starters?"

"Five hundred would be fine. But that's awfully soon, Benjamin. We don't expect—"

"Last night, an opportunity presented itself."

Maurice brightened and sat forward in his chair.

"An opportunity? Really!"

I nodded, forcing a smile.

"Did you hear that, Fred? Reporting, Benjamin?"

"Something like that."

He grabbed my hand optimistically.

"That's wonderful! I'm sure it will develop into something!"

I shrugged, and kept the smile up.

He leaned closer, trying to squeeze a little more out of the moment.

"Maybe you'd like to spend the afternoon with Fred and me at the thrift shop. I'm sure they'd find something useful for you to do. Sorting goods. Sweeping up—"

It was something Maurice suggested every few months, testing to see where I was on the subject of AIDS. I was still in the same place I'd been since Jacques's death—I wanted nothing to do with the world of AIDS in any way, shape, or form.

"Try me in another month or two, Maurice. Maybe—"

"I understand."

I carried my coffee upstairs to call Templeton, feeling more like a doomed man with every step.

There must have been a million aspiring freelance writers who would have killed for the chance to cowrite an article for *Angel City* at a buck a word, even without full credit. To me, it felt like a sentence of punishment. It meant returning to an occupation where I could never be anything more than Templeton's shadow, where my past would cling to me like sewage, where my name would always leave its peculiar stink on the story. Not exactly a fulfilling way to work, but employment nonetheless, which I badly needed at that moment.

I dialed Templeton's number with mixed feelings. She picked up halfway through the first ring.

"Benjamin. I was just about to call you."

I could hear Joshua Redman in the background, blowing

"Sweet Sorrow" on his mournful sax. It seemed an appropriate tune.

"I'm accepting your offer, Templeton. Fifty-fifty, down the middle. On one condition."

"What's that?"

"I'll need a cash advance. Say, a thousand by the end of the week."

"That sounds doable. What changed your mind?"

"The prospect of homelessness."

"Always a great motivator. Where would you like to start?"

I didn't have to think about it long.

"Daniel Romero."

A telling moment of silence followed.

"Why am I not surprised?"

"Don't start, Templeton."

"I noticed how you were looking at him last night. You think you can keep your professional distance?"

"Probably not. You have his number?"

I jotted down the ten digits that came over the phone. Then I asked her how she got them.

"Confidential source."

"Does your confidential source weigh three hundred pounds and chew sugarless gum?"

"Let me know what you learn from Romero. And remember, Justice—you're a reporter now."

"After a fashion."

"Keep me posted."

I heard a click at her end, and cut the connection at mine just long enough to get a new dial tone.

Then I punched in Daniel Romero's number, feeling my pulse race a little, which it hadn't done for a long, long time.

# Nine

D ANIEL ROMERO lived on a badly potholed stretch of Fountain Avenue in a two-story apartment building the sickly color of gourmet mustard.

Out front, some Hispanic and black kids were splashing in a play pool while an older sister kept an eye on them, then more warily on me as I mounted the front steps.

Romero's apartment was on the second floor, at the end of an exterior landing that needed sweeping. A note on his door directed visitors to the garage at the rear of the building.

I followed a cracked concrete driveway past sad-looking shrubbery and shriveled weeds struggling to survive in arid ground until I reached a row of small garages out back.

In one of them, Romero was kneeling, hand-sanding an unvarnished table, with sawdust and carpentry tools all around him. He'd shaved away his whiskers, leaving his face smooth and boyish, with a razor nick under his chin. Faded jeans and a cheap tank top hung loosely on his lanky frame. On his upper arms I counted three Indian-style tattoos, stitched in dyes of red and blue.

At his side was an old golden retriever who barked half-heartedly before getting up slowly to greet me with a busy tail.

"Hello, Daniel."

He got to his feet with some effort, his eyes big and dark in his narrow face.

"Danny," he said.

We shook hands.

"It was Daniel last night."

"I was talking to a cop last night."

The dog nuzzled my hand.

"Maggie!"

Maggie left my hand alone but stood her ground and kept her tail going, a wise old dog who knew the boundaries.

"On the phone, you said you wanted to ask some questions about Reza."

I nodded. He glanced at my notebook and pen.

"Why don't we go upstairs?"

I ran my fingers along the surface of the big rectangular table. The wood was dark and richly grained, with solid, square legs flawlessly joined at each corner and rising half an inch above the table's horizontal plane. Atop the four corner squares were bas relief carvings that appeared to be Native American, like Romero's tattoos; more carvings of similar design extended down the legs.

"Cherry?"

"Black walnut."

"It's beautiful."

"Thanks."

I touched one of the corner carvings.

"Indian symbols?"

He pointed to each of the designs.

"Earth . . . Wind . . . Rain . . . Fire."

"Any particular tribe?"

"Tokona. My father's people. Out of Oklahoma."

"This table has a lot of meaning for you, then."

I was rewarded with a small, embarrassed grin.

"Don't give me too much credit." He touched the symbol for Earth. "I had to go to the library and look 'em up."

He pulled down the warped garage door, locked it behind him, and we started back. He wasn't moving any quicker than the old dog, and used the handrail when we reached the stairs.

"You look tired."

"It was a long night."

We entered a small, drab apartment that was beaten up with age and neglect. Rust-colored water stains were visible on the cottage cheese ceiling, and the grubby green carpet felt thin and tacky under my feet. What furniture there was looked cheap and factory made, like an odd assortment of garage sale specials.

"I've sold all my handmade pieces," Romero explained. "Except the table. I'm keeping that, at least for a while."

He asked if I was thirsty. I said I was and followed him into the tiny kitchen, where he pulled open the refrigerator door. The refrigerator didn't have much in it. What it did have that caught my eye were several emerald green bottles, each with a hinged, reclosable cap.

"You drink Grolsch?"

"Reza," Romero said. "It was the only beer he ever touched."

I glanced around at the shabby surroundings.

"It doesn't quite fit."

"He didn't have much money but he had expensive tastes. Designer clothes, fancy cologne—Grolsch beer."

"Status symbols."

"I guess." He indicated the bottles. "Have one if you want. Reza won't be drinking it."

I opted for a soda; so did Romero.

"Maybe you'd like to see his room."

"Thanks, I would."

I followed Romero down a dim, narrow hallway, with the dog tagging along. I paused at the first door and Romero came back.

"That's my room." He reached down and scratched the dog around the ears. "Actually, me and Maggie sleep there. Don't we, girl?"

"Had her long?"

"Ever since I came out from Oklahoma. Found her on the street, up in San Francisco. She was just a pup."

"When was that?"

"Ten years ago, 'round in there."

"You must have been a teenager."

"Eighteen."

"What brought you to the City?"

"Life on the reservation was feeling a little cramped."

"You lived with your father then."

"Off and on. I bounced around a lot."

"Your mother?"

"Mestiza. Out of New Mexico. Small village called Milagro, up in the Sangre de Cristos."

"*Milagro.* 'Miracle.'"

"You speak Spanish."

"A little. Beautiful country up there."

"Yeah, real nice."

I saw a backpack leaning against the wall, a vintage Kelty with a rolled sleeping bag and foam pad bound to the frame.

"You spend much time in the mountains?"

"Not like I used to. You?"

"My boyfriend and I used to do a lot of backpacking."

Romero didn't say anything, just nodded a little.

"Mostly the eastern Sierra," I said. "Lone Pine up to Mammoth. All the trails."

"That's a great range—about as good as it gets."

We were standing close; his eyes were direct, curious. I hadn't talked to anyone about the mountains since Jacques died.

"When was the last time you were up?"

"Coupla years. You?"

"Not since Jacques got too sick to go. A long time."

"How is he now?"

"Dead."

"Sorry."

"It happens."

"I know." His eyes pulled away. "Come on, I'll show you Reza's room."

He shuffled down the hall to a door at the end.

Inside, a narrow bed and sizable desk competed for space with teetering stacks of *Variety* and the *Hollywood Reporter,* wedged between piles of *Premiere, Buzz, Movieline,* and *Entertainment Weekly.*

On the desk was a computer, printer, combination telephone and fax machine, answering machine, and Rolodex. In a corner of the desk, standing upright between bookends, were a number of Hollywood resource books—the *Hollywood Creative Directory,* the *Hollywood Reporter Blu-Book,* the *Studio Directory.* Also between the bookends was a copy of *The Cantwell Method,* by Gordon Cantwell, along with several other manuals on scriptwriting bearing such author names as Field, Truby, Seger, and McKee.

"Reza talked a lot about making movies," Romero said. "He was always coming up with a new idea for one."

I glanced around.

"I don't see any scripts."

"I don't think he actually did any writing. He was mostly a talker, I guess."

"And what was it he talked about?"

"Some deal he had going, some new contact, a producer or director he was trying to meet. To be honest, I didn't pay a lot of attention. I'm not really into that Hollywood stuff."

"You lived together. The two of you must have had some things in common."

"When we met, I needed a place to stay. He gave me the room and let me pay him when I could. It was an OK deal."

"You liked him, then?"

"Like I said, he helped me out." He looked around. "It's weird, seeing all his stuff, talking about him like this. With him gone."

"What do you remember most about him?"

"What do I remember most about him." Romero took his time, looking thoughtful. "I guess the way he knew how to please people, to get what he wanted. Telling them what they wanted to hear. He could play different roles to suit different people, different situations."

"A hustler?"

"Yeah, sort of."

"The way you describe him, I'm surprised he wasn't more successful. From what I hear, selling yourself is half the game in Hollywood."

"He was about to make it big. At least that's what he claimed."

"Tell me more."

"He was never much on details."

"I'd be interested in whatever you know."

"There was something, a few weeks ago. He told me he was real close to nailing down some deal. Said he'd finally gotten the break he needed. With some studio big shot."

"Involving a script?"

"Like I said, he never got into specifics. He talked plenty, but a lot of it was bullshit. He kept just as much to himself."

The light was flashing on the answering machine. I asked if I could play back the messages. Romero shrugged.

"Sure, why not?"

There was only one, delivered in an angry female voice: *This message is for Raymond Farr. This is Anne-Judith Kemmerman. You know my number. Find the balls to call me, dammit.*

"Who's that?"

Romero shrugged again. "Don't know."

"There were a number of people at the party last night looking for your roommate. I'm surprised there's only one message."

"Reza listened to a bunch of messages just before we went out. I guess he erased 'em."

I hit the rewind button, then the one marked "Messages/Fast Forward." Going back to the beginning of the tape, there were a dozen messages from a Bernard Kemmerman, who sounded more and more anxious, and less and less healthy; several more messages from Anne-Judith Kemmerman, whom I presumed was his wife; and one or two each from Dylan Winchester, Roberta Brickman, and Leonardo Petrocelli, all sounding strained and anxious to varying degrees.

At one point or another, each caller left a phone number; I wrote them all down.

"I don't suppose you know who Bernard Kemmerman is?"

Romero shook his head.

"A couple of them sounded awfully unhappy."

"I guess they did."

"You wouldn't know why?"

He shook his head again, then reached over to raise a window, letting in some air against the heat.

"What about you, Danny? Did you have any reason to be pissed off at Reza JaFari?"

For the first time, his eyes faltered.

"Not that I can think of."

"Last night, Lieutenant DeWinter pointed out that you weren't all that upset to find your roommate dead."

"Yeah, I heard him say that."

"You don't seem all that upset now, either."

"People have different ways of looking at death, I guess."

"Were you pleased when you learned he was dead?"

This time, his voice became as unsteady as his eyes.

"Of course not."

I had no doubt that Danny Romero was lying. I also saw him scared for the first time.

"You sure there's not something you want to tell me, Danny?"

We both heard the doorbell ring, then a fist pounding on wood. From the sound of it, it was a big fist with considerable weight behind it.

Romero found my eyes, but only for a moment.

"I'd better get that."

I watched him shuffle off down the hall. He seemed to be working hard to conceal a limp.

Then I heard the front door being opened, followed by the unpleasant voice of Lieutenant Claude DeWinter.

# Ten

I'M BRINGING Reza JaFari's father up. Before he gets here, there's a couple of things I want to get straight."

The lieutenant stood in the doorway, filling it so completely that Danny Romero and I faced him from his shadow.

He'd already expressed his surprise upon seeing me, and chewed me out for hanging up on him that morning. In the process, he slipped in a dire warning about meddling reporters interfering with police investigations, which failed to leave me quaking with trepidation.

"Mr. JaFari is grieving badly," DeWinter said. "He doesn't know that his kid was sick with the AIDS virus. He doesn't even know his kid was gay or bisexual or whatever the fuck he was."

"And you'd like us to keep it to ourselves," I said.

DeWinter's hard manner lost some of its edge.

"He'll find out soon enough, one way or another. All I'm asking is, give him a little time. Either of you got a problem with that?"

Neither of us did, and we said so.

"Remember, his kid lived in this place, too. Hosain JaFari has a right to come here, look around. It was his idea. I figure it might be better if I came with him. He's pretty upset."

DeWinter turned and lumbered out the door.

"Jesus."

Danny slumped into a corner of the sofa like an aging boxer who'd just had a bad round.

"What's the problem?"

"I didn't tell DeWinter that the apartment's in Reza's name. I figure he's gonna find out pretty damn soon, though."

"Is that so bad?"

"It is if you got no place else to go."

He sounded worn down, more exhausted than sorry for himself. Maggie ambled over and laid her head in his lap to be scratched. Danny obliged reflexively, but seemed far away from both of us.

"I don't need this shit." He tilted his head back to stare at the ceiling with eyes that were quickly growing troubled. "Not now. Not with—"

We heard footsteps and turned to see Hosain JaFari coming through the door, with Claude DeWinter huffing and puffing behind him.

JaFari was a neatly dressed man of about fifty, well fed but handsome, with olive skin, a thick, neat mustache, and a balding pate that looked good on him. There were also shadows under his dark eyes the color of old bruises, and in the whites, the redness of grief.

DeWinter made the introductions.

"This is Benjamin Justice, freelance reporter. That's Daniel Romero, the roommate."

As JaFari moved past me, I could see anger tugging at the muscles of his neck and face.

He stood in the middle of the living room, surveying the apartment as if taking inventory. When he was done, he aimed his eyes straight at Danny.

"What did you do to my son?"

"What do you mean, Mr. JaFari?"

"You know what I mean! Last night—what did you do?"

"I drove him to the party. That's all."

Danny's voice was flat, neither combative nor defensive.

"You were the last one who saw my Reza alive."

"Maybe I was. I don't know."

Hosain JaFari threw his hands up and swiveled his eyes about the room.

"Where are his things? His stereo? His television? The nice things we gave him? Where is his car? The good car we gave him when he turned twenty-five, to help him be successful?"

"He sold it, Mr. JaFari."

"Sold his car!"

"He sold all his stuff, everything but his clothes and office equipment."

"Why? Why would he sell the fine things we gave him?"

"He needed the money, I guess."

"You lie!"

Danny sagged deeper into the couch, closing his eyes.

"Have it your way, Mr. JaFari. If you want to think I'm lying, then I'm lying."

JaFari clenched his hands into dangerous-looking fists.

"You stole his things! You stole them and then you killed him to cover it up!"

He was on Danny in a heartbeat, grabbing his throat and pummeling him with a fist while Danny curled up and tried to ward off the blows with his upraised arms. Maggie got hold of JaFari before DeWinter and me, snarling ferociously and tearing at his arms with her teeth.

I took hold of the dog, DeWinter grabbed JaFari, and we pulled them in opposite directions.

Slowly, Danny uncurled, then began to tremble. He called to Maggie, telling her it was OK. She flattened out on the carpet under my hands, growling low, with the hair on her back up, never letting JaFari out of her sight.

DeWinter had JaFari from behind, pinning his arms at his sides.

"Take it easy, Mr. JaFari. This isn't helping anything."

He settled JaFari into a chair, where the smaller man placed his face in his hands and began to weep.

I glanced across the room at Danny.

"You all right?"

He nodded and swallowed hard, looking shell-shocked.

After a minute, Hosain JaFari raised his tearstained face. When he spoke, his voice was low, confused.

"Reza told us how well he was doing. He had a nice studio business arrangement, good salary, his own office. He wrote a wonderful script, made a very good deal for himself. He told this to his mother and me. We were so happy. Finally, our son was doing well for himself."

He looked around.

"So where are all his nice things? Where is the success he was so proud of? I see nothing."

His eyes landed back on Danny, more questioning than angry now.

"Where is his money? All the money he made from the movie people?"

Danny huddled on the couch, saying nothing.

"We're going to look into that, Mr. JaFari." DeWinter laid a huge black hand gently on his shoulder. "Maybe it wasn't such a good idea you coming here today. Maybe you should go home, be with your wife, your family."

JaFari stood with a handkerchief, blotting away the tears. His voice had become little more than a whisper.

"Yes. That is where I should be. With my family." His eyes moved to each of us in turn. "I was wrong to lose my temper as I did. Islam teaches that we must be better than that. Please accept my apology."

"I'll be in touch," DeWinter said.

Maggie followed JaFari to the door with her eyes. When he was gone, I let go of her collar, and she was up on the couch beside Danny in a bound.

DeWinter stood over him, hands on hips.

"We got ourselves a few loose ends to tie up, Danny boy."

"I answered all your questions last night."

"Maybe I got more questions."

"Is Danny a suspect, Lieutenant?"

"Are you his lawyer, big shot?"

DeWinter found a stick of sugarless gum, unwrapped it, and pushed it into his mouth. He moved slowly about the room, checking it out.

"Maybe if you treat Danny with a little respect," I said, "he won't press charges."

DeWinter whirled, chomping furiously on the gum.

"You know what I'm talking about, Lieutenant. Assault. Filed against Hosain JaFari. With you as a witness. And a couple of Polaroids as evidence."

Danny's face was reddening below the cheekbone and around one eye, and there were likely to be bruises. DeWinter didn't bother to look. He already knew.

The anger was still in his eyes as they stayed on me, but his silence suggested something closer to respect. He knew we could complicate Hosain JaFari's life if we chose to, and his own as well, tying him up with paperwork and lawyer's inquiries, and questions from his superiors he might not want to face.

"Stay put, both of you, while I look around."

He glanced into the kitchen, then moved down the hall. Danny raised his head and called after him.

"Reza's room is at the end."

The detective disappeared into Danny's room, anyway. He emerged a minute later and proceeded down the hall. A minute or two after that we heard a door being closed and he came back.

"Right now I got no solid angle on how Reza JaFari died. But that could change after the coroner takes a look at him."

He turned back to Danny.

"I want everything in this apartment that belongs to JaFari left untouched. His room kept closed. Until I come back for a better look. You got it?"

Danny nodded.

"And if you plan on making any little trips, I want you to let me know."

"I'm not going anywhere."

"Be sure you don't."

DeWinter stalked out without another word.

"I hate that guy," Danny said.

Early evening shadows slanted into the room; the air had cooled a little, but not much.

"I only have a couple more questions."

"I'm really beat."

"One or two, that's all."

He sighed.

"Yeah, go ahead."

"Is there any possibility Reza died from AIDS complications?"

"Not unless he was lying to me about how sick he was."

"What did he tell you?"

"That he was on protease inhibitors, and they were working great. His T-cell count was over six hundred. His viral load was way down at the low end, almost undetectable. He'd had a couple of minor stomach infections and some diarrhea last year, but he was asymptomatic for AIDS. Hadn't lost any weight, no cough, no steady fever, no night sweats, no thrush. You don't have blood counts like that and suddenly keel over and die from HIV."

"You seem to know a lot about it."

"I know a few things."

"Do you know if anybody was angry enough with Reza to want him dead?"

He didn't answer straightaway. His eyes shifted uneasily at first, followed by a second or two of pointless silence.

"No."

I had him in another lie, but decided not to push him into a corner. Not just yet.

"It's getting late. Maybe we can talk another time."

"I don't see why not."

The shadows had deepened in the room, and a quietness settled over us as well. It felt like it was time to go, but I didn't want to leave him.

"Would you like to get some chow? I've got a little cash."

"Thanks, but I'm really fried. I'm not used to cops chewing on my ass and pissed-off fathers pounding on my face."

"We could order in. You look like you need a good meal."

"Actually, I got dinner taken care of."

I hadn't seen much food in the refrigerator, so I took it as a sign that he wanted me gone.

I stood over him, scratching Maggie's golden head.

"You going to be all right?"

"Yeah, I'll be OK."

He offered me an unconvincing smile.

I moved my hand from Maggie's head to Danny's and ran my fingers through his shaggy hair. He didn't seem to mind.

"I can come by again?"

"Sure. Give me a call. I could use the company."

I was at the door when he spoke again.

"Hey, Ben. Thanks for helpin' me out with DeWinter."

His eyes held me for a moment. They were filled with more than curiosity this time.

I went out trying to put a name on the emotion I saw in them, without success.

A white van pulled into the driveway of the ugly yellow apartment house as I was climbing into the Mustang. The words "Project Angel Food" were stenciled on the side, along with the logo of an angel holding up a plate with a heart in the center.

The driver got out and pulled open the rear doors. He was a dark-featured Asian in his forties, probably Filipino, on the soft and effeminate side, and buoyant with energy.

I watched him remove a sealed tin container from a thermal hotbox, close the doors, and start for the stairs.

"Excuse me."

He stopped at the first step, waiting.

"Is that for Reza JaFari?"

"Someone else, I'm afraid. Same apartment, though."

His voice was light and musical. I recognized the cadences of Tagalog, the primary language of the Philippines. One heard it a lot in nearby Filipinotown.

"Someone else," I echoed.

"Yes."

Everything was coming together very quickly. Project Angel Food was a nonprofit organization that delivered free meals to shut-ins with AIDS and HIV. Jacques had been one of them, during the last year of his life.

"I guess it's for Danny, then."

He answered with a question.

"Are you a friend?"

I nodded. He glanced at the covered meal in his hands.

"We have a nice chicken marsala this evening, with broiled garlic potatoes and mixed sautéed vegetables on the side. A whole-grain roll and butter. And a delicious apple cobbler for dessert."

He raised his eyes toward the upstairs apartment.

"How is Danny doing?"

My legs felt weak, my stomach in turmoil. I wanted to throw up, to scream, to run.

"He has his ups and downs."

"Is he on his feet today?"

I nodded again.

His smile was serene, his voice as comforting as a lullaby.

"Then it's a good day, isn't it?"

"I guess it is."

Maybe it was the simplicity with which he was doing his job. Maybe it was his calm in the midst of horror. Maybe it was the incredible goodness I saw in his warm Filipino eyes.

Whatever it was, it helped me make my decision.

"If I could, I'd like to take his dinner up to him."

He handed me the box, which was warm in my hands.

"Tell him Aurelio says hello." His smile widened, his teeth white against his brown skin. "And be sure to give him a hug for me. I always give him a hug."

"Sure."

I watched Aurelio drive off, steering with one hand and clutching his list of deliveries with the other, an angel of mercy whose simple kindness shamed me.

Then I turned to the stairs.

Memories, images, feelings washed over me like a dark wave

rolling up from a cold sea filled with corpses that all had the same face. Memories of Jacques. Images of him getting sick, scared, dying. Feelings I'd tried to keep buried for years and years and years.

As I climbed, I felt myself wading into that cold, dark sea, which I'd fled with such fierce resolution. I dreaded every step, but made my legs keep moving.

At the top, I rang the bell and waited.

Danny opened the door rubbing his sleepy eyes. His face and neck glistened with sweat from the early evening heat.

"Your dinner's here."

He looked at the box in my hands. I stepped back and he pushed the screen door open.

I went in and we faced each other in the small living room.

"How long have you been sick?"

"A few years."

"You don't look so bad."

"Looks can be deceiving."

He turned away, facing an unwashed window.

"Aurelio says hello." I set the boxed meal on a side table. "He asked me to give you a hug."

"Aurelio's a sweet guy."

A long moment passed without either of us speaking.

Danny pushed the hair back off his face with both hands; the fading light caught the sheen of perspiration on his forearms, where the fine, dark hairs had lain down like wet grass after a storm.

I wanted him very, very badly but was frightened of him just as much, frightened by the poison he carried in his blood and semen, and by his mortality.

Finally, he said, "I didn't have anything to do with Reza's death."

"I believe you."

I said it knowing it meant nothing, except momentary relief for him; the most believable people in the world are often simply the best liars. I'd met my share and then some.

Danny turned to face me. His eyes showed a special fear some people would never understand; he appeared close to tears that I suspected were never very far away, but rarely spilled.

"I can't go to jail. Not now. Not sick like I am."

I moved to him and took him in my arms. I held him the way I should have held Jacques in the final months of his life, the way I should have held him all the time we were together, all the years, if I hadn't been so selfish and afraid.

Danny responded passively at first, letting me pull him in as if he didn't care, as if I'd forced him to surrender. In the end, though, I felt his arms wrap around me, holding on as tightly as I held him.

We had become fused in the sudden, perplexing way that the outlaw nature of homosexuality can thrust strangers together, welded tighter by the terrifying dimensions of a disease that either draws people closer or propels them forever apart.

I'd made my choice not to turn and run. What remained now was for me to find the courage to honor the unspoken promise.

Whatever Danny Romero was—murderer, saint, something in between—I felt bound to him until the end.

# Eleven

I TOOK a small table on the sidewalk outside Tribal Grounds, with a pen in one hand, a tall cup of the house blend in the other, and my notebook open to a fresh page.

It was a few minutes past eight. Santa Monica Boulevard was sluggish with Monday morning traffic, cars and buses filled with men and women on their way to another numbing day of work. I looked for smiles, faces of contentment. I didn't see many.

It felt odd, sitting here again in the mode of a working journalist—freelance yet—with decent money figuring in the deal. As much as a part of me resisted, it didn't feel half bad. If nothing else, at least for now, I'd managed to avoid the sad parade of lemmings, marching dutifully forward to the tick of the time clock.

I sipped some coffee, bent over my notebook, and printed a list of names.

>Dylan Winchester
>Roberta Brickman
>Leonardo Petrocelli
>Bernard Kemmerman
>Anne-Judith Kemmerman
>Gordon Cantwell
>Christine Kapono
>Daniel Romero
>Lawrence Teal
>Hosain JaFari

Each had known Reza JaFari. With the exception of Danny Romero and Hosain JaFari, each had been at the party or left messages for him in the days and weeks before his death.

Excluding Teal, I wanted to talk to each of them when I had the right questions in place. If I never saw Teal again, it would be soon enough.

I spent the next few minutes completing a list aimed at Dylan Winchester, then called him from the pay phone outside A Different Light, whose windows displayed an array of book titles of special interest to lesbians and gays. Included were unauthorized biographies of two popular actresses, Jodie Foster and Whitney Houston. There were also tell-alls on a number of late actors—Rock Hudson, Anthony Perkins, James Dean, Ramon Novarro, Montgomery Clift—who had spent their careers concealed in the Hollywood closet and tormented, each in his own way, by the need to lead a double life. Which brought me full circle back to Dylan Winchester.

I got his voice mail and left a message.

After that, I headed downtown to the *Los Angeles Sun,* stopping to put gas in the Mustang and buy a dozen doughnuts, which pretty much cashed me out. At half past ten, I was walking into the four-story building on the south side of the central city that housed the *Sun.* My notebook was in one hand and the box of doughnuts in the other.

When I entered his third-floor office, Harry Brofsky looked up from behind his desk, where he was scanning copy for the next day's edition.

"Don't get up," I said, knowing Harry had never risen for anyone in his life, not even attractive women.

"Well, well. If it isn't the stranger in a strange land."

"Hello, Harry."

I set the box of doughnuts on his desk. He looked at it above his bifocals.

"You heard."

"I heard."

Templeton had warned me that Harry was off cigarettes, stuffing himself with doughnuts as a substitute. I could see a good twenty extra pounds on him just from the waist up. When you're on the stubby side like Harry, there's not a lot of places to hide twenty extra pounds.

I opened the box.

"I hope you like glazed chocolate, Harry."

"What I'd really like is for you to take over the damn story Templeton got herself into so she can get back to what she gets paid to do here at the *Sun*."

Templeton's voice floated into the small office.

"Which is what, Harry?"

She leaned against the doorway, a tall, graceful package of dark beauty and keen intelligence, looking like she'd put her shattered romance well behind her.

Harry smiled with all the sincerity of a mob lawyer, and spoke in his most syrupy Sweet 'N Low voice.

"What you get paid to do, Alex, is to be my best crime reporter."

"He showers me constantly with praise," Templeton said, waltzing in with a file folder in one hand.

"Calm down, Harry—I've agreed to work with Templeton on the story. Have a doughnut."

He reached for the box, looking slightly embarrassed.

"I guess I could try one."

Templeton and I took chairs on opposite sides of the office, which put about five feet between us.

"How did your meeting with Daniel Romero go?"

"Dramatically."

I filled her in on Danny's violent encounter with Hosain JaFari, and the temporary leverage it gave me with Lieutenant DeWinter. I left out any mention of Danny's medical condition, figuring it was no one's business but his at this point.

Templeton opened the file folder, plucked out a legal-sized envelope, and tossed it in my lap. It was stuffed with fifty-dollar bills, twenty of them, the advance I'd requested. In the cushy old days at the Velvet Coffin—as we called the *L.A. Times* back then—it would have been a week's pay, after deductions. Now it felt like a small fortune in my hands.

"I didn't know if you still had a bank account, so I brought cash."

"You want a receipt?"

"I trust you completely, Justice."

She handed across the file folder, which was fat with notes, computer printouts, and photocopied press clippings.

"I've organized and written up all my notes. Interviews with several leading screenwriters and an official with the Writer's Guild of America West. That's the union out here for film and TV writers. You'll also find lots of lists."

I glanced through a few. There were detailed compendia of how-to books, audiocassettes, software programs, and magazines devoted to the craft of screenwriting; universities that taught cinema; stores and mail order houses that sold nothing but old screenplays; computer programs that transferred text into proper screenplay format; and countless unaccredited courses and workshops on how to write, pitch, and sell film and television scripts.

"Teaching screenwriting seems to be an industry in itself."

"Everybody's writing a fucking script in this town." Harry pulled a doughnut apart and stuffed a ragged section into his mouth, glazing the tips of his gray mustache with chocolate. "Half my goddamn reporters want to be the next Jake Novitz."

"A name that means nothing to me," I said. "Along with a few others I heard in passing at Gordon Cantwell's bash the other night."

"We have to keep in mind," Templeton said, "that Justice has had his head buried in the sand for the better part of a decade."

"Big-shot screenwriter," Harry explained. "Gets millions of bucks to write crap like *Strip Show.*"

"No more than some of the big-book authors get," Templeton said. "Grisham, Clancy, Crichton, King."

Harry poked the last of the doughnut into his mouth, grumbling between bites.

"At least their stuff has to have some description in it."

Templeton glanced over at me, enjoying herself.

"In Harry's day, writing the great American novel was the mission of every young writer. Today, it's knocking out a script that might strike box-office gold. Right, Harry?"

"Thank you for placing me in my proper historical context, Templeton."

"Always a pleasure."

I scanned her notes on recent prices paid for original screenplays.

"It's obviously lucrative."

According to Templeton's figures, only one percent of the WGA's four thousand members consistently made more than a million dollars a year. Half the active members made less than seventy-five thousand. Hundreds barely made a living at all. But if you scored the big one, it paid off: Prices for original screenplays generally ranged from a quarter of a million to the higher six figures.

"The jackpot can climb as high as several million," Templeton explained, "if an agent is able to start a bidding war for a particular property."

"Sounds like real estate."

"A screenplay's not a final version like a novel or a play. It's more like a blueprint that's turned over to others for interpretation and revision."

"So it really never belongs to the writer."

"Not once it's sold."

"Sounds like a whore's profession."

"It has that element. Which may be one reason screenwriters seem so preoccupied with money."

"It's crazy," Harry said, licking his fingers and reaching for another doughnut. "A million bucks for a hundred pages of writing that doesn't even have to be grammatically correct."

Templeton shrugged.

"It depends on what the market will bear. There are actors making more than twenty million a picture now. Movies that cost a hundred million or more to produce, with budgets going up all the time. Why should the writer be left out?"

"The screenplay drives the market?"

"The script is where it all starts. Without the right script, the star doesn't say yes and the movie doesn't get made. At least that's how it works at the studio level."

Harry talked while he chewed.

"Sounds like you've got a lot of good material, Templeton."

"Thank you, Harry."

"So what's the fucking problem?"

She leveled her eyes on his, like a bullfighter staring between the horns.

"The 'fucking' problem, as I believe you know, has to do with my troubling case of writer's block."

"Thinking through a serious magazine piece," I said, "can be a lot more challenging than knocking out a news story."

"Thanks so much for the encouragement, Justice."

Harry wiped his hands on a paper napkin, leaned back in his chair, and folded his fingers behind his head.

"So how would you write the story, Ben?" ·

"Yes, Ben," Templeton said cutely. "How *would* you write the story?"

"I'd start and end the piece at Gordon Cantwell's party."

She cocked her head skeptically.

"Frame my entire story with the party?"

"Why not? It has all the elements we need in one setting—screenwriters, agents, producers, a self-important screenwriting teacher, lots of Hollywood wannabes. Even a director whose career seems to be falling apart."

"Dylan Winchester," she said, perking up a little.

"There was a kind of fever at that party, spiked by ambition and greed. Anchor your article at the party and you'll have the focus you need to tell the bigger story."

"Fleshed out with my other research and interviews."

"Exactly."

Templeton was nodding now, looking much happier.

"I like it, Justice. I like it a lot."

Harry stood, as if his mission was accomplished.

"Sounds like a fairly simple magazine piece to me."

"Maybe more than that."

He peered down at me, narrowing his eyes.

"You've also got an unexplained death, Harry—a young screenwriter who died grabbing for the brass ring. And a number of people at the party who didn't seem terribly distressed by it."

"I thought some kid choked on his beer at that party. You're making it sound sinister."

"Justice suspects foul play, Harry."

"It's a possibility, that's all."

"How strong a possibility?"

"All I know is, there were at least three people at that party who were looking for Reza JaFari. A troubled director, an uptight agent, and a frail old screenwriter."

"Winchester, Brickman, and Petrocelli," Templeton said.

"I heard Winchester say he wanted to kill JaFari."

Templeton shot me a questioning look.

"Dylan Winchester threatened Reza JaFari with violence?"

"Figuratively, anyway."

"Why am I just hearing this now?"

"Because telling you sooner wouldn't have done anybody any good. You'd be getting it secondhand, without concrete proof. And my word, to put it bluntly, isn't worth shit anymore."

Harry sat on the corner of his desk, looking more interested.

"What makes you think this kid might have been knocked off?"

"I watched the people gathered around JaFari's body Saturday night. Not only did they not seem bothered by his death, one or two seemed almost pleased. The question is why."

"That's it?"

"I have a few other things to check out."

"Why do I get the feeling you're about to turn an uncomplicated magazine feature into a major journalistic crusade?"

"I just want to do a little digging, that's all."

He got to his feet again.

"I never discouraged a reporter from doing a little digging. Just don't dig too long. Get the damn piece finished so I can have Templeton back full time."

He glanced at his watch.

"Now, if you ladies will excuse me, I have a meeting."

"Why don't you take a doughnut with you, Harry? You look famished."

"Well, one more, maybe."

He took two. We pretended not to notice.

As he left, I opened the file folder again.

"What else have I got in here?"

"There's a list of everyone we met at the party," Templeton said, "along with their phone numbers. Except one for Dylan Winchester. Directors aren't so easy to find."

I told her about the names and numbers I'd gotten from Reza JaFari's answering machine.

"I left Winchester a message this morning. I have a feeling he's not terribly eager to talk to us. Or Claude DeWinter, for that matter."

"That's not surprising, since he was angry with JaFari."

"There's another reason, on the more delicate side."

"I'm all ears."

"At one time, Winchester and JaFari were sexually involved."

Templeton widened her eyes.

"Winchester's gay?"

"According to Lawrence Teal."

I glanced down my list of names.

"I need you to have someone in the library run two names through the database."

She flipped to a new page in her notebook.

"For starters, Bernard Kemmerman. He left several urgent messages for Reza JaFari in recent weeks. Also, Anne-Judith Kemmerman."

I guessed at the spellings and she jotted them down.

"I'll do it right now—before Harry comes back with a news story he wants me to chase."

I watched her disappear into the maze of computer pods,

where reporters busied themselves with notebooks, keyboards, and telephones. I shifted to the chair behind Harry's desk and was picking up the phone when Templeton stuck her head in the door.

"Justice—it's good to be working with you again."

The last time had been a year ago, on the Billy Lusk murder case. I'd done the bulk of the research, Templeton the writing, while Harry had front-paged her piece in the *Sun*, nailing the true culprit for a murder the cops had wrongly pinned on a sexually troubled Hispanic kid. It had resurrected Harry's career from the ashes of the Pulitzer scandal I'd caused, and boosted Templeton to the top of his reporting staff. For obvious reasons, my name had been kept off the story.

"I appreciate the chance to make a few bucks, Templeton."

"Maybe it will lead to something more than that."

I assumed she meant professionally, but I wasn't sure.

"Maybe."

Her eyes lingered on mine longer than they needed to.

"We've both got work to do, Templeton."

"Yes, we do."

She smiled cryptically, then slipped away.

I put the phone to my ear and dialed Leonardo Petrocelli's number.

# Twelve

T HE PHONE RANG several times before it was picked up by a
grandmotherly sounding woman trying to catch her breath.

"Sorry. I was out for my morning fast walk. I forgot to turn on
the answering machine."

"I believe that's a felony in this town."

She laughed, and it sounded genuine. I pictured a trim, vibrant
lady with silvery hair, not much makeup, and a jogging suit of soft
pink velour, an image I'd later learn was not far off the mark.

"I usually take my morning walk about now and then a longer
walk in the early afternoon, but Leo has a doctor's appointment
this afternoon, so I—"

I heard her cluck her tongue behind her teeth.

"I'm going on and on like a ninny and I don't even know who
I'm talking to."

"My name's Benjamin Justice. I was calling for Leo."

"Have we met, Mr. Justice? That name sounds awfully familiar."

"I believe we have," I lied.

"You must be a writer."

"That's right."

"I'm Beatrice, Leo's wife. Most people call me Betty."

"Nice to talk to you again, Betty."

"Leo just left for the guild, to straighten out some insurance
matters. You know what it's like after a lengthy hospital stay."

I flipped to a fresh page in my notebook and got my pen ready.

"His heart, wasn't it, Betty?"

"No, no. That was last year. This time it's his prostate."

"Of course," I said, and jotted it down. "I hope he's doing better."

"We're very optimistic. What's the point of being anything else?"

"Thank goodness for that guild medical plan. He's been a member—how long now?"

"Let's see," she said. "He qualified for membership in 1958. I remember, because he wrote two scripts for Warners that year which were produced, and another for MGM. My goodness, that's half a lifetime ago!"

We chatted for another minute or two, and I slipped in the name Raymond Farr to see if she knew it.

"The boy who died the other night," she said, and clucked again. "So sad. He was here once or twice some time back, not long before Leo had the surgery. Trying to learn more about screenwriting. Very likable boy, though a bit anxious."

"Speaking of anxious, Mrs. Petrocelli, I think I'll try to catch Leo at the guild. Thanks very much for your time."

I pulled a west side phone book from the stack behind Harry's desk and looked up the address of the Writer's Guild of America West. It was located at Third and Fairfax, more or less on my way home.

I guided the Mustang through the downtown traffic crush, then cruised out Olympic Boulevard through Koreatown to the city's west side. The air was warm, the day bright with the familiar glare of sunlight filtered through a gauze of smog. I kept the top down, weaving past homeless paraplegics traversing the busy boulevard in wheelchairs and small-time drug dealers perched nervously on street corners like hungry birds. The streets became residential after that and then Midway Hospital loomed, giving me a jolt.

Two or three friends had died there, part of Midway's sizable population of AIDS patients. Suddenly, the thought of Danny Romero was with me so powerfully he might have been sitting next to me. I swung right onto Fairfax, trying to put the hospital out of my mind, and kept going until I saw Farmer's Market ahead, and CBS just beyond that, which told me I was approaching Third Street.

I parked at the curb, fed two quarters into the meter, and made my way past elderly Jewish ladies hobbling along with shopping bags until I reached the double glass doors of the WGA.

I knew from Templeton's research file that this was the heart of the screenwriting profession on the West Coast. More than thirty thousand scripts and treatments were registered here each year for legal protection, by guild members and nonmembers alike, although that probably represented only a fraction of what was actually being written.

I'd expected a more venerable building, one or two stories, perhaps, with grass and trees around it and ivy on the walls and some sense of the tradition that had given the world *It's a Wonderful Life* and *Casablanca* and *The Wizard of Oz*.

Instead, I found myself entering a modern, four-story building, chrome and glass surrounded by concrete, with sealed windows, a round lobby of fake tile, and a security guard in a navy-blue blazer who looked as efficient and impersonal as the rest of the place.

As the doors closed behind me, sealing in the artificially cooled air, I saw Leonardo Petrocelli at a bank of elevators, looking like a well-preserved museum piece as he attempted to straighten up from a painful stoop.

He was dressed in a well-tailored gray silk suit with vintage lapels, accented by a burgundy tie and matching pocket handkerchief, all of it topped off by his distinctive wavy white hair.

His wife had calculated his union membership at nearly forty years. It made me wonder why he'd shown up at Gordon Cantwell's party, where most of the guests were decades younger and little more than eager novices.

"Hello, Leo."

He adjusted his glasses and squinted at me with rheumy eyes the color of weak tea.

"Forgive me," he said, regarding me as if I were a complete stranger.

"Benjamin Justice. We met at Gordon Cantwell's party."

"Oh, yes, of course." He put out a spotted hand, and I shook it. "Do you belong to the guild?"

"No. Actually, I'm here to talk with you."

"Oh." Some of the warmth went out of his voice. "What was it you needed?"

"I'm helping Alexandra Templeton with her magazine piece."

"We probably should make an appointment, then."

He tucked a file folder under one arm and pressed the elevator button impatiently. Typed neatly and pasted to the top of the file was a label with the acronym WGA.

"Am I imposing, Mr. Petrocelli?"

"I'm rather surprised to see you here, that's all."

"I only have a couple of questions."

"How did you know to find me here, Justice?"

"Your wife was kind enough to tell me."

"My wife is a kind person."

"She told me you'd been in the hospital recently."

"My wife is also a talker."

He pushed the button again.

"Damned elevators. Wait, wait, wait. They're worse than Hollywood agents."

"I hope you're feeling better."

He turned suddenly to face me, and I could see behind his frailty the old fire of a man who had once burned hot with pride and passion.

"What is it you're after, Justice?"

"You sound wary."

"I was a reporter myself before I became a screenwriter. I know how reporters work. Why don't you quit dancing and get to the point?"

An elevator stopped, but it was going down.

"Damn!"

"All right, Leo. I'll stop dancing. How well did you know Reza JaFari? The young man you knew as Raymond Farr."

The stoop disappeared as he stiffened and raised his chin resentfully.

"Not well."

"He's been to your home."

"On one or two occasions."

"Yet you were looking for him Saturday night."

"I would have liked to speak with him."

"You could have called him."

"I did call him, which I mentioned to you at the party. He failed to return my calls. I was told he might be there."

"By whom?"

"I don't see the importance of that."

"Templeton and I want to put all the pieces together."

"The pieces of what?"

"Saturday night."

"Farr's death, you mean."

"That would be part of the story, now, wouldn't it?"

"I suppose that depends on the story you choose to tell."

He faced the elevators again and pushed the button almost violently.

"You seem in a hurry to get away, Leo."

His next words came tersely, defensively.

"I never saw Farr that night."

"What was it you wanted to discuss with him?"

"Business."

"That covers a lot."

"Personal business."

The elevator doors opened and he stepped in. Before they closed, I stopped them with my hand.

"At the party, I got the impression you wanted to cooperate with Templeton on her story."

"I'd be happy to discuss the craft of screenwriting, Justice. It's a profession of which I'm most proud."

"But you don't wish to discuss Reza JaFari."

"As I said, I hardly knew him. Now please remove your hand."

I did. The doors came together, and I was left staring at my own blurred reflection.

Maurice was raking leaves as I arrived back at Norma Place. The two cats, Fred and Ginger, watched from the front porch while an aria poured from the open windows of the small house.

"Enjoying your retirement, Maurice?"

"I miss the students already—all those eager young faces. I suppose I'll get over it in time."

"Maybe this will cheer you up."

I pulled out the wad of cash Templeton had advanced me, peeled off ten fifties, and handed them over.

"My goodness," Maurice said.

"That should buy some cat food."

"I should say so. God bless you, Benjamin."

He tucked the money away and I helped him transfer a pile of leaves into a recycling bin.

"You're a film buff, Maurice."

"Not so much as I once was."

"But you've still got a shelf filled with movie books."

"A bit dated, I'm afraid."

"Could you see if you have anything on a screenwriter named Leonardo Petrocelli?"

"Sounds vaguely familiar. Let's go inside."

We brushed ourselves off and went into the dim, old house, which smelled of decades of incense and cooking. It was crowded with hospitable old furniture, a collection of kitschy bric-a-brac devoid of design or reason, and photographs of friends who had "made their transition," as Maurice liked to put it. A few of the faces were of his generation, dead from old age, but most were on the younger side, taken by AIDS. I spotted Jacques's face among them, and studied it a moment while Maurice paused to savor the swelling aria.

Moments later the music ended and I was following him down the hallway to the second bedroom, which served as a den.

He knelt down, ran a bony finger along a row of books, and found one between Leslie Halliwell's *Filmgoer's Companion* and Vito Russo's *The Celluloid Closet*. The title was *The Film Encyclopedia*, the author Ephraim Katz.

"Let's see," Maurice said, turning and scanning its pages. "Screenwriters. Leonardo Petrocelli. Here we are."

He handed the book over with his finger on a seven-line biography. It placed Petrocelli's birth in 1925, and listed nearly three dozen produced films going back to 1958, with Academy Award nominations twice in the 1960s.

"Quite successful, it appears." Maurice scanned the list of pictures while I looked over his shoulder. "My, my. He wrote some wonderful movies."

"Look where his credits end."

"Nothing after 1985."

"Which means he hasn't had a screen credit in more than a decade."

"That shouldn't surprise you, Benjamin. According to his biography, he'd be seventy-two now."

"The man was nominated twice for Oscars, Maurice. It's hard to believe his career was over at the age of sixty."

Maurice raised his delicate hand and gave my chest a little push.

"Benjamin! Don't be so naive!"

"About what?"

"Hollywood, darling!"

"To be honest, Maurice, I've never paid all that much attention to Hollywood."

"Well, you should. Without Hollywood, Los Angeles has no point!"

He knelt again and slipped the book back into its slot.

"You must realize, Benjamin, that in Hollywood, old people are taken seriously as seldom as possible, and employed slightly less."

"And Leonardo Petrocelli would be considered old."

"Ancient, I'm afraid."

"Which means Petrocelli, for all his considerable experience and skill, may be washed up."

"He'd merely be one of many, my boy."

Maurice got to his feet slowly, using the shelf to help himself up.

"And if he's anything like the older screenwriters I've known, he's more than a little bitter about it."

# Thirteen

WITH AN HOUR OR TWO of daylight left, I hiked up Doheny Drive toward the steeper roads of the Hollywood Hills, determined to put myself in some kind of shape again.

When my legs felt ready, I'd help Danny Romero do the same. Then, one fine morning, we'd choose a trailhead, hoist our backpacks, and trek off into the southern Sierra together, with Maggie trotting happily ahead.

In a city built on fantasies, I was hard at work scripting my own.

I reached Sunset Boulevard and turned east, past familiar landmarks. The Rainbow Room, where rock stars ate. The Roxy and the Whisky, where they performed before becoming stars. The wildly eclectic Viper Room, partly owned by an actor named Johnny Depp. Book Soup, with its window displays aimed at the Hollywood crowd. Tower Records, where a plywood Madonna, her arms upraised as Evita, rose several stories above the street. Tina Turner, hawking hosiery on the side of a ten-story office building that had been turned into a towering billboard, like so many others along the Strip. Across the boulevard, equally monumental, the image of the beautiful boxer, Oscar de la Hoya, photographed so suggestively that I longed to reach up and run my fingers through his thick tangle of chest hair billowing darkly against the soft studio backlight.

Then I was in that otherworldly zone of chichi boutiques and cafés known as Sunset Plaza, where the rich congregated to spend their endless money on fashionable things they couldn't possibly need. So precious was the long block that no unsightly trash cans were allowed along the sidewalk, yet not a piece of litter could be seen—not even a stray leaf from the perfectly clipped trees potted here and there among the monied, pretty people who dined outside where they could be noticed.

When I reached Chin Chin and the aroma of spicy Chinese cooking, I crossed the boulevard to Sunset Plaza Drive and climbed. I wound my way past homes that cost more money than most people make in a lifetime until I was a mile or more up, with a wide-open view of the city and legs beneath me that felt as shaky as a serving of fresh flan.

I hadn't gotten the photographs in Maurice's living room out of my head. I found myself thinking first of Jacques, then of Danny Romero, then about the disease that had taken one and might one day take the other, unless the new therapies could save him. In between Jacques and Danny there had been a dozen more I'd known well who'd been afflicted and died, all under forty, all imperfect but good and gentle men. Their names and faces were always with me, no matter how much wine I poured down my throat when evening came and the memories started to work themselves to the surface like pieces of old shrapnel.

Evening was almost upon me now. The sun was around the hills to the west, and the first lights were flickering on in the city below.

Above and around me stood lavish estates valued in the millions, many of them owned by Hollywood faggots in hiding or others who had been dragged from the closet kicking and screaming by the more aggressive members of the gay press. One famous producer—supposedly hetero—known for his liberal politics, had spent fifty million dollars to carve the top off a mountain and erect a mansion bigger than any hospice in the country. This was just his Los Angeles nest; there were also homes in Malibu, Manhattan, Aspen, and Paris.

How much outpatient health care would fifty million dollars buy? How much faster could a cure be found if each of them gave up just one of their precious houses? A few of their Keith Harings or Ellsworth Kellys? Half their stocks and bonds? They had no such obligation, of course, and some had already donated generously—advised, of course, by their tax accountants. One saw their names on the walls of clinics, or their photographs in newspapers, getting awards for their charitable efforts at lavish black-tie dinners. But why couldn't some of the filthy rich faggots who collected corporations like toys be truly heroic and give enough to dramatically change the course of the disease?

*Who am I to complain? What have I done, except hide away and wallow in self-pity? Where have I been, while tens of thousands of others have fought the battle so tirelessly, so valiantly? What am I but a whining hypocrite?*

I was suddenly thinking of Jacques again, then Danny, Danny and Jacques, back and forth until they began to blur dangerously. It made me feel angry and hopeless and afraid, all of it underscored by shame, a mix of dark feelings taking form and life inside me, and growing too big. Too big and too powerful, the way it had happened seven years earlier, when I'd gone a little crazy and written a series of articles that saw life and death and love the way I'd wanted it to be instead of the way it really had been, and I'd won the big prize for my fine work, then been exposed as the pathetic fraud I was, and my world had come crashing down.

I turned away, trying to leave the memory of it there while I hiked back down, even though I could feel it following like a cold shadow that hovered over my whole life. I needed something to do, something with purpose but no personal connection, something beyond the shadow's reach.

Back on the Strip, I headed directly for the double doors of Book Soup. I immediately felt safer, embraced by the narrow aisles stacked floor to ceiling with hardcovers and paperbacks, smelling of old wood and new paper, surrounded by words, stories, pictures, ideas.

*Work. Get to work.*

I found *The Cantwell Method* in the well-stocked writing section on the store's west side, a single copy wedged in among the other books on screenplay writing I'd seen lined up on Reza JaFari's desk, plus dozens more.

A single copy of Gordon Cantwell's book could mean one of two things: It was so popular it was nearly sold out, or so marginal the store kept only one copy on hand.

"We sell a copy now and then," the clerk at the cash register said, when I asked. "Nothing like the old days."

"The old days being when?"

"Ten, fifteen years ago. Before all the other experts started doing the same thing, only better."

I carried *The Cantwell Method* next door to the civilized comfort of the Book Soup Bistro, where I ordered smoked salmon fettucini and a decent bottle of Pinot Grigio from a tall, sleek-looking waiter named Benny. He looked like he might be half-black and half-Vietnamese, with a lovely face the shade of creamed coffee and darker eyes that knew how to say nice things without words. I took a long look at his small, round butt as he headed back to the kitchen, the way lusting straight men ogle good-looking wait-resses, thinking their wives and girlfriends don't notice.

When the door swung closed on his pretty behind, I turned to Cantwell's book.

*The Cantwell Method* was still in hardcover, 212 pages long, with an original copyright date of 1974. I found the author bio on the final page:

> Gordon Cantwell brings to the teaching of the screenwriting craft a background rich in experience and expertise. As a former development executive with one of Hollywood's most successful companies, he read and analyzed thousands of screenplays. In the process, he learned why some succeed commercially while others fail, and formulated his own spe-cial approach to screenplay structure—the key to a successful "Hollywood-style" script.
>
> Mr. Cantwell is also a successful screenwriter in his own right and has acted as a consultant to several major studios and leading production companies.
>
> The Cantwell Method is now recognized as the first and foremost approach to solving the problem of screenplay structure, and Mr. Cantwell's seminars teaching his unique techniques are conducted worldwide.
>
> Mr. Cantwell makes his home high in the Hollywood Hills of Los Angeles, in a house once owned by Charlie Chaplin.

Benny arrived with my wine and offered me a taste, but I told him to pour away. As I finished my first glass and poured my second, I felt a sense of calm settle over me like a gentle change of light, the way the dusk was slowly filtering in from the neigh-borhood outside.

Getting the gist of Gordon Cantwell's "method" didn't require many pages. Essentially, he had taken the basic three-act structure that serves as the foundation for virtually all traditional storytell-ing—beginning, middle, end—and broken the middle act in half, creating four acts.

With Cantwell's approach—hardly revolutionary—a short open-ing act set up the primary problem facing the main character and established his or her main goal. A second act deepened the pri-mary relationships between the main character and important sec-ondary characters as the hero or heroine moved forward in their quest, facing increasingly challenging obstacles along the way. At the midpoint of the story—roughly an hour into the average movie—the plot was supposed to take an unexpected turn that would throw it in a whole new direction, creating a third act that ended with the character at the greatest point of complication or choice. The short final act accelerated to the climax and resolution.

"Your fettucini, sir."

I studied Benny's smooth, brown arms as he set the dish in front of me but failed to catch his eyes as I'd hoped, and he was quickly gone. I tried the pasta, washed it down with wine, turned another page.

What struck me most about Cantwell's method was his insistence that turning points and act breaks fall on specific pages. He was rigid about it: Act I was to end no later than page twenty; the first major turning point was to come between pages twenty-five and thirty-five; the midpoint break, or end of Act II, was to fall between pages fifty-five and sixty-five, with the third act ending somewhere between pages eighty and ninety; the last act was to run no longer than thirty pages, preferably shorter, keeping the entire script to 120 pages.

Cantwell allowed for no flexibility—on one page early in the book was this admonition:

> If you are truly serious about breaking into the arena of commercial filmmaking, you must set a firm rule for yourself right at the outset—*no script longer than 120 pages.* The rule of thumb for the standard screenplay is one minute of screen time for each typewritten page. American audiences will not sit through long movies and Hollywood agents and executives do not like to read. *Keep it short!*

And this:

> To be effective, act breaks must fall exactly on the pages signified in the Cantwell Paradigm, which you'll find diagrammed on the following page. This will enable you to craft a tight, fast-moving, flawlessly structured screenplay.

I looked up to find the restaurant filled with chattering diners and the last of the lights coming on along Sunset Boulevard. I finished the pasta, emptied the bottle into my glass, downed the last of the wine, and signaled Benny for the check.

As I hit the sidewalk, neon was alive overhead and the street was abuzz with young people. I quickly put the crowd behind me, ambling down side streets that led me into Hilldale Avenue toward home. When I reached the eight-hundred block, just off Dicks Street, I found myself standing in front of the apartment house bearing the address Lawrence Teal had given me.

It was an old, Spanish-style building that looked solid and cool behind its front garden of tropical foliage. Teal's apartment number was on the door of a first-floor unit that showed light coming from a deep side window.

I found a weathered wooden gate, pushed aside some thorny strands of asparagus fern, and opened it, then made my way along the side of the building until I reached the window where the light shone.

Music came through the open side louvers, one of those synthetic tunes suitable for elevators that Jacques had called jazzak.

Then I saw Teal, naked under the harsh light of a bare ceiling bulb.

He moved, faunlike, over the hardwood floor on his muscular legs, his eyes fixed on the image of himself in a full-length mirror that leaned unattached against a bare white wall. He touched himself as he moved, every part of his body from his thighs to his face, his nipples and penis aroused and his eyes transfixed with self-love.

Then his eyes shifted, meeting mine for a split second in the glass, before darting self-consciously back to themselves.

He continued to dance, one hand drawing graceful parabolas in the air while the other stroked his preening cock, pretending not to know that I was there. I felt my own body responding and hated Teal for making me want him so much when it was Danny Romero I needed, and no one else.

If Teal stole another glance my way, looking for the admiration of his beauty in my eyes, he was disappointed.

I'd found my way back to the gate, shutting it firmly behind me, putting rapid strides between us, determined to have nothing to do with Lawrence Teal ever again.

# Fourteen

T HE AUTOPSY RESULTS on Reza JaFari came in Tuesday
morning, which was fast for a weekend death, at least in Los
Angeles.

"I think Lieutenant DeWinter pushed it through," Templeton
said to both Harry and me. "Probably for the family's sake."

We had a patio table at The Ivy in Beverly Hills. Our fellow
diners were mostly clonelike blond women in the company of
male model types in loose-fitting jackets or slightly older men in
ties, who looked and acted like they owned the city, which they
probably did.

Templeton glanced across the antiqued picket fence that surrounded the terraced patio toward the sidewalk.

"Isn't that Charlie Sheen?"

I followed her eyes to a male brunette with good cheekbones,
slicked-back hair, and a self-satisfied smirk. He was climbing out
of a red Lamborghini with two shapely younger women, while a
valet in a green jacket held open the door.

"I have no idea who you're talking about, Templeton."

"Surely you've heard of Charlie Sheen, Justice."

"Actor," Harry said as he opened a menu. "*Platoon. Wall Street.*
Heidi Fleiss."

"Ah. Now I recall the name."

It was Templeton's idea to lunch with the Hollywood crowd, to
soak up some "industry" color—and let *Angel City* pay for it—
while she brought me up to date on the Reza JaFari case.

Harry took one look at the prices and tried to bolt.

"Don't worry, Harry," Templeton said, sitting him back down. "*Angel City* gets the receipt. We're here to do some work."

"I got plenty of work back at the *Sun*," Harry grumbled. "So do you, dammit."

"That's why we're doing lunch, Harry. To get some magazine business out of the way."

I looked up from my menu.

"Doing lunch? You sound more Hollywood every time I talk to you, Templeton."

"We could have eaten downtown on the cheap," Harry complained. "Been back at the office in a wink."

Templeton patted him on the arm.

"Order something expensive, Harry. Enjoy yourself."

He slapped the menu shut.

"I'll have a burger, well done."

Templeton looked over at me.

"He's been so irritable since he quit smoking."

"I hadn't noticed the difference."

The waiter arrived and Harry ordered his hamburger. Templeton selected the Chinese chicken salad while I opted for grilled duck with sautéed vegetables and wild rice.

Then Templeton delivered her news: The coroner's office had failed to determine the exact cause of Reza JaFari's death, but placed a high probability on natural causes attributable to AIDS.

"Bullshit," I said. "Reza JaFari didn't have AIDS."

"You did your own autopsy?" Harry said.

"It comes from Danny Romero."

"The roommate."

"Right. He's certain JaFari hadn't developed AIDS yet."

"The kid's a medical expert?"

"He's a suspect, Harry. He has nothing to gain by discounting AIDS as a possible cause. Quite the opposite."

"Keep talking."

"According to Romero, JaFari's T-cell count was over six hundred. His viral load was extremely low. He was totally asymptomatic for AIDS."

"You think the coroner's office botched the autopsy," Templeton said.

"It wouldn't be the first time."

"Six hundred T-cells," Harry said. "Viral load. Forgive me for not being a trained lab technician."

"In simple terms? JaFari was healthy, his blood counts almost normal. His immune system was strong."

Templeton leaned forward on her elbows and locked her fingers under her chin.

"What I don't understand is, why would the coroner's office pass JaFari's death off to AIDS?"

"The coroner's office is notoriously overworked and understaffed," Harry conceded. "The bodies are stacked up down there like cordwood. Unless you've got a death that warrants special attention, the autopsy's probably cursory at best."

"And HIV or AIDS might provide a quick answer," Templeton said. "Inaccurate but convenient."

"I got to admit," Harry said, "the medical examiners in this city are famous for sloppy work and bad calls."

Templeton rummaged in her big handbag and extracted a file folder.

"I have something else for you, Justice."

She handed it across.

"You asked me to see what I could find on Bernard Kemmerman."

I opened the folder to a collection of photocopied newspaper clippings and database printouts, all with Kemmerman's name in them, some with his photograph.

"There was quite a lot, actually. He started out in the mailroom at William Morris in the early fifties, worked his way up, and was one of the more successful agents in town throughout the sixties."

"What kind of agent?"

"Screenwriters, directors, producers. Went into independent production in the seventies. Several major hits. In the late eighties, the studios made him an offer he couldn't refuse."

"Which one?"

"He joined Universal, moved to Paramount, ended up with Monument."

"Why haven't I heard his name before?"

"Kemmerman was one of those rare creatures on the production end who shunned the limelight."

"But he rose to the top?"

"President of production before taking a leave of absence a few months ago."

"Why the leave?"

"Illness."

"Where is he now?"

"Forest Lawn."

The food came and plates were passed around. Harry asked for ketchup and the waiter went for it. I was more interested in Kemmerman's death than my lunch.

"How long ago?"

"A few weeks. Kidney failure."

"After a transplant?"

"Never took place. Rare blood type. Couldn't find the right donor in time."

"Private service?"

Templeton shook her head.

"Very public. Kemmerman was apparently well liked and respected in the industry. According to the clips, hundreds of Hollywood's elite turned out for the service."

"A man that big, I wonder what was so urgent that he needed to discuss with a small fry like JaFari."

Harry looked up from inspecting his hamburger.

"Especially when he had more important things to worry about—like dying."

"What about Anne-Judith Kemmerman?"

"Married Kemmerman eight years ago. He was sixty-seven when he died. She's forty-four."

Harry raised his eyebrows.

"The young, rich widow—the plot thickens." He glanced around. "Speaking of which, where's my ketchup?"

I looked deeper into the file folder. Two faces stared out at me from a *Sun* society page photo taken a few years back. Bernard Kemmerman was a tan, decent-looking man behind aviator-style glasses, casually dressed; he had warm eyes and a calm, contented face.

If Kemmerman looked untypical of the hard-driving studio executive, his younger wife, Anne-Judith, fit the Tinseltown stereotype more closely. She was a knockout, glamour run amok: heavy eyeliner, bee-stung lips, Jayne Mansfield breasts, Grand Canyon cleavage, and enough stacked hair to qualify her for televangelism.

"Nice jugs," Harry said. "Her hubby must have died happy."

"Thank you so much, Harry," Templeton said, "for your sensitive male input."

I thought of the recording Anne-Judith Kemmerman had left on Reza JaFari's answering machine: *This message is for Raymond*

*Farr. This is Anne-Judith Kemmerman. You know my number. Find the balls to call me, dammit.*

The brassy voice and the tough words matched the face in the photograph, to a *T*.

"The question is," Templeton said, "what's the connection between the Kemmermans and Reza JaFari?"

"And how do you figure to find out?"

"I think we should characterize our story as a eulogy to Reza JaFari, the aspiring screenwriter. Death of a Hollywood dream, something sappy like that. Gives us more latitude to ask questions, dig around."

"You can go almost anywhere with an angle like that," Harry said.

"And certain sources," Templeton added, "might be less inclined to turn us down."

The busboy set a bottle of ketchup on the table. Harry shook it, unscrewed the cap, and dumped a load onto his patty, barely looking at us while he talked.

"Who knows? Maybe you and Templeton will end up with a story you can break in the *Sun*." He put the burger back together, trying too hard to sound offhand. "You can always do the magazine piece later, as a featurized follow-up."

I suddenly got it: There we were—Harry, Templeton, and me—sharing a civilized, sociable meal. Trading ideas while a big question mark hung over a developing story. Working as a team. The way Harry had always wanted it.

Clever old Harry. He'd pulled it off again, protesting all the way.

Templeton and I started in on our lunches, exchanging a knowing glance across the table.

Harry ate with his burger in one hand and the menu in the other, like a rich uncle out to lunch with his niece and nephew, trying to decide between the chocolate mousse and the cherry cheesecake for dessert.

# Fifteen

I SPENT THE REST of Tuesday afternoon finishing Gordon Cantwell's book and making phone calls.

First, to Anne-Judith Kemmerman, whose brassy voice was immediately recognizable as the one I'd heard on Reza JaFari's answering machine. Unfortunately, the voice came from a tape directing me to leave my name and number, which I did.

Next, to Roberta Brickman at ITA, where a temp informed me that the agent was in a meeting but would return my call as soon as possible.

Then, to Dylan Winchester, whose voice mail told me—once again—that he would get back to me.

Everybody in Hollywood, I decided, was busy getting back to everybody else.

I made one more call, and when Gordon Cantwell's recorded message came on, I hung up without leaving one of my own.

Instead, I hopped into the Mustang and drove up Beachwood Canyon uninvited, intending to take a closer look at Cantwell's house while there was still some light in the sky.

When I turned onto Ridgecrest Drive, it was getting close to seven—roughly the same time Reza JaFari had arrived at Cantwell's three nights earlier, a few hours before leaving with a coroner's tag on his toe.

A minute or two later I was crossing the footbridge to Cantwell's faux castle. A sporty red Mazda convertible sat in the driveway with the top down. A pint-sized surfboard shaped like a shark's tooth poked up from the backseat.

"Mr. Justice. What a surprise."

Christine Kapono's voice was on the cool side, suggesting the surprise wasn't a happy one.

She emerged on the front steps, looking compact and boyish in bare feet, cutoffs, and a T-shirt with the words YEAH, RIGHT printed across the chest. I could now see surfer's knobs on her knees that matched the ones I'd previously noticed on the upper arches of her feet. Her ducktailed hair was damp.

"I called," I said. "No one answered."

"I just got here. Haven't checked the messages. Probably won't."

Her words came rapid-fire, without much feeling except for irritation.

"Gordon gave you the day off?"

"I took the day off. The waves are up at Malibu. I caught a few. What can I do for you?"

"I'd hoped to set up a meeting with Gordon. I've joined Alexandra Templeton on her magazine article. I'm doing some of the interviews."

"I'm afraid you'll have to deal with Gordon's publicist, Mr. Justice. I'm no longer working for him."

"Since when?"

"Since the moment he put his hand on my butt yesterday afternoon. No one puts their hand on my butt unless I want them to."

"I think that's called sexual harassment."

"I call it male piggishness." She wasn't smiling, not even close. "It was the second time he's done it. I always give them a second chance."

"Are you going to file some kind of complaint?"

"I took care of it myself."

"Mind if I ask how?"

"The first time, I slapped him across the face and asked him politely to respect my body. The second time, I kicked him so hard between the legs that his gonads ended up where his tonsils should have been."

"Ouch."

"He reacted a bit more strongly than that."

"I imagine."

"You're not one of the pigs, are you, Mr. Justice?"

"If I am, I'll try to keep my snout where it belongs."

She finally smiled a little.

"You want to come in? I'm packing the last of my things. We can talk if you'd like."

I followed her along the downstairs hallway to the room where I'd first seen Dylan Winchester and Roberta Brickman talking heatedly on Saturday night.

Inside, cardboard boxes filled with papers sat atop a desk. On top of one stack of papers was a circular plastic organizer, loaded with alphabetized index cards.

"The proverbial Rolodex," I said.

"The key to my future."

"What is your future, Christine?"

"For now, I'm going to International Talent."

"ITA? The requisite mailroom job?"

A second or two of hesitation followed.

"Higher up, actually."

"How high up would that be?"

"I'll be working as Roberta Brickman's assistant."

"Reza JaFari's old job."

"That's right."

"That worked out well."

Kapono's voice grew cool again; the words came briskly.

"Roberta and I are good friends. She needs someone to take JaFari's place. I'm available."

"Seems like a big step, going to an agency like ITA."

She didn't hesitate this time.

"I'm smart, organized, and know who does what in this town. I'll be better at it than he was."

"You're not lacking in confidence, are you?"

"People who lack confidence don't survive long in this business, Mr. Justice."

She placed more files into one of the boxes.

"You feel your time with Gordon Cantwell was worthwhile, then?"

"All I have to say about Gordon for your article is that I worked for him for a year, learned a great deal about the movie business, and then moved on to greener pastures."

"How about off the record?"

"I'm not sure I trust reporters right now—especially male ones."

I raised my right hand in a three fingered salute.

"Scout's honor—it's off the record until you say otherwise."

"You don't look like a Scout to me."

I lowered my hand, sagging dejectedly.

"You found me out."

She grinned.

"I never liked Boy Scouts much, anyway." Her dark eyes suddenly grew mischievous. "Girl Scouts were another matter."

Her hands got busy again; she talked as she packed.

"Off the record, Gordon Cantwell is a pompous, egotistical jerk—a legend in his own mind."

She shook her head slowly, tossing papers into a waste can.

"It's amazing, really, how successful he's been for someone with so little talent for anything except self-promotion."

"But according to his bio—"

"Gordon's bio?" She laughed. "You know that bridge you walked across to get to the house?"

"Sure."

"Would you believe me if I told you it was the Golden Gate?"

"He exaggerates."

"Gordon started out as a script reader, Mr. Justice. Someone near the bottom rung who screens submissions for the development executives. He never rose higher than that."

"But he learned a lot about flawed screenplays in the process."

"Especially weak story structure, which is one of the most difficult things to grasp, especially by semiliterate writers raised on television. Gordon's very analytical, meticulous, a problem solver. No one had a systematic approach to teaching screenwriting structure back then. In trying to learn how to write screenplays himself, he devised a model neophytes could understand."

"With all the plot points figured out for just the right pages."

"You've taken his course."

"Read his book."

"So did half a million other readers during the early years. Then other teachers came along, building on what he'd started. When the software programs hit the market, it pretty much finished him."

"Still, he seems to have a coterie of loyal disciples."

"A small following of groupies who haven't seen through his bullshit yet. Gordon lives for that. He likes to believe they hang on his every word, worshiping at the feet of the master."

She lifted one of the boxes.

"Mind giving me a hand?"

"Not at all." I glanced at the overflowing waste cans. "What about the rest?"

"Out with tomorrow night's trash, I guess."

She grabbed the heavier box; I took the other one and followed her from the room.

We moved through the house to the driveway and hoisted the boxes into the Mazda.

"I'd like to take a look around, if it's OK."

"The terrace, you mean. Where JaFari died."

I nodded. She considered it a moment, looking as if she might be measuring her trust in me.

Finally: "I don't see why not. Hell, I don't work here anymore, anyway."

She led me to the south side of the house and the passage through which Dylan Winchester had made his hasty exit Saturday night. We passed through an unlocked gate, along stepping stones to the rear yard, where the lights were just coming on. I glanced at my watch; it was seven o'clock, straight up.

"Do the lights always switch on at seven?"

"Automatic timer."

We turned down the brick steps and followed the pagoda-shaped lanterns to the terrace. With the early evening light, I could see the dense brush and deep contours of the canyon below, which appeared nearly inaccessible by foot. A corner of the cottage belonging to old Mrs. Fairbridge peeked out from one of the far bends; I guessed the distance at half a mile, maybe more. An inspection of the patio revealed nothing new, although the odd odor I'd picked up was gone.

Across the canyon, the Hollywood Sign thrust itself proudly into the fleeting light.

"Cantwell must like the idea of sharing the same view Charlie Chaplin once enjoyed."

Kapono laughed.

"You're referring to Gordon's bio again."

I nodded.

"Charlie Chaplin didn't own this house, Mr. Justice. It was more like one of the Ritz Brothers."

"I guess Cantwell has a weakness for hype."

"He's a product of Hollywood. What can I tell you?"

"So was Reza JaFari. What can you tell me about him?"

"I'll leave that to the people who knew him better than I did."

"Like Roberta Brickman?"

Kapono held my gaze evenly, her face impassive.

"I should finish up my work, Mr. Justice. I'd like to be gone before Gordon gets back. You're welcome to stay and look around if you'd like."

A breeze rippled up the canyon, passing like a whisper across the ground where Reza JaFari had recently expelled his last breath.

"Thanks. I've seen enough."

As we climbed, Kapono told me where I could find Cantwell, if I didn't waste too much time getting there.

"He's playing in his regular Tuesday night softball game." She glanced at her watch. "They'd be in the fourth or fifth inning about now. Film industry guys. No girls invited, except in the stands."

"The old-boy club."

"In this case, the young-boy club. Except for Gordon and a couple of others."

"He recruits students on the baseball field?"

"He plays in the industry league because he wants to be a screenwriter, Mr. Justice. And to produce his own scripts, of course. He's always looking for a new connection, like every other would-be screenwriter in this town."

"Then he's not the successful screenwriter he pretends to be."

"As just about everyone inside this business realizes by now."

"How badly does he want it?"

"Desperately, like all the others."

We reached the top step, and she turned. Her eyes swept across the smog-shrouded city, from the downtown skyscrapers west to the ocean.

"Somewhere out there are half a dozen movie studios, Mr. Justice. Two or three more in the Valley. A dozen film-writing schools. Hundreds of talent agencies and production companies. Thousands of women and men working on the script they hope will be their ticket to the big time."

"What drives them, Christine? Why do they want it so badly?"

When she looked my way, her eyes were thoughtful, keen.

"I think fear is a big part of it."

"What is it they're all so afraid of?"

"Not knowing the right people, not getting their foot in the door. Never getting their shot. The fear that their time might run out before they make their dream happen. Bottom line? That they might end up perceived as ordinary, unimportant."

"And what's the timetable?"

"If you're not well established as a screenwriter by the age of forty, Hollywood looks at you as a loser. Someone not worth taking a chance on. They figure there's always another writer who's younger, more energetic, more productive, more in tune with the youth market. Somebody who's easier to sell."

"After forty-five?"

"Without a track record, it's tough to get the attention of an agent or producer."

"And after fifty, like Cantwell?"

"You're pretty much dead meat."

A sharp *caw* rent the air above us. We looked up to see a crow soaring across the canyon on broad black wings. It settled watchfully atop the *H* in the Hollywood Sign, where it continued to cry out. It was the same letter from which a failed actress named Peg Entwistle had leaped to her death, in 1932, earning an everlasting place in the Hollywood tourist guides.

"Is that what drives you, Christine—the fear of ending up ordinary?"

"If things don't work out, I'll always have myself, Mr. Justice. I'll go back to the islands, spend time with my family, eat fish, walk in the warm rain. Find a good wave to ride, a good woman to love."

"Sounds like a fantasy."

"To you, maybe."

"And Cantwell?"

"Gordon's like a lot of people you see here. Afraid that if he doesn't realize his dream, he has nothing, he is nothing."

"You seem to see things rather clearly."

"I'm an outsider. It's a necessity."

We crossed the lawn, retracing our steps around the side of the house. Kapono gave me directions to the baseball field where Cantwell was playing. As I slid behind the wheel of the Mustang, I asked her a loaded question.

"Ever attend any of his games?"

This time her smile was sly.

"Not unless they let me play. Which they won't. Not yet."

"May I put that in the article?"

Her smile widened to a grin.

"Just write that Christine Kapono intends to play with the big boys."

She held up her right arm, pushed up the sleeve of her T-shirt, and flexed an impressive bicep.

"And that she can swing a bat with the best of them."

# Sixteen

I DON'T KNOW YOU. Go away!"
  Constance Fairbridge peered out from behind tattered curtains, over the tops of old bottles displayed along a window ledge heavy with dust.

"It's Benjamin Justice, Mrs. Fairbridge."

"How do you know my name?"

"You told us, the night of the accident. It's also on your mailbox."

"Accident?"

"The other night, in the road."

"They should never have paved the road."

"I know, Mrs. Fairbridge. It's a shame what they did."

"Fire and brimstone!"

"The flaming torch," I said, remembering a bit of Genesis. "The flaming sword."

She opened the door, eyes wide.

"You know?"

I nodded. Her eyes narrowed fearsomely.

"Too many roads. So many houses! So much sin!"

"It's awful, what's happened."

Her eyes flew skyward, then all around.

"Dust into dust!"

"How are you feeling, Mrs. Fairbridge?"

"Behold, I am old."

"It's a pretty name, Constance Fairbridge."

She held her head up proudly.

"Constance Fairbridge, star of the silent screen."

"You were an actress, Mrs. Fairbridge?"

Her eyes became fierce again.

"Who are you? Leave me alone!"

I put up my hand to stop the door as she tried to close it.

"I'm Benjamin Justice, Mrs. Fairbridge. Just making sure you're all right."

She seemed to be peering past or through me.

"The end of all flesh."

Her eyes came quickly back, striking at me like knitting needles.

"Go! For I will blot out man!"

She shut the door, fast and hard. I stared at it a moment, then decided there was nothing to do but go.

I spotted the Grolsch bottle as I started down the steps.

It rested among a pile of others in her shopping cart near the bottom step, where she had left it Saturday night, and where I had missed the bottle in the darkness. Now, the distinctive green glass caught my eye like a precious emerald wedged in granite.

I found a clean tissue in my pants pocket, rummaged through the cart, lifted the Grolsch bottle out carefully.

The door creaked open behind me.

"My bottles!"

Constance Fairbridge came at me with an ax handle half-raised. I held the bottle up to the fading light.

"I was just admiring it, Mrs. Fairbridge. What a pretty bottle it is."

When she'd found it, she must have fastened the cap; I could see an inch of residue captured at the bottom.

"What do you want with my bottle?"

"You found this Saturday night?"

"Saturday night?"

"The night of the accident. With the car."

"I think so. Yes. Go away!"

She raised the ax handle.

"May I buy this bottle from you, Mrs. Fairbridge?"

"Take it if you must. Just go!"

She worked her gums nervously behind her wrinkled lips.

"Do you recall *where* you found the bottle?"

She turned her nose up the canyon.

"In the ravine, not even half a mile. I have my secret trails. I'm old, but I get up and down the canyon just the same."

"You collect bottles along the trails?"

"Where no one else goes. Down where the bottles go when they throw them from the road." Her eyes narrowed again. "You want to know where, but I won't tell you!"

"You've told me quite a lot, Mrs. Fairbridge."

"Take the bottle, then! Take it and go away!"

She motioned toward the Mustang with her ax handle. I wrapped the bottle in the tissue and placed it on the passenger seat, then started backing out.

"Wrath and retribution!"

I could still hear her raspy voice as I pulled onto Ridgecrest Drive.

"God destroyed the cities of the valley!"

I passed through the sandstone portals of the Hollywoodland Gates onto the final mile of Beachwood Drive, which ran in a straight line down to Franklin Avenue.

Halfway there, a red sports car suddenly filled my rearview mirror. Forming a steeple above the windshield was the sharp nose of a surfboard. I eased the Mustang to the curb as the red Mazda came up fast on my left.

Christine Kapono sped by, no wave or horn, so I figured her mind was somewhere else, somewhere that kept her foot hard on the gas pedal. I decided to find out where that was.

I followed at a safe distance, cutting along the whorish section of Franklin Avenue, with its depressingly drab apartments and hot-pillow joints, all the way west to La Brea. Then it was down to Santa Monica Boulevard, which carried us along AIDS Alley, where the male prostitutes wandered the sidewalks and hugged the shadows of the buildings, until I was into the bustling bar section of West Hollywood.

A few blocks past La Cienega, Kapono swung left and pulled into a metered space next to the one-story building that housed Eleanor's Secret.

I drove past before she was out of her car, continued to the end of the block, turned around, and came slowly back.

Women sauntered into the coffee bar in small groups, or as couples, holding hands. The patio tables out front were full, a few men, mostly women.

With a clear vantage point from the side street, I watched Kapono slip into a seat at a window table near the back. Across from her was a woman whose head was in her hands, her fingers thrust like hairpins through her frosted blond coiffure. Kapono reached across and took the woman's hands as she looked up.

Roberta Brickman's face was a portrait of anguish and exhaustion.

Kapono found a tissue, wiped away Brickman's tears, then gently stroked her face.

Funny, I thought, how Kapono has just been treated badly by a boorish man, forcing her to change jobs—yet she's comforting her new boss instead of the other way around. All in a coffeehouse in the middle of Boy's Town, named in honor of America's most famous lesbian First Lady.

It was then that Kapono glanced out to the street and caught me spying.

Her righteous look said it all: I was a reporter—a male reporter at that—whom she'd foolishly trusted.

The damage was done. The least I could do, I figured, was to give them back their privacy, such as it was.

I punched the accelerator, made a couple of turns, and headed west again, to Gordon Cantwell's softball game.

# Seventeen

T HE FIELD where the Tinseltown Tyros played softball was
located in a Little League park in Westwood, not far from
UCLA, in the shadow of the 405 Freeway.

Fittingly, a building that housed a major film and TV production company loomed monolithically across the street. Its name
was emblazoned in outsized letters across an upper story, a con-
stant reminder to the ballplayers of their true goal in mixing it up
on the field of play.

I spotted Gordon Cantwell as I slipped into a third-row seat,
next to a bespectacled black guy in a Spike's Joint baseball cap,
who alternated his attention between the script in his lap and the
action on the diamond.

Cantwell was planted deep in center field, using an orange
sleeve to mop away the perspiration that ran down from beneath
his reddish toupee. On his other hand was the big glove I'd seen
him with Saturday night, which he'd carried with the unabashed
pride of a little kid.

Now, he pounded it nervously with his fist, rocking from one
foot to the other, waiting for the next pitch.

I scanned the rest of the outfield, then the infield. As my eyes
reached third base, I spotted another familiar face, a surprising
one.

Dylan Winchester stood just off the base pad, leaning toward
home, dressed in the uniform of the opposing team. His long
auburn hair flowed from beneath a blue-and-gray cap and his
powerful legs filled his pinstriped baseball pants to the stretching

point. As the pitcher readied the ball, Winchester's green eyes moved keenly from the pitcher's mound to home plate and back again, like those of a hungry cat waiting for the right moment to pounce.

In center field, Cantwell alternately pounded his glove and adjusted the orange brim of his cap.

The pitcher whipped his arm into a circular motion, then let the ball fly. I heard the *thunk* of the padded ball against the graphite bat, followed by screams of encouragement from the dugout and the stands.

As the ball lofted, Cantwell backed up a few steps and raised his eyes to the sky above the field lights. Winchester tagged up at third as Cantwell gloved the ball, then took off for home. Cantwell took two strides with his throwing arm cocked, showing good form, and launched the ball toward home plate.

Winchester powered toward the rubber plate like a runaway locomotive. The ball took one bounce in the infield before disappearing into the catcher's outstretched glove, which he swung toward Winchester as he lowered his shoulder for the collision.

Winchester hit him ferociously, but the catcher held his ground. I winced, watching the bone-jarring impact.

The umpire jerked his thumb and hollered, "Out!"

Winchester was in the umpire's face instantly, fists clenched at his sides, cursing, showering spittle through his beard. Then he went after the catcher, who was still shaking off the pain. One of Winchester's teammates came off the bench and grabbed him from behind, pulling him away; another pushed a can of Foster's Lager into his hand. More players crowded around, positioning themselves between Winchester and the targets of his fury. Then it was over and the players drifted toward coolers for the seventh-inning stretch, as if they'd seen it all before.

I found Winchester sitting alone on a dugout bench, muttering expletives between chugs of lager.

"Hello, Dylan."

"What's up, mate?"

He said it amiably, but also as if I were a total stranger, an odd, hybrid greeting that seemed peculiar to successful Hollywood types.

"I've been leaving messages for you."

"A lot of people leave messages for me. I only look at scripts through my agent."

"From what I hear, you don't have an agent at the moment."

"You've got a pair of ears, then, don't you?"

"I'm a reporter. Ears are useful."

"Oh. One of them."

His eyes showed contempt as he tipped the can.

"We've met, you know."

"I don't think so."

"Saturday night. In the downstairs hallway of Gordon Cantwell's house. You were asking about Raymond Farr."

In his eyes, the contempt was replaced by wariness. Wariness on a bully always looks closer to fear, perhaps because bullies don't like to feel the power and control they need so badly slipping away.

"Had me a bit too much to drink Saturday night," Winchester said, trying hard to sound cocky but failing badly. "Don't remember a whole hell of a lot, to be honest."

"Do you remember saying that you wanted to kill Raymond Farr?"

He stood up fast, nose to nose with me. It was a foolish thing to do, but he didn't seem capable of diplomacy.

"Who the fuck do you work for?"

"My name's Benjamin Justice. I'm working freelance."

"Freelance."

The contempt had returned—maybe relief—followed by another chug of lager.

"I was with a young woman named Alexandra Templeton. A staffer on the *Los Angeles Sun*. We're working on a freelance piece for *Angel City*."

"So what do you want from me?"

"I have a few questions about Saturday night."

"Like I said, I had a bit too much to drink."

"You were just shooting your mouth off."

"That's right, mate. The way blokes do. No more to it than that."

"Why were you so angry at Reza JaFari?"

" 'Fraid I don't know the fellow."

"Raymond Farr, Reza JaFari. Same man. I think you know that by now."

"You think you know a lot, don't you?"

"Not nearly enough, I'm afraid."

He glared at me a moment. Then he set his can of Foster's on the end of the bench, picked up a bat, and began taking practice swings.

"Just what is it you think you need to know?"

"For starters, why you wanted to find JaFari so badly."

"That's between me and him."

"Not anymore."

He pinned me with his eyes again, carving the air between us with dangerous arcs.

"Why did you drive off so fast that night, Dylan? Without a word of good-bye to anybody?"

"Is that what happened? Don't remember. Should never have been behind the wheel of a car."

"Should I repeat my question?"

He stopped swinging the bat and looked at me as if he couldn't decide whether to answer me or kill me.

"I heard they'd found him. It sounded bad, especially after I'd shot off my mouth earlier. I figured the cops would be up there. I didn't need my name dragged into it."

"Wrong answer, Dylan. I saw you drive away from the party roughly half an hour before JaFari's body was found."

Two ballplayers passed, popping beers. They exchanged greetings with Winchester, then moved on.

"I think it's time for you to shove off, mate."

"When can we sit down and talk more privately? Say, with a tape recorder running."

"I'd just as soon not be in your bloody story, if it's all the same."

"I'm afraid you're in the story, Dylan, whether you like it or not."

He took a vicious swing. The bat sliced the air inches from my face.

"I got nothing more to say, to you or anybody else."

The swings came faster now, narrowing the tenuous gap.

"Maybe you and JaFari still had a love problem. Maybe the affair didn't really end ten years ago."

He rested the bat on his shoulder, poised for the next swing, while his furious eyes rested on mine.

"You don't write one word about that, or anything else about my private life."

"You may direct movies, Winchester. But you don't control me or the press."

"You're playing a dangerous game, mate. You know that?"

"Is that a threat, Dylan? The kind I heard you make against Reza JaFari on Saturday night?"

His neck muscles tightened into thick cords and his body shook with suppressed rage. He suddenly readjusted his stance and took a lethal swing, dipping his shoulder away from me and sending the big can of Foster's flying.

Then he heaved the bat aside and took off in the direction of the stadium exit, his hands clenched into fists so tight they were almost tiny.

I cupped my hands to my mouth and called after him.

"I'll be in touch, Dylan—let's do lunch!"

# Eighteen

I FOUND Gordon Cantwell standing behind the dugout, sandwiched like aged ham between two female slices of fresh Wonder bread.

He had one arm around each of their slim waists, using the curves of their hips to rest his freckled hands.

I reintroduced myself, and thanked him for his hospitality Saturday night as the hour grew late with DeWinter's questions.

"It was the least I could do, under the circumstances. Terrible tragedy, what happened to that young man—a night I'll never forget."

"The ball game must be a welcome diversion." I glanced at the two young women. "As well as the company of friends."

Cantwell smiled with measured solemnity.

"One has to go on."

"You seem quite devoted to the game of baseball."

"It's a childhood passion that I've never quite outgrown."

"That was a nice throw from center field. You've got an impressive arm."

The smile re-formed, this time with exaggerated modesty.

"If only I could hit the ball as well, Mr. Justice."

He laughed lightly, and glanced to each side to see the two women laughing with him.

He introduced us; they were both named Debbie. One Debbie carried a tote bag filled with scripts, the other a well-thumbed copy of *The Cantwell Method*.

"Are you in the industry?" the Debbie with the tote bag asked.

"I'm assisting on a freelance piece for *Angel City* magazine. With Alexandra Templeton. You may have heard of her."

The two Debbies looked at each other, shrugged their slim shoulders, and shook their pretty heads.

"No offense," the other Debbie said, "but I don't read *Angel City*. They say mean things about people I respect. You know, people in the industry. Successful people, like Gordon."

She cast her admiring eyes toward Cantwell, causing him to redden pleasurably.

"You're more an *Entertainment Tonight* kind of person," I guessed.

"Absolutely! Of course, I try to read the Sunday *New York Times* when I can."

"Section Two, I'll bet."

She looked nonplussed.

"I don't really know the numbers."

"*Angel City* does have a certain edge," Cantwell said, with the tone of a religious figure making an official pronouncement. "But it also manages to come up with a decent piece on the industry now and then. I'm sure you and Alexandra will contribute to the latter."

"Thanks, Gordon. I feel at least partially vindicated."

"Vindication is one of the primary themes of cinema," the first Debbie said. "I learned that in one of Gordon's seminars. I'm trying to work it into a script."

She put a hand to her mouth.

"Or was it redemption?"

"If your article is about screenwriting," the other Debbie said, "you absolutely *must* talk to Gordon. He's widely thought of in the industry as a genius."

"So I understand." I glanced his way. "Maybe we could grab a few minutes now."

"I'm afraid I'm due up to bat next inning."

"I wouldn't want to file the piece without at least mentioning you and your valuable work."

"And my book, I hope."

"The bible of screenplay structure? I don't see how we could leave it out."

His freckled skin flushed pink again. He glanced toward the field.

"I suppose we could find a minute or two."

He bid good-bye to the two Debbies and we took seats in the

stands away from the crowd. Cantwell launched into a speech about why his approach to screenplay construction was so much sounder than anything else being offered. I scribbled notes, which seemed to make him happy.

"How many students would you estimate you've taught over the years, Gordon?"

"Counting the weekend seminars, the ten-week workshops, and the mail-order courses, along with the international lecture tours, the number would certainly be in the tens of thousands. I can get a more precise figure for you if you need it."

"With that many students, it must be difficult to know them personally."

"I do my best, but, yes, it is difficult."

"How well did you know Reza JaFari?"

The question stopped him cold.

"I'm sorry," I said. "I guess you knew him as Raymond Farr."

"Are you going to write about Raymond?"

"We won't know until we actually put our story together. But we envision making you and perhaps your networking party the focal point."

"How flattering." His eyes shifted to my notepad. "But I hope you won't dwell on what happened Saturday night. My little gathering has been going on now for more than twenty years. This is the first time anything unpleasant has happened."

"Difficult to avoid mentioning, though."

His mouth tightened into a pained smile.

"I suppose it is."

"What can you tell me about JaFari's death?"

"What happened was a terrible tragedy for the family of a fine young man. Any publicity your story might generate for myself or the work I do pales in the face of the sadness we all feel."

He waited while I wrote it down word for word, repeating the second line for me and looking more comfortable afterward.

"How would you describe your relationship with Reza?"

"He enrolled a year or so ago in one of my seminars. As Raymond Farr, of course. I didn't know him particularly well."

"A good student?"

"Off the record, Mr. Justice? I wouldn't want to cause his family any more pain than they've already suffered."

I closed my notebook.

"Raymond wanted very badly to be a success, but he didn't really want to do the work it takes to be a good writer. Great talent, as you may know, is not necessarily a requirement for success in the writing field. Discipline and craft are. At the very least, one must be productive and write with a reasonable command of technique."

"And have a great deal of patience, I imagine."

"Absolutely."

"And JaFari had none of those qualities?"

"Raymond was charming, hungry for success, eager to please. Yet he lacked both the talent and the commitment to make it in one of the world's most competitive professions. He certainly wasn't alone in that respect, of course. The great majority of aspiring screenwriters never sell a thing."

"Yet JaFari kept coming to your parties."

"Everyone is welcome. I open my home each month to encourage the sharing of contacts and ideas. The young people, especially, seem to appreciate it."

He laughed in his false way, and added quickly, "Not that I'm all that much older than many of them."

"Is that where you met the two Debbies, at your party?"

"Actually, I was fortunate enough to be introduced to them at one of our ball games." He lit up a bit. "Did I mention that Michael Keaton was supposed to play tonight? Unfortunately, he was forced to cancel at the last minute. But he's played with us before. You might want to put that in your story."

"We're back on the record, then?"

"By all means."

I opened my notebook and dutifully wrote it down, while Cantwell craned his neck to see that I got it right. He spelled K-E-A-T-O-N aloud, and followed it with several of the actor's more impressive credits.

Then he stood and looked toward the field, where the umpire had called the eighth inning.

"I should get back—take some warm-up swings."

"Perhaps we can get together when you have more time."

"To be honest, I was hoping I might be able to meet with Miss Templeton again."

"You don't like my questions?"

"Not at all. It's just that—well, Alexandra is quite—"

"Attractive?"

"And very personable."

"Funny, she said the same thing about you."

His eyes flickered excitedly.

"Did she?"

"I'll tell you what, Gordon. If Alex is able to free up some time, I'll have her call Christine Kapono to set up a meeting."

We heard a bat connect with the ball, the crowd cheer, then a few groans. Cantwell lowered his voice.

"Actually, Christine no longer works for me."

I feigned surprise.

"Really? Why is that?"

He leaned close.

"Just between us, Justice? She has what you might call a 'problem' with men. If you know what I mean."

"I'm not sure I do."

He chuckled.

"Does the film *The Children's Hour* mean anything to you, Justice? *The Fox? The Killing of Sister George?*"

"I'm more familiar with *Rubyfruit Jungle.*"

"I don't know that one."

"It's a novel. Never made it to the screen. But I think I get your drift." I winked, buddy-buddy style. "Kapono's a dyke. Hates men. You canned her."

"That's awfully blunt."

"How would you put it, Gordon?"

"Let's just say I felt it would be better for her to find an environment where she would feel less tension due to gender and lifestyle differences."

"It didn't have anything to do with you putting your hand where it didn't belong?"

"I beg your pardon?"

"I'm talking about you grabbing her ass, Gordon. Just before she planted her knee in your family jewels."

His face turned sour.

"You've spoken with Christine, I take it."

"You take it right."

"When was this?"

"I ran into her up at your place a couple of hours ago."

"You were at my house?"

I nodded.

"May I ask why?"

"I wanted to look around while the light was good."

"Look around for *what?*"

I shrugged. "You never know."

"I suggest you make an appointment next time."

"It's difficult, when no one answers their phone."

"Better yet, have Miss Templeton make the appointment." He tucked his glove under one arm. "Your questions strike me as totally out of line."

Cantwell's back was to the field. Across his shoulder, I saw the second batter saunter to home plate.

"Perhaps you'd better take those warm-up swings, Gordon. Shouldn't take the plate cold, not at your age."

A viper couldn't have looked at me with more displeasure.

Cantwell turned his back and attempted a manly stride on his way to the dugout, where he picked through the bats until he found one that felt right in his hands.

He took a few awkward swings while the batter ahead of him flied out to left field. Cantwell stepped to the plate and dribbled a grounder back to the pitcher, who easily threw him out.

Then Cantwell was back in center field, pounding his glove, waiting for another chance to show the two Debbies how far and how straight he could throw a softball.

I picked up groceries and a jug of wine and returned to my apartment, to find the telephone ringing. Danny Romero's voice was at the other end.

"DeWinter's here. I'm up shit creek."

"What happened?"

"He came with a warrant to look for evidence. There's a bunch of stuff missing."

"Someone broke in?"

"This morning, when I took Maggie for her walk."

"What did they get?"

"Reza's papers, computer disks. Files, phone messages, stuff like that. They pretty much cleaned out his room."

"You told DeWinter that?"

"He's not buying it. He thinks I ditched the stuff to protect myself."

"The coroner ruled that Reza died of natural causes. I don't see why DeWinter belongs at your place at all. Or how he got a judge to issue a search warrant."

"Well, he's here."

"How are you feeling?"

"It hasn't been a good week." Then, more troubled: "I think he's going to bust me, Ben."

"Does he know you're sick?"

"I told him I got AIDS, showed him my meds. It just made him treat me worse."

"Put him on."

"I hate to get you involved in this."

"Just put him on, dammit."

I heard muffled voices, then DeWinter's terse delivery.

"Yeah, what is it?"

"Danny says you're going to arrest him."

"It's looking that way."

"What about the coroner's report?"

"A coroner's report isn't written in stone. Besides, I'm looking at new evidence now."

"What evidence?"

"I don't owe you any explanation, Justice."

"Why don't you stop being an asshole, DeWinter, and give him a break. He's got AIDS, for Christ sake."

"That makes him a choirboy, I guess."

"It means he doesn't need the aggravation."

"Neither did Reza JaFari."

"You're saying you've got something solid to link Danny to JaFari's death?"

DeWinter's voice grew smug.

"Like I said, I don't even have to talk to you."

"Fine. I'll talk to Alexandra Templeton instead. Let her know she's got a juicy story about a cop harassing a kid with AIDS."

"He's no kid. He's twenty-seven."

"We'll see how Templeton plays it on the front page of the *Sun*. How the AIDS organizations react. Then how the mayor deals with you for doing your homophobe routine in a city filled with a strong gay voting bloc. I imagine Danny's still got his bruises. Should make a nice press photo."

"Fuck you, Justice."

"That's the best offer I've had all day, Lieutenant."

Several seconds of silence followed; I could hear DeWinter breathing hard.

"I'm going off the record here."

"I'm listening off the record."

"I'm building a case against Romero that makes the coroner's findings look a little hasty."

"Tell me about it."

"One, he was the last person to see JaFari alive."

"The last person you know about."

"Two, they were two punks living together, one of whom wanted to go to a party to meet some other guy alone."

"If it was a guy."

"Three, Hosain JaFari thinks Romero stole his son's belongings."

"Conjecture."

"Four, I tell him to leave the rest of JaFari's things alone and now most of it turns up missing."

"He says someone broke in and stole it."

"That's what he says."

"That hardly sounds like enough to book him on."

"There's more."

He paused for effect, then let me have it.

"Your friend Romero had an argument with JaFari the night before he died."

"He told me they were getting along fine."

"He lied."

"How do you know?"

"The neighbors heard them screaming at each other, down in the driveway. Romero's already admitted that much."

"Arguing about what?"

"The neighbors aren't sure. But they heard Romero using words like 'murder' and 'kill.' Two of them heard your friend Romero tell JaFari he didn't deserve to live another day."

"They heard Danny say that?"

"That's a direct statement from two of the witnesses—'You don't deserve to live another day, you bastard.' "

Advantage DeWinter. I could almost see his gloating face at the other end of the line.

"I consider him a flight risk. I want him in a cell."

"Do me a favor. Hold off booking him for a while."

"Give me one good reason why I should do you the slightest fucking favor."

"Because I may have something for you that's more important than a lukewarm suspect."

There was an encouraging pause.

"And what would that be, Justice?"

"I'll deliver it personally, if you'll wait."

"You got twenty minutes. Then we're outta here."

# Nineteen

"LIEUTENANT DeWINTER. How nice to see you again. Or may I call you Claude?"

Alexandra Templeton extended her hand so that her painted nails were pointed in the general direction of Claude DeWinter's crotch. Her eyes were brown sugar, her smile as warm and sweet as oven-fresh pecan pie.

"Claude will do."

The moment DeWinter had seen Templeton step into Danny Romero's apartment, his roar had diminished to a purr.

Fifteen minutes earlier, I'd reached Templeton on her car phone and asked her to meet me there. I'd also asked her to soften up Claude DeWinter any way she could. She'd understood the implication and didn't like the idea, until I explained Danny's situation in terms both medical and emotional.

"Then Claude it will be," she said, and let her slender fingers linger in DeWinter's huge paw just long enough to give his penis a chance to twitch.

Danny was slumped on the couch with Maggie, fighting a dry cough. I introduced him to Templeton and they both said quiet hellos. After that, I dropped the social niceties.

"The lieutenant says you and Reza had an argument Friday night."

"We had some words, yeah."

"You didn't tell me about that."

"I wasn't gonna mention it. Not to nobody." He glanced at DeWinter. "But not because of what you think."

"Why, then?"

Danny got up and pulled a sweatshirt on over his T-shirt, even though the room was warm.

Then he picked up a photograph of Reza JaFari from a table-top, which I studied over his shoulder. I saw again that JaFari had been blessed in the looks department—heavy-lidded dark eyes, a nicely shaped face, a dense growth of beard that worked well against his prettier features, including the longish hair. I wondered if Danny was about to admit after all that he and JaFari had been lovers; it wouldn't have seemed unreasonable.

His voice grew quiet as he gazed at the photo.

"Reza helped me out. Gave me a place to stay, let me use the garage to make my furniture. Even loaned me money a coupla times for the wood. I was grateful to him for that."

He studied JaFari's face a moment longer, then put the photograph back in place and faced us. His next words came quickly, spit angrily from his mouth.

"What I didn't like was that he had HIV and he was still sleeping around. Without telling his partners. I think he was even lying to 'em, saying he was negative."

Templeton put a hand to her mouth.

"My God. That's evil."

Danny ignored her, directing himself straight at DeWinter.

"I didn't say anything before because I didn't want Reza's family to know. The way he talked about 'em, they seem like good people. It's bad enough they just lost him without finding out what a bastard he was."

DeWinter studied Danny a long moment without blinking.

"Suppose I believe this story about him doing what he did, and you suddenly getting soft toward his family. That still doesn't explain why you threatened to kill him."

"I didn't threaten to kill him."

"That's not what the neighbors say."

"I told him that when he spread the virus, it was the same as killing people, almost like murder. I told him he didn't deserve to live another day doing shit like that. That's what I said."

"You were angry. Angry enough to draw half your neighbors to their windows."

"I still am. It was wrong, what he was doing. Dead wrong."

*Dead wrong.* The words hung there like an indictment.

"Maybe he infected you. Maybe you decided it was payback time."

"I was infected before I met Reza, way before. I can show you medical records, if that's what you want."

DeWinter kept pushing.

"But Friday night, when you found out he was exposing people to the virus, you felt he had to be stopped."

I could see Danny wearing down. He was already worn down enough. I wanted to end it.

"He explained the argument, Lieutenant."

"He offered his version."

"At the very least, it weakens your case against him."

Templeton interceded, gently but forcefully.

"To a jury, it might even put Danny in a sympathetic light, Claude. And cast JaFari as the villain. If it ever got as far as the courtroom."

Once more, she found the right button. DeWinter stared at the floor while he fished around in his pockets for a stick of gum.

"I'll take that into consideration."

He turned to me as he fed the gum into his mouth.

"You told me you had something for me."

I handed him the paper bag I was carrying. He looked inside.

"A Grolsch bottle."

"Capped, with some liquid trapped in the bottom."

"So?"

"I think you should send it to the lab, have it tested with the bottle you found near JaFari's body."

"Those tests are back. Clean as a whistle. All they found in the bottle was expensive beer."

"Then I definitely think you should have this bottle checked."

"Where'd you get it?"

"An old lady found it. She was scavenging the canyon below Cantwell's house."

"How far from Cantwell's house?"

"A hundred yards, thereabouts."

"That's a fair distance. I don't see the connection."

"How often do you see a Grolsch bottle littering the landscape, Lieutenant?"

Templeton stepped in again.

"Claude, Justice is just asking you to have it tested. And to give Danny the benefit of the doubt, at least for a while."

DeWinter smiled a little; it was a remarkable sight.

"Why do I feel like I'm getting gang-banged, here?"

Templeton smiled coyly.

"I'll bet you can handle just about anything, Claude."

"Yeah, yeah, yeah."

He cast a harder look toward Danny.

"Nothing's changed, Romero. Ten to one you're booked and behind bars before the week's out."

"Whatever," Danny said.

What little hope had shown in his eyes was gone. I couldn't stand to see any more hope drain out of him. DeWinter had played his best card, the argument between JaFari and Danny. I decided to play mine.

"What if I told you I heard someone threaten to kill Reza JaFari Saturday night, not long before his body was found? Someone other than Danny?"

"If you did, you damn well should have told me before now."

"Then you're interested."

"Maybe you heard someone make this alleged threat, Justice, maybe you didn't. Maybe you're just trying to blow smoke to create a cover for your sick friend here."

"Then you're not interested."

"What would this alleged person's motive be?"

"I'm working on that."

DeWinter stared at me with a look that was somewhere between curiosity and disgust.

"All I'm asking, Lieutenant, is that you have the contents of that bottle tested. And lay off Danny for a while."

"And what if Danny boy disappears on me?"

"I can't. I gotta stick around."

"Why's that?"

"I'm on Medi-Cal. My treatment program is with the AIDS Healthcare Foundation. My doctor's here, my clinic. All my prescriptions come out of AHF."

"His life literally depends on them, Lieutenant."

"I think Claude understands," Templeton said. She moved to his side, touching his shoulder. "Don't you, Claude?"

He glanced at her lovely hand draped over the shiny polyester blend of his discount suit. It was probably the closest he'd been to a woman as beautiful as Alexandra Templeton in a long time. Maybe ever.

"Yeah, yeah, yeah."

He shook his head, trying not to smile, a smart man who knew exactly what was happening but was grateful even for that.

"I'll have the Grolsch bottle checked out, Justice. And I'll give

Danny boy a little breathing room. But understand, it's only temporary. And if you have any new information pertinent to Reza JaFari's death, I want to know about it."

"As soon as it's solid, Lieutenant."

"Don't wait for it to get too solid."

DeWinter hitched up his trousers, cast a last, appreciative glance at Templeton, then took his big body out the door.

Danny sat forward on the couch, massaging his temples.

"Deal straight with us from now on, Danny. It's the only way we can help you."

"Yeah, all right." He got to his feet, shifting his eyes from Templeton to me. "I got to take my meds. Thanks for stickin' up for me."

Maggie trotted after him into the kitchen. Templeton picked up the photograph of JaFari, looking for something in it she didn't understand.

"What kind of person would do what he did?"

"The same kind that sells crack to kids or cheats old people out of their life savings."

She shivered, as if the room had suddenly gotten cold, as if she might be able to shake off the truth of things and feel better.

She was twenty-six, well-read, sharp as a Buck knife. But she'd also been raised protectively by wealthy parents, educated in exclusive prep schools, and now lived high above it all in a west side condo with a half-million-dollar ocean view. Her apprenticeship as a reporter wasn't complete, nor the loss of innocence that inevitably went with it.

I put my hands on her shoulders and turned her to face me.

"You handled DeWinter well. It means a lot."

Her troubled look gave way to a wan smile.

"I guess you owe me."

"What's the debt?"

"How about dinner at Musso & Frank's? We'll sit in the same booth William Faulkner shared with F. Scott Fitzgerald when they were out here writing movies for the money and hating every minute of it."

"Those damn movies again." Then: "Rain check?"

"You have plans?"

I glanced toward the kitchen, where Danny was plucking variously colored capsules from the compartments of a plastic pill box.

"You're not falling into something that could get you into trouble, are you, Justice?"

"I like him."

"You're on assignment. He's a suspect."

"The assignment's about the screenwriting game. We're using the party as our setting. He's not a screenwriter. He wasn't at the party."

"You're walking a thin line."

"I guess I am."

"How about Thursday, then? There's a press screening of *Thunder's Fortune*. We could grab a bite afterward at Spago in Beverly Hills. My treat."

"At their prices, it has to be."

She touched my face, gave me a chaste kiss, and left me, saying good-bye to Danny on her way out.

I stood beside him as he washed down the pills one by one with bottled water.

When he'd gotten the last one down, he said quietly, "This is no way to live."

"It's better than the alternative."

"Is it?"

I reached for him, but he moved away from me, nearer the door.

"You don't need to get involved in my shit, Ben."

"I know. That's what worries me."

"Getting involved?"

"Knowing I don't have to. Knowing I can cut and run if I want."

"If that's your choice, man, I'll understand. My life's all fucked up. Worse than you even know."

*Tell me then, Danny. Tell me all your secrets.*

"You want some company tonight?"

"Yeah, sort of. But it's better if you go."

"Why?"

"Just is, that's all."

It felt like both a rejection and a reprieve. I held him for a while, pressing my lips to the smooth slope of his neck, aching for more of him, but just as afraid of him as ever.

Before I left, I told him I wanted one more look at Reza JaFari's room.

"What for?"

"I wish I knew."

I entered the room alone, and switched on the desk lamp. The thief—whoever he or she was—had left little behind except JaFari's Hollywood magazines and resource books.

Most of the drawers were pulled out. Those that weren't, I opened. I found odd scraps of paper—laundry receipts, business cards—but nothing very interesting.

Then, one by one, I went through the books, turning them upside down, shaking the pages loose. One or two Samuel French bookmarks hit the floor.

JaFari's copy of *The Cantwell Method* yielded something more—a sheet of white paper, folded four-square. I picked it up from the littered floor, opened it up.

Under the lamp light, I saw the name and insignia of the Writer's Guild of America printed at the top.

Below that was a WGA script registration receipt for a screenplay titled *Over the Wall*, signed by Reza JaFari and dated three days before his death.

# Twenty

I DROVE AWAY from Danny Romero's place, looking with longing toward his lighted window but equally drawn by the freedom of escape.

Somewhere in between was an expanding sense of loneliness,
that unmistakable craving for closeness with another human
being that too many of us feed with fast-food sex as cold at the
center as it is steamy on the surface. It's not the occasional thrill
of anonymous sex that kills the soul, any more than a Big Mac
now and then guarantees a heart attack; it's the addiction to it, as
the callings of the heart grow fainter beneath the rising cries for
the next quick sexual fix.

The opportunities were all around me, but I had no taste at the
moment for hustlers, cruise bars, or pay-at-the-door sex clubs. I
ended up back in Boy's Town, eating dinner alone at Boy Meets
Grill and washing it down with more wine than was good for me.

Five minutes after paying the check, I was standing outside Lawrence Teal's apartment, convincing myself I was there to talk to
him about Reza JaFari.

He opened the door wearing only shorts. A day's worth of
golden fuzz looked good on his pretty face, and his rosebud nipples pouted at me with pride, demanding attention.

"Hello, Lawrence."

"Hello."

His voice was as cold and hard as concrete in winter.

"I wanted to run a few questions by you, if it's all right."

"I think you should have called first."

"You want me to go?"

He looked me over with eyes that were as hungry as mine, then stepped aside to let me pass.

The living room held only two pieces of furniture—identical, stiff-backed chairs, arranged to face each other from opposite sides of the hardwood floor. A single item of decoration leaned unframed against a bare white wall: a matted, life-size, black-and-white photograph of Teal stretched balletically at center stage, his sinewy body naked from the waist up and clad in dancer's tights from the waist down, shot in the kind of moody, diffused light usually reserved for divas and prima donnas.

Behind me, I heard the door being shut, the dead bolt being turned, the chain lock being latched. The blinds were already drawn. I felt imprisoned with Teal, trapped by our mutual raw need, and with the feeling came a deeper stab of sexual desire.

He came around to face me, standing close enough for me to see a few tendrils of fine hair curling around each soft nipple.

"Wine?"

"I wouldn't mind."

"I only have red."

"Red will do."

I followed him to the kitchen, where he poured me a glass, and one for himself.

On the countertop between us lay the day's mail, including an opened envelope bearing the return name and address of Lydia Lowe, the syndicated columnist. Lowe was well known inside the journalism trade as a closeted lesbian who had made a lucrative career writing about the personal lives of others while carefully concealing her own. She worked out of New York City, relying for much of her material on a string of West Coast confidants who kept their ears to the rumor mill. Her spies included the usual coterie of nervous butterflies who depended for self-importance on digging dish and trading gossip. A pair of tickets to a Broadway show poked at an angle from the ripped envelope.

"You're chummy with Lydia Lowe?"

Teal's eyes followed mine to the envelope.

"Never met the old dyke. Went to school with one of her assistants. I feed him tidbits once in a while. Sometimes they make it into the column."

"And what do you get out of it?"

"A trip to New York now and then. Theater passes. A bottle of good brandy at Christmas."

He handed me a glass that looked stolen from a bar, filled with Chianti that smelled and tasted like cheap but decent Italian. Then he came around the corner, passing close enough for me to smell his pricey cologne.

"Is that why you dropped by, Justice? To chat about Lydia Lowe?"

"I'm more interested in Dylan Winchester and Reza JaFari."

"Why am I not surprised?"

"You told me they were lovers once. Almost ten years ago."

"Frankly, Justice, I'm tired of the subject."

"Do you think JaFari might have been blackmailing Winchester about their affair?"

"You're determined to pin JaFari's death on Dylan, aren't you?"

He brushed past me into the living room, where he sat straight up in one of the hard-backed chairs. I turned the other chair around and straddled it, resting my arms on the wooden back.

"Is it possible that JaFari was using his leverage to make some kind of movie deal? Blackmailing Winchester into helping him get a film project going?"

"In this town? Anything's possible."

Teal's voice was distant and clipped now, giving nothing away but his own self-absorption.

"You're not helping me much, Teal."

"I'm just an actor, Justice. We're not smart like you writers."

"You're extremely smart and you know it. Maybe it's the subject of Dylan Winchester that makes you suddenly turn dumb."

Teal sipped from his glass, keeping his eyes on me, saying nothing.

"Shall I try another name, Lawrence?"

"If you want."

"Roberta Brickman."

"What about her?"

"How good an agent is she?"

"If she's at ITA, she must be good."

"Is she a lesbian?"

"Not that I'm aware of. But you never know."

"How close is she to Christine Kapono?"

"I have no idea."

"Anne-Judith Kemmerman?"

"Never met her."

"But you know who she is."

"I know that she was married to a big shot in the film business."

"That's it?"

He shrugged.

"You were a lot more talkative the other night, Teal."

"I'm not used to surprise visits like this."

"You like to give the stage directions."

"That depends on who I'm with—or what mood I'm in."

"What mood are you in now?"

His blond eyebrows arched with insinuation.

"Why don't you find out, tough guy?"

"Is that an invitation?"

"Do you need it in writing?"

I set my glass on the floor, walked across the room, and stood in front of him. The heat between us was palpable.

I lifted his chin, feeling the soft bristle of his beard. Then I unbuckled, unbuttoned, and unzipped.

When I pulled down my briefs, my cock sprang up and smacked him in the face. He turned his head away as if he didn't want it. I grabbed him by the ears and pulled him on like an old boot. He sucked me eagerly until I was seconds away from ejaculating. On the HIV risk scale, we'd ventured into the middle zone, sort of like cigarette smokers who keep their habits to half a pack a day, hoping they'll beat the odds.

I drew away from Teal's pliant mouth.

"You have condoms?"

"Of course."

"Get one."

He got up and went obediently into the bedroom. I stripped and followed. He was waiting for me on the edge of the bed, his shorts off, his long, narrow feet planted firmly on the bare wood floor. A condom and tube of K-Y lay beside him.

He inspected me up and down, all six hairy feet of me, and when his eyes came to rest on mine, they reflected equal measures of hatred and desire.

I shoved him back on the bed and tossed the condom onto his flat belly. He knew what that meant.

He unwrapped it and rolled it carefully down the entire shaft of my cock. He lathered me up and down with the lubricant, handed me the tube, fell back, and raised his legs.

His ass clenched predictably when I inserted my finger into his rectum, but the jelly was in and his expectant eyes told me he was ready. I hooked one of his legs atop each of my shoulders, mounted him, and pinned his wrists above his head.

I entered him slowly but all in one movement, pushing past his tightening sphincter, forcing him to accept me or take the pain. He opened up and I went all the way in until our bodies joined and our faces were so close we felt each other's rapid breath.

He kept his eyes open, fixed on mine with undisguised contempt. But as I drew slowly out to begin a quickening series of strokes, he clamped his eyes shut and didn't open them again for a long time. Finally, he let out a low moan that came from deep in his throat, the choked sound of a man who has given in to the brutal power of pleasure, and I knew that whatever we felt about each other no longer mattered.

I pumped in rhythm to his thrusts and cries until I felt an overpowering sensation building somewhere deep between my ass and belly, then rolling up volcanically through my balls and cock. Then I was exploding with a wail and a groan and Teal was reaching to find his own cock and pull on it until it erupted with gobs of white semen that fell like pearls across his smooth chest.

As I slowly withdrew, he didn't give me the pleasure of hearing him cry out one last time, not even the usual small gasp as I pulled free. He remained still and silent, his eyes taken over again by what he really felt for me, and I for him.

"You do that well, Justice."

"It's nice when the critics approve."

I cleaned up in the bathroom, soaping off at the sink, wondering what Teal could possibly do with all the pretty jars and bottles lined up like good little soldiers on a shelf beneath the mirror. When I went back out, he was standing naked in the living room, toweling off as he stared at the moody portrait of himself dancing.

I dressed as if he wasn't there, thinking of a note in Templeton's research file bearing a quote made famous by a late, straight, drug-addled producer named Don Simpson, of *Top Gun* fame: *I don't make love, I fuck.*

I had little respect for heterosexual men who used women that way, which meant I didn't have an awful lot of respect for myself. I was smart enough to know it, too weak to change.

I zipped up and started toward the door.

"Justice."

I waited.

"A few minutes ago, you asked me about Anne-Judith Kemmerman."

"You didn't have much to tell me."

"I saw her having dinner with Raymond Farr."

"When?"

"Six, maybe eight weeks ago. At Jimmy's in Beverly Hills. I was parking cars for a special party. They were at a window table around the side, very private."

"What was the mood?"

"She seemed to be pleading with him, close to tears. Anne-Judith Kemmerman doesn't seem like the kind of woman who would beg."

"I thought you said you didn't know her."

"I've parked cars at a lot of Hollywood social functions. She's at most of them. I've seen enough of her to know she's not on the soft and weepy side."

"But not that night at Jimmy's."

"Like I said, she was close to falling apart."

"You think she and JaFari were lovers?"

"Raymond went both ways. Jimmy's is a classy place—expensive. Not the kind of place Ray would be picking up the check."

"I appreciate the information, Teal."

The corners of his mouth raised with the contempt I'd seen minutes earlier in his eyes.

"I appreciate the way you use your dick."

He turned his back, having deftly made a whore of me.

I walked over, reached around, and found his cock. It was soft again, but not small, like a giant curled up for a quick nap. I spit in my hand, then fondled him until it awoke and stretched; within seconds, it was standing tall, the swollen shaft filling my hand.

"Shall I go now, Lawrence?"

"Prick."

His teeth were clenched; the word barely made its way out.

He kept his eyes fixed on the giant black-and-white image of himself while I worked his cock, tightening my fingers on the circumcised ridge until I felt his whole body go tense and shudder while he pumped out strings of semen. When there was nothing left, his body trembled one last time and went slack with relief.

I dropped his drooping dick the way a butcher tosses aside an inferior piece of meat.

"Next time I'll be sure to call first."

I left him there admiring his own frozen beauty while his semen widened into puddles on the polished floor, feeling sick in my soul for having needed him more than my self-respect, but also wildly alive.

# Twenty-one

ROBERTA BRICKMAN was sitting at a distant corner table when I arrived at Hugo's the next morning for a breakfast interview.

It was exactly half past eight, our appointed time. She was wearing a tailored gray business suit with burnished gold buttons, and was bent over an open script, holding a coffee. She looked tense and unhappy, much the way she had at the party Saturday night.

That she had agreed to meet with me at all was remarkable. Templeton had applied the pressure, convincing Brickman that a "no comment" from Reza JaFari's one-time boss might appear awkward in an article revolving around the young screenwriter's death.

Templeton had requested Hugo's as the setting, based on her background research for the *Angel City* piece. The corner restaurant, which shared the same neighborhood as the new West Hollywood city hall, had long been a prime networking spot for youthful agents, rising producers, ambitious script readers, and hardworking development executives—"D-girls," in sexist Hollywood jargon, since most of the lower-paying development jobs were traditionally held by young women.

According to Templeton's notes, some customers went there for Hugo's two most popular dishes—Pasta alla Mamma and pumpkin pancakes—but most came to trade information on new scripts and writers that could later be cashed in for valuable career chips. Hugo's support system was especially important to the bright, determined women who had become more visible in the industry in recent years but were still fighting for their place in the entrenched male hierarchy.

Dozens of them were here this morning, sitting in groups of two and three, leaning close, abuzz with conversation. Roberta Brickman looked up from her script as I approached and glanced at her watch as I sat down.

"Maybe you should order, Mr. Justice. I don't have a lot of time."

"Good morning, Roberta."

She attempted a smile.

"Forgive my shortness. Good morning."

Her frosted blond hair was swept back and pinned in a tight swirl that looked as forcefully drawn together as the painful lines of her otherwise pretty face.

I nodded toward the screenplay.

"An original about to be put on the auction block?"

"A rewrite, actually." She closed the script and slipped it into a handsome attaché case sitting on the chair beside her. "To be more precise, a revision of a previous rewrite by another writer of an adaptation by yet another writer of a novel written by someone else entirely."

She managed a poker face, but I detected a trace of humor in her voice, which made me feel there might be some hope for her after all.

"I'd think so many cooks would spoil the proverbial broth."

"A major studio film is a huge enterprise, Mr. Justice. The stakes are very high. Tens of millions of dollars are on the line, as well as individual careers. At the same time, it's a collaborative process involving dozens of creative and technical people. A lot can go wrong, and frequently does. That's why so much effort goes into getting the script as right as possible to being with."

She sipped her coffee, then spoke precisely and forcefully, as if winding up a lecture.

"You can make a bad movie out of a good script, Mr. Justice. But you'll never make a good movie out of a bad script."

A waitress arrived while I was putting Brickman's words down on paper. She ordered the vegetable omelette with fresh OJ. I opted for ham and eggs.

"And coffee, please. The sooner the better."

I turned to a fresh page in my notebook and began the questions.

"At the party, you mentioned that JaFari had worked for you until recently. But I'm still unclear about your role as his agent."

Brickman responded in a careful monotone.

"From time to time, I gave him advice about his screenwriting aspirations. Strictly on an informal basis."

"You hadn't actually tried to sell anything of his?"

"To my knowledge, Raymond had never written anything. At least nothing of which I was aware."

"How did he come to be your assistant?"

"He started in the mailroom, as most of us have. I believe he got the job through Dylan Winchester. Apparently, they were . . . friends."

The waitress set a cup in front of me and filled it with steaming coffee. I sipped and forged ahead.

"JaFari made the leap from the mailroom to working as your personal assistant?"

"I needed someone on short notice. He seemed bright enough and he was rather ambitious, which you have to be when the hours are long and the pay is low."

"Why did he leave?"

"That's a personal matter, Mr. Justice." She quickly corrected herself. "That is, a *personnel* matter."

She glanced at her watch again. "I have a meeting at ten. Perhaps we should stick to questions of the most pertinence to your article."

"You're a busy woman."

"I'm a busy *person*, Mr. Justice. Most agents are. If they're not, their clients should probably look elsewhere for representation."

"Dylan Winchester also left ITA recently. Was his departure connected to JaFari's?"

"I wouldn't know. Winchester wasn't my client."

"You must have heard some scuttlebutt."

"I don't see what Winchester's leaving ITA has to do with the article you're writing with Miss Templeton."

"You're probably right. I seem to be getting off the track."

The waitress served our breakfasts, warmed my coffee, and left us again. Brickman cut her meatless omelette neatly into sections and ate one without salting it.

"Next question, Mr. Justice?"

"Tell me what you can about Reza JaFari. His personality, his life."

"Of course, I didn't know him well."

She reached for her glass of pulpy, fresh-squeezed orange juice.

"I was aware of him when he worked in the mailroom. I'd see him in the hallways. We chatted a few times, as people who work in the same building tend to do. Then the position in my office was posted, and he put in for it."

"There must have been a lot of competition."

"It's considered a good entry level job, a place to learn the business."

"What did you do before you became an agent, Roberta?"

She smiled pleasantly.

"I was another agent's assistant."

"So you knew what the job demanded."

"Of course."

"And Reza apparently met your qualifications."

"Obviously, since I hired him."

"You interviewed him personally?"

"Briefly, yes. I knew him as Raymond Farr, of course."

"Looked at his résumé?"

"Naturally."

"What was it about Reza that so impressed you?"

She hesitated, sipping her juice. She used up a few more seconds by raising her napkin to dab needlessly at her mouth.

"He'd been to film school, as I recall. Done some clerical work, which helps. He knew our computer system. And he could spell, which has become a rare quality among young people."

"I don't think he was that much younger than you, was he?"

"I got started in the business early."

"And rose fast."

"I work very hard, Mr. Justice. Generally, I begin my day with an eight o'clock breakfast meeting and end it with an appointment for drinks, dinner, or a screening. Weekends are spent catching up on my reading. Seventy-hour work weeks are not uncommon. Frequently they're closer to eighty."

"That doesn't leave much time for a personal life."

"In this business, one's professional life *is* one's personal life."

"Doesn't sound like much fun."

She propped her elbows on the table and formed an arch with her fingers that held up a prim smile.

"I don't mean to tell you how to do your job, Mr. Justice. But your questions seem to be wandering again."

"I'll get back to Reza JaFari, then." I glanced at a list of questions I'd put in prioritized order the night before. "Did you see any hope that he might one day be a successful screenwriter?"

"Let's just say he had a lot of work ahead of him before that might happen."

"Could you be more specific? What steps did you recommend?"

"Screenwriting is a very special medium, Mr. Justice, quite unlike narrative prose writing. Reza had almost no grasp of the techniques, no sense of the craft. And his ideas were rather mundane, often sophomoric. One thing I did for him was to put him in touch with Leonardo Petrocelli. I believe you met him the other night at the party."

"Yes, I remember."

"Leonardo had contacted me looking for representation. I checked his credits. He'd done some wonderful work in the sixties and seventies. Unfortunately—"

"He's old."

"He's been out of the loop for quite a few years."

"Euphemistically speaking."

"I don't want to see this in print, Mr. Justice."

I laid my pen aside.

"This is a business of energy and new ideas. It's driven by the youth market, because young people buy most of the movie tickets. Leonardo was a fine screenwriter in his prime. But he's of another time, another era."

"His sensibility is old-fashioned?"

"It may sound unfair, but there's a certain vernacular and tone to writing that either appeals or doesn't appeal to a new generation of moviegoers. Leonardo, as skilled a storyteller as he is, as worthy as his ideas are, works with material that is not readily salable in today's marketplace. At least not in my opinion."

"Couldn't you have sent his work out and tested some other opinions?"

"I have only so much time in the day to pitch and sell and try to make deals. I use that precious time where I think it has the best chance of success."

"Yet you worked with Reza JaFari."

Her eyes flared with irritation.

"On an informal basis, Mr. Justice, as I've tried to make clear. I suggested he and Leonardo meet and consider working together. I felt that Reza's youth and sense of the marketplace might enlighten Leo. And that Reza, in turn, might benefit from Leo's maturity and sense of craftsmanship."

"What came of it?"

"Unfortunately, Leo fell ill shortly after they met. Reza left the firm not long after that, and I've had no contact with him since."

"You went looking for him the other night at the party."

"I went to do some networking and have a drink. I heard Raymond was there and didn't want to seem unsociable. So I asked around about him."

"At the party, you said you had some old business to clear up."

"Did I?"

"But you never found him?"

"No."

"His death must have been very upsetting."

"Of course."

"You handled it awfully well, though."

"Did I? I really don't remember. That whole evening is something of a blur."

"Christine Kapono must have been a comfort."

Tension hardened Brickman's face.

"Christine is a good friend who's been there when I needed her."

"Have you needed her more than usual recently?"

Her voice sparked, along with her eyes.

"These questions are altogether improper."

"I didn't mean to upset you, Roberta."

"I'm not upset. I'm just not interested in talking about myself, that's all. I see no purpose in it."

"Any last thoughts on Reza JaFari, then—since the two of you worked so closely together?"

"He was my assistant. It was a purely professional relationship, and it didn't last long."

I glanced back through my notebook until I found one of the quotes I'd written down.

" 'In this business, one's professional life *is* one's personal life.' I believe those are your exact words, Roberta."

She raised her hand, signaling for the check.

"I really must go, Mr. Justice. If you need to round out your picture of JaFari, perhaps you should talk to someone who knew him better than I."

She handed her credit card to the waitress, and stood.

"Good luck with your article. I'm sorry I couldn't be of more help."

She grabbed her attaché case and walked briskly to the front counter on stylish maroon pumps, waiting impatiently while the waitress processed her card. Then she disappeared out the front doors, fumbling with her pocketbook, dropping it, picking it up, hurrying on.

I checked my watch. It was five minutes past nine. The offices of ITA were no more than ten minutes away, on the eastern fringe of Beverly Hills. That left Brickman roughly forty-five minutes before her next meeting.

She wasn't rushing to make the appointment; I was certain of that.

Roberta Brickman was in a hurry to get away from my troubling questions about Reza JaFari.

# Twenty-two

WITHIN AN HOUR of Roberta Brickman's hasty departure, I was looking at a *USA Today* headline taped to Harry Brofsky's office door.

*GROUCHY OLD PEOPLE LIVE LONGER*
*NEW MEDICAL STUDY INDICATES*

Harry was behind his desk, biting into an oozing jelly doughnut. It wasn't a pretty sight.

"Still off the cancer sticks, Harry?"

"What's it look like?"

"Severe oral deprivation."

"Thanks for the psychoanalysis."

"Templeton around?"

"Out on assignment—where she should be."

He pushed a Winchell's box toward me. I pushed it back.

"Thanks, I had breakfast."

"So did I—twice."

He crammed the rest of the doughnut into his mouth and sucked the sugar off his fingers, one by one. When his fingers were clean, he stared at the remaining doughnuts despairingly. He reached for one with white frosting and colored sprinkles, then withdrew his hand.

"I can't keep doing this."

"Maybe you should try stopping."

His dull gray eyes peered at me over the rims of his low-slung bifocals.

"Look who's giving pep talks on discipline."

"Just hate to see you trade tarred lungs for clogged arteries, that's all."

"You here to chew the fat or do some work?"

"Why don't you take me down to the library and get me into the files."

"For the magazine piece?"

I nodded.

"Why don't you give me a status report, since it's looking like it might turn into something for the *Sun*."

"How about talking while we walk?"

We left the newsroom and headed down a corridor of buckling linoleum that led in the direction of Data Central, as Harry liked to call the research library. We turned a corner and passed the glass-enclosed kitchen where the food editor had once tested recipes. There was no longer a food editor at the *Sun*, no recipe testing, no food section; budget cutbacks and reduced page counts had taken care of that years ago. I wondered how long the *Sun* would stay in business, and what Harry would do if it folded.

"So fill me in on this JaFari business."

I flipped open my notebook and showed Harry a chart I'd drawn linking various names to Reza JaFari and each other. Lines connected JaFari to Dylan Winchester, Roberta Brickman, Leonardo Petrocelli, and Gordon Cantwell. The line between JaFari and Anne-Judith Kemmerman was broken and tagged with a question mark, along with the word "Jimmy's." Anne-Judith Kemmerman was linked to Bernard Kemmerman by a solid line, indicating their marriage before his death. The connection from Bernard Kemmerman to Reza JaFari consisted of a broken line with a question mark and the words "phone calls" above it. Other lines connected other players to each other where appropriate: Brickman to Petrocelli, Cantwell to Winchester ("softball"), and so on.

"One tangled web," Harry said, looking at all the crisscrossing lines. "Now all you have to do is untangle it."

"And see where it leads me."

"You know the old axiom, Ben: When in doubt, follow the money."

"Except for Danny Romero, these people all have one thing in common, Harry."

"The movie business."

"Right. And they've got to be in the game for something be-

sides money. The effort's too big, and the chances of being successful too small."

"Power?"

"That's part of it, sure."

"Money equals power, Ben."

"And what does power get you?"

"In this town? Whatever you want."

"Most people want happiness, Harry."

"And what the fuck is happiness?"

"I guess that depends on the individual."

We stopped outside the door to Data Central.

"I met a screenwriter once," Harry said. "Little guy, near-
sighted, not much to look at. Insecure as hell. Worked his ass off
learning how to write screenplays until he finally sold one. Had a
couple of hits. Strictly hack stuff, car chase movies, but the sequels
and TV spin-offs made him rich. I asked him what made him want
to be a screenwriter so badly. You know what he told me? 'So I
could get some of that Hollywood pussy!' "

I laughed, loudly enough to turn the head of a librarian or two.

"I swear," Harry said. "His exact words."

We stepped into Data Central and took our places at the front
counter. The shelves to our left held an assortment of directories,
from the popular *Encyclopedia of Associations, Who's Who in America,*
and *Research Centers Directory* on down to the more esoteric *Celebrity
Register* and *Directory of American Scholars.* Across to the right, racks
were draped with several local newspapers and half a dozen major
papers from across the country. In between were four round tables, where reporters scanned various periodicals or leafed
through clipping files, making notes or carrying pages to nearby
photocopy machines.

Two or three looked up from their work, studying me as if I
were a museum exhibit.

"It's Benjamin Justice," Harry barked at them. "You got a problem with that?"

Their eyes went back to their work, while mine took in the *Sun's*
library. It occupied a space less than half the size of the research
quarters at the *Los Angeles Times* and was operated by an even
smaller staff. That had to trouble Harry. I know it bothered me
seeing him there, where I'd put him.

Harry bellowed toward the rear stacks.

"Hey, Nakamura!"

Katie Nakamura came scurrying from the index drawers that

rose at least a foot above her head. She was a tiny bundle of energy from Northwestern University, who had interned for Harry the previous summer and helped Templeton and me with research on the Billy Lusk story.

I noticed immediately that she'd let her hair grow out and lost much of the baby fat I'd seen a year ago, along with the moon-shaped face and oversized, horn-rimmed spectacles. She was changing from a chubby teenager into a pretty young woman, but hadn't given up her relentless good cheer.

"Mr. Justice! Welcome back!"

"You too, Katie. I'm surprised to see you stuck back here. Shouldn't you be out reporting?"

"I want to learn data research from the ground up, Mr. Justice. I feel it will pay off in the long run."

"Katie's studied the entire local, state, and national archival system," Harry said. "Visited half the specialty libraries in Southern California. She knows database systems like I know doughnuts."

"Somehow, I'm not surprised."

Her face turned cherry pink.

"What can I do for you, Mr. Brofsky?"

"Justice needs a few Hollywood clips."

"You're working for the *Sun* again?"

"Not exactly."

"He'll fill you in," Harry said. "Excuse me—I got news pages to put together."

When he was gone, I told Katie that I was helping Templeton with a freelance magazine piece.

"How exciting!"

"Harry's letting me use the library, if I don't abuse the privilege."

"What can I get you?"

"For starters, anything you've got on a director named Dylan Winchester."

"*Sun* clips? Or shall I search further?"

"Let's start with the *Sun*."

"I'll see what we have."

Katie came back with a file slugged *Winchester, Dylan (Film Director)*. I signed for it and took a seat at one of the circular tables, where a few pairs of eyes ventured again in my direction. I set the stack of old clippings in front of me, with the most current on top. When I'd gone through them, I'd narrowed it down to two clips that seemed worth photocopying.

The most recent, dated not quite a year ago, detailed Dylan Winchester's production troubles on his latest film, *Thunder's Fortune,* a mystical, sword-and-sorcery adventure that starred Mel Gibson. According to the article, the initial budget of $65 million had soared past $90 million, due in part to adverse weather conditions, elaborate stunts, and Winchester's demanding standards. Executives at Monument Pictures, the studio backing *Thunder's Fortune,* had been concerned with the runaway budget; one of them, Bernard Kemmerman, had personally visited the location in England trying to get the production back on track. He hadn't stayed long; sickness had forced his return home.

On my chart, I drew a line between the names of Bernard Kemmerman and Dylan Winchester.

The second clip was dated nearly ten years earlier, datelined Mexico City. It covered an independent production, an action picture called *Full Contact,* which Winchester had directed early in his career. The project had given the Aussie wunderkind his first American-sized budget—a mere $22 million at the time. The article itself was a standard production puff piece, in which the reporter wrote a lot of favorable things about the movie and its cast, and probably had a swell time hanging out in cantinas and getting a suntan at the producer's expense.

It was the name of the producer that caught my eye: Bernard Kemmerman. That, and a photo of the film's male star kissing a buxom supporting actress named Anne-Judith Carlton.

*The future Anne-Judith Kemmerman?*

I drew a broken line on my chart connecting Anne-Judith Kemmerman to Dylan Winchester, and added a question mark above it.

Then I made copies of both articles and handed the file back to Katie Nakamura.

"Our clips on the movie industry aren't too good," she said. "I could do a search of the *L.A. Times* database, although I'm told their film coverage hasn't been anything special since the eighties. If you want to do some serious research, you might try the Margaret Herrick Library at the Academy of Motion Picture Arts and Sciences."

"The foundation that awards the Oscars?"

"Right. They've got some amazing stuff over there, going back decades. The library's open to anyone doing serious research."

She wrote down the address, phone number, and library hours in neat, block handwriting and handed me the slip of paper.

"I need another favor, Katie—a home address for a man named Bernard Kemmerman."

I spelled it for her and she wrote it down.

"He was a studio honcho, Monument Pictures. Died a few weeks ago. I've already got the obit."

"Have you called the studio's publicity department?"

"Not cooperative."

"There's the *Celebrity Register*."

"They probably wouldn't have more than a publicist's or lawyer's name, anyway."

"That's true. I assume you've tried the phone book."

I gave her a look.

"Sorry, Mr. Justice."

"This is a long shot, but maybe you can check the *L.A. Times* database, real estate section. Does the *Times* still run that fluffy column about celebrity real estate deals?"

"Hot Property. Front page, left-hand column, on Sundays."

"If I remember right, when the news gets thin, the writer sometimes includes entertainment execs. Cross-check the column with Kemmerman's name and see if anything turns up. They usually list the realtor."

"I'll search back the last two years."

"Make it three and I'll buy you lunch."

What turned up was the sale of an estate not quite three years earlier to Bernard and Anne-Judith Kemmerman of a home owned by a pop singer I'd never heard of named Michael Bolton. The home was located high in the hills of Bel-Air, and had sold for $2.8 million after originally being listed at nearly twice that much.

It didn't matter that I'd never heard of the singer. The important thing was that he was apparently well known to people who cared about such things. If my luck held out, I'd find the house listed on one of the star maps sold by youngsters along Sunset Boulevard, which gave the locations of homes owned or once owned by Hollywood's rich and famous. If that didn't work, I'd contact the realtor named in the item and see if I could squeeze the address out of her.

I took Nakamura to lunch at the Mandarin Deli on Second Street in the shadow of the mighty *L.A. Times*. She ate a cold San Tong chicken salad and sipped hot green tea while asking me endless questions about the world of journalism, reminding me of the zeal that had possessed me when I'd been her age, and that I'd assumed would never run out.

She was still asking questions when I dropped her back at the *Sun*.

Just before I drove off, she reminded me about the research library operated by the Academy of Motion Picture Arts and Sciences. As I pointed the Mustang toward a northbound on-ramp of the Harbor Freeway, it seemed more and more like a good idea.

But first I wanted to find Anne-Judith Kemmerman, the grieving widow whose urgent phone calls Reza JaFari had failed to return, and who was now ignoring mine.

# Twenty-three

I T WAS MID-AUGUST, the peak of the tourist season. Star maps were being hawked on dozen of curbsides from Hollywood to West L.A.

I purchased mine from a slim, good-looking Mexican kid with eyelashes long enough to make a drag queen jealous. He stood on a corner at the west end of the Sunset Strip, where Sunset Boulevard crosses the golden border into Beverly Hills and the neighborhood suddenly becomes palatial, with picture-perfect landscaping festooned with placards warning about armed patrol guards.

I idled the Mustang at the curb, scanned the map's index, and found my luck was holding.

A home was listed for Michael Bolton, an address on Stone Canyon Road that sounded high up enough for the tennis courts and maid's quarters to have million-dollar views. The location fit into the general description of the house he'd sold to the Kemmermans. For once, one of the city's sillier newspaper features was proving useful to someone other than the celebrities and real estate agents who got free promotion from it.

I pulled back into the westward caravan of cars with the map folded to show the route through Bel-Air Estates. A few minutes later, I passed the imposing gates and colorful flower beds at the eastern Bel-Air entrance, then found Stone Canyon Road a minute or two after that, due north of UCLA.

As I wound my way into the cool shadows of lush foliage, it was like leaving one world for another. There were no modest houses here, only fine estates; everything was woodsy yet eminently tasteful, right down to the spotless stone driveways and gleaming door knockers made obsolete years ago by the security intercom systems erected at every gate.

As I got higher, the driveways didn't lead to the homes but *ascended,* with a certain sweep and grandeur that kept the rest of us properly in our place. Banana palms were everywhere, along with towering ferns and flowering impatiens and climbing bougainvillea bursting with blossoms of red, orange, and yellow.

Los Angeles was by nature a desert; a serious drought could ruin a place like this. Yet I suspected that the drought warnings and water rationings experienced by Southern Californians from time to time didn't apply to the monied class that dwelled in the rarified realm of Bel-Air. Like the gleaming, high-priced automobiles Bel-Air denizens always managed to drive in times of economic distress, their personal forests would somehow be watered and their swimming pools filled, while the rest of us took fewer showers, left our ordinary cars unwashed, and watched our unimportant little lawns die slow deaths.

I guess you could say I went looking for Anne-Judith Kemmerman with a chip on my shoulder.

The number I wanted was posted in brass on a pillar of brick, the used variety that rich people pay more for to add "character" to their homes. The pillar was one of twins mounted on either side of a wrought iron gate high enough to keep out an Olympic pole vaulter. More wrought-iron fencing ran around the front of the property and up both sides, enclosing a two-story Spanish-style home replete with arches, verandas, and enough lawn for a nine-hole golf course.

I parked on the street, pressed the intercom button, and announced myself, asking to speak to Mrs. Kemmerman.

A male voice told me she wasn't home.

I asked when she was expected back.

The voice told me he didn't know.

I told the voice I would wait.

A female voice came through the speaker.

"This is Anne-Judith Kemmerman. I'm aware of the messages you've left. If I wished to talk to you, I would have called you back."

"I only need a few minutes of your time, Mrs. Kemmerman. A few questions about Reza JaFari."

"Don't know him."

"You knew him as Raymond Farr."

"Never heard of him."

The voice was bold and vibrant, without a trace of widow's grief.

"You left messages on his answering machine, Mrs. Kemmerman. You were seen dining with him at Jimmy's. Rather intimately."

The few moments of silence that followed were interrupted by ear-splitting anger.

"I have nothing to say to you, scumbag. Get lost!"

"I'll be right here until you're ready to talk, Mrs. Kemmerman."

I settled my butt on the trunk of the Mustang where the security camera could see me, crossed my arms, and whistled an uptempo version of "My Funny Valentine."

A minute later, a man strode down the long driveway and the big gate opened between us.

He was on the short side of thirty, clad only in a hot orange Speedo and rubber sandals. He was about my size, except he'd worked hard at pumping up his muscles while I'd worked hard at letting mine go soft. His handsome brunette head sported a close, expensive cut, and a web of tight, dark hair spread out with a fine symmetry across the contours of his gym-cut chest.

I took my butt off the car and stepped to the sidewalk to meet him. He didn't stop walking until his nose was inches from mine.

"Mrs. Kemmerman told you to get lost."

I stepped back and looked him up and down. I noticed that there wasn't an awful lot filling the front pouch of his Speedo.

"I don't take orders from Mrs. Kemmerman. Or from the boy toys who work for her."

"You've got one more chance to leave the easy way, pal."

"I believe I'm standing on a public sidewalk."

I'd used the line before. It never did much good, at least not with airheads like this one, who correlated masculinity with the size of their biceps.

He pushed me hard enough to back me up a few steps.

"Now you're standing in the street. So what?"

I glanced down for another appraisal of his pint-sized basket.

"Tell me something, Muscles. Do bodybuilders like you work so hard at pumping up to compensate for certain shortcomings?"

"You're this close to feeling some pain, pal."

I looked over the rest of him.

"You'd be perfect for an *International Male* catalog, if it weren't for—well, you know . . ."

Everything tensed above his waist, causing his hairy pecs to swell.

"Of course," I added helpfully, "you could always stuff it with a sock."

He swung with his right fist. I blocked the punch by seizing his wrist, then leaned my hip into him while cinching my right arm around his neck. His weight was coming forward, which helped. I flipped him across my hip and lower back and slammed him ungently to the pavement. We'd called the move a Japanese hip roll in my college wrestling days. I'd never been particularly good at it, but it was adequate for taking down a muscle bunny whose athletic skills were limited to lifting barbells.

He got in a couple of punches that found my face, but the wind was knocked out of him and he was confused. I flipped him facedown, mounted him to tie up his legs and arms, and smacked him on the back of the head a few times to get his attention. His taut buttocks squirmed beneath me in the scanty Speedo, an unexpected gesture of romance I found quaintly touching.

I leaned down and kissed him on the ear.

"Had enough, sweetheart?"

"I'll kill you, fuck face!"

"You Rambo types drive me wild."

I placed my palm on the back of his head and ground his face into the street until I saw blood on the pavement. His mouth, especially, was a mess. I suspected Mrs. Kemmerman wouldn't be pleased.

"One more time, pretty boy. Enough?"

"OK, OK, enough."

I eased up on him just as a horn blasted behind us.

Over my shoulder I saw the former Anne-Judith Carlton behind the wheel of a new Ferrari convertible, with the sticker still on the windshield. She had big, flaming hair and enough gold jewelry around her neck, wrists, and fingers to fill half the teeth in Beverly Hills. Her breasts, more than ample in the photograph taken a decade earlier on the set of *Full Contact,* had grown to even more voluptuous proportions, no doubt through the wonders of modern technology.

I raised myself off her boyfriend and faced her through the windshield.

"We'll have to stop meeting like this, Mrs. Kemmerman."

Muscles got to his feet, hanging his head a little.

"He got me by surprise, A.J."

"Get in the house!"

He glanced at me, attempting to look surly.

"Next time, you won't be so lucky."

"Next time, I might not be so sweet."

"In the house," Mrs. Kemmerman repeated. "Take care of your face, for God's sake."

She sounded like a woman who might appreciate a small endowment on a man, something to humiliate him with when she felt the need. Muscles trudged away up the driveway, tipping his head back and holding a hand to his bloody face.

"I'm Benjamin Justice, Mrs. Kemmerman. I'm on assignment for *Angel City* magazine. Wrestling is just a hobby."

"I know who you are. I had you checked out. You're that reporter who made up some story about AIDS a few years back at the *Times*. Won a goddamned Pulitzer until you got caught and had to ship it back."

"That's me, all right."

"You work in a cesspool profession and still manage to make all the other turds smell like chocolate kisses."

"You have quite a way with words, Mrs. Kemmerman."

"Keep your ass away from me or I'll hire somebody for protection who knows how to get the job done."

I glanced at the car. I didn't know much about fancy cars anymore, but I figured a new Ferrari had to run in the six figures.

"Nice transportation, Mrs. Kemmerman. Did you pick it out before or after the funeral?"

Her tires squealed and the Ferrari came straight at me. The wheels turned at the last moment and the bumper missed my knees by inches.

I watched Anne-Judith Kemmerman disappear down Stone Canyon Road, raising one hand with the middle finger extended, her jewelry flashing like a victory trophy in the westerly sunlight.

# Twenty-four

"T HE TABLE looks better every time I see it."

Danny Romero looked up from the garage floor, where he knelt with a soft cloth, rubbing Danish oil into the dark wood.

"It's pretty much done." He ran a hand over one of the corners, checking the joints. "I always have trouble admitting that a piece is finished—I guess I want to hang on to it as long as I can."

Maggie trotted over to be scratched and I obliged. Danny rose slowly, wincing, using the table for support.

"Need some help?"

He shook his head. As he came closer, he scanned my bruised face. I felt the light touch of his fingers on a tender section of my chin.

"What happened to you?"

"I ran into a fist."

"Where?"

"Up in Bel-Air, at Anne-Judith Kemmerman's place—the woman who kept calling Reza. She encouraged me not to hang around."

He grinned.

"She's pretty tough."

I laughed.

"It was her boyfriend who did the damage. But, yeah, she is pretty tough."

"How does her bodyguard look?"

"Worse."

"Did she tell you anything that can help us?"

"She wasn't in a loquacious mood."

"I don't know what that means."

"She told me to fuck off."

"Shit."

His head turned away, then down.

"I haven't given up on her, Danny. Or the others, either. We'll find out something."

I studied his face; the hollows seemed deeper than before.

"How are you doing? You eating?"

"I've been better."

"You look pale. Worn out."

"Yeah."

"You're moving more slowly."

His eyes shifted away.

"What is it, Danny?"

Somewhere in the arc away from me and back again, he found the courage he was looking for.

"I've got an appointment at the clinic. In about an hour."

"Regular checkup?"

"No. I made it yesterday. Asked if they could squeeze me in."

That meant he was having special problems, urgent problems.

I took a deep breath, and tried to ignore the churning in my guts.

"I'll drive you."

"Thanks. Driving's not so easy for me these days."

His eyes were steady but his voice faltered, giving him away. I reached out, touched his face.

"You're young, Danny. You're strong. It's going to be all right."

"Sure."

"Be positive."

He laughed.

"I've been positive for eight years, Ben." He raised an arm, sniffed one of his pits. "I better take a shower, get ready."

He took the stairs to his apartment one painful step at a time, clutching the handrail. I followed, and waited for him on the couch, stroking Maggie's head as she rested it in my lap. Danny slipped from his bedroom into the bathroom, carrying fresh underwear and a towel, and a minute later I heard the shower running.

When he emerged a few minutes after that, shirtless in jeans, I was waiting for him outside the bathroom door. His tangled hair was wet, his upper body damp. On his left breast was a small tattoo I hadn't seen before, a bolt of yellow lightning outlined in blue.

I opened my arms to him.

"Come here."

He hesitated, then eased himself up against me while I braced against the wall. I closed my eyes, pressed my face into his uncombed hair, spread my hands across his dewy back.

It was difficult to imagine that he was sick. Touching him felt so incredibly good.

He relaxed a little, and I drew him closer still. I stroked his bony back, then more boldly lower down, kneading his slender butt with my big hands, until I felt the hardness below his belly meeting mine.

My lips rested briefly on his neck, then roved his face, tracing its shape, kissing his eyes closed, softly brushing the patches where his beard had gone unshaved.

When I found his lips, I kissed him the way I'd wanted to since the first time I'd met him: tenderly, safely, but with an unashamed yearning that grew more excited as I felt him respond. I took his face in my hands and held him away from me for a moment so I could look into his eyes, so I could tell him without words how much he meant to me.

"I should get dressed, Ben. I—"

I put a finger to his lips.

"Shhh."

I lowered my lips to the smooth expanse of his chest, kissing and nibbling at his nipples until I felt them rise up, losing their softness. My tongue searched out the rest, the gentle curves between his nipples and his ribs, the sprinkling of fine, dark hairs in the cavity where his breastbone formed, the thin path of curls that ran down his belly into the dark cushion of hair peeking over the waistline of his sagging jeans.

I popped open the buttons and pressed my face against the bulge that filled his briefs, feeling the damp heat coming off his scrotum, crazy for his smell, aching to taste him.

When I reached for the waistband, he grabbed my hands.

"No, Ben."

I felt his hands under my arms, pulling me up.

"I won't do anything that isn't safe, Danny."

"I know. It's not that."

I touched his face again, looked into his eyes.

"What is it, then?"

"It's not the right time."

"You may be sick, Danny. But you're still a handsome man. You're still desirable."

His eyes were moist with an emotion I couldn't put a name to. I felt wonderfully close to him, yet unbearably distant at the same time.

"We should go, Ben. I don't want to be late."

He pulled away, and I watched him disappear into his bedroom, where the door closed quietly behind him.

There was a deep, quiet wisdom about Danny, a calmness that belied his youth and situation. Maybe he sensed that I was trying to start something I was unlikely to finish. Maybe he knew me better than I knew myself.

When he came out, he'd slipped into a T-shirt and a pair of leather huaraches and brushed back his hair. He spoke before I could touch him again.

"I guess we should get going."

As we climbed into the Mustang, I grew heavy with the reality of what I was doing. I hadn't been in a place that cared for PWAs since Jacques had died seven years ago, and I'd vowed that I never would—not a clinic, not a hospital, not a hospice. And now I was driving straight back to that place, straight back to hell.

We drove out Third Street with the top down, listening to a Los Lobos tune Danny found on the radio while he gave me directions to the AIDS Healthcare Foundation clinic.

"I thought they were the other way," I said. "On the east side."

"They have a west side clinic now, at Cedars-Sinai. Out in your neck of the woods." He looked out at the big, elegant houses as we cruised through Hancock Park. "I've heard it's a good place to be if you get sick."

"You're not going to get sick, dammit."

"I *am* sick, Ben."

"OK, you've got AIDS. But most PWAs are outpatients now. Living with it, doing OK. You know that. That's why AHF set up these clinics—to keep people out of the hospital."

"Let's not argue."

"Have you been admitted before?"

"Not for AIDS."

"Night sweats? Diarrhea? Severe weight loss?"

"Not for a while."

"Then you're doing pretty good."

"OK, I'm doing pretty good."

He settled back in his seat, tipped his head back, let the warm breeze dry his hair.

Almost as an afterthought, he said, "Some problems with KS. That's about it."

KS—Kaposi's sarcoma—the cancerous purple lesions that appear on various parts of the body, and sometimes internally, when the immune system grows too weak to fight them off or keep them from spreading. I hadn't seen a sign of KS on Danny.

"That's one of the more treatable infections."

"Yeah." His eyes shifted my way, but only slightly. "Like you said, I've been real lucky."

No scarring shingles, I thought. No crippling, or agonizing stomach infections. No cancerous lymphoma or suffocating Pneumocystis or blinding cytomegalovirus. No dementia, that most dreaded of all AIDS afflictions. He had been lucky.

"What's your T-cell count? Your viral load?"

He closed his eyes.

"Let's not talk about it anymore, OK?"

"I didn't mean to pry."

Suddenly, he was grinning.

"Sure you did. You're a reporter. You guys pry for a living."

Then: "Turn left here."

I turned onto Gracie Allen Drive, continued to George Burns Road, and made a left at the stop sign, just before the Steven Spielberg Pediatric Research Center. All around us, other medical facilities named for their benefactors rose up, a small city devoted to the maimed and sick. I tried to steel myself for what lay ahead.

A minute later, we were pulling into a parking space in the cool dimness of an underground garage. Then we were in a corridor, passing sick people, injured people, sad-looking people. Doctors, nurses, medical administrators, messengers picking up or delivering lab specimens. The smell of pharmaceuticals, disinfectant, the battle against illness. It was all around, like the plague itself.

I felt disconnected from myself, moving robotically.

We were in an elevator, riding up. A man not much older than Danny rode with us. He had pushed the same button we had, for the seventh floor. The skin of his face was shiny, stretched taut over his skull, a sure sign of wasting syndrome. His color was ashen, his breathing raspy, his hair wispy and brittle; he covered a dry cough with a pale, bony hand.

I kept my eyes away from him.

Still, inside my head, I saw Jacques—diapered for diarrhea,

leaning on a walker, struggling for air. Living his last months, his last days without hope. Gone less than two years after his diagnosis.

*It's different now. Things have changed so much in recent years. Antivirals. Protease inhibitors. The combinations, the so-called miracle drugs.*

The doors opened at the third floor to let passengers in and out. Danny and I moved to the back. Our arms were touching, and our shoulders. I could feel his body expand, ever so slightly, as he breathed.

*AIDS is no longer an automatic death sentence. It's become a chronic, treatable disease. We've entered a new era of hope.*

*For some. For the lucky ones.*

The doors opened again and Danny nudged me, indicating our floor.

We stepped out and held the door for the sick man. He nodded his thanks and shuffled along behind us. We turned right into a carpeted corridor that led us to a door at the end. I let Danny go in first and held the door until the man behind us was through it.

The waiting room was bright and comfortable, with magazines and plants, and a game with wooden blocks in the corner for children. A clean-cut young man in a coat and tie stood behind the counter, greeting Danny by his first name like an old friend. Danny signed in and we sat down together, saying nothing, until his name was called.

A water cooler was positioned directly in front of me, posted with a sign:

THIS WATER HAS BEEN FILTERED
FOR CRYPTOSPORIDIUM AND OTHER BACTERIA
OF RISK TO IMMUNO-DEPRESSED PERSONS.

Beside the water cooler sat a young African-American woman gently bouncing a cherub-faced black baby on her big thigh. I couldn't tell if she was sick or the baby. Maybe both, I thought, maybe neither. They could have been waiting for someone inside—a husband, boyfriend, girlfriend, relative, neighbor. The endless possibilities sharpened my despair.

I heard someone coughing behind me, sensed a man filling out forms to my right. If he was filling out forms, it probably meant he was a new client, recently HIV-positive. I wondered what must be going on inside him. I wondered how he could hold the pen straight or find the composure to fill in mundane words on empty lines. I wondered how he managed to stay sane.

"I stuff myself constantly." The voice came from a thin young man sitting nearby, directly to the older man sitting next to him. "Cookies. Pastry. Ice cream. I still can't put on weight."

"The AIDS diet, honey," the other man said. "Eat all you want and still look like Kate Moss. Somebody should patent it."

One or two others in the room laughed. I didn't understand it. They were supposed to be depressed, desperate, terrified.

Instead, they were making jokes.

I crossed to the cooler, filled a cup with cold water, drank it with an unsteady hand. I sat back down, trying to breathe deeply and slowly and not think about what was all around me.

*AIDS World. The last place on earth I want to be.*

Minutes passed that way, and more minutes. Then Danny was mercifully touching my shoulder, telling me we could go.

When we were walking back down the carpeted hallway, he said simply, "I have to go into the hospital."

My insides felt like the bottom had dropped out. We reached the elevators. Danny pushed the down button.

"When?"

"Monday."

"Why?"

"Tests and treatment."

His way of not being too specific.

We both knew what anyone close to AIDS knew—that a trip to the hospital, even the first, might be the last.

The elevator doors opened, we entered, and Danny pushed the button marked P2, our level. As our doors started to close, the doors across the way slid open.

A woman stepped quickly out, her slim legs descending from a gray business suit with gold buttons into sleek maroon pumps. Her head was bent deliberately low and covered with a large silk scarf; her eyes were hidden behind immense dark glasses.

She hurried toward the hallway and turned right, never slowing. I stuck my hand between our doors just before they closed.

"Hold the elevator, Danny."

I made a hasty exit and crossed into the corridor, just in time to see Roberta Brickman reach the end, where she opened the clinic door and stepped inside.

# Twenty-five

AURELIO DROPPED OFF Danny's dinner from Project Angel Food while Danny and I were sitting on his apartment landing, watching the sun go down.

It was one of those evenings when the heavy pollution has the ironic effect of enhancing and transforming the colors of the western sky, what Angelenos like to call a "smog sunset."

As we watched the colors deepen, Danny became talkative and reflective.

"I miss seeing the stars, Ben. Down here in the city, what with the pollution and all the lights, it's like there's no stars at all anymore."

"We'll get to the mountains, Danny. Soon."

"You think so?"

"Promise."

I stayed while he ate, swapping fishing and hiking tales that were at least half true, while dusk helped camouflage the grubbiness of the neighborhood, though not the drone of traffic, television sets, and bickering voices rattling out of the surrounding apartments like verbal gunfire.

He fell asleep on the couch with Maggie at the other end. I laid a blanket over him, kissed him gently, then drove to Canter's Delicatessen in the Fairfax district to grab a bite of my own.

The big downstairs rooms were filled with the usual chatter of customers and bustle of busboys and the mingled odors of corned beef, steamed cabbage, and lox. I had a small booth to myself near the back and one of the older waitresses who had worked at

Canter's for three or four decades. She wore a faded paper flower pinned to her rayon uniform, talked fast like she was annoyed with me, and called me sweetie.

I spent the next couple of hours bent over my notebook, working out possible scenarios in the Reza JaFari case, while I gnawed on a pastrami on rye smothered with horseradish hot enough to make my eyes water.

On the page where I'd drawn my chart of names, I inked in another broken line between Danny Romero and Roberta Brickman. Above it, I drew a question mark, along with the words *AHF Clinic* in parentheses.

Collecting the facts was only part of the job. The other was linking them, along with the people involved. Connecting the dots, Harry called it—figuring out what held all the information together.

*Who. What. Where. When. Why. How.*

The elements of every reporter's story.

I had the who, what, where, and when—Reza JaFari's unexplained death the previous Saturday night on Gordon Cantwell's terrace roughly between 7 and 8 P.M. If it was murder, though, I needed a second who, along with a why and a how.

Unless, of course, the who was Danny Romero, as Lieutenant DeWinter wanted to believe. If that was the case, only how remained.

I closed my notebook sometime after ten, asking myself if someone as decent as Danny could take a human life, and already knowing the answer. Any of us, even the most gentle, is capable of killing, if pushed to it. Armies are filled with gentle men, prisons with gentle women. I'd been a gentle boy before grabbing my father's police revolver at the age of seventeen and emptying it into his chest for raping and degrading my little sister. I knew as well as anyone how quickly one can cross the line, how blindly and insanely, into that dark, cold territory of righteous, vengeful violence. I knew how wonderful it could feel for the moment, like an orgasm arising from the most troubled region of the soul, before the deed was finished and the haunting set in.

Danny, a man with AIDS, face to face with the horror of the disease. JaFari, an infected man who was knowingly exposing others to the virus. Motive, opportunity, lack of alibi. It wasn't hard to connect the dots, as DeWinter already had.

I paid the check and drove from Canter's feeling unsettled in all kinds of ways, and badly in need of a drink.

Back in West Hollywood, the Norma Triangle was dark and quiet. So was the house on Norma Place as I pulled into the driveway.

As I trudged toward the rear stairs, I sensed movement in the yard. The leg of a patio chair scraping concrete, perhaps. Or a foot.

*It could be one of the cats, jumping from the chair with its back paws. Or a possum sniffing around.*

I stopped at the corner of the house.

"Maurice? Is that you? Fred?"

No one answered, but a shadow moved. The edge of a shadow, really, as a figure pulled into the deeper night shade beneath the big jacaranda and the vine-covered lattice awning.

I backed up a few steps to the Mustang, laid my notebook on the hood, pried a brick from the border of the front garden.

When I edged slowly back up the drive, it was along the far side, close to a neighboring fence.

As I came even with the back side of the house, there was movement again. This time, the figure stepped boldly from the shadows toward me.

"I've been waiting for you, Justice."

Christine Kapono took another step or two until she was recognizable in the dim light of the distant streetlamps.

"Why didn't you answer when I called out?"

"I wanted to remind you what it feels like to be uncomfortable—even scared."

I set the brick aside.

"I guess you succeeded."

"Good."

Kapono was dressed all in black—a black T-shirt that showed off her muscular upper body, black pants, black Doc Martens that gave her feet a military look.

"What's going on, Christine?"

"I want you to lay off Roberta."

"Templeton and I have a story to put together."

"There are other people you can talk to for your story."

"But no one who had quite the relationship with Reza JaFari that Roberta did."

Kapono's narrow eyes narrowed even further.

"That's her business, not yours."

"Maybe. Maybe not."

"I saw you spying on us the other day. Outside Eleanor's Secret."

"That was unfortunate."

"That you were spying on us? Or that you got caught?"

"Both."

"I also heard about your breakfast meeting at Hugo's, the way you questioned her."

"Roberta confides quite a lot in you, doesn't she?"

"I'm serious, Justice. Leave her alone."

"She strikes me as a highly capable person who can handle things on her own."

"So am I. As a female, I grew up fighting for my place in the water, demanding my right to catch waves. As a dyke, I had to fight even harder. When I'm forced to fight back, I'm not afraid to let it get ugly. So don't underestimate me."

"Believe me, I don't."

"Roberta's dealing with some personal problems right now. She doesn't need any extra stress."

"There are things about Reza JaFari I need to know."

"Why is it so important that you write about him?"

"Because he was at Gordon Cantwell's party—the center of a lot of people's attention. He's dead. There are a lot of unanswered questions in the balance. Call me goofy, but I have this thing about unanswered questions."

A few seconds passed while she regarded me with angry, unblinking eyes.

Finally, she said, "I'll make you a deal."

"I always listen to offers."

"Leave Roberta's personal life out of your story and I'll help you any way I can."

"Roberta's a successful agent, Christine, associated with one of the biggest agencies in town. I don't see how her personal life—"

"Have you ever been to the bar at the Peninsula after five P.M., Justice?"

"Can't say I have."

"It's filled with movie people. You know what they're talking about?"

"Oscar ad campaigns?"

"Other people. Who wrote what, and what star is interested in it. Who did a great rewrite job, who screwed one up. Who botched a pitch meeting, who's out of favor with such-and-such a studio, who snorts too much crystal. Who's got herpes, and who's got a three-picture deal."

"What's that got to do with Roberta Brickman?"

"She could be badly hurt by a story like this, in ways you may not even suspect."

"The truth is always the best policy, Christine."

Kapono laughed curtly.

"Maybe in your business. In my business, a friend is someone who stabs you in the *front*. If you can't tell the right lies to the right people at the right time, you're considered an amateur."

"Lovely business."

"If I help you, you'll lay off Roberta?"

"I'll be as sensitive as I can."

She turned away from me and stared into the shadows of the yard as if looking for ideas, answers—anything to lead me away from Roberta Brickman.

"You care a lot about Roberta, don't you, Christine?"

"I think you already know that."

"Are you in love with her?"

"Roberta doesn't feel about me the same way I do about her."

"Meaning you're just good friends."

Kapono faced me, a small woman who managed to seem considerably bigger.

"For the record, Justice, Roberta is not a lesbian. I am, and I don't give a damn who knows. There was a time in the industry when gay women survived only if they did the lipstick number and played it straight. Those days are pretty much past, except for the leading actresses, the ones who depend on men's romantic fantasies to make a living. So I don't give a flying fuck who knows about my private life.

"But Roberta's got enough to deal with right now without having rumors circulating that she's a dyke."

"I'm interested in facts, not rumors."

"Maybe I can pass some your way. If you're willing to give Roberta some space."

"I'll do my best, Christine. But if I feel I need to talk to her again, I will."

A distant fury colored Kapono's face and voice, the way an approaching storm darkens an island sky.

"Be careful what you ask her, Justice. And how you ask it. I don't like to see Roberta get hurt—not by anyone."

"Is that how you felt about Reza JaFari when you learned what he'd done to her?"

The darkening storm settled in Kapono's eyes, which settled in turn on me. Then I was watching her black-clad figure march down the driveway, where the night quickly swallowed her up.

My watch told me it was close to midnight. Up in the apartment, a jug of wine waited with my name on it. All I had to do was mount the stairs.

Instead, I climbed back into the Mustang and flicked on the headlights.

Then I was heading back to Beachwood Canyon, where nothing beyond the gothic-looking gates seemed to follow a straight line, not even the legendary Hollywood Sign.

# Twenty-six

I PASSED the white mailbox marked Fairbridge without slowing.

House lights blinked at me from inside the leafy fortress. I wondered what Constance Fairbridge might be doing up at this hour, and made a mental note to check on her when my work up the road was done.

When I reached Ridgecrest Drive, I turned right and climbed. Moments later, I was looking at the nine-letter sign spelling out *H-O-L-L-Y-W-O-O-D* just below the highest ridge of Mount Lee. Several twists in the road later, Gordon Cantwell's house came into view.

During my last visit, Kapono had indicated that the city picked up the trash on Cantwell's street on Thursday mornings. That made tonight "trash night" in city jargon. Large plastic bins with hinged lids were lined up alongside the road.

I slowed as I approached the medieval silhouette of Cantwell's house.

There were no vehicles visible in his driveway or along the immediate roadway. Lamplight glowed dimly from behind drawn curtains. I sensed no movement inside or around the house.

Two oversized trash bins stood next to the driveway. Next to the bins were four plastic trash bags stuffed almost to bursting and bound at the top.

I continued up the hill past Cantwell's property line, switched off the headlights, then shifted into reverse and backed the Mustang quietly down until Cantwell's trash collection was just behind me.

A car approached from down the hill but moved past without slowing.

I got out with a flashlight, checked for more cars coming, saw none, and went to work.

The first bin was all yard waste. The second held what appeared to be everyday trash, along with the pile of old paperwork Kapono had left behind, but nothing that looked like the remnants of Saturday night's party. I'd dug through it to the bottom when a pair of headlights appeared down the road. I killed the flashlight, stashed it, and leaned against the Mustang as if I were waiting for Cantwell to return.

The car slowed to a stop. The driver was an older man wearing a Dodgers baseball cap. He lowered the passenger window and leaned across the front seat.

"Car trouble?"

"Waiting for Gordon."

"The fella in the funny house there?"

"That's the one. Thanks for asking, though."

He gave me a small salute and drove on.

When his taillights had disappeared over the hill, I went back to work.

It might have taken hours to properly go through the four fat trash bags that remained, and I would have left a mess besides. I glanced at my watch and decided to simply take them all with me.

I opened the Mustang's trunk and stuffed a trash bag into it. Then another and another, until there was no more room.

Headlights appeared again from below. I pushed the trunk shut, grabbed the last trash bag from the roadside, and tossed it into the backseat.

The headlights approached slowly.

I leaped into the Mustang and glanced back, hitting the ignition switch at the same time. I flicked on my lights.

The approaching car seemed to respond, speeding up. In the dark, from this distance, it was impossible to make out the shape or model of the vehicle. All I could see were two bright headlamps reflecting off my rearview mirror.

I turned the wheel and pulled away from the curb, one eye on the road and one on the lights behind me.

They came faster, then suddenly stopped where Cantwell's driveway met the street.

At the top of the hill, I slowed almost to a halt.

The other car sat right where it was, its headlights watching me like the eyes of an animal whose nest has just been robbed.

I drove over the rise, turned around, shut down my headlights, and came slowly back.

The twin beams on the other car were no longer visible. I glimpsed a pair of red taillights just before Cantwell's garage door came down electronically, sealing the vehicle in.

Logic told me that Gordon Cantwell had seen me hauling away his trash in the middle of the night, or seen someone. Whether he had recognized me or not, I couldn't know.

I kept my lights off until I was past his house and taking a curve. I flicked them on without slowing, quickly putting distance between myself and Cantwell's place.

When my high beams hit the white mailbox, I slowed and turned into the drive.

I rolled the Mustang slowly under the heavy canopy of leaves, listening. I heard nothing except the crunch of gravel beneath the tires.

Then I was in the clearing at the end, facing the ramshackle garage with the rusty gas pump next to it. To my left was the old house. A porch light was on above the steps. Another light burned inside, on the lower floor.

I shut off the ignition and climbed out.

"Mrs. Fairbridge?"

Then I noticed the bottles. The prettiest ones still lined the window ledges inside the house, but those along the porch and railings were gone. The shopping cart, filled to capacity, had been pushed across the small clearing and sat in a narrow grassy space between the dilapidated garage and the antique gas pump.

"Mrs. Fairbridge?"

I remained still for several seconds, listening for her voice. What I heard instead was a solid *thunk* on the back of my skull that was followed by a roar of pain.

I turned, raising my arms. Constance Fairbridge was at the other end of her ax handle, bringing it down for another blow. I snatched it from her brittle fingers.

"Mrs. Fairbridge!"

Her eyes were all rage and fear, without a sign of recognition or reason.

"Thief! Devil!"

She was backing toward the house, keeping her wild eyes on me. Brambles, leaves, and twigs covered her heavy coat; dried mud caked her running shoes. Her hair was a tangled, filthy mess.

"It's me, Benjamin Justice."

"There is no justice but the Lord's!"

I felt the back of my head. There was no blood that I could find, but a bump was rising fast. My neck felt stiff; my head throbbed.

"Let me talk to you, Mrs. Fairbridge. We'll talk about the silent movies."

She was up the steps, on the porch.

"Go away!"

"Constance Fairbridge, star of stage and screen. Remember saying that to me yesterday, when I came to visit?"

She raised her voice to a shriek; the power behind it amazed me.

"Sodomites! Whores! Murderers!"

I watched her creep along the porch toward the front of the house, pointing a skinny finger at me.

"Go and repent while time remains!"

"I'm going, Mrs. Fairbridge."

"The cities must be destroyed!"

I placed the ax handle at the foot of the steps, climbed into the Mustang, and backed it down the drive. Back through the dark zone beneath the oaks. Back to the road, to the city.

Away from the woman named Constance Fairbridge, who now dwelled in a frightening world created by her own troubled mind, where I clearly wasn't welcome.

# Twenty-seven

I AWOKE Thursday morning with a serious lump on my head, which reminded me of Constance Fairbridge, which aroused my curiosity.

Of all the names in my notebook, she stood out as the one about whom I knew the least.

I took my curiosity down to the house, where I drank a cup of Maurice's fresh-ground coffee while he went looking for a copy of the *Filmgoer's Companion*.

Fred sat in his underwear at the kitchen table, scratching his big belly and reading the sports page. He nodded when I said good morning; that was it. He generally got more sociable as the day progressed—by late afternoon, you might even get a few words out of him, if his mood was good.

Maurice came padding back in rubber sandals and a silk robe, his bracelets jangling and his long white hair pulled back into a ponytail. He placed a vintage edition of the book on the countertop.

"Constance Fairbridge, you said."

I nodded, stirring the scrambled eggs and chopped parsley he'd started on the stove. Next to them, potatoes and onions sizzled in olive oil, seasoned with salt, pepper, and a dash of rosemary. Somewhere in the mix of aromas was more coffee brewing.

"Constance Fairbridge," Maurice repeated. "Rings a bell. Distant, but with a definite little clang."

He turned the book's musty brown pages.

"I'm consulting my oldest *Halliwell's*. Sometimes the more recent volumes eliminate the lesser-knowns."

"You're assuming she was a lesser-known."

"Trust me, darling, if she'd been an important star, I'd know the name. Isn't that right, Fred?"

A grunt came from the breakfast table.

"Here she is," Maurice said. "Coming just after the two Fairbanks."

He handed me the open book, his finger pointing to a brief entry.

**Fairbridge, Constance (1908–).** American ingenue of the '20s and early '30s known for her fluttery eyes and lovelorn expression. Most notable role was in *Damsel in Distress* (1926), which vaulted her briefly to stardom. Her potential as a leading lady was never fully realized, her career cut short by the advent of the talkies. Later appeared in supporting roles in B movies of the '40s and '50s, then bit parts in TV before permanently retiring in 1959 following the suicide of her only child, minor actress Gloria Cantwell.

A list of her primary credits followed, along with their year of release, but I wasn't paying much attention to that.

My eyes were fixed on the last few words of her biography: *. . . following the suicide of her only child, minor actress Gloria Cantwell.*

Maurice scooped the hot food onto two plates, and began to butter whole grain toast.

"Did you find what you needed?"

"Maybe more." I refilled my coffee cup. "Does the name Gloria Cantwell ring a louder bell?"

Maurice looked up from preparing a third plate.

"Gloria Cantwell, the actress?"

I nodded.

"Dear boy, I *knew* Gloria Cantwell."

On the third plate, Maurice arranged a piece of dry toast, a slice of canteloupe and a peeled banana, a chunk of skinless broiled chicken, and a sprig of parsley for color.

"We weren't what you'd call bosom buddies," he went on. "But I got to know her a bit when I was hanging around with Sal and Jimmy."

Sal Mineo and James Dean, part of the underground gay Hollywood scene of the early fifties, where Maurice had dallied before settling down with Fred.

"I was dating Randolph Scott at the time, just after the release of *The Bounty Hunter*. All on the hush-hush, of course—Scottie was pathologically discreet, he lived his whole career in fear of being exposed. Now and then, I see him on TV in *The Last of the Mohicans,* the nineteen thirty-six version. Standing tall in his buckskins, with that lean, rugged face—"

Maurice paused to fan himself.

"Oh, my, I believe I'm getting hot flashes."

Fred harrumphed, snapped and folded the sports section, and buried his face in it again.

"Then I met Fred," Maurice added diplomatically. "And Randolph Scott was just another name in my little black book."

"According to this edition of *Halliwell's,*" I said, "Constance Fairbridge was Gloria Cantwell's mother."

"Of course—that's where I heard the name!"

"Did you ever meet her?"

"Mrs. Fairbridge? No. I don't think she approved of her daughter's lifestyle. Gloria was always throwing parties up at that strange house she owned in Beachwood Canyon."

"The one shaped like a castle."

"Yes! How did you know?"

"I was there last Saturday night."

Maurice froze with the diet plate halfway to the table.

"The party where the boy died?"

"The very same."

"How absolutely creepy."

Maurice placed the plate in front of Fred.

"Fred's cutting down on his cholesterol and calories. Doctor's orders. Aren't you, Fred?"

Fred put the sports page aside and stared at the plate as if it were infested with cockroaches. His fleshy face bristled with two or three days of nearly white beard. His big, hairy gut expanded to deliver a put-upon sigh.

"Eat," Maurice said. He kissed Fred tenderly on one of his stubbled cheeks, then patted his stomach. "We're going to get you back into shape."

Fred growled but picked up his fork; Maurice had that way of getting you to do small things for him that added up to something significant.

"You, too, Benjamin."

He nudged me toward a table setting where he'd lodged a plate of eggs, potatoes and onions, buttered toast and jam, and a glass of fresh-squeezed grapefruit juice with the seeds carefully strained off.

"I promise to eat every bite, Maurice, if you tell me more about Gloria Cantwell."

Maurice, seated now, paused with his fork poised near his lips.

"She was quite beautiful, I remember that. Also neurotic, chronically depressed. Utterly wild with men. Fatally attracted to Jimmy, I'm afraid."

"She and James Dean were lovers?"

"They probably slept together a few times. Jimmy didn't discriminate all that much between women and men, at least not when I knew him."

"Did she ever marry?"

"When she was still a teenager, before she met Jimmy. Sixteen or seventeen, I think."

"The husband?"

"Victor Cantwell. Small-time producer. Rumor had it that Cantwell raped her, then agreed to marry her when she got preggers. Promised to make her a star, which never happened. He didn't have the clout and she didn't have the talent."

"What happened to Cantwell?"

"They divorced a few years later. He died of a heart attack not long after. She got the house and the life insurance money. Worked now and then in small parts. Mostly, she liked to bed as many good-looking men as possible."

"What about the child?"

"The boy? He lived with Gloria. Until she committed suicide in fifty-five. After that, I'm not sure."

"You still remember the year?"

Maurice smiled ruefully.

"It was the year *Rebel Without a Cause* came out—the same year Jimmy died. Gloria took her life a few days after the crash, out of her mind with grief. Drank a lethal dose of cyanide mixed with gin. She'd always kept some around, waving the bottle, threatening to end it all."

"Quite the drama queen, I gather."

Maurice's face creased with sympathy.

"Unfortunately, it wasn't all talk."

"Her suicide must have made headlines."

"Not really. All the big news was about Jimmy dying in a fiery desert car crash. Gloria Cantwell was just a footnote to the James Dean story."

"The boy's name was Gordon?"

"I think that's right. Yes, Gordon. Gordie, Jimmy called him."

"What else do you remember about him?"

"I recall a bespectacled, redheaded child. Precocious, sad, lonely. Gloria shunted him off to his upstairs room whenever there was a party."

Maurice paused, two fingers pressed thoughtfully to his lips, which were close to smiling.

"He loved baseball, I remember that. I recall one time when he sneaked down from his room with a ball and glove and got Jimmy to play catch with him—until his mother saw them and sent the boy back up."

"She wanted James Dean all to herself?"

Maurice nodded.

"I'm sure she did the same when she had other men over. And there were lots of men in her life, believe me. That's not gossip—she even tried to seduce me on one occasion!"

Fred stifled a laugh and Maurice cast him a reproachful look.

"Meaning the kid didn't get much attention."

"Gloria was a selfish woman—coy, demanding, manipulative. The type who would squeeze you like a tube of toothpaste one moment, smothering you with love, then turn vicious on you the next. I don't suppose it was a lot of fun being her only child."

We ate in silence for a while until Maurice suddenly put down his fork.

"Isn't Gordie Cantwell the fellow who threw the party Saturday night?"

I nodded while I chewed my eggs.

"Then he's still in the same house? And there's been another untimely death there, all these decades later? My goodness gracious—no wonder you're so interested, Benjamin."

"By the way, I locked four bags of Gordon Cantwell's trash in your garage last night. Hope you don't mind."

"Of course not. But why?"

"It's trash from the party. I plan to sort through it when I get the chance. See if anything interesting turns up."

"You're really quite involved in all this, aren't you?"

"I guess I am."

I stared into the morning brightness of the little house, connecting two more names in my mind. Gordon Cantwell to Constance Fairbridge. I hadn't expected that one.

Maurice wiggled his finger at my plate.

"Eat all your onions, Benjamin. They're good for you."

I picked up my fork and did as I was told.

# Twenty-eight

LATE THURSDAY MORNING, with the questions in my notebook outnumbering the answers, I paid a visit to the Margaret Herrick Library.

The address written down by Katie Nakamura led me to an unfenced section of park land in southeast Beverly Hills where the boulevards of San Vicente and Olympic joined.

The centerpiece was an imposing concrete structure that resembled an ancient Spanish cathedral. I recognized it as the landmark building that had once housed the city's water-processing plant, a seventy-year-old white elephant that preservationists had fought to save from the wrecking ball in the 1980s, when I was still a working newspaperman and paying attention to such matters.

Clearly, the preservationists had won. The old water building now rose up before me renovated and expanded, its Spanish-Romanesque style intact, including the picturesque tower that had been constructed in 1927 to disguise a smokestack. Tree-lined walkways, broad lawns, and a rose-filled plaza added further touches from another time.

A brass plaque mounted near the arched entrance told me I was about to step inside the Academy of Motion Picture Arts and Sciences Center for Motion Picture Study. I passed through big wooden doors framing windows of wrought iron and glass, crossed a lobby of French limestone the color of sand, and signed in with the uniformed guard. He examined my driver's license, instructed me to fill out a security form, and pointed me toward the second floor.

I mounted stairs carpeted in the color of old money, and passed another plaque that told me I was on the Kirk Douglas Grand Staircase. After that came more bronzed names of Movieland notables who had made generous donations to ensure the center's longevity. The stairway—solid and attractive but hardly grand—led me into the Cecil B. De Mille Reading Room, a pleasant space of soft light, arched white ceilings, and hushed whispers that reminded me of a church at weekday.

Bookshelves laden with thousands of volumes devoted to movies lined both sides of the long room. In the middle, a few dozen men and women sat at rectangular tables, poring over pages with the pious concentration of monks.

I handed in my security form and driver's license at the orientation desk and was given a library card, useful only for that day. My next stop was the reference desk at the room's north end, where I requested files on Gloria Cantwell and Gordon Cantwell.

The librarian was a pleasant, efficient woman wearing fifties-style horn-rim glasses and a perky hair bob of the same period. She asked me if it was my first time at the library. I told her it was.

"Feel free to look around if you'd like," she said. "I'll be a few minutes."

I crossed through the De Mille reading room and passed under an archway into the smaller Special Collections Reading Room. It was square with round tables, and housed the more rare collections of producers, directors, stars, and other prominent movie figures, the contents ranging from personal papers to annotated shooting scripts to costume sketches and rare photos.

In a locked display case outside the Karl Malden Conference Room, I saw the leatherbound shooting scripts of John Huston, George Cukor, Lewis Milestone, and other noted filmmakers. Oscar statuettes, some showing their age, also decorated the shelves, bearing such film titles as *All About Eve* and *Diary of Anne Frank* and names like Bette Davis, Katharine Hepburn, and Edith Head.

Inside the conference room, a large, circular window on the east wall had been redesigned with interior framing to resemble a film reel. Next door, a smaller space was devoted to microfilm and microfiche reading, with screens and printers where the studious could survey indexes of the thousands and thousands of pieces of Hollywood history that were housed in the deeper recesses of the building's forty thousand square feet.

Everywhere I turned, I saw another vintage movie poster,

framed and flawless—*The Red Shoes, The Maltese Falcon, Wuthering Heights, Duck Soup, The Best Years of Our Lives, The Lady Vanishes.* They reminded me of Gordon Cantwell's house, with its countless tributes to a time and way of making movies that would never come again.

My several minutes were up, so I strolled the length of the library back to the reference desk, where I put my back against the counter and waited.

That's when I glimpsed a pair of eyes watching me from behind a distant row of stacks.

The eyes were masked behind dark Oakley lenses and looked away the moment I fixed on them. The figure, barely visible through the slats between the shelves, disappeared a moment after that.

I started to cross the room to see who the watcher might be when the librarian's voice called me back.

"Mr. Justice?"

She held out the two Cantwell files I'd requested.

I took them, thanked her, and carried them with me across the room to the row of stacks where I'd spotted the mysterious face, or at least a masked portion of it. The space between the shelving was flooded with soft window light, but otherwise empty.

I scanned the room; the stylish Oakley frames were nowhere in sight, and the faces meant nothing to me.

Maybe it was my imagination, I thought. Maybe the troubling questions surrounding Reza JaFari's death were starting to make me jumpy.

I found a seat and opened the file on Gloria Cantwell. Her movie credits were skimpy, all bit parts, except for featured roles in a few forgettable monster flicks from the early fifties. The clippings were comprised of two short pieces from the old magazine *Photoplay,* accompanied by busty-starlet photos and several later news items about her death at the age of twenty-seven.

The news articles reiterated pretty much what Maurice had already told me: She had ingested cyanide mixed with gin during a late-night drinking binge while her ten-year-old son, Gordon, had slept. According to her part-time housekeeper, the binge had started three days earlier, soon after Mrs. Cantwell learned of James Dean's death in a fiery automobile crash. The housekeeper had discovered the body when she let herself in the following morning. She had awakened the boy and taken him out the back door to a neighbor's house, sparing him the sight of his mother's corpse on the living room floor. No note was found, but the police recovered a bottle of the poison with enough missing to have killed her quite easily, along with an empty fifth of gin smelling of what one detective identified as the distinctive scent of cyanide.

The file photos of Gloria Cantwell were all retouched publicity stills. They showed a striking young woman with wavy auburn hair, pale green eyes, high cheekbones, and a sensual mouth glossed darkly in the Jean Harlow style.

Her mother, Constance Fairbridge, was mentioned only briefly as a former silent screen star who occasionally worked in television. Victor Cantwell got a few lines as her ex-husband, whose paltry credits supported Maurice's description of him as a small-time producer lacking the power to make his child bride a star.

The file on Gordon Cantwell was considerably deeper and quite up to date. Virtually all of the material—press clippings and publicity handouts—concerned Cantwell's success as a pioneering instructor in the art of screenplay structure. The clippings were from sources worldwide, publications large and small, many of which seemed beyond the reach of the ordinary clipping services that a nonprofit institution like the library might employ. I suspected that Cantwell, given his penchant for self-promotion, had supplied most of them himself.

The clips repeated what I had already read in the author bio included in *The Cantwell Method*—his early years as a development executive, his success as a screenwriter, his devotion to passing on his knowledge to a new generation of screenwriters—with a similar and surprising lack of detail.

I finally found something more specific in one of the earlier press releases, dated 1978. In it, Cantwell listed Film World Productions as the company where he had performed his executive duties. I also found three titles mentioned as films produced from Cantwell's original screenplays. None of them turned up in the most recent edition of Leonard Maltin's *Movie & Video Guide,* or in any of the other comprehensive movie resource books available at the library.

I returned both files to the reference desk and asked the librarian if it would be possible to see copies of Gordon Cantwell's screenplays.

"You'd have to check those out at the Special Collections desk, Mr. Justice."

"Gordon Cantwell's scripts are considered that valuable?"

The librarian dropped her eyes discreetly.

"Actually, we've had to make special accommodations for Mr. Cantwell's script collection."

"I'm not sure I follow."

"Mr. Cantwell has been very good to the library. He's helped us gather some historical material and donated a number of rare movie posters. When he offered his own papers and scripts, it put us in a bit of a quandary."

"How's that?"

She folded her hands on the counter, looking a trifle embarrassed.

"None of Mr. Cantwell's scripts has ever been produced. I'm not sure they were ever sold or even optioned. We didn't want to turn him down, but we can't house unproduced screenplays in our general collection—you know, a concern over plagiarism, theft of idea, that kind of thing."

"So even though the scripts are of no real importance, you placed them in Special Collections, where they're protected from general inspection."

"That's correct."

"But in his file, his early publicity materials list several produced films."

She smiled apologetically.

"Perhaps Mr. Cantwell is prone to overstatement."

"Would you happen to know anything about Film World Productions?"

"I haven't heard of them. Is it a new company?"

I opened Cantwell's file and showed her the reference in Cantwell's earlier promotion material.

"Ah, yes. I do remember now. That was the company where Mr. Cantwell worked as a young man, before he wrote his book and started teaching. It wasn't exactly a bona-fide production company. That is, they never actually produced any pictures."

"What did they do, then?"

"Film World Productions was part of Film World Catering. That was their real business."

"A catering company?"

"Back in the nineteen sixties and early seventies, they were quite successful supplying meals to the casts and crews of movies on location. Someone in the company thought they might venture into film production. I believe Mr. Cantwell was hired as a reader to sift through scripts. It was basically a one-person operation. As I said, they never did produce any movies."

"In his biographical material, Cantwell calls himself a film development executive, not a reader."

She smiled again, more broadly this time.

"We're talking about Hollywood, Mr. Justice. The land of make-believe. The place where illusion is an art form."

I thanked her for her help, turned in my library card, reclaimed my driver's license, and descended the Kirk Douglas Grand Staircase to sign out with the guard.

As I crossed the plaza toward the street, I stood back to take one last look at the renovated building.

As I glanced up at the reel-shaped window of the Karl Malden Conference Room, I noticed a pair of eyes peering at me from behind a familiar pair of dark glasses. The sun was in my face and the window in shadow, making it impossible to discern any facial features between the window's spokes. I couldn't even tell if they belonged to a man or a woman.

Then, just as quickly as I glimpsed them, they were gone.

# Twenty-nine

"YOU'VE HAD COMPANY."
    I stood in the living room of Alexandra Templeton's cushy Santa Monica condominium, looking down at her glass-topped coffee table.

Two cups of fine china rested in saucers on the spotless glass. A heavy Waterford crystal bowl filled with brightly colored peonies anchored an upper corner. Next to it was a hardcover copy of Toni Morrison's latest novel, parted by a bookmark of African design fashioned from pure silver.

Lipstick was visible on the rim of one cup. It matched the shade Templeton was wearing as she emerged from her bedroom looking cool but elegant in an outfit of silk that billowed as she moved. The blouse and pants were creamy white, contrasting nicely with her dark skin, and must have cost her half a week's pay. Unless, of course, it was Daddy's credit card that paid for them.

"Claude DeWinter was here. He sends his regards."

"I'll bet he does."

Templeton kneeled before the glass cabinet that housed her sizable CD collection, changing the subject.

"We have a little time before we have to leave for the screening. Shall I put on some music?"

"You're seeing Claude DeWinter?"

"He dropped by to talk about our story."

"Really."

"I'm cultivating a source, Justice. Something I learned from you."

"What's wrong with the telephone?"

"He also happens to be good company. At the moment, I can use some."

She opened the glass doors of the cabinet, running her fingers over the CD cases.

"Any special requests?"

"Sarah Vaughan. *Black Coffee.*"

Templeton raised her eyebrows, then the corners of her mouth.

"All those regrets? No thanks."

She found a disc she preferred and slipped it into the machine. Moments later, the room was filled with the sound of Oscar Peterson's piano and Stan Getz's tenor sax rendering a pleasant version of "I Want to Be Happy."

"Claude DeWinter is a hulking, bullying homophobe, Templeton."

She crossed the room without looking at me and straightened the Romare Bearden collage hanging above the fireplace. On the mantelpiece was a framed photograph of her parents, a handsome couple with short-cropped natural hair glistening with Luster's Pink, and contented smiles backed by T-bills and a good stock portfolio.

"Do you recall the final line from *Some Like It Hot,* Justice?"

"Sorry, I'm not much of a film buff."

" 'Nobody's perfect.' "

"Meaning you're willing to overlook DeWinter's use of the term fag, along with his other homophobic traits."

"I've heard you use the word yourself."

"That's different and you know it."

"Is it?"

"So you'd have no problem if I started hanging out with someone who used the word nigger and spouted white power slogans?"

She regarded me icily.

"I'll start paying more attention to how Claude talks. Call him on his shit if it comes up. Satisfied?"

"I still don't understand what you see in the guy."

"Maybe I'm not as good at being alone as you are."

She stepped out sliding glass doors to the balcony. I followed, leaning on the railing beside her with enough space between us to accommodate the tension. From our sixth-floor perch, we looked out at the shaggy heads of palm trees silhouetted against an orange sun making its slow descent into the blue Pacific. Out of view were the posted signs on the beach warning visitors to stay out of the water because it was so loaded with bacteria, garbage, and carcinogens. From here everything just looked pretty.

"Maybe you should practice a little solitude, Templeton. Instead of going after the first man who comes sniffing around."

"Am I getting advice from the same person who had his hand on Lawrence Teal's crotch five minutes after meeting him?"

"That's also different."

She glanced over.

"Oh, really? Why—because you're a man?"

"No. Because Teal and I are both sluts."

Her toughness finally gave way to a smile.

"I just don't see you and Claude DeWinter as a couple, that's all."

"I know what I'm doing, Benjamin. And one thing I'm *not* doing is jumping back into a relationship."

I glanced at my watch, tired of a conversation that was only making me irritable.

"Maybe we should get going. Wouldn't be polite to walk in after the movie starts—not even at a press screening."

"Who's driving?"

"It might be better if we took separate cars."

She pulled back in surprise.

"I thought we were having dinner at Spago afterward. Making an evening of it."

Spago was one of those Beverly Hills restaurants with expensive art on the walls, color-coordinated portions on the plate, and a wine list with prices that made me laugh out loud. Templeton and I had dined there once or twice. She'd always picked up the check.

"Something's come up."

Her voice grew brittle.

"Sorry, I expect a better explanation than that."

"While you were changing, I checked my messages. There was one from Danny. He asked me to come by."

"So you're breaking your dinner date with me?"

"He sounded in bad shape, Alex."

"Physically?"

"Emotionally."

"Fine. Go see your friend. I'll dine alone."

She brushed past me, into the living room.

"Templeton—"

She grabbed her purse and keys and stood waiting.

"Let's go, Justice. Like you said, we don't want to be late."

"He's sick, for Christ sake."

"Yes, I know."

"You're acting like a spoiled brat."

"That's my prerogative, isn't it?"

I stepped in, facing her with only a foot or two between us.

"You're scared to be alone tonight, aren't you?"

"Don't be ridiculous."

"Correct me if I'm wrong, but I believe you split up with What'shisname exactly one month ago today."

She glared, but it looked shaky.

"You always have to go right for the jugular, don't you, Justice?"

"It's bloody, but it saves time."

"All right, I'm feeling a little blue. More than a little. Are you happy?"

"That's a funny way to put it."

Her face and shoulders went slack, and she exhaled sharply.

"God, I hate the idea that a lying, cheating member of the male species can make me feel like this."

I slipped an arm around her, stroking her arm on the other side.

"I can put Danny off until tomorrow, if you want."

"No. Go see him. He's got bigger problems than I do. Besides, you'd rather be with him than me."

We stood quietly for a minute listening to the music. The tune now was "Bewitched, Bothered and Bewildered." Templeton leaned into me, her head on my shoulder.

"Tell me, Justice—why the hell do we let men do this to us?"

*Thunder's Fortune*, Dylan Winchester's new film, was being previewed for the press in the theater of the Academy of Motion Picture Arts and Sciences building in Beverly Hills.

The academy occupied a modern but undistinguished three-story structure on a stretch of Wilshire Boulevard located not quite a mile from the more ornate building that housed its library and research center. Screenings for the media were frequently held there, although the studios liked to fill the extra seats with employees and others in the industry likely to be sympathetic and less critical of the movie under review.

Winchester's film may have gotten bad press during its production, but you wouldn't have known it by the line out front, which stretched half a block. Maybe it was because Mel Gibson was star-

ring, or because of interest in the bloated budget. Or maybe because the tickets were free.

Templeton and I made our way toward the entrance while she
searched the crowd for famous faces, joking that if we ran into
Denzel Washington, I was to catch her before she hit the sidewalk.

She leaned into my ear, whispering.

"I see James Caan. Up there, by the door."

The man she was pointing out was stooped and frail-looking,
his face haggard and drawn—Sonny Corleone a quarter of a century and too many hard years later. It made me realize how much
time had passed since I'd been to the movies with any real enthu-
siasm, yet how deeply certain images were etched in my consciousness. Sonny, exploding with two-fisted anger. Sonny, sending his
treacherous brother-in-law on a car ride to his own execution.
Sonny, writhing in a hail of deadly bullets at a turnpike tollbooth.
I'd seen *The Godfather* on my fifteenth birthday, mesmerized along
with my best male buddies. We'd had pizza afterward, doing
Brando imitations with our cheeks stuffed with crust and making
jokes about the blow job Sonny got on his sister's wedding day.
Everybody was raving about Al Pacino's performance, but it was
the raging, self-destructive Sonny I'd secretly identified with, and
still did.

"Justice?"

I blinked, turning my head. Templeton was peering curiously
at me.

"You still here?"

I smiled dumbly.

"I was back in Buffalo, eating pizza."

She rummaged in her purse until she found the special passes
arranged by a publicist at Monument Pictures. They allowed us to
bypass the long line of ordinary ticketholders and take our place
among the critics, entertainment reporters, and VIPs.

As we did a slow shuffle toward the door, I filled Templeton in
on my confrontation with Christine Kapono the previous evening
and what I'd learned that morning about Gordon Cantwell's family connection to Constance Fairbridge.

"Which reminds me," I said. "I've got to talk to Cantwell—
warn him about his grandmother."

"What about her?"

"I'm afraid she's two enchiladas short of a combination plate."

"We realized that the first time we met her."

REVISION OF JUSTICE | 191

"It's getting serious. I stopped by her place last night to check up on her. She tried to scramble my brains with an ax handle."

Templeton showed her pass at the door and we moved inside.

"First you get attacked by Mrs. Kemmerman's bodyguard. Now Constance Fairbridge. How are you holding up?"

"I'm beginning to feel like James Caan looks."

We crossed a spacious, carpeted lobby with a horde of men and women chattering like monkeys at a banana sale. It wasn't hard to sort out which ones were the lower-paid members of the press, meaning print. They took everything that was handed to them— programs, posters, publicity photos—freebies that could later be peddled or traded at the movie memorabilia shops along Hollywood Boulevard.

The big lobby was currently devoted to a collection of posters from black-themed films—*Carmen Jones, Porgy and Bess, Nothing but a Man, Sounder, Claudine, Cooley High, Shaft, Do the Right Thing, Waiting to Exhale*. It felt like a history lesson as we passed, and Templeton slowed her pace, looking deeply thoughtful as she studied the framed one-sheet for *Malcolm X*.

Then we were climbing a broad staircase and turning onto the second landing, where I pulled up, touching Templeton's arm.

Claude DeWinter stood at the top, off to the side, his eyes scanning those of us coming up.

"I thought you said—"

"I didn't know he was going to be here, Justice." Her voice sharpened. "Don't look at me like that—I didn't know."

DeWinter spotted us, and a moment later we were standing next to him. I noticed that he'd gotten a haircut and put on a decent suit. All in all, despite a hundred pounds of flesh he didn't need, he wasn't such a bad-looking man.

"Claude—what a surprise."

"Hello, Alexandra."

He pasted her with a smile filled with longing, which lasted until he turned my way.

"Looking for someone, Lieutenant?"

"I might be."

"Dylan Winchester?"

"What do you figure, smart guy?"

"My guess is he won't show up at the screening of a film the studio took away from him. Too humiliating."

"I'll keep that in mind."

"You *are* here looking for Winchester, then."

"I'd like to talk to the man, yes." He turned to Templeton. "Winchester's not a suspect, mind you. I just have a few questions."

"I understand, Claude."

DeWinter's friendly eyes returned to me, getting unfriendly again.

"If you knew where to find Winchester, you'd tell me, wouldn't you, Justice?"

"Not necessarily."

"Why is that?"

"He's not a suspect, Lieutenant. Isn't that what you just said? On the other hand, he is on my list to be interviewed."

DeWinter looked at me like he wanted to kick me down the stairs.

"I certainly wouldn't want to interfere with your journalistic endeavors, would I, Justice?"

I glanced at my watch, then at Templeton.

"Maybe we should find our seats."

"Would you like to sit with us, Claude? We could save a place for you."

Templeton's melodic voice drew DeWinter slowly back. He looked almost dreamy when he spoke to her.

"Unfortunately, I can't stay. Heavy caseload. Maybe another time?"

"I'd like that. We'll talk soon?"

"Absolutely."

DeWinter's limpid eyes lingered on her as we moved away.

"You're turning him to jelly, Templeton."

"I'm just being friendly. I thought you wanted me to soften him up—so he'd cut Danny Romero some slack."

"You're tickling his balls, and you know it."

"When did you get concerned about Claude DeWinter?"

"I just hate to see the guy being set up for such a big fall. Even if he is a sonofabitch."

"You're sure you're not jealous, Justice?"

Her voice was playful, but the words were out of bounds.

"You're sure you're not trying to *make* me jealous, Templeton?"

She stiffened at that but otherwise failed to respond, which told me I was closer to the truth than she liked. She showed a reservation pass to an usher, who pulled away a strip of tape cordoning off one of the upper rows in the middle section.

Our seats allowed us an unrestricted view of the theater, a space well designed for optimum acoustics and sight lines, holding several hundred seats. The aisles were crowded with people glad-handing acquaintances, scanning the audience for familiar faces, or suggesting to others that they get together for lunch. On either side of the stage stood a human-sized replica of Oscar, painted gold, reminding visitors of where they were.

Finally, the theater darkened, the curtains parted, and the music came up. The movie opened with a flashback action sequence in which a medieval knight was chased down on horseback and killed by his enemies, but not before he slipped his treasured medallion into the hands of his young son.

Then came the opening credits.

Monument Pictures Presents
MEL GIBSON
A Dylan Winchester Film
**THUNDER'S FORTUNE**

The movie was one of those fast-paced, sword-and-sorcery epics featuring state-of-the-art special effects, death-defying stunts, and pumped-up music that makes dialogue largely superfluous and virtually guarantees big international grosses. The story had Mel Gibson in the role of a mystical stud muffin who wields supernatural powers over evil as long as his father's magic medallion hangs safely around his neck.

His lust-interest was an athletic young actress with a heaving bosom but not much to do except lop off heads with her jeweled sword and clinch her co-star for a hot kiss now and then between bloodbaths staged with a sensuality more commonly reserved for steamy love scenes. The script also gave Gibson a younger side-kick, played by a gorgeous Hispanic actor whose chiseled face and chest got as many close-ups as the female lead. In fact, the camera lingered lovingly on the anatomy of both men at least as much as it did on hers, and was as much about male power and male beauty as it was a mythical tale of good versus evil. The homo-erotic undertones were difficult to miss, no matter how hard Dylan Winchester had worked to create a film that concealed, rather than revealed, his own personal truth.

Yet on its own terms, the picture worked well enough. Its production values were first rate, the story wasn't half bad, and Gibson's screen presence was undeniable. I wondered what had happened during the film's editing to cause Winchester's banishment by the studio. Whatever the reason, it wasn't apparent on the screen, at least not to my untrained eye.

At the film's conclusion, polite if unenthusiastic applause rippled through the theater. After an endless list of credits that indicated nepotism was alive and well in the film industry, the lights finally came up. Templeton was the first to speak.

"I haven't seen that many shots of Mel Gibson's butt since *Bird on a Wire*. Not that I'm complaining."

"You should check out *Braveheart,* then."

The voice was deep but fey, and unmistakably that of Lawrence Teal. We turned to see him in a seat directly behind us.

"What a coincidence," I said, in the chilliest voice I could muster.

"Like I told you, Justice—Hollywood's a small place."

"What brings you here?"

"Lydia Lowe wanted a report on how the screening went. She's putting together an item on Dylan's rift with the studio. I copped a press pass."

Templeton leaned over the seat.

"You work for Lydia Lowe, the syndicated columnist?"

"Teal feeds tips to one of her assistants."

"I guess we're all reporters, then, each in our own way." Templeton beamed a smile at me. "No wonder you and Benjamin have become such fast friends."

I returned the smile, but it was the *fuck you* variety that Templeton was so adept at herself.

"Let's get out of here, shall we?"

To my displeasure, Teal stood with us. We made our way to the aisle and joined the crowd moving slowly toward the exit. Teal positioned himself on one side of me, with Templeton out of earshot on the other.

"I'd like to see you tonight."

"Thanks, Teal. I'll pass."

"You have a date?"

"Something like that."

He lifted his nose.

"Aren't we popular all of a sudden. Who's the lucky boy?"

"No one you've slept with, Teal."

We threaded our way through the upper lobby. Encased behind glass were more of the ubiquitous movie posters, this time promoting film noir classics going back to the forties. *Laura. Cape*

*Fear. Double Indemnity. The Big Sleep. Chinatown. The Postman Always Rings Twice.*

"Unless I'm mistaken," Teal said, "you'd like to talk to Dylan again."

"I wouldn't mind."

"I happen to know where he is."

"I'm listening."

"He's got a hideaway, out of town but not that far."

"I thought you wanted to protect him."

"The cocksucker hasn't returned one of my calls since the party. He's treating me like shit."

"Even after you removed his cigar from the murder scene? Or doesn't he know that yet?"

Teal shot me a nasty look.

"Do you want to find him or not?"

"Of course I do."

"My place, then."

"I told you, I'm busy." Then, reluctantly: "It'll have to be later."

We started down the stairs.

"How much later?"

"Midnight."

"I'll be waiting."

"And how do I know you have the information I need?"

We crossed the bottom steps and faced each other in the big foyer. Templeton strayed ahead, studying the incomparable face of Dorothy Dandridge on a lobby card from *Island in the Sun.*

"Dylan usually spends his weekends at his ranch near Palm Springs. I heard through the grapevine that he's been holing up there since that big cop started looking for him. It's up in the mountains, real private. Famous for its weekend, all-boy pool parties. I used to be invited myself, when I could pass for a teenager."

" 'The mountains' covers a lot of territory."

"You'll get the exact location tonight." His voice grew tough, insinuating. "Don't be late."

He waltzed away, nodding to Templeton before disappearing into the crowd.

All around us was the sound of Tinseltown buzz—critics jabbering in self-important tones, reporters adding their cynical jibes, publicists standing around nervously, getting paid to smile and say encouraging things about the movie. Everybody behaving as if Hollywood were the center of the universe.

I wanted out, as quickly as possible. When I saw Claude De-Winter crossing the lobby, I wanted out even faster.

He took a place between Templeton and me like he held the deed to it, mashing gum between his busy jaws.

"I thought you'd left, Lieutenant."

"I did. I came back."

His eyes settled on Templeton like bees on honey.

"I was hoping we might grab something to eat. That is, un-less—"

Templeton shifted her eyes toward me without ever quite re-moving them from DeWinter.

"As a matter of fact, I'm unexpectedly free."

Her voice performed a tight wire act with consummate skill, tempting DeWinter while taunting me. For an uneasy moment, she reminded me of Teal.

I flung my next words at her like a handful of well-aimed darts.

"You must take the lieutenant to Spago, Templeton. Introduce him to a good Bordeaux. Although he may want to lose the gum before the first course."

I turned toward the nearest exit, before Templeton's glare gave me a bad chill.

Then I was in the Mustang, pulling out of the academy's under-ground garage, making a turn, driving hard toward central Holly-wood.

Away from the chattering monkeys. Away from the insidious Lawrence Teal. Away from the offensive Claude DeWinter, and the games Templeton was playing with both him and me in an effort to shore up her shattered confidence.

After sacrificing two hours to watch a movie about bloody be-headings and magic medallions that someone had deemed wor-thy of spending $90 million on, I longed to have contact with something solid and real, something that mattered to me.

# Thirty

I T WAS HALF PAST TEN when I reached Danny's apartment on Fountain Avenue.

His pickup truck was parked on the street but the windows at the top of the stairs were dark.

I found a note on the door, scrawled in pencil by a hand that didn't look all that strong:

> I'm in the garage out back. Danny.

The garage door was down, but I could see light through the cracks. I rapped with my knuckles and heard Maggie's woof from inside, followed by Danny's voice.

"Who is it?"

"Ben."

"You'll have to pull it open."

When I did, I found Danny stretched out on a mattress on the concrete floor. He was propped up on big pillows, clad in baggy sweatpants, with an old blanket heaped to the side. Maggie stood guard at his feet, but when she recognized me her tail went into action and she showed me the canine grin peculiar to golden retrievers.

A table lamp sat on the floor near Danny's head, casting its paltry light over the lower portions of the dingy garage. In his hands was an illustrated guidebook, *California's Eastern Sierra,* open to a photograph of a small blue lake fringed with pine. Nearby was his pillbox, along with a bottle of juice, a box of tissues, and a bowl of water for the dog.

"You sleeping down here?"

He nodded.

"Worried that somebody might break in again?"

"Naw—it's my legs."

"What's the problem?"

"I can't get up the stairs anymore."

*At the hospital, they'll find out why. They'll stop it, reverse it. You'll be OK. You have to be.*

I lowered myself to the edge of the mattress.

"Why didn't you tell me how bad it was?"

"I'm pretty good at taking care of myself." Maggie snuggled up next to him, resting her chin on his hip. "At least I have been until now."

"AIDS Project Los Angeles has a buddy program."

"Yeah, I've kinda avoided that." He tried to laugh, but couldn't. "I've avoided a lot of things, I guess."

His eyes swept the marginal comforts he'd transported downstairs.

"Aurelio came back after delivering his dinners, helped me haul this stuff down."

"You should have called me sooner."

"You've got plenty to do without taking care of me."

"Hey, it's only temporary—until you get better."

Danny's voice had lost any sense of resistance. Yet I heard a different kind of strength; he sounded oddly at peace.

"I'm not afraid of dying, Ben." He looked away, into the garage, where his finely crafted table took up most of the space. "I'm afraid of dying badly."

"You're not dying, Danny. You're going to get through this. PWAs aren't dropping like flies anymore. They're living a long, long time now."

"Some. The ones that got early treatment, took care of themselves."

He turned to look straight at me.

"I'm dying, Ben. You'd better accept it. Because I have."

Then he startled me with a smile.

"At least I got my table finished. I wanted to do that."

"You're not dying, dammit!"

He picked a burr from the fur on one of Maggie's ears.

"I've got to find a home for Maggie. Someplace where she has a yard. An apartment's no good for a dog like her. Even if she is old."

"A garage is no good for you."

"It's not so bad. There's people with AIDS worse off than me. Living on the street, in the shelters."

"You're not sleeping here tonight. Or ever again. Not on a thin mattress on a dirty concrete floor."

"I don't have a lot of choices, Ben."

"You've got more choices than you realize."

I held out my hands to him.

"Come on, get up."

"Where we goin'?"

"Home."

We arrived back on Norma Place inside the hour. Danny and Maggie sat beside me in front; in the back were his assortment of meds, personal papers, clothes, toothbrush, razor, the guidebook of the eastern Sierra, and a big bag of Maggie's dry food.

"I feel funny about this," Danny said. "We should have at least called first."

"Believe me, it won't be a problem."

I knocked lightly on the back door. Fred was asleep but Maurice was still up, watching a videotape of *My Beautiful Laundrette*.

"That East Indian lad," Maurice said, after opening the door. "That face! Those eyes! My heart was doing somersaults!"

When I explained the situation he darted past me out the door. By the time I reached the car, he was already helping Danny out.

"A garage floor? When we have an empty bed in the extra bedroom. Shame on you!"

"Danny, meet Maurice."

"I have," Danny said, and laughed.

"Warn the dog about the cats," Maurice said. "Fred and Ginger aren't terribly friendly with their canine cousins."

"Maggie's good with cats. I think she'll be OK."

"Oh, my goodness—the cats! That could be dangerous for you, couldn't it?"

Maurice was talking about toxoplasmosis, which could be fatal for someone with a severely diminished immune system.

"I have to be careful," Danny said. "Especially around litter boxes—the feces in the dust. But I'll be all right."

He was able to walk, but it was an effort. Maurice and I each took one of his arms, while Maggie trotted into the yard and lifted her leg against a honeysuckle vine.

Danny stopped when we reached the back steps.

"It's going up that's the biggest problem."

I bent down and scooped him off his feet, one arm circling his back, the other cradling his legs, while he draped his arms around my neck.

Feeling his weight, his flesh pressing against mine produced a shiver of pleasure that felt bigger and more powerful than my fear of him. He laughed as we crossed the threshold.

"I feel like a bride on her wedding night."

"The two of you do make quite an attractive couple," Maurice said. "I'm taking a photograph first thing in the morning."

I carried Danny through the kitchen and down the hall toward the front of the house, while Maggie followed. Maurice scurried ahead to open the bedroom door and turn down the sheets.

"I can walk on my own now."

I inhaled Danny's scent while I still had him close, the musky odor that comes when your last shower and dose of deodorant have worn off and you start to smell human again. It was wildly intoxicating, better than any cologne.

I kissed him on the cheek and set him gently down. He hobbled ahead of me into the bedroom at the end of the hall.

Maggie hopped up on the bed the moment she saw it.

"To the manor born," Maurice said.

"You don't have a problem with dogs in the house?"

"Not a bit. Fred loves them. He's always thought of himself as a dog man. You'll meet him in the morning—very butch."

Maurice gave me a wink.

"At least he likes to think so."

Danny stood awkwardly in the center of the small room.

"I don't know what to say."

"No words needed, dear. Just make yourself at home."

Maurice pointed out the TV set and VCR, and a modest collection of feature films that featured humane portrayals of gay male characters—*Ernesto; Maurice; Victim; Another Country; Sunday, Bloody Sunday; Victor, Victoria; La Cage aux Folles; Parting Glances; My Own Private Idaho; Philadelphia; Longtime Companion; Beautiful Thing*. Films that Maurice found heavily flawed by homosexual stereotype or veiled with homophobia—*Death in Venice, Midnight Cowboy, Partners, A Different Story*—were excluded from his collection. Anything by William Friedkin was banned—Maurice could not forgive the director for *Boys in the Band* and *Cruising*—and *Making Love* was missing because Maurice found it as boring as it was well-meaning. His generous demeanor masked a ruthless, unyielding critic.

"Bathroom's down the hall," he said. "I'll put out a fresh towel. Consider the kitchen your own. If you need anything, Fred and I are on the other side of that wall."

He gave Danny a hug, and my hand a quick squeeze, then left us, closing the door softly behind him.

"I never met anybody like him before," Danny said.

"Maurice makes a habit of taking in strays."

"Are you one of 'em?"

I nodded.

"So was Jacques, before me."

"You think about Jacques a lot, don't you?"

"More than I should, probably."

He looked at his feet a moment, then back up.

"Try to think about me like that once in a while. You know, when I'm gone."

His eyes suddenly glistened with tears and when I took him in my arms, I could hear him crying softly on my shoulder.

*Finally. Finally, he's letting some of it go.*

"Listen to me, Danny. You're going into the hospital on Monday. They're going to find out what's wrong, then turn it around. After that, you're coming back here—back where you belong."

After his tears had ebbed, he separated from me.

"I should get some sleep."

I glanced at the double bed.

"There's room for both of us." I grinned. "If Maggie's willing to sleep on the floor."

"I'll see you in the morning." He kissed me on the lips, sealing it. "Thanks again for helping me out."

I left the door ajar on my way out, so Maurice could hear if he was needed during the night.

As I passed through the pantry, the short hand on the kitchen clock was pointed straight up at twelve, the long hand straight down. I was late for my appointment with Lawrence Teal.

I strode down the driveway, out to Norma Place, over to Hilldale Avenue and up to the intersection of Dicks Street, where I knocked on Teal's door.

He was naked when he pulled it open, except for a leather cock ring binding the base of his scrotum and penis. He'd shaved away all his pubic hair, turning himself into a tightly muscled man-boy.

Each of his nipples was pierced with a silver ring, still swollen from the piercing.

He shut and locked the door, faced me, and slapped me hard across the face.

"That's for being late."

Various pieces of paraphernalia were laid out in orderly fashion on the living room floor—bondage straps, a leather harness, rubber dildos in a range of sizes, handcuffs, a whip.

Teal ordered me to get on my knees. I kneeled.

"Open your mouth."

I did as ordered, and he moved toward me. Leading the way was an erection big enough and stiff enough to hang a Stetson on.

I'd never been that fond of role-playing in sexual situations, certainly not the rigidly defined, master-slave variety. But I'd rarely shied away from a new experience, either.

When I left Lawrence Teal's apartment just before dawn, I knew a great deal more about him, especially his capacity for inflicting pain.

I also came away with directions to Dylan Winchester's Palm Springs ranch.

The sun was coming up when I finished showering off the sticky remnants of Teal's dark pleasure, and traces of my own.

I didn't bother trying to sleep.

# Thirty-one

I SPENT most of Friday in grease up to my elbows, working on the Mustang, while Danny handed me tools and offered his sympathy each time I took another piece of skin off my knuckles.

As the afternoon cooled, Fred fired up the barbecue to grill chicken drumsticks, which we ate with generous helpings of Maurice's baked beans and cole slaw, and corn on the cob that Danny cooked in tinfoil. Fred, who was given a dieter's half portion of everything, kept his grumbling to a minimum, and I did the same with my consumption of wine.

Maggie lay on the patio at Danny's feet, while the cats sat next to Maurice on the chaise lounge, their eyes narrowed to slits of pure contentment. When the sun began to fade, Maurice brought out his old Rolleiflex and took a photograph of Danny and me together, with Maggie between us leading the smiles.

I cut up a cold, sweet watermelon for dessert and as I watched Danny chomping through his slice, I assured myself there was no way in the world he was dying. Maurice talked for a bit about how it felt like the old family was back together, and though he didn't mention Jacques by name, I knew he was on everybody's mind. The neighbors were playing vintage Van Morrison albums that evening—*Astral Weeks, Moondance*—and as the music drifted over the vined fence, we all grew sleepy listening to rocking Irish soul.

I asked Danny again if we might sleep together, and this time he agreed. He leaned on me going up the stairs, and we nodded off together nuzzling each other in my big bed, me in boxers,

Danny in his baggy sweatpants, both of us with erections I was too tired to do anything about, even if he'd let me.

Just after breakfast the next morning, Saturday, we set out in search of Dylan Winchester, leaving Maggie in the care of Maurice and Fred.

We rode east out Interstate 10 with the windows open and our shirts off, letting the warm air wash over us like a blessing. During much of the two-hour drive, Danny napped with his head on my shoulder while I kept the radio low, listening to old Art Pepper tapes that swung on the mellow side.

As we headed into the furnace of the high desert, I felt cleansed by the broiling air, while the sight of the cactus-covered landscape delivered the welcome shock of open space.

From time to time, Danny woke and smiled sleepily at me. Once or twice, he poured me a paper cup filled with iced lemonade from a thermos Maurice had sent along with tuna sandwiches and homemade oatmeal cookies.

It was as if time had been suspended.

Danny and I were younger, two lovers on our first adventure together. There was no AIDS, no T-cell or viral load count, no hospital bed waiting for him on Monday.

If he was terminal, I didn't see it. If these were his final days, his final weeks, I still needed convincing.

The highway rose and fell and rose with a rhythm that lulled and entranced us. Then, to the north, metallic windmills appeared ominously on a ridge like a platoon of soldiers swarming out of the hills, their arms collecting wind for hydroelectric conversion. As we rolled on, hundreds more spread out ahead of us like an army across the arid valley floor.

The resort communities of Palm Springs, Cathedral City, and Rancho Mirage sprouted up to the southeast, oases crowded with motels, restaurants, clubs, and boutiques, many of which catered to the lesbians and gay men who came in by the thousands for long weekends. In recent years, the area had become a haven for queers, with hundreds of gay cops trekking there annually for their Pigs in Paradise celebration and more than twenty thousand lesbians gathering during the Dinah Shore pro golf tournament each spring to drink and dance and tan topless beside dozens of hotel pools. I'd always avoided the Springs, and its pricey, suntanned veneer. Suddenly, it seemed like a good idea.

I turned to Danny impulsively.

"Let's spend the night in Palm Springs. We'll sleep in tomorrow and eat breakfast in bed and lay around the pool like a couple of tourists."

"Like a couple of soft queers from the city, you mean."

We both grinned.

"Why not? That's what we are."

"I'm strapped for cash. Until my next SSI check."

"I've got enough."

"Sure, if you really want to."

"I want to."

A few miles outside the city limits, we turned off toward the mountain community of Idyllwild, following Lawrence Teal's hand-drawn map.

We left behind a shoulder-high forest of cholla cactus, yucca, and thorny buckhorn and climbed into pine country. The air grew cooler with each passing mile, the vistas broader. To the east, we saw the startling green of the wealthy golf and tennis communities beyond Palm Springs and, above them, dozens of tourist-filled hot-air balloons drifting in a rainbow of colors.

Then we took a sharp curve and all that disappeared while the mountains wrapped themselves around us.

A few minutes later, I spotted another turnoff indicated on Teal's map and took it. We drove for a mile or two on a narrow paved road, pushing our way deeper into the national forest that wound around a few pockets of private land.

One of the parcels belonged to Dylan Winchester. I knew it by the carved wooden sign hanging over the massive front gate: WILD HORSE RANCH.

The gate was comprised of six-foot walls of indigenous mountain stone with wooden doors between them that bore Aztec-style carvings. The walls ran in either direction for a hundred yards or more, before giving way to a lower fence of barbed wire partly camouflaged by trench-irrigated pine. It struck me that Winchester had gone to some expense to protect his hideaway from prying eyes.

I parked, got out, and inspected the big gate. It was locked tight. An intercom microphone was perched on a steel arm that rose from a small concrete island in the middle of the driveway entrance.

Just then, a powder blue MGB convertible came speeding down the road from the direction of the Springs. Inside were three boys wailing the words to "Y.M.C.A." with all the energy of the Village People, if not the harmony.

Their rendition faded as the sports car slowed and pulled up alongside me.

"You a friend of Dylan's?" the driver asked.

He was a slim, pretty kid, probably on the short side of eighteen, with medium-length dark blond hair and a wispy mustache and goatee that looked like spun gold.

"Old mate from Down Under," I said, attempting an Aussie accent. "Wanted to surprise the old bloke. Brought him some videos from Thailand—very hot stuff."

The boy grinned.

"We'll get you in."

He pressed a button on the intercom, leaned toward it, spoke his name, and moments later I heard the gate locks unlatch.

"I'll handle the gate, mate."

I pulled it open and the MGB shot through, its horn tooting as it disappeared up the drive.

When I'd closed the gate behind the Mustang, I followed the path of the other car. The asphalt-covered drive ended in a circle outside the main house, where several cars and vans were parked under a stand of ponderosa pines.

Two long-legged Akitas came bounding out from around one side of the house, barking like they meant business, but they quieted down when I offered each of them half a tuna on whole wheat.

The two-story house was put together with indigenous rock, like the walls below. It looked to be a century old, or close to it; on the second story was a wide veranda shaded by a gabled roof.

Stables, corrals, and grazing land occupied the property to the north. The rest of the acreage was meadowlike, running for a half mile or so up and around the house, then rolling into low ridges until it blended into the rising slopes of the San Jacinto Wilderness.

I left the car under branches heavy with needles, while Danny hunkered down for another nap.

The front door was locked. I looked through the adjacent windows across a large, cabinlike living room paneled in warm wood with beamed ceilings. I could see straight through the rear windows, onto a patio and pool area. Several young men were splashing, diving, or stretched out on lounge chairs. All but one or two were buck naked.

To the southwest, beyond the yard, was a rise that looked like it might provide a clear vantage point from which to survey the entire property. I left the yard, hiking across hard ground strewn with rock and chaparral, watching for rattlesnakes. The dogs followed, sniffing for more tuna.

As I reached the top of the rise, I saw a boy trotting a sleek, dark mare out of the distant woods coming in my direction. He pulled the horse up as he got close. He was naked, riding bareback, as taut and slender as a swimsuit model, with Asian eyes and cheekbones, and straight dark hair falling to his shoulders.

He stared passively at me for a moment, then kicked his long legs against the horse's ribs and made a streak across open ground toward the house, his hair flying behind him, his bare rump lifting and settling on the horse with the easy rhythm of someone who was born to ride.

He galloped the horse past the house, where he turned her skillfully toward the mountain slopes, leaving a trail of golden dust in the early afternoon sunlight.

I followed the first leg of his trail while the dust settled and the dogs ran ahead, listening to the splash of naked bodies in the pool, and wondering if Dylan Winchester was among them.

# Thirty-two

I HADN'T SEEN so many naked teenaged boys since high school, when I'd lined up with the wrestling team for a physical, waiting for my turn to face the doctor and cough.

They were scattered over Dylan Winchester's patio, around the pool, or in it. Every one was on the lean and pretty side, past puberty but not by much. It looked like Winchester had created his own modest version of the Playboy Mansion, populated to suit his boy's camp tastes.

"You here to party?"

The question came from a slender black kid with bright, friendly eyes, molasses-colored skin, and a gold ring decorating his right ear. A neat patch of tightly curled hair cropped up below his waist; below that was a set of plump, purplish genitals with some growth still ahead of them.

"Don't you guys worry about UVA rays?"

He grinned.

"Dylan keeps plenty of sunblock on hand." The grin widened. "Sometimes he even helps us put it on."

"Every inch, I'll bet."

"Yeah—you know Dylan."

"Where is he, by the way?"

"I think he's inside. You know—with Fernando."

"Right, Fernando."

"We don't see too many older guys up here." His brown eyes moved shyly away, then found me again. "I like older guys."

"I'll keep that in mind—?"

"Horace."

"Horace."

I crossed the patio past the pool and the sharp smell of chlorine. The lanky blond boy I'd seen earlier behind the wheel of the MGB stood on the end of the diving board, raised up on his toes, arms pointing skyward, showing a golden cushion of soft hair under each arm. The board sprang and the boy performed a nicely executed jackknife, while his buddies cheered and applauded.

"There's beer in the fridge!" Horace called after me, and I gave him a wave without turning around.

I entered the living room, saw no one, and crossed to a hallway. The first door I came to was ajar, and I pushed it slowly open.

"Oh!"

There was a freckled redhead inside, standing before a bathroom mirror, a disposable razor in one hand and his flat chest lathered with foam.

"You startled me."

A thin red line trickled from his left nipple.

"Horace told me I'd find Dylan down this way."

"End of the hall. He's with Fernando. Better knock first."

"You're bleeding," I said, and left Red looking down.

I passed a screening room with overstuffed leather chairs and sofas arranged for viewing. Across the hall was another bedroom, its door wide open. Inside, two boys slept naked in each other's arms, intertwined in the fashion of young lovers who have managed to sneak away to their own private world, safe from the torment of guilt and shame, if only for a stolen piece of time. I pulled the door quietly shut, giving them their peace and privacy, wishing I'd been as lucky at their age.

Then I was facing the door at the end of the hall. From inside came grunts and cries that sounded like two grown men in the heat of sex. I turned the doorknob slowly, soundlessly easing the door open.

Dylan Winchester was bent over the end of the bed, his bearded face and powerful chest on the mattress and his hairy butt raised in the air. His swimming trunks lay in a small pile around his ankles. His eyes were closed, his jaw locked.

Fucking him was the most flawless male specimen I'd ever laid eyes on.

He was roughly my height, as darkly bronze as I was blond and fair. His face was angular and smooth, with a bit of soft shadow on his upper lip and chin, and a profile that looked like the ideal Aztec warrior in every gay man's collection of Latin fantasies.

His shoulders were broad and his arms lean but well muscled, cording up as he gripped Winchester by the hips and thrust into him with strong, controlled strokes. I couldn't see a hair on his sculpted chest, none on his rippled belly, and only the softest trace on his long, brown legs.

Yet every inch of him was clearly a man, fully in command of the brawnier man beneath him.

Each time he stroked, he arched upward on his toes, thrusting his hips smoothly, while the muscles of his legs and butt tightened into knots of power.

It went on like that for another minute or two. Then the bronzed Adonis was grunting through clenched teeth and the hairy Australian was hollering the word *yes* over and over, his fist flailing at the stiff meat between his legs, until they were thrashing against one another, pelvis pounding ass, crying out like wounded animals.

When it was over, Winchester flattened out on the bed, his head turned my way but his eyes still closed, his thick forearms spread before him on the bed as if raised in surrender.

His lover moved with him, pressing his chest to Winchester's back, while placing tender kisses in the damp tangle of Winchester's auburn hair.

I let them enjoy another minute of bliss before I spoke.

"I hope I'm not interrupting."

Winchester's green eyes shot open and a millisecond later flared with rage.

"What the fuck!"

The Aztec god pinched the end of the condom between his fingers to hold it in place and pulled slowly out.

He backed away as Winchester came at me with his fist cocked.

"I'll bash your bloody face in!"

"That wouldn't solve anything, would it, Dylan?"

He grabbed my shirt front and held his fist at the level of my mouth.

"You've got two seconds to explain yourself, mate. Then I'm going to fucking kill you!"

"The last person you threatened to kill was Reza JaFari, and he ended up dead. I haven't told the police that yet, but I could. Then there's the matter of the cigar you dropped down on the terrace, roughly ten feet from JaFari's body."

Winchester trembled with unspent rage, but loosened his grip and lowered his fist. He glanced over his shoulder at the younger man and jerked his head toward a side door.

"Give us a minute, will you, luv?"

"You're certain you want me to go?"

Fernando spoke perfect English but with a Mexican accent as pretty as a Luis Miguel ballad.

"I'd best keep this between me and the bloke here."

Fernando wrapped the condom in tissue, deposited it in a waste can, slipped on a skimpy thong, and opened the side door. I heard the sound of splashing and laughter that ended as the door was closed.

"Talk to me about Reza JaFari, Dylan. No more bullshit. His connection to you, to the Kemmermans, all of it."

Winchester slipped into a monogrammed velour robe, then sat on the edge of the bed, running his hands through his hair. I waited a moment, but he didn't speak.

"It seems to me you've got two choices, Dylan. Talk to me, or talk to DeWinter with a lawyer present."

When he looked up, I saw the face of a man who felt a lifetime of self-indulgence and deception catching up with him.

"If I talk to either of you, it's the end of my bloody career."

"I didn't say I'd print it."

"You didn't say you wouldn't."

I crossed to the windows and drew back the curtains. Most of the boys were in the pool now, engaged in a free-for-all wrestling match, with an erection popping up now and then as someone got lifted or tossed.

"Boys will be boys," I said. "Hmmm—not a bad title for a life-style piece."

I faced Winchester, with the pool of naked boys cavorting behind me.

"You know—how a famous Hollywood action director spends his weekends away from the rat race."

"You fucking vulture."

"I've already spoken with Horace. I love the anecdote about the sunblock, how you like to lather up the boys from head to toe. Then there's Red, who shaves his chest to keep you happy. Like my old boss likes to say, the story's always in the details."

"I should break your bloody neck for trespassing. Take the consequences."

"My photographer too?"

Winchester was on his feet.

"You brought a bloody photographer?"

"He's waiting in the car out front."

Winchester stomped from the room and down the hall. At the front window, I pointed to Danny sleeping in the Mustang.

"He got some lovely shots of the Asian kid who rides a horse like Geronimo. And half a roll out by the pool. We'll black out the faces of the kids. Use studio publicity photos of you. Maybe we'll find a shot of you and Mel Gibson looking chummy."

The rage slowly seeped from Winchester's eyes. His muscular shoulders sagged heavily. He suddenly looked years older, weary from all the lies he'd carried for so long.

"I could use a beer."

Fernando stood in the kitchen doorway as we approached.

"Fernando, meet Benjamin Justice. Reporter. Got me by the *cojones*, I'm afraid."

Fernando nodded, but neither smiled nor extended his hand.

"Keep an eye on the boys for a while, eh? Put a capper on the beer. Get some food in 'em. That mountain road's no place for a kid with a steering wheel in his hands and a belly full of suds."

Fernando sliced me with a scathing look on his way out. Winchester watched him go.

"Have you ever seen anything more beautiful?" His eyes came around and studied my face carefully. "Or maybe blokes ain't your cuppa tea."

"We drink from the same cup, Dylan."

His head swung back in the direction of his departing lover.

"He's got a Mexican heart, that one. Big, open, full of passion. Christ, there's nothin' like a Mexican if it's love you're after."

"Is that what you're after?"

He was gazing out at the pool now.

"I fool around with the kids. Look at 'em 'til my eyes get sore. But I don't fuck 'em, or put my mouth on 'em."

He looked back my way.

"Fernando laid the law down about that a long time ago. He's worth it, too, I'll tell ya."

I watched Fernando cross the patio to an outdoor shower on the far side, slip out of his thong, and lather himself with soap. In the sunlight, the droplets of water were like pebbles of crystal on his dark skin. I finally pried my eyes away; it was almost painful.

"He's exquisite, I'll grant you that."

"Tell me something, mate. Since you seem to be every bit as queer as me, why do you want to do this to me?"

"I don't want to screw up your life, Dylan. But there's someone who means more to me than you do who could find himself in all kinds of trouble unless I put some facts together about Reza JaFari."

"This someone is a bloke, I take it."

"Yes."

He nodded slowly, as if he finally understood there was no point fighting me.

"So that's it, then."

He opened a can of Fosters's and drank half of it down in silence. Then I followed him up a stairway and out to the veranda, where we settled into a pair of Adirondack chairs and looked out at the mountains.

"Ten years ago, me and JaFari, we had a little thing going."

I pushed the story ahead, drawing on my conversation at Rimbaud's with Lawrence Teal.

"You met at a party up at Nando Sorentino's, dated Teal for a few weeks, then dropped him."

"You should be workin' for the fuckin' CIA."

"Hollywood's a small town, Dylan. People talk."

"Damn the fucking town. Sometimes I wish I'd stayed Down Under, makin' me little films."

He tilted his head back and guzzled more beer.

"Tell me what happened in Mexico, Dylan. When you were on location shooting *Full Contact*. Then connect it to what's happened in the last couple of months up here."

Winchester raised a hand to shield the sun and stared off across his land. The long-haired Asian boy had ridden back into view, joined now by the black kid named Horace on a saddled white stallion.

They waved in our direction. Winchester saluted them with his can of beer the way promiscuous straight men send calculated compliments and winks to impressionable young women.

We watched them turn their horses and disappear over a rise, the sharp hooves stirring up the earth.

"Once you get a taste of a beautiful lad," Winchester said, "it's like a hunger that gnaws at you forever."

"Tell me about Reza JaFari, Dylan."

He spoke as the dust settled in the distance on his lovely fantasies.

"Everybody knew him as Ray Farr back then. You already know that, I guess. He was a good-lookin' kid with stars in his eyes. I had a romp with him. Then I went into pre-production on *Full Contact*. It was my first American movie with a decent budget, and I poured myself into it."

"But JaFari still wanted to see you."

"He'd gotten this idea he was in love with me."

"Kids can do that the first time around, especially when they want the life you have. It's what makes them such easy scores."

"Whatever," Winchester said tersely. "Raymond got a little crazy about it. I had to change my phone number, have him barred from the studio. Then I didn't hear from him for a while, and I took the production down to Mexico."

"Where you met Fernando."

"He was an extra. Rode a horse like the wind. I'd seen a lot of beautiful kids in my life, all over the world, but I'd never dreamed there was a kid who looked like that. He was a virgin the first time I had him. Never been with a lady or a bloke. But it was pretty obvious right off which way his dick was pointed.

"So I'm down there directing this bloody movie, looking at rushes at night, doing script changes, fucking this gorgeous kid until dawn. It was nuts, but I was a young tyro, a bloody Aussie wunderkind. I could do anything, you know?"

"Except handle Ray Farr?"

"He showed up one night, at this little hotel down near Oaxaca where the cast and crew was staying. Caught me in bed with Fernando. Went totally fucking berserk. Smashed things, put his fist through a plate-glass door."

"He was left-handed?"

"How'd you know?"

"The scars on his left wrist and hand."

"Tore himself up something awful. Blood pouring out of him. Looked like one of the FX guys had rigged him up for a blood effect. We stuck his hand and arm in a bag of flour to slow the bleeding until we could find a doctor to close him up. But he'd lost a lot of blood. Hospital couldn't help him. Farr had a rare blood type—we learned later he was part Jewish."

"JaFari was Jewish?"

Winchester laughed.

"He didn't even know it. His father never let on—raised him thinkin' he was pure Muslim. It was a real shock to him at first."

"So he was stuck down in southern Mexico, where he couldn't get the right blood—"

"Everybody volunteered—cast, crew, Mexican extras. Nobody matched. Then they typed Bernie Kemmerman. Bullseye! Bernie gave several pints, way more than was safe. Kept passing out but he'd come around and tell 'em to draw another pint. Then he reached into his own pocket and hired a military plane. His blood kept Ray alive long enough to get him flown back to the States, where they patched him up."

"Kemmerman saved JaFari's life."

"That he did, mate. He also kept the whole thing quiet—with the studio, the press, my agency. Saved my fucking career is what he did."

"You must have felt you owed Bernard Kemmerman a lot."

Winchester drained the can.

"I loved the bloke. A lot of people did. He was the only decent man I ever met in this whole fucking business."

"And a few months ago, when he needed a new kidney to stay alive, he remembered that Reza JaFari was the same blood type. He came to you, hoping you'd put him in touch with JaFari."

"I'd gotten Farr a job with ITA, thinkin' he might make something of it. So I knew where to find him. Bernie was pretty sick by then, so most of Farr's dealings were with Anne-Judith—Bernie's wife."

"JaFari agreed to be the donor?"

Winchester nodded.

"I don't know exactly what happened after that, 'cept Ray started stalling, while Bernie got sicker and sicker. But that wasn't the worst of it."

"The worst of it was, JaFari was infected with HIV."

"Infected, but never told 'em. They found out late in the game. Somebody tipped 'em with a phone call. By then it was too late. Bernie died waiting for the kidney that bastard JaFari had promised him, knowing Bernie couldn't use it because of the HIV."

Winchester's voice was heavy with disgust.

"Bernie saved Ray's life ten years ago and then Ray let him die. Don't think I don't blame myself, neither."

"Is that what derailed your career these last few months?"

"Like I said, a lot of people liked and respected Bernie. Word got out—about me and about Ray, about Ray's HIV. The whole thing blew up in my face."

"The agency fired JaFari and dumped you at the same time. Then the studio took *Thunder's Fortune* away from you."

"All because of that lyin' little bastard JaFari."

"Maybe he learned how to lie from the people he looked up to most. His father. You."

He slid down in his chair, showing me his troubled profile.

"Go fuck yourself, Justice."

"You had plenty of reasons to want JaFari dead."

He crushed the beer can slowly with his meaty hands. Then he gazed at me with eyes gone dull from alcohol.

"I got me a temper, Justice. I won't deny that. But I don't go around killin' blokes."

He heaved the crushed can over the railing, his face sullen.

"Not even the ones who deserve it."

# Thirty-three

D ANNY AND I never got to enjoy our idyll at the Springs.
By Saturday evening, he was so racked with pain, just getting in and out of the car was an ordeal. So I drove him straight home that night, and left him in the care of Maurice.

I spent most of Sunday with my answering machine on, reading *The Little Prince*—Jacques's favorite book—to Danny while he lay in a nembutal haze in the small bed at the end of the hallway. It felt like a lost, precious day, a bridge in time I didn't want to cross.

I slept alone upstairs Sunday night, ignoring the blinking message machine, and was back down to the house at daybreak, frightened irrationally that Danny might not be alive.

He was already awake—on his feet, actually, and feeling better—and insisted on showering and dressing for the hospital without my help.

By then, Maurice had coffee ready. I took a cup back upstairs and drank it while I cleared the weekend's phone messages.

The first was from Gordon Cantwell.

*Justice. Gordon Cantwell here. I'm willing to overlook our misunderstanding at the ballpark the other day if you are. I wouldn't want to see it get in the way of an accurate and thorough article on an industry of which I'm such an integral part. Along those lines, you may wish to catch the front page of Monday's* Daily Variety—*the story about Tom Cruise's new project over at Paramount. Take a look, then give me a call. You've got the number.*

Cantwell's message was delivered in a manner that tried, but failed, not to sound supremely self-satisfied.

The next message was from Alexandra Templeton. For the most part it was conciliatory, though served with some leftover chill from our verbal tiff on Friday evening.

> *Hi, it's me. Gordon Cantwell called, trying to maneuver me into meeting him for another interview. I told him you were more or less in charge now, that he should talk to you, take it or leave it. He mentioned some kind of major studio deal he feels we should highlight in the article. My guess is you'll be hearing from him. I'll be at the office or out on assignment. Hope you got your interview with Dylan Winchester, and that Danny's feeling better. Kisses.*

One more message followed.

> *This is Lieutenant DeWinter, Homicide Division, Los Angeles Police Department, calling for Benjamin Justice. Mr. Justice, I do hope you know the whereabouts of your friend, Daniel Romero, because he seems to no longer be around. No more games, Justice. Call me ASAP, before a huge load of shit hits the fan.*

He repeated his phone number twice and punctuated his warning by replacing the receiver rather indelicately.

While Danny put together a small bag for the hospital, I hiked up the hill to the newsstand at Book Soup for a copy of *Variety*. I also grabbed the *Hollywood Reporter* in case the story was carried in both trade papers. It was, but the *Reporter* placed it on an inside page.

The *Variety* piece was right where Cantwell had said it would be—front page, center—below a grinning photo of Hollywood's reigning box-office star that must have pleased his orthodontist. The three-tier headline summed things up.

*CRUISE GRABS RIGHTS*
*TO CANTWELL SCRIPT*
*FOR $1.5 MILLION*

The article noted that Cantwell was to be paid the money up front, with built-in bonuses that could bring the total to $3 million. Cantwell was to serve as coproducer, earning another $250,000, and had a pay-or-play deal to perform rewrite and polishing chores on the script that added another $225,000. His agent and lawyer were included as executive producers for undisclosed fees that presumably ran into the six figures.

Cantwell was also entitled to a cut of the net profits, although the Hollywood studio system was notorious for rigging the books in such a way that even the most successful films somehow never showed much profit. That was one reason—other than simple greed—that writers' agents tried to get as much cash up front as possible.

All in all, Cantwell had done very well for himself. Though neither Cruise nor his people were quoted in the story, they apparently had thought very highly of the script.

Its title was *Nothing to Lose.* The storyline was summed up this way:

> Cantwell described the project as a psychological suspense thriller about a cancer-stricken prison convict who escapes on a cross-country run, hoping to see his newborn son one time before he dies, with a violent, vengeful warden in pursuit.
>
> Although originally intended for a more mature actor, Cantwell said *Nothing to Lose* will be retailored for Cruise, giving him an estranged young wife and a baby he has never seen, rather than an estranged adult son and grandchild, as first written.
>
> Cantwell called the script his "masterpiece," a screenplay that "encompasses strong character, suspenseful plotting and a moving emotional subplot," and brings together everything he has learned about the art and craft of screenwriting.

Then, this quote:

> "After years away from screenwriting to teach the craft to students worldwide, this script marks a new phase in my life. From now on, I will devote my time to writing and producing stories for the screen that I hope will live up to the principles embodied in *The Cantwell Method,* and that will find their place in the annals of movie immortality."

The article jumped to an inside page that offered a brief summary of Cantwell's background, as well as those of his attorney and agent.

I was about to set the slick tabloid aside when another headline caught my eye.

*LUNCHEON TO BENEFIT*
*ORGAN DONOR RESEARCH*
*CHAIRED BY KEMMERMAN*

The social item that followed described a charity luncheon to be held that afternoon at the Beverly Hills Hotel. Anne-Judith Kemmerman was the chairperson, an appropriate choice given the recent death of her husband from kidney disease.

I called Cantwell from the apartment, finally catching him at home. I congratulated him on his movie deal, stroked his ego a bit, and asked when we could get together. He suggested we meet for dinner that night at a West Hollywood restaurant called Morton's. I asked him to bring along a copy of his now-famous screenplay. He said he would.

Danny and I shared a solemn, awkward breakfast, and another quiet hour sitting on the front porch swing, watching the neighborhood wake up. Then it was time to take him to the clinic, where he would be processed in before his transfer to the big hospital next door.

Maurice hugged him and promised to come visit. Fred told him not to worry about Maggie, he'd feed her properly and take her on regular walks.

Danny knelt, scratched her ears, and told her to be a good dog while he was gone. He hugged her longer than seemed necessary, which didn't settle me any.

The five-minute trip to the clinic felt like hours. I rode up with Danny in the elevator to the seventh floor, where they put him in a wheelchair and handed him a file to carry in his lap. There were people scurrying and fussing over him, taking care of details, which took some of the edge off my apprehension. Then I was back in the elevator with him, my hand on his shoulder, as we descended to the third floor for his transport to the hospital facility next door.

The doors opened and an attendant pushed Danny out.

He gave me a brave smile, and the thumbs-up sign.

Then I watched him being wheeled away down a dim corridor and out sliding glass doors to the annex bridge, where a blast of sunlight consumed him.

# Thirty-four

T HE BEVERLY HILLS HOTEL sat on twelve lushly land-scaped acres along palm-fringed Sunset Boulevard.

The Pink Palace—as it was fondly known—looked swell for a resort built in 1912, which can happen after a two-year renovation that comes with a $140 million price tag. Even in Beverly Hills, that's an expensive facelift.

I arrived in the early afternoon, striding into a sanctuary that felt largely unchanged by time. Marilyn Monroe had once sipped milk shakes here. Marlene Dietrich had been banished from the Polo Lounge for wearing pants. Elizabeth Taylor had cavorted with various husbands in a bungalow that now went for $2,000 a night, while the Presidential Suite inside the main building topped the rate chart at $3,000. Business had reportedly fallen off some since the hotel's reopening in 1995—something about the owner, the Sultan of Brunei, and his outspoken views on the Palestinian conflict—but the Pink Palace was still regarded by many as one of the prestige watering holes for the showbiz set, regardless of bloody territorial issues half a world away.

The valets out front were handling a string of mostly black or white vehicles, of which Rolls and Mercedes were the dominant brands, a limousine or two among them. John Travolta stepped from a vintage white Bentley, buttoning a jacket over his ample stomach, looking as content as you'd expect from a man with a revived career, a good Scientology scorecard, an attractive family, and millions in the bank.

I'd parked the battered Mustang on the street and come up the curvacious drive on foot, for reasons having less to do with shame than with the need to pass myself off as respectable. I'd even borrowed a tie from Fred, one that was so old it was back in fashion, and tucked my long expired *Los Angeles Times* I.D. card in my pocket just in case.

I got into step behind Travolta, nodding and smiling as I strolled, until I was in a lobby done in glowing shades of apricot, with curvy ceilings and enormous crystal chandeliers festooned with delicate rosebud lights.

Travolta made straight for the Polo Lounge, leaving me on my own.

Lots of well-dressed ladies were gliding into the Crystal Ballroom on the west side of the lobby, which seemed like a good bet. I followed them in, past a placard telling me I'd found the organ donor fund-raiser, stopping just short of the registration table.

Sizable round tables filled the apricot-tinted ballroom, which featured a swirling Art Nouveau ceiling and balconies with elaborate black-and-gold railings. Waiters scurried about, filling water glasses and laying salad plates in front of well-dressed women who all seemed to have the same ghastly, anorexic look.

Anne-Judith Kemmerman was one of the few exceptions; she was radiant and voluptuous in the old Sophia Loren style, though her stacked hair was closer in spirit to Dolly Parton. She stood at the center of the dais, speaking into a microphone about the need to raise money for organ donor research, while stressing that "every dollar counts." It seemed like a silly thing to say to a roomful of women attired in dresses and jewelry collectively worth millions, but I doubted it troubled even a single well-coiffed head in the lavish room.

Several more ladies came through the door behind me, talking in hushed whispers. As they crowded the registration table, I took the opportunity to slip by unquestioned.

I had no game plan, other than to somehow corner Mrs. Kemmerman and make her squirm. DeWinter had made it clear that Danny's grace period was quickly running out, and I had decided Mrs. Kemmerman was going to talk to me whether she liked it or not.

Her eyes found me as I weaved my way through waiters and tables, heading toward a small open area just below the podium. When I was roughly halfway across the room, her speech became slow and halting, and finally stopped altogether.

As she grew quiet, so did the room.

Her eyes were on me, mine were on hers, and I assumed every other eye in the place was on the two of us, which was the way I wanted it.

"I just have a few questions, Mrs. Kemmerman."

"How did you get in here?"

"It must have been my trustworthy face."

Her eyes flitted from table to table.

"Will someone please call security? This man is not supposed to be here. He's quite dangerous."

No one in the room made a definitive move. The real Anne-Judith Kemmerman suddenly emerged.

"Somebody get off their goddamned ass and find security!"

Two or three women ran scurrying for various exits, as fast as their three-inch heels and corsetlike dresses would allow.

"All I want is a little information, Mrs. Kemmerman."

"You're in serious trouble, mister. I'll have you by your goddamned balls!"

"Shall we discuss the sordid details of the Reza JaFari case, Mrs. Kemmerman? Right here, in front of all these nice people? Or shall we do it more privately?"

"You fucking bastard."

I heard a commotion and assumed security personnel were in the room, coming for me.

"Either you talk to me, Mrs. Kemmerman, or I take what I know about you and your husband's death straight to the tabloid TV shows."

Her face lost some of its color. I felt strong hands grab my arms. Mrs. Kemmerman gulped some ice water, then set her glass down, looking seriously troubled.

"It's all right. I'll handle this."

"Are you certain, Mrs. Kemmerman?"

It was a man's voice, just off my left ear.

"Yes. Let him go. I'll speak to him privately."

"If you're sure, Mrs. Kemmerman."

"I'm sure."

I felt the hands relax and bodies step away.

Mrs. Kemmerman came down off the dais, brushing quickly past me. If her eyes had been fingernails, my face would have been raked and bleeding.

I followed her through the roomful of stunned faces, then the lobby, and onto a patio shaded by an enormous pepper tree almost as famous for its longevity as the old hotel itself.

I had to work hard to keep up with her. She turned down a walkway under spreading banana leaves, striding past gardens of azaleas, camellias, roses, and magnolias bursting into thousands of pink and white blooms.

She didn't say a word until we were inside a bungalow with the door locked. Even then, she waited until I spoke first.

"I have a pretty good idea what went down between your husband and Reza JaFari, Mrs. Kemmerman. But I'd like a few more details."

She found a cigarette and lit it with trembling fingers.

"You've humiliated me in front of some of the most important club women in this city. Barbara Davis was out there, for Christ sake!"

"Tell me what I need to know. Then you can hurry back and salvage some of your precious social standing."

"You're lower than a leech, Justice."

"That's what people keep telling me."

She sucked in a lungful of nicotine, which seemed to calm her.

"Help me out on this, Mrs. Kemmerman, and your involvement may never have to get into print. Stonewall me for one more second, however, and I promise you that half the world will learn the truth."

"And what exactly is that, Justice?"

She faced me, gambling against what she hoped was my bluff, her burning cigarette held aloft like a battle flag.

"Bernard Kemmerman offered Reza JaFari a studio production deal in exchange for a healthy kidney."

Her eyes smoldered hotter than the end of her cigarette.

"Goddamn you."

"He used his position of wealth, power, and privilege to buy his way right past that donor waiting list you're championing with such well-publicized nobility."

She turned away from me, forcing me to talk to her back.

"Forget all the fine movies he made, Mrs. Kemmerman. All his good deeds. The goodwill he engendered during his career. In the end, your husband will be remembered for an act that epitomizes Hollywood's corrupt elitism."

"It wasn't like that." Her words came sharply, but the ones that followed were delivered more gently. "*He* wasn't like that."

"I'm here to listen, Mrs. Kemmerman."

She paced the room, sucking down more nicotine.

"The deal wasn't entirely bogus. JaFari pitched Bernard a very good concept."

"Go on."

"A few days later, maybe a week, JaFari came back with a script. Bernard said it was quite good. A bit old-fashioned, but very strong. With some minor revisions, he felt sure he could get it packaged and green-lighted at the studio."

"In exchange for one of his kidneys."

"You have to understand, we were desperate at that point."

"Your husband was critically ill."

"Yes." Her voice trembled. "We sent JaFari to our personal physician for a complete physical, including blood work. We were told he was healthy, that everything was fine. Bernard went ahead with plans to have the studio purchase JaFari's script and get him an office on the lot. Then the surgeon who was to perform the operation informed us that JaFari needed to be tested for HIV before we could proceed. We'd assumed it had been done with the standard blood work."

"But under California law, an HIV test can't be done without the express permission of the person to be tested."

"We didn't know that. So we went back to JaFari to ask that he be tested. He began to stall, demanding that his production deal be finalized, that the check be delivered. I met with him personally, begged him to be tested."

"That was your dinner meeting at Jimmy's."

She nodded.

"Days went by, then weeks. Finally, we couldn't even reach him—all we got was his answering machine. Then we got an anonymous phone call warning us that he was HIV-positive."

"Must have been shattering."

"I didn't want to believe it. But Bernie did. He said it explained a lot of things. We tried desperately to find another donor with the same blood type, but it was too late."

She crushed the cigarette out in an ashtray the way she must have wished she could obliterate the past.

"Bernie died a week later."

She turned her back to me again and her shoulders began to shake, as if she might be crying. I remembered that she had once been an actress.

"JaFari helped to kill the man who had once saved his life," she said. "What accounts for someone like that?"

"A town where integrity is an afterthought, if it's even thought of at all?"

She spun on me, tears spilling.

"Bernie had integrity. Ask anyone who knew him."

"You're crying now, Mrs. Kemmerman. But otherwise, you seem to be bearing up awfully well. Or maybe it's just that a new Ferrari and a gym-bunny boyfriend are good grief therapy."

She took two strides and was in my face.

"Listen, mister. Bernie may have been my senior by twenty-odd years. But he was the great love of my life. I tended to him for years, long after he was well enough to take care of certain husbandly duties, if I make myself clear. But I loved him to the end and waited until he was gone before I sought satisfaction elsewhere.

"Yeah, I bought a new car. Yeah, I found a young stud who could put something hard between my legs after years of going without. Maybe that's how I deal with my grief. So who are you to judge, Mr. Pulitzer Prize Winner?"

"You must have hated Reza JaFari for what he did."

"More than words can ever express."

"Your mascara's running, Mrs. Kemmerman."

She pulled herself up straight, then disappeared into the bathroom, where she blew her nose and attended to her face.

I stood at the window and watched an actor famous for his suntan standing on the lawn. He took a couple of practice swings with an imaginary golf club and lifted his sharp profile to study the flight of the nonexistent ball. By the pleased look on his face, the invisible ball had landed somewhere south of Sunset Boulevard. I tried but couldn't remember his name.

Mrs. Kemmerman came back in and poured a short bourbon without offering me one.

"I don't suppose I could make it worth your while not to print the story."

"Buy me off?"

"I'm not without resources."

"I realize it may sound naive, Mrs. Kemmerman, especially in this setting, but I'm more interested in getting to the truth than getting rich."

"We all act out of our own self-interest, Justice. Why is the truth so important to you?"

"An hour ago, I helped check a young man into Cedars-Sinai.

He's seriously ill. He's also very close to becoming a prime suspect in Reza JaFari's death."

"This young man apparently means a lot to you."

"I don't think he did it."

"There's enough evidence to convict him?"

"Maybe only to arrest him and hold him for a while. But that would be hell enough. He's got AIDS."

"You think I might have arranged JaFari's murder, don't you?"

"It's a possibility."

She wandered to the window and looked out, while I stood beside her. The dreamy golfer took another swing.

"George Hamilton," she said. "I played tennis with his ex-wife once."

She was silent for a minute and seemed to be thinking.

"I killed Reza JaFari, Justice—is that what you wanted to hear?" She sipped her drink, then smiled bitterly. "I killed him about a hundred times, in my dreams."

"That doesn't help me much."

"I don't know what I can do that would help you, Justice. I would if I could. If only for your friend's sake. After what Bernie went through, I have a certain sensitivity to that kind of suffering."

"Can you tell me more about the script JaFari submitted to your late husband?"

"Not much. Bernie didn't say what it was about. Just that it would make a terrific movie."

"You didn't read it yourself?"

"I never read any of the scripts sent to Bernie. He got truckloads of the damned things. I could probably find a copy for you among his papers. If you thought it would help."

"It might."

She stared out the window again. Out on the lawn, the actor with the suntan had fired up a cigar and moved on, taking his imaginary golf clubs with him. A Latino gardener under a broad-brimmed hat had taken the actor's place, pulling small weeds and picking off pink and white azalea blossoms that were not quite perfect.

"It's funny, this writing business."

"How's that, Mrs. Kemmerman?"

"Seems like half this city is either waiting for the right script to fall in their lap or out hunting it down. All these writers with all their great ideas. Yet so much of it depends on luck, or timing."

She tipped her glass, finished off the bourbon, then glanced my way.

"Take this script that JaFari gave Bernie. Bernie said it was a natural, one of the best things he'd seen in years. Yet he'd heard essentially the same idea before, thirty-something years ago, back when he was an agent."

I perked up.

"Really?"

"Back in the sixties, Bernie said. He had a client who'd come up with the same story, right down to the characters and the way the story played out. But the guy'd never written it. Ideas for movies are a dime a dozen, Bernie always said. There's no such thing as a new idea—they've all been done before, one way or another. It's how they're executed that counts."

"And who reads the script, and when."

"Like I said, luck and timing. Who knows? If Bernie's client had written that script thirty years ago, maybe it would have gotten made. Maybe the guy would have won the fucking Academy Award."

"You don't recall the name of the writer, do you, Mrs. Kemmerman?"

"Italian, I remember that much. Nice name. Had some music to it."

"Leonardo Petrocelli?"

She looked over, raising her plucked brows.

"Yeah. Yeah, that's the name. You know the guy?"

"We've met."

"Damn, this town is small."

"I keep hearing that, too."

The phone rang. She picked it up and talked briefly. I could make out enough to know someone was calling to make sure she was OK. Then she hung up.

"You through with me, Justice? I'd like to get back to my luncheon and see if I still have any friends left."

"Are they really your friends, Mrs. Kemmerman?"

She plastered me with a look that told me she didn't need any advice about her social life.

"I guess they'll have to do, won't they?"

"I'll walk you back."

"If it's all the same, I'd rather not be seen with you again. Ever."

I closed the door behind me and started back in the direction of the main building.

As I passed the window where she stood, Anne-Judith Kemmerman was staring out distantly, as if I wasn't there. Thinking of someone she'd lost, perhaps, and better times. I knew the feeling.

The gardener looked up from the clumps of azaleas as I went by, dipping the brim of his straw hat in respect, before putting his hands back into the rich, dark soil.

# Thirty-five

T HE BEVERLY HILLS phone book listed an address for Leonardo Petrocelli on Roxbury Drive, a street Gore Vidal once described as "not so much a drive as a state of mind."

The number listed for the Petrocellis, however, put their house in the flats south of Wilshire, where Roxbury was not so much a drive as wishful thinking.

The real estate prices here were considerably lower, with a corresponding drop in acreage, design, and snob appeal. They were still nice homes, however, with neatly clipped lawns, healthy trees along the well-swept sidewalks, and sparkling windows showing off interiors worthy of *House and Garden,* if not *Architectural Digest.*

The Petrocelli residence was a cozy-looking Country English in the middle of the block, with leaded windows and a shingled roof steeper than a playground slide. A winding brick walkway meandered through staked rosebushes abloom with yellow petals to the low-walled front porch.

I found a space at the curb, then followed the path up the front steps, where a copy of Walter Mosley's *A Little Yellow Dog* sat on a canopied swing with a pair of reading glasses resting on top.

The door was slightly ajar but I rang the bell anyway.

I waited, then rang it again and pushed the door open, calling out Petrocelli's name. No one answered.

Almost no one in Southern California walks away from his house with the front door unlocked, let alone open. I felt my internal antennae rise, picking up a signal I didn't like.

I crossed the lawn to the driveway and found my way to the

backyard, which was uninhabited. When I pounded on the back door, I still got no response. Then I looked in a rear window and saw Petrocelli.

He lay face up, his eyes and mouth open wide, his face contorted in apparent agony. If he was napping, his office floor seemed an odd place to do it.

I dashed back to the front door, arriving just as a small woman with white hair turned briskly up the walk. She was wearing a powder-blue jogging suit and clean white walking shoes, and was slightly out of breath.

"Mrs. Petrocelli?"

"Hello. Are you here to see Leo?"

"Mrs. Petrocelli, I think your husband's had an accident."

A second passed as my remark registered. Then she was hurrying past me into the house.

"Leo? Leo!"

I stayed right behind her.

"In the back, Mrs. Petrocelli. His office. I saw him through a rear window."

She dashed ahead of me into the room and before I reached the door I heard her scream his name.

"Call 911, Mrs. Petrocelli."

She was kneeling over him, stroking his face.

"Mrs. Petrocelli?"

She looked up with frightened eyes.

"Call 911. I'll see to your husband."

She started across the room; I touched her arm.

"Not here. Better use another phone."

She was gone on her springy shoes, soundlessly.

Petrocelli had stopped breathing and I found no pulse in any of the usual places. His skin bore a slightly pinkish tint, not unlike Reza JaFari's the night of his death. Somewhere in the room was the unfamiliar scent I'd pick up near JaFari's body.

There were brown stains on the beige carpet, streaking away from the body as if they'd been made with a splash. Otherwise, the room was neat as a pin. If there was anything odd about it— other than a dead man laying at my feet—it was the file cabinet. One drawer had been left open a few inches, another was closed but with one of the file folders caught between drawer and frame.

I began CPR and was still at it when the paramedics arrived. It was déjà vu all over again, as the quipsters like to say—a sequel, Hollywood-style, but without the requisite happy ending.

Mrs. Petrocelli huddled next to me the whole time, holding her husband's cold hand and calling his name again and again. It sounded like a stuck record, except that the sound got more frightened and more lonely each time I heard it.

I asked the paramedics to treat the space as a crime scene and to call in a homicide detective, which didn't exactly allay Mrs. Petrocelli's anxiety.

She seized my wrist with her tiny hand.

"What are you saying?"

"I'm just being cautious, Mrs. Petrocelli."

I told her who I was and reminded her that we had spoken a few days earlier on the phone, when her husband was running an errand at the Writer's Guild.

"I think we should get out of here and let the paramedics do their work."

"No, I'm staying."

"There's nothing you can do here."

She didn't move.

"Maybe I can ask a favor of you, then."

She gave me a questioning look.

"I know it's not a good time. But if you could—"

She had knelt down beside her husband again, shoulder to shoulder with one of the paramedics.

"Please save him," she said. "Please."

The paramedic gently pushed her aside, reaching for a medical kit.

"Mrs. Petrocelli." I lifted her by her arm. "We're in the way here."

"I feel I have to do something."

"Take a minute and do something for me, then. While they work to save your husband."

"What is it?"

"Over here."

I led her in a wide path around the area where her husband lay to his writing desk and the adjacent file cabinet.

"How well do you know your husband's office?"

"I do all his filing. I tidy up here almost every day. He won't let the housekeeper touch it."

"If you would, take a quick survey and tell me if you find anything missing."

"You think someone might have—?"

"It's possible."

Her scared eyes were back on her husband.

"Mrs. Petrocelli—it might be important."

Her mouth tightened awkwardly into a brave smile.

"All right."

"Without touching anything, please."

Her eyes roved his big desk, where several scripts with different-colored binders were stacked to one side against the wall. Various books were held up by heavy bronze bookends—Lajos Egri's *The Art of Dramatic Writing*, William Campbell's *The Hero With a Thousand Faces*, Eugene Vale's *The Technique of Screenplay Writing*, Strunk and White's *The Elements of Style*, a good thesaurus, an unabridged Oxford dictionary. In a far corner lay a tattered copy of the shooting script for *Network*, autographed by its author, Paddy Chayevsky. An old Smith Corona electric anchored the desk front and center, where a computer might have been in the workroom of a younger writer. On the wall were several plaques—Oscar nominations and Writer's Guild awards.

"Leo's scripts are gone."

"Which scripts would those be, Mrs. Petrocelli?"

"Copies of his most recent one, including the master."

"Did it have a title?"

"*Over the Wall*. Though he's not thrilled with it."

"Sounds like it might be a prison movie."

"Yes, in a way. But it's really more about what happens after the convict escapes. He's terminally ill, you see, and he's never seen his grandchild. So he escapes in the hope he can hold his grandchild in his arms just once before he dies. There's this mean prison warden who goes after him—but I'm sure you don't want to hear me tell you the whole story. Leo is so much better at it than me. He can sum it up for you in one line."

"I believe they call that a logline description."

"I think you're right. Leo says that's what they want these days—a one-line concept." She smiled with a bit of mischief. "He says it's because these young executives are functionally illiterate, and have the attention spans of gnats. That many of them can't even write a memo that meets basic grammatical standards."

"Times have changed, I guess."

Her eyes grew worried again, edging toward the paramedics.

"Why isn't Leo waking up? Why is it taking them so long?"

I steered her by the elbow toward the four-drawer file cabinet.

"If you would, Mrs. Petrocelli, take a quick look through his files."

I pulled open each drawer for her, using a tissue to keep my fingerprints off the handle.

"There are so many," she said. "I don't—"

She paused as she looked through a drawer marked WGA.

"How strange—all his Writer's Guild files are gone."

"Did he keep his script registration receipts in this drawer?"

"No. He keeps those in a wall safe. He's always been very protective of those."

"He would have registered his latest script?"

"Oh, yes. I went down to the guild with him. He's very proud of that script."

"When was that?"

"He's had the idea forever but never got around to writing it. Then, right after he was diagnosed with prostate cancer, he just sat down and wrote it out, all in a fever. Finished a rough draft in two or three weeks. Then he went in for the surgery."

"That was about the time he met Reza JaFari, wasn't it? Pardon me, Raymond Farr."

"Thereabouts, yes. Why?"

"Just curious."

I escorted her from the room, doing my best to block her view of her husband, and into the living room.

"What time did you go out this afternoon, Mrs. Petrocelli?"

"Shortly after noon."

I glanced at my watch.

"You were gone two hours?"

"I went out for a light lunch, then a long walk. I walk for half an hour each morning, and try to do an hour in the afternoon."

"But not Leo?"

"I try to get him to go, but his knees aren't good. He walks up to Wilshire Boulevard each morning to buy the trade papers, but that's about it. I do wish he'd get more exercise."

She glanced down the hallway, where one of the paramedics was shaking his head.

"Was your husband expecting any visitors this afternoon?"

Her eyes stayed on the paramedics, while her voice grew small and distant.

"Not that I know of, Mr. Justice."

Through the window, I watched an unmarked police car pull into the driveway. A good-looking, crew-cut detective got out the driver's side. He was about my age and height, with roughly the same coloring, but knew how to dress.

I stepped out to meet him on the porch. I told him how I happened to be there and suggested he treat the carpet stains near the body as potential evidence. He was a low-key, amiable guy who asked the right questions and listened well.

He went inside and spoke briefly with Mrs. Petrocelli. When he went down the hallway to check on her husband, she followed him, and a moment later she burst into tears.

I didn't need to hear or see any more to know that they have given up on Petrocelli. I found a phone and called Claude De-Winter.

I got his beeper but he got back to me within the minute, demanding to know the whereabouts of Danny Romero.

"He's in the city, DeWinter. He's not going anywhere. Stop worrying."

"I get paid to worry."

"I hope you get paid a lot."

"Stop fucking with me, Justice. Where are you?"

I told him.

"Petrocelli? The old writer who was at the party?"

"That's the one."

"So what's he telling you that he's not telling me?"

"He's not telling me anything. He's dead."

The line was silent for a second or two.

"My guess is he died the same way JaFari died, assisted by the same person. You want the address here?"

"What do you think?"

I gave it to him, and he asked me to stay put until he got there. I said I would, and used the time to poke around.

For the most part, the kitchen was as spic and span as you'd expect of someone who kept her husband's office shipshape and wore squeaky-clean walking shoes. Still, I saw a few telltale signs of disorder that reminded me of the mishandled file drawers in Petrocelli's office.

A jar of instant coffee sat on the white tile counter, the lid slightly askew and a sprinkling of dark crystals visible at its base. In the drainer were two coffee cups and a spoon. They appeared to have been washed and rinsed, rather hurriedly from the looks of the water drops splashed around the sink and on the floor below.

I put my hand to a tea kettle on the stove and found it warm.

In a waste can beneath the kitchen sink was a dish towel, wadded up and shoved deep beneath a pile of trash. I shook it gently open; brown stains covered most of it, similar in color to those on the carpet in Petrocelli's office. From the towel, I picked up a now-familiar scent. When I held the towel to my nose, the odor deepened. It was a sharp, bitter smell that vaguely reminded me of almonds.

I found a plastic Baggie in a drawer, dropped the towel into it, and delivered it to the crew-cut detective, letting him know what I'd seen in the kitchen. I also asked him if he'd smelled anything unusual in the room where Petrocelli died. He said he hadn't, and wanted to know why I'd brought it up. When I told him, he came back with three words.

"Sounds like cyanide."

"Then why can't you smell it?"

"Only one in three people have the nose to pick up the scent. If that's what it is, I guess you're one of them. Thanks for letting me know."

When I went back out, Mrs. Petrocelli was sitting on the couch sobbing. A black policewoman was sitting next to her, holding her hand. I noticed two patrol cars out front, and more uniformed cops down the hall. The Beverly Hills PD worked fast.

The sobbing diminished, becoming choked and intermittent. Then all I heard was soft weeping, no louder than a whisper.

"Mrs. Petrocelli?"

She looked up.

"I'm sorry. Just one more question."

She nodded remotely.

"When you left for your walk this afternoon, did you leave two coffee cups and a spoon in the sink?"

"I did up all the dishes before I went out."

"No coffee cups?"

"I keep a very tidy kitchen, Mr. Justice. Leo likes that."

"I'm sorry about your husband. He seemed like a very fine man."

"I have to call the children. That's going to be the hardest part."

I nodded, feeling clumsy and useless. I found a corner to myself and made some notes. The crew-cut detective came back out, and I told him about the missing files and scripts. I suggested he have Mrs. Petrocelli open the wall safe so he could take the remaining WGA file with him as possible evidence. I also suggested that Mrs. Petrocelli might be safer staying elsewhere, in case the intruder came back for the file he or she had missed.

As we finished talking, Lieutenant DeWinter arrived. He was chomping gum and carrying an unpressed jacket over one shoulder. The two detectives walked alone down the hall and stuck their heads in the door to look at the body.

When they came back the younger cop thanked me for my help, then went away again.

"I guess you got yourself a fan club," DeWinter said.

"They appreciate raw genius when they see it."

"Maybe you should have been a cop."

"My old man was a cop. Until I was seventeen, I figured I'd be just like him."

"What made you change your mind, hotshot?"

"I caught him raping my little sister. I pumped six loads into his chest from his thirty-eight Detective Special, then used it to turn his face to mush. It put a kink in my career plans."

DeWinter swallowed hard, possibly his gum.

"What a load of bullshit."

"Have it your way, Lieutenant."

I started to leave him, with no particular destination, but he held my arm.

"You do time?"

"Justifiable homicide."

"Sounds fair."

"Not to my little sister."

I'd said all I cared to on the subject, so I changed it.

"What about the Grolsch bottle I gave you, Lieutenant? The one the old lady picked up in the canyon."

"What about it?"

There was a new kind of uneasiness in his voice now.

"The lab results—are they back?"

"Not yet."

He reached for a new stick of gum faster than usual.

"It's taking a while, wouldn't you say?"

He folded the gum up against his teeth a section at a time until he'd fed the whole stick into his mouth.

"The bottle's been misplaced."

"Say what?"

"Relax, Justice. We'll find it."

He said it without his usual bombast.

"Nice work, Lieutenant."

I opened my notebook and started writing.

"You can't wait to write this story, can you, Justice? Another Keystone Kops caper. Another broadside against the LAPD."

"Maybe you should worry less about your image, Lieutenant, and more about how your department handles evidence."

"Maybe I should worry about how you happen to be in the immediate vicinity of another stiff."

"I dropped by about an hour ago. Found the front door ajar. Went around back, looked through a window. Saw Petrocelli face up on the carpet, where he is now."

"You and Petrocelli buddies?"

"I had a few questions about his relationship with Reza JaFari."

"I interviewed Petrocelli the night we found JaFari's body. He told me he barely knew him."

I slapped my notebook shut and gazed stupidly at him with a Howdy Doody smile.

"Gee, Lieutenant. I guess that's all we need to know, then."

I started past him but felt his big hand on my arm again. That didn't surprise me, but the respect in his voice did.

"Maybe we should stop fighting each other, Justice."

"Why should we do something as reasonable as that, Lieutenant?"

"Frankly, I could use your help on this."

"No kidding."

"Tell me what you know."

"I gave you the Grolsch bottle, Lieutenant. Maybe you should go find it and make sure it gets to the lab."

"Even if it does, that bottle could have come from anywhere. It's got no proven connection to JaFari's death. And if it does turn out to have some connection, let's not forget that I found bottles of Grolsch in Daniel Romero's refrigerator."

"JaFari's refrigerator, Lieutenant. Danny Romero was just staying there."

"And where's he staying now?"

He'd worked me nicely into a corner. I decided to gamble on the truth.

"The infectious diseases ward at Cedars-Sinai."

"Since when?"

"Couple hours ago."

"And before that?"

"Palm Springs, with me."

"What were you doing at the Springs?"

"Getting some sun."

"Why do I have this feeling you're blowing smoke up my ass?"

"Do you really want to pull Romero out of the hospital, Lieutenant? Based on the evidence you have against him?"

"I want to talk to him again. Clear up a few things."

"The last thing Danny needs right now is you leaning on him. He's not going anywhere, believe me."

"That's what you said the last time."

"He's sick, he can barely walk." I did my best to find the centers of his eyes. "A few more days, that's all."

"I can't spend much more time on this case, Justice. Not after the coroner wrote it off to natural causes, even if that's bogus. As it is, I'm squeezing this one in between other assignments."

"Why?"

"If I told you, you'd laugh."

"Try me."

"Because I want the same thing you do."

"The truth."

"Yes—if only to give Hosain JaFari some peace. If I ever lost a kid of mine under similar circumstances, I'd want somebody to do the same for me."

I believed him, even though I still didn't like him much.

"How's Mr. JaFari holding up?"

"Better than before."

"Maybe he'll talk to me now about his son."

DeWinter slid the jacket off his shoulder and reached into a pocket. He handed me a business card.

"That's the family restaurant. A few blocks from here, on Wilshire. Be nice to him. I hear otherwise, and I stop doing favors for your friend in the hospital."

I glanced at the card, slipped it into my shirt pocket.

"Was Reza JaFari cremated?"

"Muslims don't cremate."

"They planted him, then?"

DeWinter nodded his big head.

"Did you keep tissue and blood samples? Or did you lose those too?"

"We got 'em."

"Find the Grolsch bottle, Lieutenant. Have the contents checked for cyanide. Then decide if maybe you should order the blood and tissue samples tested."

"And if nothing turns up?"

"I'll buy you a decent tie."

I got as far as the front door when I heard my name.

"Justice—"

"Yeah, Lieutenant."

"My old man was a cop, too. A good cop."

"A perfect father, too, I'll bet."

"Damn close."

"That's nice, Lieutenant. We'll have to get together some time and swap family memories."

Then I was out the door and heading down the winding walkway between the pretty yellow roses, while a coroner's van pulled up out front with a body bag for Leonardo Petrocelli.

# Thirty-six

HOSAIN JAFARI'S restaurant occupied a corner of Wilshire Boulevard in the golden triangle district of Beverly Hills, a few blocks west of the fabled shops on Rodeo Drive.

A sign overhead told me the restaurant, like the family, was Persian. Another in the window bore one word: CLOSED.

I walked around back just the same. There was a black Cadillac parked in the alley and the delivery door was propped open behind a locked outer door with security bars and a screen. Through the screen I could see a narrow concrete corridor stacked with cartons and crates, lit by a dim yellow bulb. I rang the bell.

A few seconds later I saw Hosain JaFari coming toward me, clutching a meat cleaver in his right hand. He wore a fresh white apron, stained with blood and sauces, over gray slacks and a white dress shirt. The sleeves were rolled up, showing his thick, hairy forearms.

"We ordered no delivery today."

"It's Benjamin Justice, Mr. JaFari."

He came closer to the sunlight and I could see the toll that grief had taken. The passion in his dark eyes had dimmed; his face, even his stocky body, seemed softened by sadness if that, in fact, was the burden he was carrying.

"We met last week at your son's apartment."

"Yes, I remember. What do you want with me, Mr. Justice?"

"To talk about Reza, if you're up to it."

"Please, leave us alone."

"I may be writing about your son, Mr. JaFari. I hoped you might tell me more about him."

"You plan to write about Reza? Why?"

"He seems to be in the middle of an interesting story."

"He was of my flesh and my blood. Not a piece of information for your article. I ask you to leave him in peace. Can you not do that?"

"I'm afraid I can't."

His eyes searched my face.

"You seem very determined about this."

"I am."

"The one great thing about this country, Mr. Justice, is the freedom. The exchange of information, ideas."

He reached for the screen door, unlatched it.

"I am not happy about this story you plan to write. But if you must do it, then let us talk."

His civility was encouraging, but my wariness remained. I remembered the way he'd exploded at the end of a short fuse, attacking Danny Romero with his bare hands.

I stepped down and waited while he locked the door behind us. Then I followed him along the cool, dank passageway. A familiar smell pervaded the air, a pungent mix of meat juices, grease, garbage, and disinfectant. It reminded me of every restaurant I'd washed dishes in as a kid back in Buffalo, except spicier.

JaFari led me into the kitchen, where a rack of beef ribs lay on an expansive butcher block table. He raised his arm and brought it down with a *whack*, wielding the cleaver with power and precision.

"How did you know I was here, Mr. Justice?"

"I was passing by. I saw your car. Do you by any chance know Leonardo Petrocelli?"

"Petrocelli?" He pronounced it carefully, in his clipped accent. "I'm sorry. The name means nothing to me."

"I was just at his house. He knew your son."

"My son was acquainted with many people." JaFari sighed deeply, painfully. "And I knew almost none of them."

"Petrocelli died earlier today. Or perhaps he was killed."

"He was a young man?"

"No."

Without being asked, JaFari said, "I was with my family all morning, Mr. Justice. We were at the *masjid*, the mosque, to worship. Then I took them home. Then I came here."

His eyes roved the kitchen.

"I cook. My wife, she is good with the customers. My children with the service. Me, I cook. So I come here alone and I prepare food and I try not to think about what has happened to us."

"What time did you arrive here, Mr. JaFari?"

"You talk like a policeman."

"You seem uneasy with the question."

He reached for another slab of meat, threw it down in front of him, and hacked it into pieces.

"I have been here for perhaps one hour. Maybe longer. I did not look at my watch."

"Chopping meat?"

"Also preparing the vegetables, the sauces."

"Your restaurant is closed."

"My family will come here later. We will eat together, as a family should. Some close friends will join us, perhaps."

"You said you were with your wife and daughters this morning, then came here about an hour ago."

"Yes."

"That leaves a gap in between, doesn't it?"

"No, I do not think so."

"What were you doing, say, between noon and one P.M.?"

I saw his fist tighten on the meat cleaver, his face set with anger.

"I was praying, Mr. Justice."

"Alone?"

"Yes."

"You told me you prayed this morning, at the mosque."

"I said that I went to the *masjid* to worship, Mr. Justice."

"You happened to be praying alone, then, in the early afternoon?"

"As a Muslim, I pray five times each day. Before sunrise. Noon. Afternoon. Sunset. Before bed. Always I have prayed, even before my son—"

The words stopped.

"Was murdered?"

"Is that what you feel happened, Mr. Justice?"

"I think it's probable."

"The official people believe it was this terrible disease, this thing called AIDS, that killed him."

"Do you believe that, Mr. JaFari?"

"I no longer know what to believe, except that there is a better life after this one, and my son is now there. As I will one day be, if I live in this one as I should."

He looked away from me, grabbed another rack of beef, turned it so the ribs were perpendicular to his waist.

"I bring my family here to make a better life, Mr. Justice. But now our dream is shattered. The paradise we hoped to find here does not exist. I was foolish to think it did."

"What were you expecting, Mr. JaFari, when you left your homeland?"

"Not all this violence, this spiritual emptiness, this greed. I accept my part, my blame. Never should I have brought my family so close to this place called Hollywood, this terrible seducer that drew my son away from us, where he got this evil sickness they say killed him."

He looked at me again, his eyes revealing his pain, yet hiding something as well.

"Yet I am not sure he even had this disease. How would he get it?"

"You knew him, Mr. JaFari, I didn't."

He shook his head slowly, resolutely.

"He was my son, but I did not know him. Now I do not know how to think about him. Who was this beautiful boy who became a man I did not know?"

"Perhaps if he hadn't grown up having to lie about who he was, what he felt, deception wouldn't have come so easily to him."

He raised the cleaver and resumed hacking. Each time he brought it down, I sensed more fury in his movements.

"Do you wish to insult me, Mr. Justice? On top of all that has happened?"

I kept my eye on the heavy knife in his hand, knowing how thin a line I was walking.

"I understand that in your culture, homosexuality is considered a very great sin."

"By Muslims? Of course. The *Qur'an* says very clearly that God created women to be the mates of men, that we must not abandon them to be with other males."

"Yet between grown men and boys in the Middle East, it goes on all the time, hidden and not spoken about."

"This kind of talk disgusts me, Mr. Justice. I see no reason for it."

"The boy brothels of Thailand and the Philippines are filled with wealthy visitors from around the world, Mr. JaFari, along with the houses that offer young girls. Many of those visitors are married men from the Arab region. Sexual hypocrisy among certain sheiks from the oil countries is almost a way of life. It's an old, old story."

He stopped chopping, took a deep breath, then showed me the calm, dark centers of his eyes.

"There are more than one billion Muslims in the world, Mr. Justice. Most of them live outside the Middle East. Only a minority are Arab."

"Yet Reza grew up there."

"Until he was fourteen, yes."

"In an atmosphere of sexual repression."

"What is your point, Mr. Justice?"

"Perhaps if your son had felt more free to be himself, less need to lie, he would have turned out differently. Perhaps he'd even be alive."

"If he was the way you suggest, homosexual"—he spoke the word as if it were poison on his tongue—"then it is perhaps better that he is dead."

"And what about the part of him that was Jewish, Mr. JaFari? Do you feel the same way about that?"

He stared down at the bloody meat for a long moment before glancing my way.

"How do you know about this?"

"I'm a reporter, Mr. JaFari. I ask a lot of questions. Sometimes, if I'm lucky, they lead to interesting answers."

He slammed the cleaver down into the wood, hard enough that it stuck. His eyes slid away from me as he spoke.

"You blame me for what has happened to my son?"

"I know that it's usually the children who suffer the most from their parents' lies. They lose trust. They lose faith. They learn to imitate."

JaFari grabbed a pile of sliced ribs and tossed them one by one onto the hot grill. Tongues of flame appeared, licking the red meat.

"When I met my wife, I did not know she was a Jew. We fell very deeply in love."

"It's permissible for a Muslim to marry a Jew?"

"We have our differences with the ways Jews and Christians have interpreted and modified the teachings of the ancient prophets. But a true Muslim accepts them as People of the Book, recognizing that Jesus and the biblical prophets were true prophets of God, divinely inspired."

"And intermarriage?"

"If a Muslim woman marries a Jewish man, he must convert to her faith. But a Muslim man such as myself may marry a Jewish woman without her giving up her religion."

"Your wife remained Jewish, then."

"Secretly, for her safety. I wished my children to be raised as Muslims, so we never told them. It is one reason we came here, where my wife could feel safer, away from the political hatred in my country. In her heart, she is a Jew. But for me, for our marriage, she pretends otherwise."

He grew silent and thoughtful before he spoke again.

"I suppose you are right, Mr. Justice. We should have told the children long ago. It is not something of which I am now proud."

"Reza knew, Mr. JaFari."

He stopped tossing meat on the grill to look curiously at me.

"Reza? That he was part Jewish?" He shook his head. "No, that's not possible."

"He had an accident, Mr. JaFari. Ten years ago, in Mexico. There were blood tests. He found out."

He lay the last piece of meat on the grill, poking at it mechanically as he looked increasingly troubled.

"You are certain of this?"

"Completely."

He spoke so quietly now I had trouble hearing him over the sizzle of the meat.

"This I never knew."

He walked to a sink, washed his hands, filled a glass with water, drank it down.

"A Jew gave blood, Mr. Jafari—saved your son's life."

"This is also true?"

"Yes."

JaFari stood facing the sink, his head hanging.

"All this time, Reza knew."

"Along with the deception he'd grown up with back in his homeland, where older men, married men, had used him like a woman."

He winced as if my words were a whip.

"And this you also know to be true?"

"He spoke about it to a friend of his named Lawrence Teal."

JaFari looked over at me, imploringly.

"You will write about all this? Is it necessary? To hurt his family again, after they have suffered so much already? I say this not for me, Mr. Justice, but for my family, especially for my wife."

"I'll try to sort out the truth in this whole mess, Mr. JaFari. Then I'll write what feels necessary to tell the story."

JaFari returned to the grill, where he flipped the seared ribs with long tongs, causing the flames to jump and the meat to hiss. I sensed the anger rising in him again.

"When you write about my son, Mr. Justice, will you write about his life here—about the part we didn't know? About this disease they say he had?"

"Possibly."

JaFari stepped past me and opened the door of a massive refrigerator. On the top shelf, he reached for a plastic bucket filled with a brown sauce.

As he brought the bucket down, I glimpsed a six-pack of beer deep in the shadows of the cooler. Two bottles were missing.

As a devout Muslim, Hosain JaFari would neither drink alcohol nor serve it in his restaurant. That made the presence of the beer surprising enough. But it was the brand and the bottles that intrigued me—the Dutch import, Grolsch, in the emerald-green bottles with the trademark clasping caps.

I turned my eyes away as JaFari shut the door, and I couldn't be certain if he caught me looking or not. But there was a new tension in his manner as he set down the bucket of sauce and picked up the cleaver again, even though there was no more beef to be cut that I could see.

"I have many things to do, Mr. Justice. Perhaps it is time for you to go."

I walked down the dimly lit passageway to the rear door with JaFari a step or two behind me, the lethal cleaver hanging at his side, sticky with blood.

Then I was in the alley, listening to the screen door being secured behind me, relieved to be out of there in one piece.

# Thirty-seven

G ORDON CANTWELL was waiting for me when I arrived at
Morton's, standing at a solid oak bar with no cheap brands
behind it and a leggy blonde perched on a stool at the corner,
where she could be seen by most of the room.

It was a few minutes past eight. Cantwell was doing his best to
chat the lady up, leaning close while she sipped a yellow liqueur
that looked like it might be Pernod.

He was dressed entirely in black—slacks, shirt, jacket, Hush
Puppies, all looking freshly purchased—and his reddish beard
had a neat, new shape. As he chatted animatedly, it was with a
sense of confidence I hadn't seen in him before. He seemed blissfully unaware that his clothes were all wrong for summer, that
his nose hairs needed trimming, and his toupee needed serious
readjustment.

Also, that the woman was totally uninterested. Her eyes left
Cantwell frequently to check the entrance, perhaps for a date she
was expecting, or a celebrity worth looking at, or an agent or
producer who wouldn't mind spending a few minutes over a
drink with an attractive young woman with Hollywood ambitions.

I'd heard about Morton's, where Hollywood's elite gathered to
see and be seen, and where the less elite were seated in the back,
near the kitchen.

As I approached, Cantwell greeted me with a great brio.

"Benjamin! So good to see you!"

He had me by my upper arm, which he used like a wrench to
turn me toward the woman.

"Benjamin's here to interview me for *Angel City*. About my project with Tom, the one I was telling you about."

"Tom Cruise," the woman said, as if mildly amused.

"Exactly."

Cantwell smiled like a well-fed cat; I could almost hear him purring.

"Nice to meet you, Ben." The woman slipped off her stool without shaking my hand. "You'll excuse me?"

She turned in the direction of the rest rooms.

"I was going to give you my number," Cantwell called after her, patting his coat pockets hurriedly.

"I'll catch you later," the woman said, and disappeared around a corner.

"Nice lady." Cantwell worked hard to keep the cool in his voice. "Actress. Diana something."

"I'm sure she'll connect with you later."

"No doubt." He winked. "She seemed like the hungry type."

"Speaking of hungry . . ."

What I really wanted was a drink, but not at the well-stocked bar, where soft backlight turned rows of bottles into lovely shapes full of terrible temptation.

Cantwell took the cue, signaling the host with a gesture toward the dining area.

The host was a trim, clean-cut young man without a hair out of place who might have stepped from a *GQ* ad. He led us across a floor of large tiles in earth tones with inlaid wood, finally stopping at a table in the northeast corner of the room. It was the table nearest the swinging kitchen doors, where a small army of waiters, waitresses, busboys, and runners glided in, out, and about in a silent, skillful ballet.

The host pulled out a chair for Cantwell.

"Don't you have anything closer to the front?"

"I'm afraid all our other tables are reserved, Mr. Cantwell."

"I saw one near the bar that's been empty for some time."

"That's being held for Mr. Eastwood."

Cantwell's eyes scanned the room. They had grown nervous, the confidence waning.

"I see a booth on the side."

"For Penny Marshall. I'm sure you understand, Mr. Cantwell."

"Do you read the trade papers, by any chance?"

"Not as a rule, Mr. Cantwell."

"Perhaps you should."

The unflappable host pulled back the chair another inch and stood holding it as if nothing short of a cannon blast would move him.

"Next time," Cantwell said, "I'm sure you'll be able to find me a better location."

"We'll certainly do our best, Mr. Cantwell."

Cantwell took his seat like a field general who had survived a small skirmish but suffered an embarrassing wound in the process. I pulled back my own chair and sat opposite him.

"Next time, I'll show up with Tom and Nicole," Cantwell said. "That should get his attention."

The restaurant looked like a hothouse for social climbing, where one's status could either blossom in the heat or wither quickly and die. It was comprised of a single room with a high, arched ceiling of natural wood planks and beams that allowed the chatter to rise, accentuating the impression of general hubbub without interfering with ground-level conversation. Three towering potted plants were spaced at even intervals down the center, dividing the room like demarcations on the power scale.

Large abstract and impressionist artworks adorned the white walls, along with six huge mirrors toward one end. Behind us, in the deepest corner, was a framed word painting several feet high, its message arranged on three lines:

*MEN PROGRAMMED*
*TO CRAVE WOMEN*
*AND VICE VERSA*

I guessed it was political art of some sort, probably created by someone known primarily to critics and people who have the money to buy such things. As a diner, I was more accustomed to wall slogans in the vein of TOP SIRLOIN DINNER $7.95.

A waitress arrived, laid menus on the pastel linen tablecloth, and recited the specials. She was a pleasingly plump woman with a pretty face and a straightforward, intelligent manner, wearing a white apron over her white blouse, black necktie, and pants. She went away and came back a minute or two later with her pencil and notepad ready.

By then, I had my own notebook open on the table, and a pen beside it.

For appetizers, Cantwell ordered an artichoke heart salad for thirteen dollars, while I took the chilled asparagus for slightly less. Two entrée items caught my eye—dry aged New York steak and

China air-dried duck, each running close to thirty bucks—but just the names made me reach for my water glass. I opted for the moister-sounding Atlantic salmon, while Cantwell selected the Maryland crab cakes, which simplified the wine order. He allowed me the honor, and I asked the waitress to bring us her best bottle of Pinot Grigio for under fifty dollars, not wanting to soak *Angel City* or Cantwell too much, depending on who reached for the check.

"I noticed you didn't bring the script," I said.

"Ah, that." Color seeped into the spaces between his freckles. "Paramount asked me to keep it under wraps for a while. Feeling a bit protective, I guess. Major project and all."

He dropped his eyes uncomfortably before continuing.

"May we go off the record for a moment?"

"It's becoming a habit of mine."

"To be frank, Tom's people weren't too happy to see the stories in the trade papers."

"I didn't see anything that should upset them."

"The problem is, we don't actually have a deal memo yet—there are still a few details to be worked out."

"You're telling me you jumped the gun."

Cantwell leaned toward me, very man-to-man.

"Perhaps I was a bit hasty. But I can assure you it's a done deal—slam dunk all the way."

The waitress uncorked the wine and poured an inch into my glass, turning the bottle just enough at just the right moment so that not a drop was lost.

I sniffed and sampled it for her benefit.

"Let the nectar flow."

When our glasses were half-filled and she was gone, I offered Cantwell a toast.

"To your future as a screenwriter and producer, Gordon."

We tapped glasses and drank. Cantwell set his down, but I kept mine hoisted.

"And to the memory of Leonardo Petrocelli."

Cantwell had reached for the bread basket. He held it in midair a moment, not looking at me, before setting it back down.

"Something's happened to Leo?"

"You didn't hear?"

"No."

"He was found dead at home this afternoon."

"My God! Poor Leo."

"To be more accurate, I was the one who found him."

"His heart?"

"They're not sure at this point. I imagine they'll be doing an autopsy."

"An autopsy? Is that customary? Someone of that age, who's had so many health problems?"

"I believe foul play is suspected—some things were missing from his office."

"Burglary, then." He shook his head. "God, this city. Nobody's safe any more."

"They think it happened in the early afternoon. You were probably doing lunch with Tom and Nicole."

Cantwell laughed.

"The life of a screenwriter isn't nearly as glamorous as one might expect, Mr. Justice. I was home alone all day, writing. I'm already at work on my next script."

"You're a very productive man."

"You know what Oliver Stone said when he was asked the secret to being a successful screenwriter."

"I'm afraid I don't."

" 'Keep your butt in the chair!' "

We laughed together. Then Cantwell grew more serious, and raised his glass.

"To Leo, then. A fine writer in his day. A good man."

We clinked glasses again. I finished mine off and poured another. The waitress set our appetizers before us, freshened Cantwell's glass, and disappeared again.

"By the way," I said, "I've been doing some research at the Margaret Herrick Library."

"Fine place. Great organization."

"I hadn't realized that Constance Fairbridge was your grandmother."

"Yes, as a matter of fact." He buttered a slice of sourdough bread. "You're looking into my family background?"

"Templeton and I feel you're an important part of our story, Gordon. We like to be thorough."

"I'm flattered."

He speared a chunk of artichoke heart.

"Grandmother was rather well-known toward the end of the silent era. I guess you could say my roots in the cinema go back almost to its beginning."

I wrote that down while he looked on, pleased.

"Are you and Mrs. Fairbridge close?"

The section of artichoke heart disappeared into his mouth; he talked as he ate.

"More so in years past. She took me to the movies constantly when I was a little boy. But she was never quite the same after—"

He looked as if he'd bitten off more than he wished to chew.

"After your mother died?"

Cantwell swallowed with some effort, then cleared his throat with wine.

"Yes. Her mind—Grandmother hardly knows me anymore."

"She does seem awfully confused at times."

"You've met her?"

"The evening of the party. As Templeton and I were driving down the hill. We literally ran into her as she crossed the road. Then, more recently, when I went to check on her, she chased me off."

"God, she's still wandering around at night. Those damn trails of hers, up and down the canyon. I've tried to get her to stay in. You struck her with your car?"

"Almost. She wasn't hurt—not even her bottles."

He laughed, shaking his head.

"Those bottles." He dabbed his mouth with his starched linen napkin, then spread it in his lap. "I'll drop by first thing in the morning, see how she's doing. I've tried to get her into a home, where she'd be safe."

"Not to mention the rest of us."

Cantwell smiled grimly.

"Poor Grandmother."

We finished up our appetizers and the empty plates were whisked away by efficient brown hands.

"Your mother's death must have been awfully hard on you as well."

Cantwell chewed slowly, saying nothing. Toward the front of the room, Jack Nicholson stood to leave boisterously with four others. To my surprise, Cantwell didn't even notice. A half minute passed that way.

"Gordon?"

His eyes flickered in my direction but didn't stay.

"Any time a child loses a parent," he said, "it's traumatic."

"But in your case, the circumstances were—"

"Of course, it was horrible."

"You were ten, I believe."

"Ten, yes. To be truthful, I doubt I'll ever get the memory of it out of my mind." Cantwell's eyes lost their focus as he spoke. "Seeing her there, lying on the floor in her blue nightgown, her face against the cold tiles. No response when I cried out to her. Her skin so cool when I touched her. The radio in the background—Frankie Laine singing the theme song from *High Noon*."

His eyes returned to the present, looking as moist as the grilled salmon that was being placed in front of me on a bed of sautéed lentils.

"To this day, I still can't listen to that song."

He waited to speak again until his plate of crab cakes was in front of him and the waitress was gone.

"Yes, my mother's death was quite a shock, Mr. Justice. After my father abandoned us, she was everything to me."

"I'm surprised you kept the house, given the memories it must hold."

"Grandmother wanted to sell it, but I begged her not to. She rented it out over the years, putting money into my trust. But she refused to set foot on the property. To her, the house represented . . . I'm not sure how to put it—"

"Sin?"

"You've heard her rantings, then."

"They're hard to miss."

"She never approved of my father. From what I've heard, he was a violent man. He was older, my mother just a teenager. Then, after the divorce, Grandmother seriously frowned on my mother's lifestyle."

"From all accounts, she liked a good party."

"She was fond of male company, Mr. Justice—let's put it that way. After Mother's death, Grandmother withdrew into her own world, spouting Bible verses, gradually losing touch with reality."

"But you moved back in."

"As soon as I could afford to keep it up. I always loved that house. I suppose, in a way, I consider it a shrine to my mother's failed dreams."

"Perhaps that's why you've worked so hard to be a success—to find a place in Hollywood she never did."

He brightened at the thought.

"You may be right—I never thought of it that way. I believe this magazine article of yours is developing quite nicely."

He glanced at my plate.

"Shall we eat, Mr. Justice, before our meals get cold?"

He dug into his crab cakes, while I reached for my fork. As he ate, he raised his eyes to look out across the room.

"I believe that's Quentin Tarantino. Yes, yes, it is. I believe he's looking this way."

Cantwell raised his hand and waved tentatively to an odd-looking man with messy hair and a long, pointy jaw who was seated at a table in the center of the room. Cantwell raised his hand and waved more vigorously. The man appeared to be looking past us, to the rear booths or perhaps the big painting above them.

"Yes, he's nodding," Cantwell said, although the man wasn't nodding at all. "We met a few years ago at Sundance. He speaks highly of my book." He glanced at my open notebook. "That's T-A-R-A-N-T-I-N-O."

I dutifully wrote it down.

When I'd set my pen aside, Cantwell said, "What else would you like to know, Mr. Justice? Hopefully, something of a more upbeat nature."

"You might tell me how you came to write *Nothing to Lose,* since it seems to be the screenplay of the moment."

"It's really a case of paying your dues, working hard at your craft, understanding the marketplace. And, of course, coming up with a dynamite concept."

"That's what makes it so perfect for our story." I picked up my fork. "Why don't you start from the beginning?"

Cantwell started talking, and I started eating.

# Thirty-eight

I WOKE the next morning to the sounds of a hammer and saw, and looked out to see Fred fencing in the rear yard.

I poured some coffee, then helped him finish the fence and install a swinging gate, while Maggie watched from the patio with her head on her paws, looking melancholy.

By early afternoon, dry, hot winds were kicking up, shivering the brown fronds that drooped like broken wings from the shoulders of the tallest palms along Norma Place.

I showered off the sweat and dust of work, pulled on fresh jeans and a T-shirt, slipped into a pair of old running shoes, and set out on foot for the hospital. In a knapsack, I carried trail guides and topographical maps for the southern Sierra, a couple of pens, and my notes on the Reza JaFari story.

Half a mile later, due south, I stepped through sliding glass doors into the antiseptic cool of Cedars-Sinai Medical Center. On the sixth floor, a nurse handed me the disposable latex gloves, face mask, and gown required of visitors to the infectious diseases ward.

I pulled on the protective garb in the corridor outside Danny's room, while the able-bodied shuffled past me in robes and slippers, hauling their IV drips resolutely along with them the way tiny children clutch their favorite wheeled toys.

It was then that the reality of what I was doing hit me hard enough to awaken old terrors.

Last night I'd been at Morton's, dining on chilled asparagus and grilled salmon, washing it down with good wine, finishing up with a rich crème brûlée, surrounded by the well-known and the *fabulously* dressed as they chatted about net points and gallery openings and where their favorite chef had gone.

Now, three blocks away, I was face to face with a modern plague that had already infected more than 20 million people worldwide, killing hundreds of thousands, with the infection rate projected at more than 25 million by the end of the century. As I slipped into the disposable gown, I had trouble reconciling hundred-million-dollar movie budgets and five-hundred-dollar dinner tabs with the horror and the heartbreak hidden just around the corner, in places like this.

I shoved my hands deep into the latex gloves, stretching the fingers taut, fighting the emotional vertigo that comes with trying to straddle a fractured existence, suspended between the sanity of living a lie and the madness of accepting the truth. Harry Brofsky and Alexandra Templeton had lured me out of my isolation with the best of intentions. But now I felt myself teetering dangerously on the edge again, tempted to flee, the way I had seven years ago, after Jacques had passed and my world had imploded.

I wanted to be courageous, for Danny's sake and for my own. But I didn't feel courageous at all, not for a moment. I felt small and weak and cowardly. I wanted to run.

I took a deep breath, pushed open the door to Danny's room, and stepped back into the world of the sick and dying.

Danny was propped up in a raised bed, wearing a thin cotton hospital gown, with the sheets pulled up to his waist. A needle was taped into a bruised vein in his left arm, connected by an IV tube to a hanging bottle. He had regained a little color but otherwise looked frail.

The bed next to him was empty and made up; someone had either just gone home, to ICU, or to a mortuary.

Danny smiled.

"Thanks for coming by."

"I told you I would."

"How's Maggie doing?"

I lowered the railing on the bed and sat.

"She and Fred have bonded."

His smile widened into a grin.

"No shit?"

"He dotes on her like she's his first kid."

"That's great."

I bent over and kissed him lightly on the lips.

"I brought trail guides, topo maps. I thought maybe we could plan a trip—for down the road, when you're back on your feet."

He looked at them as I held them out, then away.

"What is it, Danny?"

Even as I asked, I didn't want to know. When he looked at me again, his eyes became steady with wisdom and resolve.

"It's time you know what's going on, Ben. It's not fair otherwise."

"I thought I did know what was going on."

"Not all of it."

"What, then?"

He gestured with his head.

"Pull the sheet down."

I set the books and maps aside and took the edge of the sheet at his waist. As I drew it down, past his midsection where the hospital gown covered him, I saw what he wanted me to see—what he'd kept so well hidden until now.

His legs.

His grotesquely swollen, horribly disfigured, torturously infected, cancerous, black and purple legs.

I lowered the sheet all the way past his feet. The mass of lesions emerged from under his hospital gown and stopped at his ankles. His long, narrow feet were oddly unmarked; they were pale, delicate, almost pretty compared with the ugliness above.

The legs seemed like appendages from a different creature—elephantine in size and shape, lizardlike in texture, a lumpish mass of dying tissue and mottled blood aswirl in dark colors.

How long does one stare at such a thing? Where is the point between looking, as requested—and gaping?

I didn't know. With all I'd seen in other hospitals—with Jacques and a dozen friends who'd died slowly, miserably—I had no preparation for this. It sickened me.

"Pretty gross, huh?"

Danny smiled a little, trying to make it easier.

"KS?"

He nodded.

I'd witnessed cases of Kaposi's sarcoma, plenty of them. Jacques had developed the lesions toward the end, on his feet and neck, but relatively mild radiation treatments had eliminated them without much trouble. This was beyond anything I'd ever seen. With all the new drugs, the preventive therapies—I didn't understand.

"How did it get so bad?"

He shrugged his slim shoulders.

"I let it get out of control."

"You didn't get treatment for it?"

"I didn't get treatment at all, for anything. Not until it was too late."

"Why?"

"You know that word they use a lot—denial? Simple as that. I couldn't face the damn truth of it."

I understood how scared a man or woman could be, getting the diagnosis. Especially in years past, when it carried with it the surety of death. Medical science had never seen a disease quite so terrible, quite so devastating in the countless ways it could ravage and kill. I understood, as much as I raged silently against what he was telling me.

"I got nobody to blame but myself, Ben. After I tested positive, I went six, seven years without getting help. I did everything you're not supposed to. Dope, booze—anything to stop feeling, you know?"

I knew.

"When the first lesions showed up, I just blew it off, man. Wore long pants and pretended I didn't know they were there. When I finally got real sick and went for treatment last year, they'd spread almost all the way up."

My eyes followed the lesions up to the hem of his gown.

"Go ahead. Take a look. It's OK."

I lifted the gown to his chest.

The tumors had spread halfway between his knees and his hips. His penis and testicles had been spared, like the rest of him above; they hung untouched and peaceful below a nest of soft, dark hair as if they belonged to someone else. Someone healthy. Someone touchable.

"If you'd gone for treatment right away—"

"I might not even have AIDS yet. You and me might be packin' in right now to some choice lake up in the mountains."

"If you'd gotten on anti-virals—"

"If. *If* don't matter no more, Ben." He let out a small, ironic laugh. "Woulda, coulda, shoulda. It's too late for any of that shit."

I pulled off my mask and latex gloves and put them aside. Then I pushed his gown up higher, above his chest.

I reached first for his right nipple, pinching gently until I felt it come to life, then the left one. I ran my knuckles across the fine hairs gathered at his breastbone, and traced a line under the gentle curve of his pectorals, watching his nipples grow harder still.

"Just this once, Danny, don't ask me to stop."

He said nothing, keeping his expectant eyes on mine.

I stepped away to draw the curtain shut around us. When I turned back to him, his penis had thickened, resting nervously against his thigh.

I lifted his testicles, letting their soft weight fill the cup of my hand before I teased and fondled them. His cock twitched, then rose, pulling up out of its foreskin collar. When it was full and firm, I closed my fist around it and stroked gently, more a caress than a tug, causing Danny to cry out my name and grab my wrist, while he kept his eyes riveted to mine.

What was happening didn't feel like sexual desire to me, or even the sharp thrill of foreplay. It was something beyond that.

I wanted desperately to give him pleasure, to take him away from his discomfort and deformity for a while. I wanted him to remember for a moment that he was queer, and not to be ashamed of that, because that was a part of who he was and how he felt and it was nobody else's business to tell him who he was or how he should feel, whom he should love or how, in what way he should give or receive pleasure or affection, what he should do with his own body, or someone else's if they were willing.

Above all, I wanted him to know that someone still found him desirable, even if his body was no longer perfect.

I bent to brush his proud cock with my lips, to run the crimson head over the contours of my face like a caressing finger, to kiss the rigid shaft up and down until it quivered on the brink of spilling over, to let Danny know how much I cherished him, even as I was losing him.

*The legs. The lesions.*

They were a part of him too. The part of him that represented the horror I had tried to distance myself from for so many years, but no longer could.

My hands abandoned his genitals, gliding between his thighs until they felt the smoothness give way to the hard, shiny mass of dark lumps that his legs had become.

I ran my hand down the encrusted skin of what had once been his strong hiker's thighs, over a knee black with disease, down the cancerous ridges of his shins. Here and there, stray hairs had somehow survived, clinging like hardy weeds to the rugged landscape of his decaying flesh.

I cupped one hand under his calf, the other under his heel, and lifted his leg. I pressed my lips to the most hideous part of him, the most private part, which in some strange way had become the most beautiful.

Then I lowered his leg to the mattress and kissed my way back up to his lips, slowly, gently, savoring the taste of him with my tongue where it was safe. When I reached his midsection and upper body he was still hard, cock and nipples both still excited.

"I love you, Danny."

"You're a fool, then."

One of his hands found mine, and our fingers intertwined.

The fingers of my other hand closed around the shaft of his cock, rising and falling faster now with a relentless rhythm, tightening each time it reached the sensitive ridges of the crown, my eyes gauging the anguished pleasure on his face.

I kept at it like that minute after minute, patient and steady, until the sensation became too much for him and his semen spurted out of him, spilling onto his belly, causing him to first gasp, then whimper.

He threw his head back and clamped his eyes shut, wringing every bit of sensation he could from the moment, while tears squeezed from the corners of his eyes and ran in rivulets down his face to the pillow. Then he relaxed and I folded myself up beside him, my face against his chest, listening to the wild beating of his heart, feeling the warmth of his fever, the sweat.

He stroked my head, and his breathing gradually calmed. For minutes nothing was said. His melting semen trickled down, and I used a towel to catch it before it reached the sheets.

"Anything else I can do for you, handsome?"

"Yeah, as a matter of fact." His voice was solemn now. "But I don't think it's something you want to hear."

"Try me."

"Maybe you should get cleaned up first. Before a nurse comes in and gets an eyeful."

I pulled his gown down and the sheet up, then deposited the towel in a laundry basket marked DANGER—INFECTIOUS DISEASES before washing up at the sink.

When I was done, he patted a section of the bed, and I took my place again beside him.

"I need you to help me die, Ben."

I brushed the damp hair off his forehead and recited the convenient words I'd spoken before, to others.

"If it comes to that, I'll be there for you."

"That's not what I mean."

Suddenly, I was teetering on the edge again, and it was crumbling away beneath me.

"Maybe you'd better tell me what you mean."

"They want to cut off my legs, Ben."

I didn't move, didn't even blink. I felt like I was dropping through space, nothing to grab hold of, a free fall into nowhere and no sense of time.

I swallowed with effort, took a breath.

"They want to take the left leg first. Then, as soon as they can, the right one. As high up as possible, above the knees. They say if they don't, I won't live more than a month or two. And it won't be too much fun while it lasts."

There was no air in the space where I was falling, no light. I rose from the bed, found a part in the curtain, and pulled it open. Each breath was coming faster and deeper than the last.

"I'm not going to let 'em start cutting me up like that, Ben, a piece at a time. Not just to buy me a few extra months."

I landed. The fall was over. Now everything inside me was collapsing, disintegrating.

I made myself face him.

"We can get you into a hospice, a care facility."

He shook his head.

"No, Ben."

"There are plenty of good people who will—"

"No!"

I gnawed my fist, tasted blood. I took my hand away but didn't know what to do with it, where to put it.

"You want to go home? Back to Oklahoma?"

"Never felt like home. Not for a long time, anyway."

"The Sangre de Cristos, Milagro, back to your mother's people?"

He reached for the trail book and topo maps I'd brought, clutching them to his chest. I started to understand.

"The Sierra."

"There's this pretty little lake out of Lone Pine, not even two miles up the trail. Maggie and me used to go there all the time, on our way over the high passes. It's right here in the book."

"You're in no condition to hike."

"The doctors say they can get me up on my feet and walking pretty good in a few days. If you help me, I know I can get up to that lake. If we have to, we can rent us some horses. I got a check coming from the government. You can have it, to pay for things."

"Just to see that lake one more time?"

"Not just to see the lake, Ben. Don't you understand what I'm asking you?"

I did, all at once, completely.

"Oh, Danny."

"I've stockpiled, Ben. Barbiturates. I got enough to do the job easy."

"Danny, Danny—"

"The pills are in a plastic bag, hidden at the bottom of Maggie's dry food."

"We need to discuss alternatives—"

"I don't want alternatives! The only choices I got are to lose my legs to buy me a little time, go into a hospice now and let 'em shoot me up with morphine 'til I'm gone, or do it myself, staring up at a ceiling that don't mean nothing to me. I don't like none of those choices. Maybe some people can go out that way. But not me."

Tears brimmed over from his pleading eyes.

"Please help me, Ben. I want to do it on my own terms. I want to die looking up at the stars."

He dropped his chin, wiped away the tears.

"Can't see no stars from this damn city."

He looked up, straight into my eyes.

"I know it ain't fair to ask. But you're the only one I got. The only one I know to do this for me. All my other friends, they're all dead, or disappeared somewhere."

I wanted to speak, to stop him from saying more, but no words came.

"You don't have to stay with me, Ben. You can leave me up there. I got the whole thing planned out. The search and rescue guys can bring out my body, over the back of a mule. I don't want to cause you no trouble."

A ragged cry tore up out of my chest, sounding like it came from another dimension, escaping my throat before I could stop it.

I ripped off the paper gown, then grabbed my knapsack, intending to run from the room. But there was no way out.

Lieutenant DeWinter filled the doorway, dressed in the same kind of protective garb worn by the policewoman behind him.

I crumpled my gown into a ball, making it smaller and smaller and smaller.

"What are you doing here, DeWinter?"

"I'm here to place Danny under arrest."

DeWinter stepped past me. I followed him toward Danny's bed.

"You told me you'd give me a few days."

"That was yesterday."

"What happened?"

DeWinter ignored me, looming over the bed.

"Hello, Danny."

He glanced at the maps in Danny's hands.

"Planning on taking a trip?"

I forced myself between DeWinter and the bed.

"I worked with you, Lieutenant. We had a deal."

"We found the Grolsch bottle, Justice, the one we'd misplaced. Got it to the lab. The contents tested positive for cyanide, like you figured they would."

"And the samples from JaFari's body?"

"Yeah, we tested those too."

"Cyanide traces."

"Correct."

"That doesn't implicate Danny."

"There's more."

I waited.

"I went back into the apartment with my warrant for another look. Guess what I found in Danny's backpack? Half a pint of cyanide in a plastic bottle."

I looked at Danny. He was as calm as a mountain lake on a windless day.

"If it was there," he said, "I didn't put it there. That's all I can tell you."

"The bottle had only one set of prints. Those prints matched the ones I took off one of your empty prescription vials."

"Whoever broke in before could have gone back and put the cyanide in one of Danny's water bottles."

"That's possible."

"If Danny used cyanide to kill JaFari, he wouldn't leave it where you could find it."

"He would if he's careless."

"Where's the motive, Lieutenant?"

"I think we've nailed that one down too. You see, we found another set of Danny's prints—taken eight years ago."

He was looking straight at Danny now.

"When I was arrested up in San Francisco."

"Bingo, Danny boy."

My eyes moved from DeWinter to Danny.

"Arrested for what?"

"Tell him, Danny. Tell him about the man you beat half to death with a piece of wood the size of my arm."

"It was somebody I was involved with."

"Somebody who was putting his ding dong up your poop chute," DeWinter said.

Danny ignored him, talking to me.

"He told me he'd tested negative, that he'd taken follow-up tests. Been celibate for a year, he said. Told me he didn't like to use condoms, that they took away the pleasure, some shit like that. I was nineteen, a kid who didn't know much except that he was in love. I believed him. I trusted him."

"He infected you."

Danny nodded.

"After I got tested and found out, I put it to him. He admitted he had HIV. Said he didn't care who he infected. Somebody did it to him, and he was going to take as many guys with him as he could."

"Which is exactly what you and Reza JaFari argued about," DeWinter said, "the night before he died. It set off your rage all over again, and you figured a way to take him out. Drove him to the party, took some beer with you. One of the bottles was spiked with cyanide. Cyanide kills fast. You left him down there on Cantwell's terrace and slipped out of the house without being seen a couple hours before the party started.

"You took the poisoned bottle with you and left a second bottle in its place, half empty, as if JaFari had been drinking from that one. You wiped your prints off the first bottle and tossed it into the canyon as you drove away, figuring it would never be found."

"I argued with Reza, yeah. I hated what he was doing. But I didn't kill him. I dropped him off and came back later to give him a ride home. Just like I told you before."

"Tell it to the jury, Danny."

DeWinter signaled the policewoman, who came around the bed with a set of steel handcuffs.

"You can't take him out of here," I said. "He's too sick."

I pushed past DeWinter, toward the policewoman.

I felt DeWinter's huge hand on my collar, pulling me back. He spun me around and slammed me against the nearest wall.

"If you're smart, you'll stay where you are, Justice. We've got another set of cuffs if you're in the market for jewelry."

I watched the policewoman slip one cuff onto Danny's left wrist, ratchet it down, then attach the other to the bed rail.

"You're staying here under twenty-four-hour guard until your doctor says you can be moved," DeWinter said. "Then you're going to the jail ward at County-USC."

"He's dying," I said.

"He can die just as well there as here."

DeWinter began reading Danny his rights.

The room felt like it was spinning at crazy, topsy-turvy angles. The last thing I saw before I escaped was the resignation on Danny's face, a mask of passivity and hopelessness that couldn't quite hide the deeper fear.

Then I was running. Along the corridor, past startled nurses, through a door marked EXIT, into a stairway, and down.

Down and down and down, until finally I was bursting into dazzling sunlight, desperate for the kind of drink that would take me far, far away, to the land of the numb and the blind.

# Thirty-nine

OUTSIDE THE HOSPITAL, blustery winds continued to scorch the city, blasting every bit of moisture from the air.

I waded into the early evening traffic on San Vicente Boulevard, forcing cars to slow, daring them not to.

Rising above me was the Beverly Center, a seven-story shrine to merchandise where the fashion-addicted could worship at the alter of materialism. Fortunately, along with its quick shopping fix, the complex offered alcohol for those of us who needed something stronger than a new set of throw pillows or Calvin Klein cologne to get us through the night.

I made straight for the Hard Rock Cafe, which anchored the ground-level northwest corner.

Above the restaurant, a big-finned Cadillac convertible—metallic blue detailed with orange flames—could be seen plunging into the rooftop, like a symbol of civilization plummeting toward self-destruction. Below the Caddie, one electronic scorecard ticked off each new addition to the world's population while another kept track of the corresponding loss of rain forest acreage. The computer-fed numbers never stopped changing—a new addition and a new substraction each second—the management's way of keeping the public dutifully informed while advertising its admirable social conscience.

Inside, the early dinner crowd munched burgers and french fries, surrounded by loud music and a display of rock 'n' roll memorabilia that hung from the walls like sacred artifacts.

The bar was big and oval, womblike, with reassuring rows of

glittering bottles behind it, presided over by a tall, blond bartender with a good chest and shoulders and a solid shadow of
beard that gave some character to his well-cut face.

I leaned into the railing and demanded a double Cuervo Gold
straight up. My tone was urgent enough for him to give me a long
look before he reached for the bottle.

When he set my drink in front of me, I ordered another double. When he brought that one, the first one was gone.

"I was wondering something," I said.

"What's that, partner?"

His deep voice came with a soft drawl—Texas, maybe—and his
eyes were baby blue. He had a fine face, but no better than the
thousands of others that crowded the file drawers of casting offices around town in the form of glossy eight-by-tens.

I shifted my gaze out to the dining room.

"Where does the beef for all those burgers come from?"

He grinned.

"Cows, I 'spose."

"You don't think any of those cows grazed on land cleared
from natural forest, do you?"

"Never really thought about it."

"No, I don't imagine you did."

I emptied the glass with one motion, set it down sharply, and
ordered another.

I could feel the alcohol seeping through me now the way good
jazz makes its way through a lonely house in the dead of night,
finding and filling the cold, dark corners.

The bartender hesitated a moment, then went to pour the
drink. He had strong hands but worked gracefully with the bottle
and glass, like a seasoned priest handling the items of religious
ritual.

When he set the third double in front of me, he said, "Maybe
you better slow down, fella."

He said it so nicely, so thoughtfully, I felt obliged to comply. I
sipped some of the golden liquid off the top, closing my eyes and
rolling it around my tongue. It had been more than a year since
I'd anointed my body with hard liquor, and I trusted it to do its
job the way some trust God to end suffering.

I opened my eyes. The bartender was still there.

"I used to be a newspaper reporter."

"Is that right?"

"Until I won a Pulitzer prize and they found out I'd made the story up. That kind of put a damper on the old career."

"I guess it would."

"Covered a big conference once on the environment, back in the eighties. Sponsored by the entertainment industry. How to save energy, stop pollution, take personal responsibility for saving the planet, that kind of thing. I'm talking now about the real planet, not Planet Hollywood, the restaurant. I wouldn't want you to get confused."

He didn't seem to like that.

"Why don't you finish your story, partner, so I can get back to work."

"I didn't cover the speeches that day."

"No?"

"I counted cars."

"No kidding."

"I stood at the parking entrance with my notebook open in one hand and a calculator in the other, watching guests arrive. Celebrities, producers, agents, big-shot executives. Want to know what I found out?"

He glanced over his shoulder at his other customers.

"If it doesn't take too long."

"Approximately eight hundred arrived by cab, limousine, or in private automobiles, most of which were of the expensive, gas-guzzling variety. Seven arrived on motorcycles. Three came on bicycles. One arrived in an electric-driven car. Carpooling appeared to be at a minimum."

"That so."

"They didn't like me reporting that. They wanted me to cover the speeches. The next year, I didn't get invited back."

He glanced again toward the other end of the bar.

"So what's the point, partner?"

"I'll bet you're an actor, aren't you?"

"When I'm not workin' here."

"Looking for an agent, I'll bet."

"As a matter of fact, I am."

"Hoping for a regular gig on a daytime soap."

"I wouldn't mind."

I smiled a little, comfortably drunk and very pleased with myself.

"Now how did I know that?"

I tipped the glass, draining it, and requested another.

"Maybe you should get some food in you before you drink any-thing more. Or some fresh air."

"One more. Then I'm gone."

I said it in a way that let him know I was starting to feel combat-ive, and the battle wasn't worth it.

He went away, poured the drink, and brought it back.

"Last one," he said. "On the house."

I drank half of it down while he looked on.

"You know that hospital over there?"

"Cedars-Sinai? Sure."

"I got a friend over there. He's dying."

"That's tough."

"The cops won't let him go home. You know why?"

"I sure don't."

"They think he murdered somebody. So they got him hand-cuffed to his bed. You know what else?"

The bartender shook his head.

"Maybe he did murder somebody."

"I'm sorry to hear that."

"Not as sorry as I am."

I finished the drink, set the empty glass on the bar, and did my best to focus on his photogenic face.

"I hate this fucking world."

I shoved some money at him and turned to go. He caught my arm and made me take back everything except what I owed him for the drinks.

"Get yourself a cab. There's a line of 'em at the curb, right out front."

His strong hand felt good on my arm. It was a beautiful hand, tanned and burnished with dark blond hairs the sun had turned golden at the tips. Or maybe it had been a tanning salon. Either way, I would have liked to see the rest of him.

"I'm walking thanks just the same."

I could hear my words slide together into one; they sounded as if they were far away, at the end of a long tunnel, spoken by a voice that wasn't mine.

I made my way toward the door, negotiating the space fairly well until I reached the ramp leading up to the foyer. I tilted sideways as I started up and landed against a wall, hard enough to rattle Pete Townshend's autographed guitar.

A pretty hostess in a long summer dress took my elbow and guided me to the door.

Outside, the heat smothered me, making the hair all over my body crackle. The office buildings had emptied and the streets were bumper to bumper with cars and the sound of anxious drivers using their horns like anger. On the sidewalks, the pedestrians seemed in just as big a hurry, moving together like a school of stupid fish lost in a sea of asphalt, concrete, and glass. Hovering over it all were the enormous billboard images of beautiful young men and women in fleshy, narcissistic poses designed to make the rest of us feel inadequate and ugly—and desperate to buy the brand names attached to the seductive pictures.

Money. In the end it was all about money. And the high priests of wealth had most of us tithing our lives to it.

I sat down on a bus bench and pulled my notebook from the knapsack. I found the page where I'd charted the names, determined to figure out who had murdered Reza JaFari and Leonardo Petrocelli, and how.

*Please God let it be someone other than Danny.*

My mind felt thick and fuzzy, ten or twelve ounces of Cuervo Gold on an empty stomach.

I shook my head, blinked, ran my eyes down the list.

> Dylan Winchester
> Roberta Brickman
> Leonardo Petrocelli
> Gordon Cantwell
> Christine Kapono
> Lawrence Teal

> > Reza JaFari
> > (Raymond Farr)

> Danny Romero
> Bernard Kemmerman
> Anne-Judith Kemmerman
> Hosain JaFari
> Constance Fairbridge

I finished drawing in the lines that connected the names to Reza JaFari, and to one another, noting the reasons they were linked. The only name not connected directly to JaFari's was that of Constance Fairbridge.

I also made a note beside certain names indicating those who might have had a motive for wanting JaFari dead. I came up with at least six.

Leonardo Petrocelli and Bernard Kemmerman I crossed off the list, since both were now dead themselves, and no longer reasonable suspects.

Then I turned to a clean page and drew a new list. It took a while and the printing wasn't too straight.

> Reza JaFari (Raymond Farr)
> Dylan Winchester
> Roberta Brickman
> Gordon Cantwell
> Christine Kapono
> Lawrence Teal

> > > Leonardo Petrocelli

> Danny Romero
> Bernard Kemmerman
> Anne-Judith Kemmerman
> Hosain JaFari
> Constance Fairbridge

Where appropriate, I drew a line connecting each name to Leonardo Petrocelli. This time—again, because they were dead—I crossed out the names of Reza JaFari and Bernard Kemmerman.

Then, as before, I started down the list looking for motives.

The answer I was looking for was right before me on the page—who, what, why, where, when, even the crucial how—but the alcohol overwhelmed me before I got to it. My attention drifted to nothing in particular. I no longer remembered quite what I was looking for, or what had led me to this point.

Tequila, as they say, has a way of sneaking up on you.

I found myself staring off at the hills rising to the north above Sunset Boulevard, about a mile away. The hills Jacques and I had hiked so often before he'd gotten sick, the same ones I'd been climbing in recent days to ready myself for the glorious treks I would take with Danny Romero. The hills where you could stand above all the noise and lights and madness for a little while and feel yourself rooted to the earth.

I shoved the notebook into my knapsack, got up, and started putting one foot in front of the other in an attempt to reach the corner. I got there and crossed against the yellow light, which turned red before I reached the other side. The cacophony of horns picked up until they merged into a single din.

*Fuck 'em.*

Harry's favorite phrase, when the assholes were ganging up on him. Good old Harry. I hadn't seen him in awhile. Too long. I had to make a point of getting in touch.

I wanted another drink, quickly, so I stopped at Morton's, halfway home. I drank two more doubles of Cuervo Gold served by another good-looking bartender who knew enough not to talk too much in a place like this.

Whoopi Goldberg and Robin Williams were coming in as I staggered out. I pushed hard on the door, making them step back. A middle-aged man in a well-tailored suit who was with them said something, so I flipped him off.

I didn't give the slightest shit about any of them. I was as big, as important, as powerful as any other sonofabitch on the face of the earth. I could do anything. *Anything!*

In the parking lot, I unzipped and peed on the gleaming grillwork of a Rolls Royce Silver Cloud. Then I heard Spanish-speaking voices behind me and felt hands grab me by the shoulders and hustle me rudely back toward the sidewalk while I dribbled urine on my pants that smelled of last night's asparagus.

I zipped up, feeling badly, knowing that the dutiful valets would have to clean off my piss, that the big shot who owned the big car would probably never even know about it.

I was not being an exemplary model for the white race. I had to try to think through my actions more clearly.

Next time, I'd be sure to piss on the big-shot driver.

I continued up Robertson to the supermarket on Santa Monica Boulevard, where I found a fifth of Cuervo Gold for eleven bucks with a two-dollar rebate coupon hanging like a noose around its slender neck.

It was amazing how much salvation eleven bucks could still buy.

I staggered over to Hilldale Avenue with the bottle in a paper bag. I drank a third of it sitting on a low wall in the skimpy shade of a sickly-looking bottlebrush tree. It was staked up pathetically to keep it from falling, someone's idea of city landscaping. Across the street was an art gallery whose rooftop was split architecturally like curling paper by a huge, plunging blade.

*Cutting edge. Clever.*

I tried to focus again on my notebook. The answer had been right there on the page; I could vaguely remember that much. But it was slipping away from me again, farther and farther away as I dipped deeper and deeper into the bottle.

Men floated past me on their way down to the boulevard. Men

in shorts and tank tops and tight jeans. Trim, good-looking men, most of them. White, black, brown, Asian. A wave of men, heading to the bars while the gusting wind stirred up lust along the streets like whirlwinds of dust.

I pulled off my shirt and felt the hot air ruffle the hair on my chest and belly and arms. It felt almost as good as a man's hands, the way it had felt on the ride to Palm Springs with Danny beside me. But now Danny was rotting in a hospital bed he couldn't leave. I couldn't be with Danny, couldn't touch him, couldn't even talk to him.

I could have Lawrence Teal if I wanted him, though. Teal lived only two blocks away. I got to my feet, wanting him.

I would go to Teal's apartment and fuck him so hard he would beg me to stop and when I did he'd beg me to start up again.

I was stupendously drunk now. I wanted sex. The elixir, the solution, the escape.

I turned up Hilldale, trying to walk a straight line and looking ridiculous the way self-deluding drunks always do. I drank my way to Teal's front door, and pounded on it with the empty bottle.

I'd decided not to fuck Teal after all.

I would get him all worked up, hard as a rock, slip a condom on him and pull him into me, his big cock all the way up my ass, as deep as it would go. I'd close my eyes and grab his ass with both hands, and pull him all the way in and make him keep plowing, until he became Danny Romero in my mind, until his strong, dancer's legs became Danny's legs, and I was crazy with pain and pleasure and filled with the fantasy that it was Danny inside me and no one else.

Teal would give me his body and in the process give me Danny Romero without knowing it. That's what Teal would do for me.

The problem was, Lawrence Teal wasn't home.

I smashed the bottle on his doorstep, then peed into the planter outside his door, deciding what to do next.

I would hike, up into the hills above the noise and lights and madness.

I stashed my knapsack behind the planter and weaved my way up to Sunset Boulevard. Bright neon was flickering on all along the Strip, a blur of neon, with the cars going past in a rush of motion that created its own impersonal music.

Then I was crossing from the House of Blues to Queens Road, just before the Comedy Store, climbing, feverish and numb, the relentless winds shaking the trees around me, turning the weeds and brush to kindling.

I was far too drunk to realize I was being followed as I staggered up the odd, disjointed section of Hollywood Boulevard that took me west toward the highest ridges. Too blitheringly blasted to sense the danger, even as darkness settled over the hills and the headlights flicked on a hundred yards behind me.

The driver waited until I was near the top, on a stretch where the houses were few and the road the darkest, before making a move.

By then, I was deep inside myself, staring out at a million city lights. The car rolled slowly past. I glanced over, mildly interested in the manner of desultory drunks. It was a utility sports vehicle, gray, with windows tinted so densely that nothing was visible within.

When it was gone, I gazed out again at the vast plain of lights, wondering how many people were out there—in homes and hospitals and hospices, alleyways—taking their last gasp of breath, their last gulp of life at that exact moment.

How would Danny go? Where? In the jail ward of County-USC, shackled to his bed? On an operating table, while they hacked off his legs, trying to keep him alive long enough to stand trial? In a jail cell, huddled in a corner, legless and alone?

From the edge of the hillside, I screamed until my lungs ached. Dogs started barking in the canyons and I screamed again, grinning as their howls answered back.

Then I sensed the headlights on my face and turned to see the gray wagon coming at me.

It came off a curve faster than it had reason to, accelerating on the straightaway that we now shared.

There was no doubt that it was coming for me.

I dashed across the road, falling to my knees, scrambling up, flinging myself against the hillside, clutching at the highest roots, pulling myself up.

The car swerved, coming across the road. I pulled myself higher, hugging the crumbling earth.

The wagon sped by, caroming off the hillside, missing me by inches.

I slipped to the road and looked around for escape. There was nothing but open roadway before me and behind me, with steep slopes up and down on either side.

The car had turned around and was speeding back.

I ran along the edge of the road, slipped behind a boulder as the car came screaming back, its front left bumper and headlight clipping the rock, crunching metal, shattering glass, making sparks.

It disappeared around a curve but I could hear its shifting transmission and knew it would come again.

Down the road, maybe two hundred yards, I saw the lights of a house suspended on stilts out over the canyon.

I ran for it, stumbling, falling, getting up, running on.

Behind me, the headlights reappeared and I knew the house might as well be in Omaha.

The car bore down on me as I reached a section of road where the mountain was steepest. There was no climbing up.

It kept coming, angling toward me as I stood at the edge of the downslope, the ground around me growing brighter as the headlights closed the space between us.

The moment before I would have been struck, I flung myself over the side.

It felt less like falling than ground coming up at me, something huge and alive that was determined to punish me for being so stupid and self-destructive. Basketball-sized rocks pounded my body, thorny brush ripped at my skin.

I grabbed at anything I could to slow my fall, tearing the fleshy parts of my hands, banging and bruising the bones.

Then I wasn't moving anymore.

I lay facedown, my head pointed up toward the road, arms and legs splayed, mouth tasting the gritty powder of arid earth.

I was surprised by how sober I felt, how clear everything around me had suddenly become.

From my awkward position, I could see the vehicle that had almost killed me taking curves as it sped its way down the hillside. I watched the taillights until I couldn't see them anymore.

My body suddenly convulsed and my mouth erupted with vomit. I turned my head, spewing bile into the dry soil, until nothing more came out of me.

Then I began the long crawl back up to the road.

# Forty

M Y GOD, JUSTICE. What happened?"
      I heard Templeton's voice, opened my eyes, and imme-
diately wished I hadn't. The pain was almost as bad when I raised
a tender hand to ward off the punishing light.

Templeton sat on the edge of the bed like an angel come to
take me home. I made the mistake of moving my battered lips.

"I took a swan dive up in the Hollywood Hills."

Out on the landing, Harry sucked on a burning cigarette as if
he'd never given them up. He was wearing his rumpled blue-gray
suit and a narrow tie that was decades old, which told me it must
be a workday.

I pulled a pillow over my eyes, resisting the urge to throw up.

"The door was open," Templeton said, "so we came in."

"We've been calling." It's was Harry's voice, from the doorway.
"You haven't been answering."

"As you can see, I'm a bit under the weather."

"You want to tell us what happened?"

I lifted the pillow. Templeton's face was still there, peering
down at me with concern.

"I spent the evening with my old friend Mr. Cuervo. Had a
grand old time. Then someone tried to redesign my body with
their grillwork."

Templeton's eyes widened.

"Someone tried to *kill* you?"

"Diligently."

Harry tossed his butt down, ground it out with his foot, and stepped inside.

"What the hell's going on, Ben?"

"You're smoking again, for one thing. Those high-risk lifestyle choices can be dangerous, Harry."

"Cut the crap. Talk to us."

"Take it easy, Harry. He's hurt."

"Stop coddling him. He's reeling from a binge. Otherwise, he's got a few scrapes and bruises."

Templeton looked me over.

"More than a few." She wrinkled her nose. "But you do smell something awful, Justice."

Harry stood over me, hands on hips.

"This kid Romero was placed under arrest last night for murdering Reza JaFari. You knew about it. We never heard squat from you."

"On *suspicion* of murdering JaFari, Harry."

When Templeton spoke, some of the sympathy was gone from her voice.

"He's right, Ben. You didn't call either of us. The only reason we found out in time to make this morning's paper—"

"You put Danny's name in the paper?"

"He's under arrest."

"He's *dying*."

"That doesn't make him less of a suspect," Harry said. "You should have called us, dammit. Lydia Lowe devoted her entire column to it—beat everybody with the best details. Even though we run the damn column, her contract requires us to credit her for anything she breaks. I got scooped in my own paper by a second-rate New York gossip monger."

Lydia Lowe. The best details. Lawrence Teal. The notes I'd stashed behind his planter. I'd fucked up again. And this time Danny had paid.

"You don't know the half of it, Harry."

His voice rose.

"Suppose you fill me in."

"Sorry, Harry. I'm not using Danny to fill another news hole for the *Sun*. Call it irresponsible sensitivity, if you must. Flagrant decency. But I'm opting out."

"You're a reporter, Justice."

"Was."

Harry turned away, fumbling for his pack of smokes. When he

turned to face me again, an unlit cigarette dangled from his lips, bouncing like a conductor's baton while he talked.

"I tried to help you out, Ben. Get you some work. We both did. This is how you pay us back?"

"I'm working on a story for *Angel City*, Harry. A feature story, not news, which may or may not have Danny Romero's name in it, depending on how Templeton and I decide to write it. That's the difference between a news story and a magazine article, Harry. It's not hard, cold facts, cut and dried for quick public consumption. We'll tell it from our perspective, the way we choose to, the way we see it."

"I don't need any Journalism 101 lectures, especially from you, Justice. If anybody has a right to climb up on a soapbox, it's me."

I propped myself up on sore elbows and leveled my bloodshot eyes at him.

"I've got no obligations to the *Sun*, Harry. Or to you."

Harry spun on the heels of his old loafers and made for the door.

"Fuck him. Let's get out of here."

"Harry, wait!"

Templeton stood, taking a position halfway between the two of us.

"He didn't mean it. He's hungover, that's all."

I pushed myself up farther on my swollen hands and eased my aching back against the wall. My face was on fire, my head roaring with pain. Templeton slipped a pillow behind me.

"Harry's right about one thing, Ben. Danny's part of the story now. You can't change that."

"DeWinter called you, didn't he?"

She nodded.

"You two engaged yet?"

"Let's not start up again, Justice."

"How much did he tell you?"

"Not a lot. Just that Danny had been arrested, based on evidence found in his apartment. He was vague on the details. We only got twelve inches out of it."

"What page?"

"Inside," Harry said. "Page three."

"Photograph?"

"We didn't have a shot of Romero. I wanted to send a photographer to the hospital. Templeton talked me out of it."

"And they say reporters have no heart."

Harry plucked the cigarette from his lips, his gray eyes fixed on me from the middle of the room.

"We're not asking you to write the damn story, Justice. Just give us the leads when they come your way. Templeton can handle it at the news end."

"Harry's got a point, Ben. We're working as a team. I have a right to know what's going on."

"Fine." I closed my eyes, feeling the nausea rise in me like a fast tide. "From now on, I'll keep you posted on all the sordid little details."

Harry stepped closer to the bed.

"Let's start with last night, when some guy tried to flatten you like the roadrunner."

"I didn't say it was a guy, Harry."

"A guy, a broad, whatever. Does it have something to do with this JaFari business or not?"

"I didn't have time to ask. I was too busy throwing myself off the side of a cliff."

"Stop pulling my chain, Ben. It's time to tell us what you know."

"No, Harry, it's time to heave again."

I rolled out of bed and stumbled into the bathroom, just in time to deposit a fresh batch of bile into the toilet bowl. I stayed there for several minutes, on my knees, wretching up a noxious liquid that added a new band to the color spectrum. When there was nothing left, the dry heaves took over, each convulsion wringing my guts a little tighter.

When that was past, I looked up to find Harry standing in the doorway. Vomit dripped from my chin. I wasn't feeling particularly proud of myself.

"Templeton went for coffee and muffins."

"God bless Templeton."

I staggered to the shower, turned it on, stripped off last night's clothes. My body was scraped and bruised from forehead to feet, sticky with dirt-caked blood. I soaped down, wincing as I washed the rawest spots, then rinsed my rancid mouth and spit enough times to clear away the taste.

Harry was holding a towel for me as I stepped out. Being a nervous heterosexual, he didn't quite know where to put his eyes. He took the opportunity to go to the sink and inspect my medicine chest.

As I toweled off, the shakes set in. I couldn't remember how much I'd had to drink the night before, but judging by the violence of my tremors, it was obviously too much by plenty.

Harry came back with cotton balls, a small bottle of antiseptic, and Band-Aids, and began dabbing at my wounds. It was the first time Harry had ever seen me naked, and physically the closest we'd ever been. I found something touching in that, even though I was worried I might throw up on him.

"I guess you and this Romero kid are pretty tight."

"I'd say that's accurate."

"You've known him what, two weeks?"

"Not quite."

"He's a prime suspect in a murder case, for Christ sake."

"Maybe that's part of the attraction."

"Then you need a good shrink."

"That goes without saying."

Harry hesitated a moment, showing a bad case of nervous eyes.

"Plus, from what I hear, he's got AIDS."

"Advanced, as a matter of fact."

I tucked the damp towel around my waist, moved around Harry to the sink, found a toothbrush and toothpaste, and scrubbed out my putrid mouth. My eyes were glassy, my skin pale. The shakes hadn't stopped. Whoever had tried to kill me last night, I thought, had probably saved my life.

Harry followed, stretching a Band-Aid across a ragged cut on my shoulder.

"Doesn't sound like the kind of relationship that's going to help you get your life back on track."

"You're offering advice to the lovelorn now, Harry?" I spit into the sink. "Harry Brofsky, who's been married three times—each blessed union more truncated than the one before?"

"I'll concede I'm no expert in that department—"

"It's always nice when we agree on something, isn't it, Harry?"

I bent to rinse my mouth with a cupped hand. When I raised my head, I saw Harry's eyes in the mirror looking for mine.

"I can probably get your name somewhere on this story, Ben. A tag credit, something. It could be a fresh start in the news business."

"I'm no good for it anymore, Harry. The kind of reporting where you feel no connection to the people or events you're writing about. Even if somebody wanted me for it."

"I want you for it."

"I know, Harry. I appreciate it."

"You'll work more closely with Templeton? Get this cop involved if things get dangerous again?"

"Yeah, I guess I can do that."

I grabbed a brush, turned to the mirror, took a few swipes at my disappearing hair. Then I went back out and looked through a basket piled with clean laundry while Harry stood behind me in the doorway.

"So what the hell *are* you going to do with your life, Ben?"

"I don't know, Harry." I threw him a weary smile over my bandaged shoulder. "But thanks for asking."

I found a clean pair of briefs, unhooked the towel, and dropped it to the floor just as Templeton came through the front door.

"Didn't see a thing," she said, and turned quickly into the kitchen.

I wasn't sure if I should be grateful or insulted. I slipped into the briefs, then jeans and a T-shirt, and joined Harry and Templeton in the kitchen.

We washed down the muffins with coffee standing up at the counter because there was no table and no chairs. I gave them details on the JaFari story, not everything but enough to help, wishing more than ever that I hadn't left my notebook where Lawrence Teal had surely found it.

"I'd keep close tabs on the death of Leonardo Petrocelli," I said. "It's a Bev Hills case, but they're in touch with DeWinter on it. I'd be shocked if the two deaths aren't connected."

"DeWinter didn't mention that to me," Templeton said.

"Maybe you should start sleeping with him."

"Why? Because it works for you?"

Harry glanced at his watch, then at us, looking impatient.

"Let's not fight, children. Ben, anything else?"

"Not until I get the right answers from the right people."

"Any names I know?" Templeton said.

"Roberta Brickman, for one—the agent."

"What makes you think she'll talk to you again?"

"My irresistible charm."

"Who else?" Harry said.

"Hosain JaFari."

"The victim's father?"

I nodded.

"I'd like to know why a Muslim who prays to Allah five times a day has a six-pack of Grolsch beer cooling in the fridge, with two bottles gone."

Templeton's beeper sounded. She put her muffin aside, wiped her fingers on a paper napkin, and checked the number. She called back, listening intently, nodding more than she talked.

Then she hung up, gulped some coffee, and grabbed her hand-bag all in one fluid motion as she spoke to Harry.

"We've got to go."

"What's up?"

"Major fire in the Hollywood Hills. The desk is holding two columns and a banner on the front page. They need me at the scene and you downtown."

She was on her way to the door. Harry followed with a question.

"What part of the Hollywood Hills?"

Her answer seemed intended for both Harry and me, and came with an echo of curiosity, maybe something more.

"Beachwood Canyon."

# Forty-one

I WASN'T SURPRISED to find my knapsack missing from behind the planter on Lawrence Teal's front porch.

I rang the bell. When Teal failed to answer, I pounded on the door, then kicked it a few times, hard enough to rouse the dead. When that didn't work, I left a note:

> Teal—
> Call me ASAP if you value our special friendship.
>                                                   Justice

My next stop was the well-stocked Beverly Hills Public Library, where I spent some time looking for information on the Tokona tribe of Oklahoma and the New Mexican mountain village of Milagro.

When I'd learned what I needed to know, I walked three blocks from the city's Art Deco civic center to the pretentious, post-modernist building that housed International Talent Associates. It was located on a leafy section of Maple Drive, rising five stories, with an exterior comprised of contrasting stone banding, dramatic gabled ends, enlarged and overscaled windows, and a courtyard fountain filled with coins and secret wishes that probably had more to do with wealth and power than art.

I entered a lobby bigger than any house I'd ever lived in. It featured a glass-roofed atrium and a David Hockney mural that covered much of the atrium's four-story limestone wall. A security guard in a business suit sat behind a chest-high circular station at center stage. By the way he looked me over, I figured my battered face wasn't too reassuring, and my chances of getting past him close to nil.

I told him I was there to see Roberta Brickman. He asked if I had an appointment. I told him I didn't.

"Your name, sir?"

"Benjamin Justice."

He was reaching for the phone when a rumbly voice next to me said, "It's all right, Henry. I'll take him up."

I looked over to see a portly, middle-aged man in leather sandals, faded jeans, a Greek peasant shirt, and enough Indian jewelry around his neck and wrists to open a Grand Canyon curio shop. His head was shaved as smooth as a Fabergé egg, while a heavy, reddish-blond Fu Manchu mustache flowed into an equally thick goatee. Perched on his nose were rectangular, rose-colored granny glasses.

"Very well, Mr. Novitz."

I followed Novitz to a bank of elevators and sneaked a glance at the directory while he punched the up button. Roberta Brickman was listed with a fourth-floor office.

The doors opened and we stepped in. He hit five and I hit four. The doors closed but the machinery was so smooth and silent it felt as if we were standing still.

"You could fucking die waiting to talk to an agent," Novitz said. "They take two weeks just to get back to their mothers."

I assumed I was talking to the famous Jake Novitz, whose name had come up during my discussions with Templeton and Harry about the big-bucks screenwriting trade.

"You must be a writer," he said.

"How did you know?"

"Those clothes." He laughed as he said it. "And the fresh notebook. Pitch meeting?"

I nodded. The doors opened.

"Don't let 'em kill your spirit," Novitz said. "You gotta write nine crappy ones for 'em so you can make one good one. Never forget that they're just a bunch of salesmen who happen to drive nice cars."

He laughed again as the doors closed between us.

I found Roberta Brickman's office near the end of a corridor that seemed to run a city block.

Inside the outer office, facing me from a marble-topped desk, was Christine Kapono.

She was dressed in sharp-looking business clothes and had ac-

cented her boyish face with small gold earrings and a touch of lip
gloss, creating a conservative but attractive package.

Now all she needed was a smile.

"Hello, Christine."

"How did you get in here?"

"Mr. Novitz brought me up."

Her short laugh came with a hint of derision.

"*Jake* Novitz? I don't think so."

"I need a few minutes with Roberta."

"She's in a meeting."

"I can wait."

"It's a long meeting."

I stepped past Kapono's desk toward the door behind her. She
was up just as fast, putting herself between me and the door, looking about as movable as an Otero sculpture. I remembered what
she'd done with her knee to Gordon Cantwell's private parts, and
decided not to push my luck.

Just then, the door opened. Roberta Brickman stood behind
Kapono with a script open in her hand, writing on the title page
with quick, resolute strokes.

"Another revision of a revision of a revision?"

When Brickman looked up, I saw a most unhappy face.

"I'll call security," Kapono said.

"Please."

Kapono moved away from us to her desk. My eyes went back to
her boss.

"Danny Romero was arrested last night on suspicion of murdering Reza JaFari."

"Yes, I saw Lydia Lowe's column."

"You must be very relieved."

"Why do you say that, Mr. Justice?"

"You and JaFari were quite close at one time. Now they have a
prime suspect in his murder."

"He worked for me briefly, that's all. I already told you that."

"It was a lie then and it's a lie now."

I hadn't seen too many women wound tighter than Roberta
Brickman, but my words managed to twist her coils one more
revolution.

"You sound awfully sure of yourself."

"Do I have to spell it out, Roberta?"

I took her silence as a yes.

"You were a workaholic, a slave to your job, lonely. Back and forth between your townhouse and your office, with appointments in between. Not much else going on. Reza was good-looking, available, more than willing. You slept with him. He infected you with HIV."

I heard Kapono hang up the phone. The two women glanced at each other, looking fully united in their mutual loathing of me. It didn't slow me down.

"You're being treated at the AHF clinic at Cedars-Sinai. Probably because it guarantees total confidentiality."

Brickman's face paled; she began to hyperventilate. Kapono stepped to her side, regarding me with more fury than a man ever wants to see in a woman's eyes.

"Why don't we talk inside, Roberta? Privately."

Brickman nodded stiffly.

"I'll stay with you," Kapono said.

"No. I'll be all right. Hold my calls. And call off security."

Brickman stepped back and I went in. She closed the door behind us and showed me to a black leather couch, taking a chair that faced it at an angle. Between us was a low table of solid gray marble that held an arrangement of pale lavender cymbidia, along with a copy of the *Sun* folded open to Lydia Lowe's syndicated column.

"You're very good at finding things out, aren't you, Mr. Justice?"

"Better than some, I suppose."

"Is it so necessary to hurt me like this?"

"I don't like being lied to, Roberta."

"I owe you nothing. Not even the truth."

I stood up.

"Fine. I'll work with what I have, then."

I waited, watching her eyes flicker uneasily.

"Sit down. I'll talk to you."

I sat. She looked away toward a Jackson Pollock print with a design of controlled chaos that seemed well suited to her situation.

"You realize what happens to my career if this town learns I have HIV."

"At one time, maybe. I'm not so sure about now. From what I hear, there are quite a few HIV-positive executives who are quite public about it, and continue to work successfully."

"I'm not the noble type, Mr. Justice."

"Maybe you're just not ready yet."

"Shouldn't that be my decision?"

"Under ideal circumstances, yes."

She got up and paced.

"Why am I so important to your story?"

"You had reason to wish Reza JaFari dead. As much reason as Danny Romero—more, the way I see it. And you deliberately misled me. Reporters take that as a sign of possible guilt."

"Even those who lost their respectability years ago because of their own lies?"

"Even those."

She stopped pacing, went to a big window, and looked out at the vast green expanse of the Los Angeles Country Club. Out on the course, wealthy golfers skitted between holes in little carts or swung their iron sticks as if everything in the world was just fine.

"Does every personal detail have to be included in your article?"

"Not necessarily."

"Why should I trust you?"

"No reason. Other than I've got you in a bad position, and there's no way you can win."

"Is that what reporting is, Mr. Justice? Winning? Beating your subjects at a game of secrecy and disclosure?"

"Sometimes."

Several miles to the northeast, smoke from the fire Templeton and Harry had rushed to cover could be seen billowing up in the hills between central Hollywood and the Los Feliz district on the city's east side.

When Brickman spoke again, her voice was less guarded, less harsh.

"Perhaps there's something to be gained from being more open with you."

"You'd be surprised how liberating the truth can be."

She took a moment to compose herself. Then she faced me.

"You're right, I was lonely. The more lonely I got, the harder I worked. The harder I worked, the less time I had for myself. Despite some obvious rewards, it was a miserable way to live."

"And then Raymond Farr appeared, applying to be your assistant."

"He was an attractive man in many ways. There were other candidates who were better qualified, but he wasn't so lacking that hiring him looked all that bad. I encouraged his writing aspirations, agreed to help him if I could. He seemed grateful, almost childlike."

Her expression suddenly grew cold, almost grim.

"He had that ability to project what others wanted to see in him. I realize now how skilled he was at it."

"I've heard that about him."

"He moved from the mailroom to my office about six months ago. We started sleeping together a few weeks after that."

"You assumed he was straight."

"Why not? He'd come on to me from the first moment I met him, and he was very good in bed. He told me he was HIV-negative but I insisted we use condoms just the same. Then, one night—"

She began pacing again, growing agitated.

"This is very embarrassing, talking this way."

"There's not much I haven't heard, Roberta. Or done myself, for that matter."

"One night, Raymond was rather rough with me. We hadn't lubricated properly. The condom broke."

She laughed bitterly.

"I remember saying to myself afterward, 'Thank God he's HIV-negative.' A week or two later, I got sick. Diarrhea, low-grade fever, a minor rash. Flulike symptoms, which I later learned flare up briefly after exposure to HIV. My doctor found nothing to explain it in the normal blood work. She asked me some rather personal questions. I mentioned the incident with the broken condom. She suggested I get tested.

"I thought it was ridiculous, since I felt fine after a few days. But I got tested anonymously, just in case, at one of the nonprofit clinics. The results came back negative. Of course, I was overjoyed."

"Then you took a follow-up test."

She stopped in the middle of the room, hugging her arms with her hands, her eyes working the ceiling.

"Three months later. The second test came back positive. It had taken that long for the virus to show up in my system. Seroconversion, I think they call it."

"You must have been devastated."

She was shaking.

"I knew it had to be Raymond. I hadn't been with anyone else in more than a year."

She came back to the chair and sat facing me, trying to steady herself.

"Yes, Mr. Justice, I've thought of killing him. Many, many times." Her smile wasn't pretty. "Apparently, someone else took care of it for me."

"Someone who cares a great deal about you, Roberta? Someone who was already angry at the way certain men use and abuse women?"

"If you're suggesting that Christine—"

"She's very fond of you. And she was up at Cantwell's house that evening, preparing for the party. She had all the opportunity in the world."

"If it weren't for Christine, Mr. Justice, I don't know what I would have done. She got me to APLA for counseling. Helped me find a support group for HIV-positive women. Held my hand and let me cry on her shoulder when all I could think about was how I was going to kill myself. She's still there for me when I have bad moments."

"Some people who are infected are living ten, fifteen years, even longer without getting sick. With the new therapies, a few patients who tested positive have actually reverted to negative."

"I realize that now. Christine helped me to realize it. She's been a godsend."

"That doesn't rule her out as a suspect."

Her voice grew cool, distrustful again.

"I suppose we're all capable of murder, under the right circumstances. But in my gut? I don't believe she did it, not for a moment."

"You've thought about it, though."

"If you have any other questions, Mr. Justice, you'd better ask them."

"Did you call the Kemmermans, warning them that Reza JaFari was infected with HIV?"

"I'd heard some buzz that Raymond had struck some kind of production deal with Bernard Kemmerman. The lawyers were putting together a deal memo and word leaked out. It didn't make sense. As far as I knew, Raymond had never written a script. If he had, he would have shown it to me, asked me to sell it for him."

"You started putting two and two together."

"Everyone knew that Kemmerman was desperate for a kidney.

By then, I knew how far Ray would go to get what he wanted. Yes, I guess you could say I put two and two together."

"This was after you introduced Farr to Leonardo Petrocelli?"

"A month or so later."

"Is it possible that Petrocelli was using JaFari as a beard?"

"You mean—?"

"A front—someone to pitch his ideas for him, work as a cover. Someone younger, with lots of energy and a gift for gab. Someone who could gain access to producers who wouldn't give the time of day to a screenwriter with white hair."

"In exchange for a piece of the action, if they happened to cut a deal."

"I imagine that's how it works."

Brickman considered it a moment, her eyes wandering.

"It would have been humiliating for someone like Leo. On the other hand, he was rather desperate. The business has been quite hard on him in recent years. I suppose I've played my part."

"Then he and JaFari may have had some kind of private arrangement?"

"It's certainly a possibility."

"He may have had access to Petrocelli's latest work."

"Again, it's possible."

I stood.

"I'm sorry I had to be so tough on you, Roberta."

"It's a reporter's job, I guess." She reached toward the table. "I assume you've seen Lydia Lowe's column."

"May I?"

She handed me the newspaper. I scanned the column from the top.

As if AIDS hasn't caused enough tragedy on its own, the deadly virus has now played a dramatic supporting role in a sordid murder carried out amid the glitter and glamour of Hollywood.

The murder victim was a handsome, talented young screenwriter named Reza JaFari, the 27-year-old son of poor, hardworking Iranian immigrants, who was known to the Hollywood community by his adopted name, Raymond Farr.

JaFari's dreams of creating movie magic and giving his beloved parents a better life died with him earlier this month when he was poisoned at a showbiz party high in the Hollywood Hills, literally in the shadow of La-La Land's famous Hollywood Sign.

Attending the party thrown by legendary screenwriting teacher Gordon Cantwell—now working on a major project with Tom Cruise—were such Hollywood luminaries as director Dylan Winchester, ITA agent Roberta Brickman, and veteran screenwriter Leonardo Petrocelli, a two-time Oscar nominee who himself died in ill health only yesterday.

Initially, the cause of JaFari's death was attributed to AIDS complications. Since then, the police have uncovered new evidence, and further lab tests have pointed to cyanide poisoning.

Yesterday, the police arrested the victim's roommate, an unemployed drifter named Daniel Romero, also 27, on charges of murdering JaFari.

What the police are not telling you—and what we are reporting exclusively in this column—is that they discovered cyanide among Romero's possessions in the low-rent Hollywood apartment the suspect shared with the victim.

Even more shocking: Romero is believed to have carried out the heinous crime in a crazed attempt to eliminate JaFari because his blood was tainted with the HIV virus.

Romero, who is currently hospitalized with AIDS, was arrested eight years ago for the attempted murder of another HIV-infected man, charges later reduced in a plea bargain to simple assault.

According to confidential sources, Romero argued violently with JaFari the night before his death.

Police have offered no motive for Romero's violent behavior, but sources close to the case have indicated the troubled young man may harbor a deep animosity toward anyone afflicted with HIV, somehow blaming them for his own condition.

Police also refuse to speculate on how many more victims may have fallen at the

hands of Romero over the years, crimes
that may have gone undetected.

AIDS is already one serial killer visit-
ing untold tragedy on Hollywood and the
rest of the world. Let's hope that Daniel
Romero doesn't prove to be another.

"She's quite the spin artist, isn't she?"

I looked up from reading the column and thinking about what
I was going to do to Lawrence Teal when I got hold of him.

Roberta Brickman was standing halfway between me and the
open door, where Christine Kapono waited loyally in the background.

"Is there anything else, Mr. Justice? I have a rather busy
schedule."

"Any chance you could get me a copy of Gordon Cantwell's
script—the one he sold to Paramount Pictures and Tom Cruise?"

"*Nothing to Lose?*"

I nodded.

"May I ask why?"

"It may provide another piece of the puzzle."

Brickman's eyes shifted with curiosity. So did Kapono's.

"You really don't believe Romero killed Raymond, then?"

"Maybe I just don't want to."

"He's a friend?"

"More than that." I glanced at Kapono. "So perhaps you understand."

"I know some people at Paramount," Brickman said. "I'll see
what I can do."

Kapono stepped away to let me by, her eyes burning holes in
my back as I left the office. When the elevator doors opened, she
was standing at the other end of the hall, making sure I used
them.

I stepped in to find Jake Novitz inside, also on his way down.

"How'd the meeting go?"

"All things considered," I said, "pretty well."

"It's all a fucking head game, a goddamn crapshoot. Remember what Bill Goldman wrote in *Adventures in the Screen Trade?*"

"I'm afraid I don't."

"Sure you do! Most perceptive line about the business to ever
come out of a screenwriter's mouth! 'Nobody knows anything.' "

Jake Novitz, the wealthiest screenwriter in Hollywood, roared
with laughter.

"That's the secret—none of the bastards knows a fucking
thing!"

# Forty-two

B Y LATE AFTERNOON swirling winds had dispersed the smoke from the Beachwood Canyon fire, and much of it was filtering down over the Norma Triangle.

I could smell it as I pulled up in front of Lawrence Teal's apartment.

The front door was open and a grandiose opera was blasting from his stereo. I stepped in without bothering to knock. The smoky light outside cast a lovely, decadent pall over the spartan living room and the life-sized portrait of Teal dancing self-worshipfully for the camera.

He was in the bathroom, shaving at the sink. His back was to me, and he watched my reflection in the glass as I came up behind him. His hair was wet and his body damp; a towel was knotted at his narrow waist, hugging his hips and showing off his butt like the short, tight skirt of a shapely woman.

I reached around, pulled the towel free, and let it drop to the floor.

"You looked at my notes."

He glanced at me in the mirror but kept shaving, saying nothing. As the blade drew clean strokes upward through the white foam, my hands drew downward strokes along his sides and hips.

Then I reached around the front of him and found his big, droopy testicles.

"I'm talking to you, Teal."

He lifted his chin and began scraping at the hairs on his neck.

"You looked at my notes, then relayed the choicest information to Lydia Lowe."

He turned his chin to one side, shaving carefully in the area around his Adam's apple as if I weren't there. I squeezed his balls hard enough to force a squeal out of him.

"Bastard!"

Blood seeped through the foam on his neck, turning it pink.

I tightened my grip.

"Finish shaving, Teal. The world's out there waiting breathlessly to see your perfect face."

He hesitated, trying to gauge the extent of the anger in my eyes.

"I'm finished."

"No, you're not."

I made my fist smaller still. He shut his eyes until the shock of pain had passed. Then he raised his chin again, and lifted the razor reluctantly to his neck.

He was taking his third stroke when I closed my fist as tight as I could. He sounded like a wounded castrato when he cried out. Fresh blood streaked his neck.

He dropped the razor into the sink, and gripped the rim with both hands, hissing for air, fighting the pain.

"Please."

"All done, are we?"

He nodded rapidly. His eyes in the mirror were fearful, but just as arrogant and angry, which pleased me.

When I let go, he sagged over the sink, breathing erratically.

"We were talking about my notes, Teal."

"Lydia didn't write anything that wasn't true."

"Just used the facts creatively."

"I guess you could say that."

"I did say that."

"So what's your point?"

"They were my facts, Teal. Not yours. Not hers."

He bent to rinse his face. When he reached for a towel, he made sure to keep some distance between us. A degree of confidence returned to his voice, as if he was testing me, even challenging.

"If your notebook was so important, Justice, maybe you should have been more careful with it."

He moved cautiously around me to the mirror, where he patted his face dry before sticking the nicks with tiny pieces of tissue. I ran my fingertips over his smooth buttocks, then up the golden valley in between, as if his physical gifts had overpowered me yet again.

"At any rate," Teal said, growing almost cocky the more I touched him that way, "there's nothing we can do about it now."

Above the sink, the expensive-looking bottles and jars stood gleaming. Teal opened one, shook some drops into one hand, set the bottle on the sink, rubbed his hands together, and began applying the lotion to his face.

I smacked the bottle with my open hand, sending it flying against the tiled shower wall, where it shattered loudly.

"That was Clinique!"

"I'm an Aqua Velva man myself."

With one sweep of my arm, I sent the rest of the jars and bottles crashing.

Teal's eyes flashed foolish defiance.

"Go ahead, Justice. Break everything! It can all be replaced with the check I get from Lydia Lowe."

I grabbed his biceps, which was small and hard.

"Maybe I'll break your arm, Teal. Think that's fair? For what you did to Danny Romero?"

He mustered more defiance, pulling free, thrusting out his chin.

"Who cares? Danny Romero's a walking corpse."

My fist caught him flush on the nose. He took two steps backward and plopped down on the toilet seat. A fat drop of blood appeared at each nostril, then broke, starting twin streams.

He sat for a minute holding his hand to his face, then stared into his cupped hand, which was filled with blood.

"You broke my nose!"

He reached for a towel, pressed it to his face.

I took a step forward, causing him to cower.

"When you gave Lydia Lowe that information, you knew she'd crucify Danny."

"You broke my nose!"

I hated the notion that he could not see anything, anyone beyond the limits of himself. I backhanded him hard across the middle of his face. He began to cry.

"Get up, Teal."

He huddled against the toilet, trying to hold back his tears. Crimson drops fell into his crotch, where the hair he'd shaved away was beginning to grow back, looking like a two-day beard.

"Leave me alone!"

I grabbed him by the arm and hauled him to his feet.

"I killed a man once, Teal. You didn't know that, did you?"

"No."

His voice quavered.

"He hurt someone I loved very much. The way you hurt Danny."

"I didn't know Lydia would write the column like she did. I swear I didn't."

I pulled him so close I could see the tiny gold flecks in his blue eyes. Snot thickened the red streams pouring from each nostril; he tried to suck it back.

"So what do you think I should do to *you*, Teal?"

A sob escaped him.

"Please—don't hurt me any more."

I flattened a hand on his back and slammed him into the wall. He started wailing.

"Shall we get out your toys, Teal? Your handcuffs and whips? Would you like that?"

His voice was small, a child's.

"No."

"We don't need those, do we?"

"No."

"You bet we don't."

He was wailing again as I dragged him into the bedroom. I flung him against the white walls, causing him to groan each time he hit, leaving a bloody swipe where his face had landed.

The opera was swelling, filling the house. A booming baritone and kettledrums behind it. I kept grabbing and slamming Teal until there was a swath of blood connecting every wall in the room.

Then I pulled him through the apartment, out the front door, and threw him in a weeping pile down the steps.

He scrambled to his feet and dashed into the street, where he stood naked, waving his arms, crying out for help. His scrotum and penis were tiny now, shriveled from fear and adrenaline, like those of a little boy.

The last of my pleasurable rage dissipated, replaced with a sense of shame that felt heavier and more deeply a part of me.

*I'm still my father's son. I'll always be my father's son. I have to hurt people to feel strong.*

Police sirens grew loud, coming up the hill.

I turned back into Teal's apartment to find my notebook while I still had time.

# Forty-three

I FOUND what I was looking for by the telephone in Teal's dining room, open to the page about the cyanide discovered in Danny Romero's backpack.

By then, the sirens had stopped.

Out the window, I saw Teal sitting on the curb, wrapped in a blanket, being tended by a paramedic. Two uniformed deputies were approaching cautiously up the front walk with their hands near their unclipped holsters.

My notebook was too big for my pockets so I slipped it into the waistband of my pants, against the small of my back, the way reporters often do. Then I raised my hands and stepped out to the porch.

One of the deputies unhooked a set of handcuffs from her belt. I turned around and put my hands behind me, palms together, the position I'd seen my father order suspects into when I was a little kid and wanted to be just like him when I grew up.

The other deputy, male, asked me what had happened.

"The guy at the curb did something he shouldn't have. I got mad and broke his nose. Then I painted the walls with his face."

The deputy read me my rights. Fifteen minutes later, I was in a holding cell at the West Hollywood sheriff's substation down the hill. Before I was allowed a phone call, I spent an hour chatting with a friendly transsexual who had a compulsion for shoplifting perfume with Elizabeth Taylor's name on the bottle. I figured Harry and Templeton were tied up with the fire, so I placed my call to Claude DeWinter. I told him where I was and that I'd appreciate it if he'd get me out.

"Sit tight," he said. "I'll be down."

Before another hour passed, he was at the substation getting me released on my own recognizance. When he saw me, he greeted me with a question that didn't need an answer.

"You're trouble, you know that?"

He thanked the deputies for making things easy for him and walked me out to the parking lot. I told him I needed a cup of coffee.

"From what I hear, you've got an even stronger taste for alcohol."

"You've been talking to Templeton again."

"Is that what set you off today? Too much hooch?"

"I only punch people when I'm sober, Lieutenant. I'm weird that way."

"You're weird in a lot of ways, Justice."

He looked up the street toward Santa Monica Boulevard.

"So where do you get a decent cuppa coffee around here?"

"Just about anywhere, if you can stand breathing the same air as homosexuals."

"I'll manage."

I took him to Tribal Grounds, where we both ordered Kona Roast Supreme because it sounded potent. We took a table inside the patio, just off the street, out of the wind.

"Thanks for springing me, Lieutenant."

"I owe you."

"You heard from Beverly Hills homicide, I guess."

"This morning. That spilled coffee on Petrocelli's carpet came back positive for cyanide. Same with the stained cloth you gave them all neatly bagged. They love you over there."

Then: "You have any more hunches you want to share?"

"I might."

We sat for another minute or two not saying much, letting the caffeine do its job while we watched the last of the sunset reflect off the towering blue and green exterior of the Pacific Design Center a long block away.

When his cup was empty DeWinter unwrapped a stick of sugarless gum, rolled it up like a rug, and popped it into his mouth.

"About this Petrocelli business. You think whoever snuffed Petrocelli also took care of Reza JaFari."

"Seems likely, don't you think?"

"Very likely. I just don't know why."

He chewed his gum thoughtfully, waiting for me to say something. I didn't.

"My guess is that you have both a good idea who and a good idea why. If I didn't think that, you'd still be cooling your heels in the can."

"Like I said, I appreciate you getting me out."

"I appreciate the further cooperation you're going to give me."

He folded his gum wrapper into a neat, tiny square and placed it on the edge of his saucer.

Then he looked at the young men passing in both directions on the sidewalk.

"I never knew until I came to L.A. how many frigging queers there really are in the world."

"Neither did I, Lieutenant. That's why I stayed."

He thought about that a moment.

Then: "Tell me what you know, Justice."

"Funny, an old editor of mine named Harry Brofsky was saying exactly the same words to me this morning."

"I don't think there's a damn thing that's funny about it. Neither does your buddy Romero."

"How's he doing?"

"I wouldn't want to trade places with him."

"You've got your suspect, Lieutenant. What do you need me for?"

The streetlamps flickered on along the boulevard. A bare-chested blond gym boy with a tiny silver barbell in each distended nipple and another through his navel sauntered past. His arm rested comfortably around the narrow waist of a powerfully built black man nearly as dark as DeWinter.

The big cop sat immobile but his eyes followed the two men until they were out of sight.

"Interested, Lieutenant?"

He shot me a look, took my cup, got up, and went for refills. When he came back, he said, "I know that Romero was in Cedars-Sinai hospital going through intake when Petrocelli drank a cup of coffee laced with cyanide."

"Which leaves you with three possibilities, Lieutenant. One, Danny's innocent. Two, he's got an accomplice. Three, somebody did a copycat on Petrocelli. My guess is you're leaning toward number one, and you don't feel too good about it."

"Romero's still my best suspect."

"But you'd like a better one."

"I think you know some things you're not telling me."

"I like to have my cards in order, Lieutenant, before I lay them on the table. In my situation, I have to."

"How long?"

"I'm getting close."

DeWinter looked out at the street again while he sipped his coffee. The smell of smoke was all around us.

"Hell of a fire up near Griffith Park."

"Looks that way."

"The Santa Ana winds always stir up trouble. Make people crazy."

"The way I look at it, we're all crazy, Lieutenant. Some are just stitched together a little better than others."

He was quiet for a moment, finishing his coffee. He looked tired, reflective, less mean.

"You're still going to have to deal with this assault rap, Justice. I can't do much for you beyond what I've done."

"I've been in worse jams."

"Alexandra tells me somebody tried to run you down last night."

"Did she."

"She's worried about you, Justice. Thinks you've got some kind of death wish."

"Templeton's got a motherly streak."

"She's a fine woman."

"Many men seem to think so."

"But not you?"

"I suppose I appreciate her mind and soul more than her body."

He shook his huge head.

"That's just something I can't understand."

"No one's asking you to, Lieutenant."

He bent his head, rubbed the back of his neck.

"I don't suppose you'd tell me what she really feels about me."

"She's really got her hooks in you, doesn't she?"

"Pretty damn deep."

"You sure you want to know?"

"I'm twice divorced. Both times, they left me. I can take rejection."

"She's on the rebound, Lieutenant."

He smiled painfully.

"I was afraid of that."

I stood, in need of Tylenol, food, and sleep, in that order.

"I'll call you as soon as I have something concrete. In the meantime, I have a request."

"What's that?"

"Take the cuffs off Danny."

"I already have." DeWinter lifted himself out of his chair. "If you continue to work with me, I'll go you one further. I'll kick him loose, into your custody."

"You sure you want to do that, Lieutenant?"

"Alexandra talked me into it."

"I guess I owe you both, then."

We stepped out to the sidewalk, where the passing men had to change course to get around DeWinter's massive frame.

"You know, Justice, I used to be a drinker myself."

"Is that right?"

"Still go to meetings once in a while."

"I've never been fond of groups myself."

He nodded slowly, then said, "Call me if you have something. Don't make me wait."

He hitched up his pants.

"And, Justice, do us both a favor—be careful."

He laid a hand on my shoulder just before he walked away.

When he was gone, I could still feel it there, along with my surprise.

# Forty-four

THE WINDS RAN WILD all night, howling through the trees along Norma Place and beating in noisy gusts against the old apartment.

I kept Maggie with me upstairs, afraid she might break loose from the yard.

The tequila still had hold of me and after some dinner I drank a tall glass of wine slowly to settle myself down. I spent the evening clicking through the TV channels, watching coverage of the fire and seeing if the JaFari story turned up. It did.

Pieces of it were on every newscast, along with Danny's mug shot taken eight years earlier when he was arrested for assault. He looked incredibly young in the photo, stunned by the sudden knowledge of how cruel people can be, and perhaps by his own capacity for violence. I saw less of Jacques in Danny now, and more of myself.

Most of the newscasts referred to him as "the HIV Killer," sensationalizing the story for maximum ratings; a few showed more responsibility, stating only that he was under arrest in the JaFari case, and refusing to speculate further.

The phone rang at half past ten, a call from Claude DeWinter.

"I don't know if you're planning any visits to your friend Romero, Justice. But you'll need to be prepared."

"The TV people?"

"They're all over the hospital, trying to get live pictures. Some print people too—the tabloid scum, especially. I've doubled the police guard outside Danny's room. You're cleared with the cops on the watch. If you go, take some ID."

DeWinter also warned me that Teal might tip the hounds to where I lived. I told him I didn't think so.

"Why's that?"

"If Teal connects me to Danny, he connects me to himself. I have a few stories of my own I could tell. I don't think Teal wants certain aspects of his private life made public. If I'm right, he won't even press charges on the assault."

"You've got my numbers, Justice. Watch your back."

I shut off the TV as another HIV Killer story came on, with the camera zeroing in on Danny's eyes for effect, the way TV loves to do. I fell asleep with Maggie beside me on the pillow, where Danny's head should have been.

When I woke at sunup she was sitting at the window, looking down the driveway toward the street. Waiting for Danny.

*Danny.*

He was central to all my thoughts now, yet I'd neither seen nor talked to him since fleeing the hospital Tuesday afternoon. I had to go back; I knew that much. And I had to help him die, one way or another. The way I hadn't been able to help Jacques when his time came, because there had been a big hole inside me where my courage should have been.

If I couldn't be there for Danny, I was lost again. Maybe forever.

I stood on the landing while Maggie trotted down the stairs to pee. Sirens screamed nonstop across the city, which told me the Beachwood Canyon fires were raging out of control in the hills four miles away.

I ran the kitchen tap until the water got hot, mixed a cup with instant coffee, and switched the TV back on.

Coverage of the fire had pushed Danny off most of the newscasts. Houses were burning and dogs and deer were running terrified down into the busy streets. People who had lost their homes huddled, weeping, before the cameras. TV reporters collared weary firefighters, pressing them about the cause of the fire, and when they couldn't get the answer they wanted, speculating endlessly and repetitively to fill airtime, as TV reporters tend to do.

I thought about Constance Fairbridge alone in her old house with nothing but her precious bottles and little animals around her. Cantwell surely would have checked on his grandmother, I thought, but I wanted to be sure. I called information, got no listing for her, and left a message on Cantwell's machine reminding him how vulnerable her property was to fast-moving flames, and how fragile her mind had become.

I also left a beeper message for Templeton, who called me back within the hour. She didn't have much time to talk.

"Harry's out here at the command post with me. But we're still overwhelmed. The *Times* has more than a dozen reporters on the fire. We've got three."

"Life's never been fair," I said. "Or *Time,* for that matter."

She wasn't in the mood for bad journalism jokes, so I cut to the chase.

"I think somebody should check on Constance Fairbridge. Maybe you can give her address to one of the firefighters. Make sure she's safe."

Templeton promised she would. I gave her the street number and our conversation was over.

I left Maggie with Fred, then drove two miles south to the Margaret Herrick Library.

I checked in with the guard, climbed the Kirk Douglas Grand Staircase, and filed my request with the Special Collections desk. A few minutes later, I was at a corner table, starting in on a stack of Gordon Cantwell's earlier scripts, which totaled nearly a dozen.

I read the first one all the way through—line by line—but it took me nearly two hours and after that I began to skim. They all seemed like the same script, anyway.

Man or woman faces tremendous, life-changing challenge in Act One, which ends by page twenty. Important turning point ten to fifteen pages later. Midway through Act II, a plot twist that throws the story in an entirely different direction, with new obstacles and challenges. Act II ends between pages seventy-five and eighty-five, with the hero or heroine facing the final, most daunting leg of the mission. Act III ends between pages one hundred and one twenty, sometimes with a tidy, half-page resolution tacked on, tying up all the loose ends and offering a pat lesson about morality and character.

The Cantwell Method.

He had it down to an airtight formula, which I'm sure he would have called classic story structure. Perhaps it was; I was hardly an expert.

But for all their technical precision, Cantwell's scripts were hopelessly contrived. The story lines were hackneyed, the characters cardboard, the dialogue flat and unbelievable.

I kept looking, but I found no real energy or emotion or heart.

No sense that Cantwell was driven to create his stories by any genuine feeling for his characters or their problems. Not an inkling of humanity in a single line. It was all cold at the core, hollow.

Everything felt driven by plot—plot worked out according to the rigid Cantwell Method—with the most interesting scenes suspiciously reminiscent of others already captured on film. An elevated railway and car chase borrowed from *The French Connection*. A war room sequence from *Dr. Strangelove*. A restaurant confrontation from *Five Easy Pieces*. A deathbed drama from *Terms of Endearment*. A teary farewell scene from *Shane*. And on and on and on.

Cantwell may have placed all his plot points on the proper pages, but his scripts were as predictable as political campaign promises. Reading them, I was no longer surprised that none of them had been sold or produced, and that Cantwell had felt the need to inflate his credits.

I returned his old scripts to Special Collections, checked out with the guard downstairs, and pushed through the big doors to the rose garden plaza outside.

In the skies to the northeast, a monstrous column of smoke rose before becoming lost in the general haze that covered much of the city. My eyes were stinging as I entered the garage at street level, passing the parking tollbooth and turning down the rear aisle toward the middle section where the Mustang was parked.

I was almost there when I saw the gray sports utility vehicle with the dark windows waiting at the end of the aisle, tucked into the last slot almost out of sight. Its left headlight was smashed and the frame twisted from its impact with the boulder two nights earlier in the hills above Sunset.

I stopped at the Mustang, opened the trunk, tossed my notebook in, and lifted a crowbar out. Then I turned and started running straight toward the wagon.

Its tires squealed as it pulled out.

This time I was well out of its path, the hunter instead of the hunted. I ran at it from the side, swinging the crowbar with a crushing blow across the highest arch of the windshield, which shattered into tiny pieces held together by a protective plastic shield. All I wanted was to create one small hole in that windshield, an opening, a glimpse of the driver's face.

The wagon shot across the aisle away from me. I sprinted after it, cutting through parked cars, angling in on it again and whacking the windshield one more time.

Again, it splintered but held.

The driver lost control and slammed into a concrete pillar, crushing the nose and grillwork. Steam hissed from under the hood. The vehicle jammed into reverse, its wheels spinning on oil and slick concrete. I swung the crowbar on the driver's side, caving in the window, giving me a good look at a face I'd seen countless times—on billboards, posters, magazine covers, cereal and toy boxes, and rubber masks like the one I was looking at now.

E.T., Hollywood's most famous and widely merchandised extraterrestrial, gaped at me from behind the wheel.

I reached to tear away the mask, but the wagon was moving again.

I heard the transmission slip into a forward gear and jumped to the safety of another pillar. E.T. glanced my way as the wagon sped by, his wrinkled features puckered into a silly rubber smile. I took off after him again.

The wagon careened toward the exit, smashing through the wooden arm of the toll gate, speeding toward the street. I sprinted after it, pushing the startled toll collector aside.

The fleeing vehicle shot into the nearest traffic lane at the same moment a big horn let out a warning blast that didn't stop. The double-bugle horn was still sounding as the concrete-loaded dump truck beneath it plowed into the wagon, driving it over the curb and into a power pole, crumpling it like a cheap toy.

The horn was stuck and still blowing as the trucker backed his rig off the crushed wagon, while traffic came to a stop in both directions.

I was the first person to reach the driver's door. It was caved in, like the front corner of the wagon on that side. Folded up on the dashboard was a pair of Oakley sunglasses.

E.T. was pinned by twisted metal and the steering wheel, which had caught him under the chin, crushing his windpipe. I heard choking sounds inside the mask and ripped it away.

Anne-Judith Kemmerman's musclebound boyfriend worked his jaw frantically up and down, gasping for air. His eyes bulged, and gagging sounds came from his compressed throat like the last gasps a fish makes fighting to stay alive out of water.

The man was an idiot, a murderous idiot driven by testosterone and puerile male pride to try to kill me. Still, I took no pleasure in watching him die.

That felt new to me, strange. Maybe I'd finally tasted enough vengeance in my life, gotten my fill.

The trucker was beside me, then a growing crowd. I asked for a pocketknife, so I could open an emergency airway in Muscles's throat. By the time I got the knife, he'd stopped moving and making his ugly noises. I reached in, felt for a pulse, found none.

I closed his eyes and told the gawkers to stop staring and move away. I had no business doing it, but there must have been something in my voice that suggested authority, because they did.

Then the police came, and more questions.

When they were done with me, I phoned Claude DeWinter and told him what had happened. He asked me if the Beverly Hills police knew about the connection of the dead driver to Anne-Judith Kemmerman.

I told him they did, then went home.

Back on Norma Place, I found a nine-by-twelve manila envelope waiting for me on the apartment steps.

My name was handwritten on the front. A return address for International Talent Associates was printed in the upper left-hand corner. Inside was a handwritten note from Roberta Brickman paper-clipped to the front cover of a script.

> Dear Mr. Justice:
>
> Here is the script you told me you were looking for. I hope it proves useful to you in some way.
>
> Although I found our meeting yesterday quite painful, I also felt better afterward for having talked more frankly with you.
>
> This is not for publication, but I thought you might like to know that I'm seriously rethinking my future. That's the positive side to being infected with this virus—it forces one to decide what truly matters.
>
> I'm considering a career change, perhaps to AIDS fund-raising or education work. I plan to live a very long time, but I'm not sure I want to spend that time making deals.
>
> Please extend to Alexandra Templeton my good wishes for the article the two of you are working on.
>
> Regards,
> Roberta Brickman

The script bore the name and logo of Paramount Pictures in embossed gold against pale blue. I opened it to the first page. Centered, in capital letters and boldface type, was the title: **NOTHING TO LOSE.**

I put my key in the door and let myself in. Across the room, the red light was blinking on my answering machine.

I poured a glass of wine and sat on the edge of the bed, staring stupidly at the flashing light, wondering if it was a message from Anne-Judith Kemmerman professing her innocence, but too wrung out to really care.

# Forty-five

"HELLO, DANNY."
He looked up as I stepped into his room. The color was back in his face, the strength in his voice. It was Thursday evening. Just four days of the right treatment had made a noticeable difference.

"Hey, stranger."

His hospital gown was lowered to his waist while a doctor sat on the bed, moving a stethoscope over his chest.

"Dr. Bergman—this is my buddy, Ben."

The doctor studied my face while he worked on my name.

"Benjamin Justice—the reporter?"

"Ex-reporter, for the most part."

"I'll be through here in a moment, Justice."

His voice was cool, close to rude.

"It's OK, Doc. He's a friend."

Bergman eyed me critically. He was a small, intense, bearded man in his forties with a prominent nose that propped up a stylish pair of spectacles. He removed his stethoscope from his ears, folded it into a pocket of his white coat, then turned to help Danny back into his gown.

"Would you mind closing the curtain, Justice?"

I pulled it closed as Bergman lowered the sheet and lifted Danny's gown, inspecting him below the waist.

I stepped through the curtain and crossed to the window, where I could see orange flames massed against the dark hills above Franklin Avenue. The wind had scattered embers like seeds into the surrounding mountains, where smaller fires blossomed like bright flowers.

A minute later, I heard the curtain being drawn open around the bed. When I looked back, the doctor was sitting beside Danny again, laying a fatherly hand on his head.

"You're doing much, much better, Danny. I'm checking you out of here tomorrow, since that's what you want. You should be walking fairly well for a while."

He pressed one of Danny's hands between his own.

"I guess you have some decisions to make, don't you?"

"I've pretty much made 'em, Doc."

"If you have any questions, or just need to talk, call me. If I'm busy, they'll find me."

"Thanks for everything you've done for me, Doc. You always made me feel real special."

"You are special."

The doctor kissed Danny on the forehead, then nodded curtly to me on his way out the door, where two uniformed cops stood drinking coffee.

I took his place beside Danny on the bed.

"I'm sorry about the mess I caused. All the reporters—"

"Fuck 'em. Isn't that what you always say?"

I grinned in spite of myself. He reached for my hand.

"I missed you the last coupla days. A whole lot."

"I had a few things to sort out."

His eyes moved keenly over my face and arms as he did an inventory of the latest damage.

"You're all banged up, worse than before. What happened?"

"I fell out of bed."

This time, he grinned.

"Somebody probably pushed you out. For gettin' fresh, like you did with me the other day."

We both laughed, but it didn't last long.

"Look, about what I asked—"

"I'll do it."

"No, Ben. Not if—"

"I'll do it, Danny. If that's what you need from me. I ran out of here the other day thinking I never could."

"What changed your mind?"

"Remembering what it feels like to let someone down. Knowing how hard it is to live with yourself afterward."

"If we're gonna do it, I don't want to wait around. I want to get to it as soon as we can."

*Get to it.* The conversation was starting to feel unreal again.

"Why so fast?"

"I don't dig the idea of sitting around for a week or two thinking on it. I'm feeling OK about it. I'm ready."

He squeezed my hand. He had to know that I was having a lot of trouble with this.

"You're calling the shots, Danny."

"They're checking me out of here tomorrow. It'd be cool if we could be on our way tomorrow night. Hike into the mountains Saturday. Take care of it Sunday."

*Take care of it.* How easily he talked about it.

"Sunday," I said. "Three days."

I watched him shrug.

"Seems like a good day—religious and all." He pursed his lips bravely. "The day we're supposed to get closer to God."

I wanted to smile for him, but couldn't.

"Sunday, then."

A female nurse came in to check Danny's IV drip, then padded out silently in her white shoes.

"How's your friend Alexandra?"

"Out covering the fire. With Harry."

"I guess it's pretty bad."

"They've evacuated a lot of the homes up in the hills." I shook my head. "Do you really want to talk about the fire?"

"What I really want to do is close my eyes while you're sitting with me. Go to sleep knowing you're here."

"That's easy enough."

I pulled a chair up next to the bed, while he settled his head against the pillow. I eased myself quietly into the chair and opened Gordon Cantwell's script again to the title page.

### NOTHING TO LOSE
*An Original Screenplay*
by Gordon Cantwell

In the lower right-hand corner was a WGA script registration number and a date that set it at ten days before.

I turned to the next page, saw the words FADE IN, and started reading. Two hours later I was on page ninety-nine, with the cancer-ridden convict about to undertake the final and most dangerous phase of his journey, and the determined warden closing in with the police.

Danny slept. I put the script aside and went for coffee. Before another hour had passed, with the coffee gone, I reached the bottom of page 131 and the words FADE TO BLACK.

I turned to a fresh page in my notebook and jotted down my final notes.

Even as a Hollywood outsider, I could understand why Tom Cruise and Paramount Pictures had been willing to pay so much for Cantwell's screenplay, even if they had to lop twenty-five years off the protagonist's life to accommodate the youthful star. The characters were complex and believable, the story suspenseful and poignant, the dialogue spare but realistic, the hero's goal worth fighting for. The weighty theme—a dying criminal trying to redeem his misspent life before time runs out—added special substance to a story that was already well crafted and compelling.

In every respect, *Nothing to Lose* was different from and far better than anything Cantwell had previously written.

Danny opened his eyes as I was scribbling the last of my notes.

"You're still here."

"I'm staying the night—unless they throw me out."

"You don't have to do that."

"I know."

He kept his eyes on me, searching for something.

"You're sure about this?"

I nodded, hoping we wouldn't have to talk about it anymore.

He asked for his water and I held it for him while he sipped through a bent straw. On his chin and upper lip his whiskers were coming in again.

"I'll give you a shave in the morning."

"That'd be nice."

I put the glass back and folded up my notebook.

"You'll return home looking very handsome. Fred and Maurice never turn away a handsome man."

"They were here a couple times."

"Fred and Maurice? When?"

"The last coupla days. When you were gone, sortin' things out."

He smiled, looking incredibly at ease with things.

"Fred says they'll keep Maggie for me, if she ever needs a home. Says he's wanted a dog for a long time. I think she'll like it there."

I looked away because I could feel tears coming. I was afraid that if I started, I wouldn't be able to stop.

Danny reached through the railing of the bed and touched my hand.

"It's gonna be all right, Ben. It's gonna be fine."

# Forty-six

I SNEAKED DANNY out of the hospital early the next day, by-passing the reporters and photographers who hovered in predatory packs around the main entrance.

I had the top up, with Danny under a blanket in the backseat, and cruised away from the hospital and through Boy's Town without incident. As I turned off Santa Monica Boulevard toward the Norma Triangle, I was doing my best not to think beyond today.

Maggie started running around barking when she saw him, which eased him back into life on Norma Place almost as if he'd never been gone.

We celebrated with a champagne breakfast, but after that I had work that couldn't wait, so I turned Danny over to Maurice and Fred. A few minutes later, they drove away in Fred's Jeep with Maggie in the back.

Neither Maurice nor Fred knew what Danny and I had planned. Danny wanted it that way, to keep them clear of possible legal complications and his good-byes to a minimum. I would tell them after it was over. They'd been through it themselves, several times, as they eased the passing of dying friends. They knew the rules and would understand.

I unlocked the garage and dragged out the four trash bags I'd collected the previous week at Gordon Cantwell's house. I spread a big plastic sheet in the yard, emptied the contents of the bags into the middle of it, and began to sort through it item by item, scrap by scrap.

Most of it was comprised of aluminum and glass beer and wine empties, followed by fruit-juice and bottled-water containers. Those went into the recycling bins Maurice and Fred kept beside the garage, along with a dozen jars and cans that had held an assortment of nuts and other goodies. There were also a couple of dozen empty bags that had contained taco chips and various other snacks, which I crammed into the regular trash.

When I finally came upon my first Grolsch bottle—emerald green, etched with imprints of barley and hops, a hinged cap dangling from its top—it was like discovering a precious lost jewel for which a setting was already waiting in the mosaic of Reza JaFari's murder.

By the time I'd sorted through every speck of trash, I'd found three more of the green bottles, along with a receipt for a six-pack of Grolsch and a bag of taco chips from a market near the mouth of Beachwood Canyon.

I checked carefully and found no more Grolsch bottles—just the four.

By then, Fred's Jeep was pulling into the driveway, followed by Danny's pickup, with Danny at the wheel and Maggie beside him. In the bed of the truck was the table he'd been working on when I first met him.

Danny climbed out and stood aside, while Fred and I lifted the table out and set it on the ground.

"What a lovely table," Maurice said. He thumped on Danny's chest with a gentle finger. "You have a real talent for woodworking, young man."

"I been doin' it awhile."

"And where would you like to keep this fine piece?"

Danny turned to me.

"I want Ben to have it."

His gift caught me by total surprise.

"Are you sure?"

" 'Course I'm sure." He ran a finger along the table's polished edges. "It's supposed to be for eating. But I figure you can use it to write on too."

"Benjamin's going to be doing quite a bit of writing from now on," Maurice said. "I just know it."

"I carved my name underneath," Danny said. "Along with the date. I just wish I had chairs to go with it."

"Fred, don't we have a set of old chairs in the garage?"

Fred nodded and disappeared with Maurice through the old rolling doors of the garage. Danny's eyes connected with mine.

"Now that you got a table and chairs, I guess you can have people over for dinner."

"That means I have to cook."

"What's so bad about that?"

"Feels a little too civilized, I guess."

"Maybe that's not such a bad idea, Ben. Getting acquainted with people again. Letting 'em into your life."

"I *have* let someone into my life."

"And when he's gone, you gotta move on, meet somebody else. 'Cause that's the way he'd want it."

We watched Maurice and Fred haul four chairs from the garage and set them in the driveway. They were straight-backed walnut pieces with seats upholstered in a paisley design. Maurice found a rag and went to work dusting them off. Then they each carried two chairs over, positioning them around the table.

Maurice was beaming.

"Perfect! Ethan Allen couldn't have done better!"

Fred helped me haul the table up to the apartment. Danny and Maurice followed with the chairs. Danny climbed the stairs without pain, looking almost strong.

We got the table through the door by turning it sideways, and set it upright in the kitchen, next to a window that looked down on the yard.

"I'm going to wash that window first thing tomorrow," Maurice said. "Fred, you can build a little flower box. Benjamin can look out on geraniums every morning while he drinks his coffee and thinks about what he's going to write!"

He and Fred took their plans with them down the stairs, leaving Danny and me alone for the first time since he'd come home.

"When I was in the hospital, I wrote letters to people. There weren't that many, but I wanted to say good-bye just the same. Maybe we can mail 'em on our way out of town tonight."

"If that's what you want, Danny."

"I got all my papers in order and I left a forwarding address to the house. I'm giving you power of attorney, which means you can cash my last Social Security check when it comes in. Maybe you can give the money to Fred, to help pay for Maggie—she'll need her shots. Or the search and rescue people, if there's a bill."

"Don't worry about that."

"I gave Fred my tools, and I'm signing the pink slip for the truck over to you. It's not worth a whole lot but it runs good. I rebuilt the engine last year, put in a new transmission."

I knew what he was doing—trying to get everything said, so it wouldn't get in the way later. After Jacques died, I'd found all his possessions in boxes, neatly labeled with the names and places where each box was to be sent.

I folded my arms around Danny, pulling him close. Each time it was harder to let go. I wanted to somehow draw him into me until he disappeared and became part of me, so I could hide him from the disease, from what was coming. He must have sensed that I was holding on too tight, because he pulled away.

"I'm gonna take Maggie for a walk. Stretch my legs. Spend some time alone with her."

"OK."

I kissed him but he wouldn't let it last. Then he was out the door and down the stairs.

I pulled out one of the chairs and sat down at my new table. It felt as smooth and solid and durable as any table I'd ever worked on, and it was far more beautiful. I'd never owned a piece of furniture so fine.

I liked the idea that it would be around long after Danny was gone. Or Maurice or Fred or me. The fact of it was, none of us was meant to last as long as a well-built table. None of us was guaranteed to last any time at all.

I opened my notebook and worked on a final set of notes, putting all my information in order to be sure it added up correctly.

An hour had passed that way when Danny came in with a tall glass of cold juice for each of us. He stood over me a moment, touching me affectionately but fleetingly, as if preparing me for the leavetaking he'd already accepted within himself.

Maggie came padding in and they lay down on the bed. Danny was asleep almost immediately, curled into an S, with Maggie tucked inside.

I went back to work.

I looked through my notes one more time, double-checking to see that all the dates and times and places were marked and in chronological order. Yet it didn't feel quite complete; I still had a nagging question or two.

Dusk had fallen; the room was in shadow. I heard the jingle of Maggie's dog tags as she raised her head alertly to the sound of something outside.

I stepped to the window and looked down the drive. Hosain JaFari was striding toward the apartment, looking grim and determined.

I hushed Maggie and fixed the lock on the screen door, ready to close and lock the inside door if necessary.

Footsteps sounded on the stairs, short and heavy. Moments later, the shadowed face of Hosain JaFari was peering in.

"Mr. Justice?"

I stepped into view.

"I'm right here, Mr. JaFari."

"Lieutenant DeWinter told me where I might find you. When I explained to him my need, he did not think you would mind."

"I'm sorry about the way the media has handled the story of your son's death, Mr. JaFari. It must be very painful for you."

"We are in God's hands, Mr. Justice. It is all beyond our control."

"You said you needed to talk with me."

"Yes, about something I believe you saw in my restaurant. In the food locker."

I kept listening.

"As a Muslim, I am forbidden from drinking alcohol, or from serving it in my place of business. Yet I keep several bottles of beer there, on a refrigerator shelf, toward the back."

"Well hidden, Mr. JaFari?"

He hesitated, a mix of feelings clouding his face.

"You see, I kept the beer there for Reza, for my son."

"At his request?"

"No—it was my idea. You see, my son is not so religious as I. He likes this beer very much. Though it was wrong, I kept some for him at the restaurant. Trying to make him feel more welcome. Even my wife did not know."

"Your son was more important to you than even the vows of your religion?"

"It was a choice I made, for the sake of our relationship."

"You must have loved him very much, then."

He dropped his eyes, and when he spoke, his voice trembled with emotion.

"Yes, I loved my Reza very much."

"Did he visit you often, Mr. JaFari?"

"Not so often as I wished. I would cook him a good meal, serve him the beer he liked, try to talk with him. I told him he was welcome to bring his friends, but in all these years, he brought only one."

"When was that?"

"A few weeks ago. I remembered this only when I saw the bottles of beer in my restaurant kitchen. Reza and this man came late in the evening, after we closed."

"What can you tell me about him?"

"He was someone from the movies, with whom Reza had some business. They sat at a table in the corner, by the front window, talking very low but with great excitement. I heard him tell Reza to speak to no one about their project, to trust no one."

"They drank beer?"

"Yes, the imported beer, the Grolsch. I made a joke about it—I told Reza's friend that was the only beer my high-class son would drink. That he would touch nothing else."

"Do you recall this man's name, Mr. JaFari?"

"No, I cannot say that I do. It was just the one time, Mr. Justice."

"Gordon Cantwell, perhaps?"

"Yes, Cantwell. That was his name. Do you know this man?"

"Better all the time."

JaFari dropped his eyes respectfully.

"At any rate, Mr. Justice, I wanted to speak one more time with you. Face to face, as men should. To explain the beer but also to apologize for any rudeness I may have shown to you."

"And I as well, Mr. JaFari."

"Good luck to you, Mr. Justice."

"And to you, sir."

He turned and trudged down the stairs, leaving me with all the answers I needed. I sat at the table, jotting down what he had told me in the place where it belonged, feeling my heart pound.

I was erasing the last of my question marks when the phone rang. Christine Kapono's husky voice was at the other end.

"Gordon called me a few minutes ago. He wanted to know where his passport was."

"What did you tell him?"

"I gave him a general area to look, but in the wrong room. To buy some time."

"You have any idea where he might be going?"

"He keeps a small house in Bali. Also, a bank account there."

"Cantwell takes trips all the time, Christine."

"Not when he's just signed the movie deal he's been waiting for all his life. Not after somebody's just been murdered at his house—somebody he may have been doing secret business with."

"You've been doing some deduction of your own."

"The way you've been asking certain questions, Justice—let's just say I figured you'd want to know about the passport."

"You figured right."

"You've been pretty hard on people. I still don't like it, but I'm beginning to understand it a little."

"A little's better than nothing."

"Kick ass, Justice."

"Hang ten, Kapono."

I cut the connection, heard a dial tone, called information, and asked for the number of the Indonesian consulate. I used it, got through to the right person, and learned what I'd already suspected—Bali had no extradition treaty with the United States.

After that, I punched in Claude DeWinter's number at the LAPD. His partner told me DeWinter was in the john. I left a message asking DeWinter to meet me at the Beachwood Canyon fire command post, and to step on it.

I slipped my notes into a file folder marked *JaFari-Petrocelli,* grabbed my old *L.A. Times* press card, woke Danny, and told him I'd be back as soon as I could.

Dry northerly winds were blowing with a fury as I reached the street.

Then I was in the Mustang, driving fast, toward fire and brimstone.

# Forty-seven

T HE POLICE had barricaded all the routes between Hollywood Boulevard and the hills, from Vine Street to Western
Avenue.

I approached each checkpoint through choking gray smoke,
flashing my outdated press pass and talking like I knew what I was
doing. Each time, the cop on duty had more important things to
do and waved me through.

I found Harry at the Beachwood Canyon command post near
Franklin Avenue and Beachwood Drive. He was standing in front
of the Scientology Celebrity Center with a finger in one ear to
block out the wail of sirens and a cellular phone at the other,
dictating a story to a rewrite man at the *Sun.*

To the north, in the hills, the fire crackled and groaned and
roared like an angry giant impatient for its next meal. The tallest
flames danced a hundred feet in the air, shifting with the wind
but generally moving northward. Judging by the smoke, they appeared to have spread as far east as Griffith Park, where the
world's largest urban parkland—more than four thousand
acres—lay waiting to be devoured.

Harry closed down the antenna on the phone as I approached.
"Where's Templeton?"

He pointed behind me.

Templeton ran toward us, clutching her notebook and tape recorder. Strands of stray hair fell across her face, which was
smudged with soot, like her clothes; her eyes were red from the
smoke, and maybe from lack of sleep.

"They just arrested a suspect on arson charges."

"Name," Harry said, getting back on his phone.

"Constance Fairbridge."

I was staring at Templeton, but her attention was on Harry.

"Spell it," he said.

She did.

"Age?"

"I'm not sure."

"We've got a new lead," Harry said into the phone.

"Eighty-nine."

Harry cocked his head at me in surprise.

"How do you know?"

"She's Gordon Cantwell's grandmother. Silent screen actress."

"Ben suggested the firefighters check on her," Templeton said. "They found her filling bottles with gasoline from an old pump on her property, using rags for fuses. She told them she'd placed the bottles all up and down the canyon."

"She confessed?"

Templeton nodded.

"I'm putting your name in the story, Ben. At least as a source."

"No, Harry. Give it all to Templeton."

"Damn you, Ben—"

He held his hand over the phone.

"You've got a chance to scoop the *Times,* Harry. Move!"

He started talking to the desk again, while I pulled my notes on Constance Fairbridge from the file. I read the most pertinent facts to him while he relayed them downtown.

When I was finished, Harry said to Templeton, "Tell me about the confession."

Templeton glanced at her own notes.

"Fairbridge told the arson investigators she'd set the first fire late Tuesday night. Said it was God's will, that he had spoken to her. According to the investigators, she was semicoherent, reciting from the Book of Genesis—"

"Slow down," Harry said.

He talked into the phone for half a minute, then asked Templeton for more.

"Fairbridge said something about having to destroy the sin of the world, all the cities, so the world could return to its natural state."

"Anything else?"

Templeton ran a finger over her reporter's shorthand.

"Just the animals would come back, she said. No people. No sin. No murder."

"No murder?"

Harry looked from Templeton to me.

"I'm way ahead of you, Harry."

I gave him the rest of the story, slowly, all the way back to 1955, while he fed the details to rewrite so the desk could remake the front page.

We heard a different siren, the *wa-wa* of a police car, and saw Constance Fairbridge being driven off in the backseat of a black-and-white. Her eyes were closed and her withered old hands, secured with plastic cuffs, were clasped together in front of her in prayer.

Print photographers and TV camera crews chased the car, pushing and shoving for a better picture, until the black-and-white had worked its way past the cluster of emergency vehicles and picked up speed.

Harry was about to close up his phone again.

"Call Katie Nakamura at the library," Templeton said. "I asked her to find the photo file on Constance Fairbridge a couple of days ago. She's got it on her desk."

Harry got back on his phone. I handed Templeton my file marked *JaFari-Petrocelli*.

"There are two sets of identical notes in here. They lay out the two murders, JaFari and Petrocelli, step by step, the way I see it. Give one set to Claude DeWinter when he shows up. Tell him to get up to Cantwell's as fast as he can."

Harry had his hand over the phone again.

"Anything else before they move the story?"

"I want a short piece on the front page clearing Danny Romero. Boxed, with the mug shot that's been all over the TV news. Reminding readers that Lydia Lowe instigated the whole thing. After you go to press with it, I want it on the wire."

Harry nodded and got back on the phone. I started for the Mustang. Templeton reached for my arm but missed.

"Where are you going?"

"Up to Cantwell's."

"Stay here, Ben! Wait for DeWinter!"

"No time."

"They won't let you through!"

"Wanna bet?"

I was in the Mustang, fueled by a heavy dose of adrenaline.

Smoke and sirens and voices swirled around me as I pulled out, keeping the pump primed.

It was slow going at first, maddening as I weaved my way through dozens of ambulances and fire vehicles toward Beachwood Drive. When I got there, wooden barricades blocked my way.

A young policewoman who couldn't have been too long out of the academy put up her hand to stop me.

"My baby girl and my wife are up there," I said. "They've got no way to get down."

"We're evacuating the area, sir. I'm sure they're all right."

"You can't see the house from the road. No mailbox. It's very private."

She looked up the hills toward the flames.

"How far up do you live?"

"Not far. A mile or so. Just inside the gates."

The fire was well beyond that, and moving away from us.

"All right. But just up and back. Don't try to save anything but your family."

She pulled the barricade aside and I shot through.

The houses and apartments along the lower stretch of Beachwood Drive were untouched by the flames, all the way to the Hollywoodland Gates and a half mile beyond.

I was forced to slow as I climbed higher, driving through smoke as heavy as a coastal fog. I crept along Beachwood until I found the narrow side street I wanted. After making my turn, I followed the twisting road up into the hills with one hand on the wheel and the other on the horn, honking at every turn to alert any vehicles that might be coming down.

The landscape remained free of fire all the way to Constance Fairbridge's property.

Just beyond her mailbox—perhaps a quarter mile—I began to see destruction. I passed the smoking frames of burned homes, the charred skeletons of trees, animals lying beside the road, their eyes starkly open while smoke rose from their smoldering fur.

All along the route, firefighters worked with hoses, axes, and shovels around the houses and on the hillsides, while helicopters buzzed overhead, making water drops. Everyone was moving quickly amid the din of screaming sirens and urgent voices, yet there was an odd calm and order at the center of the pandemonium, like a battlefield under a strong commander.

When I turned onto Ridgecrest Drive, I entered the heart of

the inferno. Brush and trees blazed on both sides of the road, and several houses were fully engulfed. Firefighters made their stands at the homes that could still be saved, hacking down trees, cutting away brush, pouring streams of water siphoned from swimming pools onto the rooftops.

Now and then a firefighter yelled or waved at me to stop. Each time I ignored the warning and kept going. Embers settled on the Mustang's ragged top and started to burn through. I lowered the top as I drove, folding it up like an accordion, smothering the hot spots.

Now the heat seared my exposed flesh. The hair on my arms and hands curled and crinkled like fine electric filament before disintegrating into ash carried off by the crackling wind.

Then I was suddenly out of the flames, into a section of the canyon the fire hadn't yet reached.

Moments later, I pulled to the curb and leaped from the Mustang.

Then I was dashing across the footbridge and up the stone walkway that led me to Gordon Cantwell's castle of make-believe.

# Forty-eight

W HEN I PUSHED, the front door opened soundlessly.
From the foyer, I surveyed all the downstairs rooms that were visible. Cantwell was nowhere in sight.

The crackle and pop of fire drew my attention to the north side of the living room. Inside the big fireplace, the gas jet spewed a pale yellow flame, and a messy stack of files and documents burned bright orange on the grate.

I shut off the jet, grabbed a poker, and stuck it among the smoldering papers; most were blackened and curling into ash. I snatched to safety what I could, including the WGA medical file that had disappeared from Leonardo Petrocelli's office the afternoon he was murdered and some personal documents that had Reza JaFari's name all over them.

I looked around again, but there was still no sign of Cantwell.

Several pieces of luggage sat at the bottom of the stairs. On top of the largest was Cantwell's passport and a plane ticket to Bali. I hid them behind the framed *Gone With the Wind* poster above the mantelpiece, where I hoped he wouldn't find them, if it came to that.

Then I made my way quietly through the house, eyes and ears alert for human movement.

I took the stairs two at a time on quiet feet, then moved cautiously down the hallway to the right. The door was open to the room at the end, and I stepped in. It appeared to be the master bedroom, with views across the burning canyon to the Hollywood Sign, which the flames had yet to reach.

Clothes were strewn about, drawers and closet doors left open. No Cantwell.

At the other end of the hallway, I found the door shut but not locked. It opened to a small, six-sided, tower-shaped bedroom, with arched windows cut into the three outer walls, which looked out across the canyon like the larger bedroom windows down the hall.

Stuffed toys snuggled together in a pile on the bed—Mickey and Minny Mouse, Donald Duck, Dumbo, Sylvester, Bambi, Tweety Bird, Goofy. In a corner were a child's baseball bat, glove and ball.

Several framed photos—actors' glossy eight-by-tens—hung on a windowless wall, bearing such autographs as James Dean, Marlon Brando, Pier Angeli, Nick Adams, Natalie Wood, Dennis Hopper, Sal Mineo, Rock Hudson, Sterling Hayden, Peter Lorre.

Above the bed was another glamour photo, this one blown up to portrait size. I recognized it instantly from an old one I'd seen at the Margaret Herrick Library—the photogenic face of Gloria Cantwell.

She was posed to offer the camera her choicest features, yet I saw little in the face beyond beauty and vanity, and perhaps an abject neediness the cold mask couldn't quite conceal.

Then I saw Gordon Cantwell himself.

He was visible through the window nearest the bed, crossing from the patio to the back lawn, dressed in a white linen summer suit. He stopped with his back to the house as he looked out at Mount Lee and the big letters: *H-O-L-L-Y-W-O-O-D*.

Beyond him, down the canyon and over the distant hills, flames approached like an enemy army, as relentless as the wind that drove them.

I made my way back down the stairs and through the house, until I was standing a few feet behind him.

Sprinklers were on all around the borders of the yard, wetting down the surrounding slopes, including the dense hedge of thorny cacti that ringed the rear of the property.

Across the way, as the wind shifted, the flames turned and charged the slopes of Mount Lee, moving toward the sign.

Cantwell looked on calmly, as if he were observing an action scene on a movie backlot that was well underway and beyond his control.

"Going somewhere, Gordon?"

He didn't turn right away; half a minute passed before he

spoke. We watched the flames reach the foot of the sign, scorching the concrete base and sheet metal letters, where the white paint began to crack and peel.

"When I was a boy, I used to sit at the window of my room at night. I'd stare out at the sign, hour after hour, letting my imagination take me away."

Cantwell glanced up at the second story of the house, where a circular turret with small arched windows stood at the northeast corner, the child's bedroom I'd been in only minutes before. From here, it reminded me of a room where a fairy tale princess might be kept prisoner, plotting her escape.

"I'd think about how famous I was going to become, all the grand movies I would make, the wonderful life I'd have."

"All the respect and love you'd get. The love you never got from your father or mother."

He didn't reply to that, just looked across at the huge icon of his lifelong dreams, barely visible now through the thick drifts of smoke rising from the flaming ravine below.

"They put it up in 1923, you know. The original sign had thirteen letters, not nine. It spelled Hollywoodland."

"They say thirteen is bad luck."

"Perhaps. But I always thought that Hollywoodland was a prettier name. They removed the last four letters fifty-two years ago, when I was just a toddler. Had it been up to me, I would have left the sign just as it was."

"Hollywoodland was the name of a real estate company, Gordon. The sign was a billboard, advertising a housing development. You must know that."

I saw color come into his neck and ears.

"James Dean and I used to play catch out on the front lawn."

"Until your mother caught you at it and shut you away in your lonely tower."

His voice took on a more insistent cadence and tone, as if he were determined to wear me down.

"My father was a producer, you know."

"A few B pictures was all. Between girlfriends."

He turned to face me, his face red, his jaw set.

"The house was always full of people, music, laughter."

"People who enjoyed your mother's booze, sometimes her body, while you listened jealously from the top of the stairs."

His breathing was audible now, but he had no more words.

"The fantasy's over, Gordon. It's time to deal with reality."

"Fantasy, reality. Who's to say which is which, Justice—or where the line is drawn?"

His face grew cruel, hateful—deadly.

"You, Justice? I don't think so."

Beyond and above him, a helicopter dropped in low, loosing a cascade of water over the sign, dampening the flames at its base and clearing away much of the smoke.

"I came to pitch you a story idea, Gordon."

Cantwell's face changed again, even more quickly than before. This time he seemed pleased.

"A story idea? For me?"

"A murder mystery with a Hollywood background."

"Do you have something in writing? I could read it on the plane."

"You're planning a trip?"

"I'm off on a lecture tour. One last whirlwind of seminars to share the Cantwell Method with the world before I go into pre-production on my film with Tom."

"Taking all your money with you?"

"I'm afraid the money hasn't come through." He laughed lightly. "Everything moves so slowly in this town—especially the money."

The talk of money seemed to jar him back to the truth of things.

"You'll have to excuse me, Justice. I really must be on my way."

I stepped into his path.

"My pitch will only take a couple of minutes. I think you'll find the story interesting."

He glanced at his watch.

"I suppose I could hear a bit of it. If you don't stretch it out. I should warn you, stories about Hollywood rarely make good films. Very few measure up to *Sunset Boulevard*."

I couldn't tell if he was playing along or really believed in what we were doing. In all probability, I thought, neither could he. He seemed to be in and out of reality now, not unlike his grandmother.

"My story is about a man who wants to write and produce movies, Gordon. More than anything. The problem is, as hard as he tries, he's never more than mediocre as a writer, if that. So he ends up teaching. He's bright, analytical, adept at borrowing the concepts of others, gifted at self-promotion—he makes a success of it. But as he gets older, into middle age, he realizes his dream is passing him by, that he's pretty much over the hill by Hollywood standards.

"Then one of his students shows him a script that's better than anything he himself has ever written—a script so good in every respect he's certain he can sell it, get it made. He convinces his student not to show the screenplay to anyone, not even to speak of it. Or so he thinks. Then he murders his student and registers the script as his own, under a different title—never realizing that the student has already shown it to someone else, trying to cut a deal that didn't work out.

"Never realizing, with his ridiculously inflated view of himself, that his student was just as ambitious and conniving and deceitful as he."

"You're taking much too long to get to the point, Justice. The best pitch is one that sums up the story in a single line."

"Dying criminal makes a daring escape from prison, trying to reach his young son before his time runs out. Something like that, Gordon?"

He seemed faintly amused.

"Yes, exactly. A strong concept, suggesting narrative thrust and a clear goal. One that's easily visualized by the marketing people, yet with plenty of room to explore theme and character."

"There's a subplot I haven't told you about."

"Perhaps you should try me again when you've worked it out more clearly."

He started past. I placed a hand squarely on his chest.

"Just a minute longer."

He glanced at my hand, then at his watch.

"Very well. But only another minute."

"With his student out of the way, the teacher sells the script to major players for serious money. Being the egomaniac that he is, he can't resist bragging to the world about it. Unfortunately for our larcenous teacher, another screenwriter sees the story in the trade papers—an older writer who has more talent and skill in his little finger than either the teacher or student between them ever dreamed of having.

"He recognizes the storyline as his own, right down to specific plot points and scenes. Being a gentleman, he calls the teacher and, without accusing, inquires about the coincidence. Of course, the teacher realizes he has to kill again."

Cantwell regarded me with eyes that seemed very much in the present. Cool, calculating eyes.

"And how does he do that?"

"He agrees to meet the older writer at his home to talk things over. Asks the writer to tell no one about their conversation, in the interest of discretion. He poisons the older man's coffee with cyanide, the same poison he used to kill his student. Hoping the old man's poor health will act as a camouflage, the way the student's HIV infection had earlier fooled the coroner."

"It's clever, if a bit far-fetched," Cantwell said. "But where's the proof?"

"Some of the evidence is in the screenplay itself. The film script in question has all the depth and craft and maturity the murderer's own scripts lack. And most of its plot points are on the wrong pages—violating all the hard-and-fast rules the teacher has laid down in his book on how to write the perfect screenplay."

"Interesting. Though I'm not sure it will translate well visually."

"That's what rewrites are for, aren't they, Gordon?"

He smiled, but without any warmth.

"And how did this man, this teacher, murder the young writer?"

"I think you know how."

He began to fidget for the first time. His eyes darted from me to the house, then to his watch and back to me again.

"I'm afraid that's not good enough, Justice. With a murder mystery, you have to let the audience know how the primary murder was accomplished. Or else you've cheated them. If you can't tell them exactly how it was carried out, you haven't got a story."

"What if an old woman finds the Grolsch bottle used in the murder of the first victim. An old woman, by coincidence the murderer's grandmother, who lives down the road and wanders the canyons at night collecting discarded bottles."

"That's an interesting twist."

"Unfortunate for the villain, though."

"How far is this bottle from the murder site?"

"At least a hundred yards, probably farther."

"Quite a distance."

"Not if the murderer is blessed with an exceptional throwing arm, the kind that can nail a runner at home plate from center field."

Cantwell was looking less and less happy with my story.

"Finished, Justice?"

"Not quite. Suppose this particular bottle ends up in the hands of the police, who have it tested for cyanide. Let's say a snoopy reporter collects all the trash from the party where the first murder occurred and goes through it looking for clues. What if he finds exactly four empty Grolsch bottles, along with a receipt for a six-pack of same.

"A fifth bottle was found near the first victim's body—no doubt planted by the killer to explain any traces of beer the coroner might find in the victim's system. The sixth bottle is in the hands of the police, laced with cyanide. All six bottles accounted for."

"Why would the murderer use cyanide? Why not a knife or a gun?"

"That's the creepiest part, Gordon, the final, gothic touch."

"I'm breathless with anticipation."

"The murderer had used cyanide once before, forty-two years earlier."

"That would be 1955, I believe."

"When he poisoned his own mother while she was on a drinking binge—crying her eyes out for James Dean when she should have been paying more attention to her troubled little boy."

This time, Cantwell said nothing. Pebbles of perspiration appeared on his forehead, just below his toupee, and his eyes grew more anxious.

"At dinner the other night, you described your dead mother to me in elaborate detail, Gordon. How she looked, the position she was in, what she was wearing, what was playing on the radio. But according to the housekeeper who found your mother's body, she woke you and got you out of the house without your seeing so much as the hem of your mother's nightgown."

The drops of sweat had broken and started to run. Cantwell mopped his face with the back of his sleeve. He was breathing hard.

"You were a precocious, neglected, angry little boy, Gordon. You found your mother's cyanide, the bottle she'd waved around during her histrionic suicide threats. You slipped some into her gin when she was too drunk to notice, and watched her die. Then you went up to your tower, climbed into bed with all your stuffed toys, and stayed there until the housekeeper found you the next morning, pretending to be asleep.

"Is that why your grandmother cracked up, Gordon? Why she never set foot in this house again? Did she suspect what her grandson had done? Did it make her crazy?"

"It's your scenario, Justice. You come up with the conclusion."

"I think she guessed what you'd done but couldn't accept it, so she snapped. I think that's part of the sin she wanted to burn away when she set fires all over this canyon the last couple of days. The sins of her promiscuous daughter, of her rapacious son-in-law, of their only child, born of Satan."

Cantwell cocked his head, looking at me strangely.

"Grandmother started the fires?"

"The police arrested her a short time ago. She confessed."

The color drained slowly from his face.

"This is the first I've heard of it."

"Here's another plot point, Gordon—the meddling reporter also found the WGA script registration slip you failed to find when you burglarized Reza JaFari's apartment. It proves that JaFari registered the script before you did. It was registered under the title *Over the Wall*—Leonardo Petrocelli's title.

"The copy of Petrocelli's registration receipt—the one you also failed to get when you rifled his files—is safe with the Beverly Hills police, proving that he registered the script before either of you. If that's not enough, there's the pile of papers I pulled out of your fireplace a few minutes ago, linking you to both victims.

"You felt things closing in the last few days, and decided you'd better get out—even if it meant leaving behind your precious movie deal. That's why you've got a passport and plane ticket waiting inside the house."

"You must know that I have a good deal of money put aside, Justice."

"You seem the type who plans well."

"Enough money to make you very comfortable."

"If I let you go."

"Why not? What did I do that was truly so terrible? Reza JaFari was a lazy, untalented little snot. Petrocelli a sick old man whose career was long behind him."

"Expendable."

"We're all expendable, Justice. A few are lucky enough to achieve enough success, grab enough power to rise above the rest. But in the end—"

"We all take the fall."

"Look at you, Justice. You traded your integrity for a Pulitzer prize. Surely, of all people, you understand."

"Maybe it wasn't the prize I was after. Maybe I had other reasons."

"You see? You're justifying your actions. We all do, no matter how big or how small our crimes."

"And your reasons, Gordon?"

His mouth twitched beneath his flickering eyes. The truth seemed to be gnawing at him from inside.

"Greed, I suppose."

"I don't think it was greed at all, Gordon."

"Don't you?"

"I think time was passing you by. You'd grown frantic. You saw one last chance for success and recognition, which meant everything to you. Even in the depths of your self-delusion, you realized you'd become something of a Hollywood joke—the man who taught others how to write screenplays but couldn't make a living at it himself."

"I have to be going, Justice." His voice sounded hurt, constricted with humiliation. "Trust me, you'll be amply rewarded."

My hand was still on his chest.

"If you hurry, Gordon—"

He suddenly looked hopeful.

"Yes?"

"If you hurry, there's still time to call the airport and cancel your reservation."

His illusory hope vanished, replaced by the dangerous cruelty I'd seen before.

"Very clever story, Justice. Nicely thought out. You even came up with a punch line."

"I hoped you'd like it."

"Unfortunately, the story has one major flaw."

"What would that be, Gordon?"

"You haven't explained how I was able to murder Reza JaFari while I was playing center field in a celebrity softball game—halfway across town in front of packed bleachers. Not to mention in the company of several notable celebrities who know me on a first-name basis."

"An ironclad alibi, Gordon?"

"Unless I'm mistaken, JaFari died between seven and eight in the evening. That would have been the third through the sixth innings, when I was either in the dugout, at bat, or in center field under some very bright lights. I'd been on that field, quite visibly, since warm-ups began at five P.M."

He smiled, pleased with himself again.

"How you murdered JaFari," I said, "is the best part of the story."

"But that's the part you haven't worked out. So, you see, you've really got no story at all."

He started to step around me. I moved to the side, staying in front of him.

"I've not only worked it out, Gordon, I've written it all down and delivered it to Lieutenant DeWinter. He's on his way up here right now to take you into custody."

"You're bluffing, Justice. It only works in bad movies."

At that moment, we heard the *wa-wa* of a police siren cutting through the more distant wails of the fire vehicles.

Cantwell glanced past the house down Ridgecrest Drive, where DeWinter's unmarked car sped up the hill, followed by a black-and-white with its lights and siren going.

Cantwell tensed, looking more desperate than before, if that was possible. Then he turned his back on me to look out across the canyon.

The flames on Mount Lee had moved on, leaving the ground charred but the Hollywood Sign intact, standing like a mocking symbol of Cantwell's collapsing dreams.

The wind had shifted yet again, driving the flames in the ravine up the steep slope toward Cantwell's property. The sirens grew louder above the crackle and roar.

Cantwell whirled and drove his fist at my face. I slowed the punch with my forearm but he caught me on the side of the head and I went down.

I grabbed his ankle as he ran for the house and pulled him back. We wrestled and kicked, flailed at each other with our fists, clawed at each other's eyes, rolling across the lawn toward the lower edge of the yard.

Ordinarily, a man of Cantwell's size and condition wouldn't have been much of a problem; a few wrestling moves, reasonably well executed, usually prove an excellent equalizer. But Cantwell was fighting for his life and it was all I could do just to keep him from killing me.

As we tumbled to the edge of the yard, he landed a kick to my face and broke free. By the time I was on my feet, he had a rock in his hand. It was a solid hunk of granite about the size of a football that I knew would crush my skull if it found its target.

As he raised the rock overhead, I kicked him square in the chest, ducking away as the rock came down.

He tottered on the edge a moment, flapping his arms awkwardly like a baby bird, then fell backward.

He hit the wet slope hard and tumbled into a patch of cactus, screaming as the needles pierced his flesh, tearing at him as he tried to pull away. He settled back, whimpering, imprisoned in the bed of thorns planted by his mother half a century ago.

"Justice!"

I turned to see Claude DeWinter moving toward me from the house, followed by Templeton and several uniformed cops.

Then Templeton was beside me, reaching for me.

"You OK?"

I nodded.

We turned to look down at Cantwell as he made one final, agonizing effort to free himself.

He braced with both arms, moaning long and low as more needles turned his hands into pincushions. Then he pushed, crying out as he struggled to his feet, leaving his toupee behind, stuck to the thorns of a fishhook cactus.

He looked up at DeWinter a moment, then at the other cops waiting to take him away.

He turned his back on us, facing the Hollywood Sign and the flaming chasm in between. Then he was moving down the slope, stepping through the cactus as if it weren't there, ignoring its barbs and spikes, straight into the heart of the fire.

He fell as he reached the deepest part of the ravine but got to his feet, aflame from head to toe, flailing his arms like a human torch.

Somehow, he began to move again, struggling up the other side as if trying to reach the sacred ground where the Hollywood Sign beckoned like a false god.

Halfway up, Cantwell fell to his knees, raising his flaming arms skyward. A moment later, I heard an anguished cry before he collapsed and tumbled backward, into the consuming fire.

# Forty-nine

Y OU STILL haven't explained how he did it."
The top was down and Danny was gazing up at a sky filled
with more stars than I could ever remember seeing.

"You really want to know?"

"I just want to hear the sound of your voice, that's all."

It was sometime between midnight and dawn. I'd forgotten my
watch, and the clock in the Mustang hadn't worked for years.
Time didn't really mean a whole lot now, anyway.

We sped north along Highway 395, the jagged peaks of the
southern Sierra to our left, the barren White Mountains of Ne-
vada ahead to our right, running parallel to the infamous Los
Angeles aqueduct, which sucked the precious water from the
Owens Valley in a scandalous engineering feat whose dark origins
went back almost to the turn of the century.

Somewhere along this route, in a town called Independence,
Charles Manson had first been jailed after directing the slaughter
of actress Sharon Tate and several others in 1969. Somewhere in
the landscape of sagebrush and rattlesnakes and mounds of po-
rous volcanic rock were the ghostly remains of Manzanar, the
camp where thousands of innocent Americans of Japanese ances-
try had been imprisoned during World War II. There was a hot
springs out there too, once sacred to the local Indians, now littered with beer cans and condoms. A lake where a group of escaped convicts had been hunted down and hanged back in 1871.
A gas station, long abandoned, with the improbable name Green
Acres on a swinging sign blistered by the unforgiving desert sun.

It was a haunted, lonely land that Danny and I were crossing in the predawn hours, miles of unrelieved desolation, yet oddly beautiful and calming.

"So tell me," Danny said. "How did Cantwell murder Reza?"

He slouched in the passenger seat as I drove, propped against a pillow. He'd said good-bye to Maggie back at the house, insisting she stay behind, worried that she wouldn't leave him when the time came.

"You remember that Saturday night, two weeks ago?"

He smiled sleepily.

"How could I forget it? That's when I met you."

"It was Cantwell who made the appointment to meet Reza at the house at seven, well before the party started. He never intended to meet Reza, of course—that was the plan. He told Reza to tell no one, and to come alone—they had important business to discuss. He said to grab a bottle of beer from the fridge, go down to the terrace, and wait. When JaFari went to get his beer, he found a couple of six-packs of a cheaper domestic brand and a single bottle of Grolsch. Naturally, he chose the Grolsch.

"What he didn't know was that Cantwell had opened the hinged cap, laced the beer with cyanide, and carefully recapped it. JaFari took his beer down to the terrace as instructed and waited for Cantwell. While he waited, he got thirsty."

"It was warm that night," Danny said. "Reza probably chugged it."

"Even better, from Cantwell's standpoint. Cyanide works fast. Depending on how strong a dose it was, JaFari probably died within an hour, possibly much sooner."

I slowed as we approached the town of Lone Pine, in the shadow of Mount Whitney, which rose 14,495 feet like a jagged tooth to the west. We passed through a stoplight or two, and then the town was behind us, with nothing but miles of open highway ahead.

"By shutting off the automatic timer on the outdoor lights, Cantwell kept the yard dark until he arrived home from his baseball game. He figured that in the dark no one from the party would venture down the hillside to the terrace before he got there with Templeton. Dylan Winchester went down anyway. That's the movie director."

"Yeah, I remember."

"Winchester found JaFari's body, dropped his cigar without realizing it, and took off in a panic."

"But what about the beer?" Danny sounded more sleepy now than interested. "If Cantwell and Alexandra were together when they found Reza's body—"

"Cantwell came home carrying a grocery bag that contained the other five bottles of Grolsch, hidden under a bag of chips. He made a quick stop in the kitchen, where he slipped four of the bottles into the fridge. He concealed the other one in his baseball glove, which he tucked under his arm. Then he switched on the lights in the yard. He led Templeton down the steps to the terrace, where they discovered JaFari's body together.

"Cantwell sent Templeton to call 911. While she was gone, he threw the poisoned bottle deep into the canyon. He then dumped out most of the beer in the fresh bottle to account for what JaFari drank, and left that bottle near the body. He made a mistake when he pressed the fingers of JaFari's right hand around the new bottle to leave prints, not realizing JaFari was left-handed.

"Cantwell knew that cyanide is often overlooked in autopsies. It might have been a perfect murder, except for an eccentric old woman with a penchant for picking up bottles—Cantwell's grandmother."

I looked over at Danny. His eyes were closed, his breathing deep and steady.

I'd brought along a small box of tapes and searched around in it for just the right one. I passed over some Mingus, Wayne Shorter, and Billie Holiday before I found the one I wanted. It was an album recorded in Europe by Eric Dolphy, a saintly reed man who blew notes of incredible purity and who died young, not much older than Danny was now. I slipped it into the tape deck.

"Glad to Be Unhappy" came on, a tune both sad and sweet, with Dolphy playing a flute that soared and fluttered and wept.

I tried to find courage in the music, in the exquisite beauty of it that was also disturbing and made me tremble and want to cry. A line from Walter Mosley came into my mind: *I felt something deep down in me, something dark like jazz when it reminds you that death is waiting.*

The first light of dawn was coming up over the White Mountains, tinting the valley floor and everything in it a gentle pink. I could see the peaks of the Sierra more clearly now, magnificent and ageless, cradling the pretty lake where Danny had chosen to take his final sleep.

An unpaved road appeared ahead on the left. I slowed to read the sign, then turned, heading west toward the high country.

Billowing dust trailed behind us until the dirt road gave way to rough pavement.

Danny shifted and mumbled but didn't wake.

I reached over to brush the hair off his forehead, to touch his peaceful face, to study him a moment, hoping I could remember him like that.

I never told him I'd done some checking on his background, unearthing more of his lies. There was no Native American tribe known as the Tokona. Nor was there a village in the Sangre de Cristo mountains called Milagro, not that I could find. I wasn't even sure he had ever ventured into the High Sierra before, except in picture books.

Danny was like a lot of us who come to Los Angeles, seeking something better to replace what we were handed. We come to reinvent ourselves, to build a new identity from the outside in, to create and occupy a role that gives us hope. Sometimes it succeeds, usually not.

Danny, in the brief time he had, may have succeeded better than most. In the end, he had created something simple but worthy and lasting. He had given and accepted love, experienced the beauty and wonder of life, touched a heart or two.

Who Danny really was, where he came from, what had driven him to flee his past and write a new one—all that remained a mystery to me. It didn't bother me to know he had lied. I understood.

Around us, the morning went from pink to golden. We kept moving higher into the mountains, into cooler air and the sweet smell of pine. Danny slept on and I listened to the jazz.

I wanted nothing more than to just keep driving with him like that. Up an empty road, with the sun behind us and the high peaks ahead and an Eric Dolphy tune floating away on the wind.

Just Danny and me. Together, forever.

But life doesn't work like that, not even sometimes.

I guess that's why they make movies.